THE WORLD'S CLASSICS

ELIZABETH GASKELL

Ruth

Edited with an Introduction by
ALAN SHELSTON

Oxford   New York
OXFORD UNIVERSITY PRESS

Oxford University Press, Walton Street, Oxford OX2 6DP

Oxford New York Toronto
Delhi Bombay Calcutta Madras Karachi
Kuala Lumpur Singapore Hong Kong Tokyo
Nairobi Dar es Salaam Cape Town
Melbourne Auckland Madrid

and associated companies in
Berlin Ibadan

Oxford is a trade mark of Oxford University Press

© Introduction, Select Bibliography, and Notes
© Alan Shelston 1985
Chronology © Oxford University Press 1981

First published 1853
First issued as a World's Classics paperback 1985 with editorial apparatus

British Library Cataloguing in Publication Data

Data available

Library of Congress Cataloging in Publication Data
Gaskell, Elizabeth Cleghorn, 1810- 1865.
Ruth. (The World's classics)
Originally published: 1853
I. Title
PR4710.R8 1985 823'.8 84-20670
ISBN 0 19-281669-1 (pbk.)

9 10 8

Printed in Great Britain by
BPCC Paperbacks Ltd
Aylesbury, Bucks

RUTH

MRS GASKELL was born Elizabeth Cleghorn Stevenson in 1810. The daughter of a Unitarian who was variously a preacher, experimental farmer and writer, she was brought up after her mother's death by her aunt in Knutsford, Cheshire, which became the model not only for Cranford but also for Hollingford (in *Wives and Daughters*). In 1832 she married William Gaskell, a Unitarian minister in Manchester: she had a son, who died in infancy, and four daughters. Her first novel, *Mary Barton*, published in 1848, was much discussed and brought her to the attention of Charles Dickens, who was looking for contributors to his new periodical, *Household Words*, for which she wrote the famous series of papers subsequently reprinted as *Cranford*. Her later work includes *Ruth* (1853), *North and South* (1854–5), *Sylvia's Lovers* (1863), *Cousin Phillis* (1863–4) and *Wives and Daughters* (1864–6). She wrote many stories and occasional pieces, and a major biography, *The Life of Charlotte Brontë* (1857). She died in 1865.

ALAN SHELSTON is Senior Lecturer in English Literature at the University of Manchester. He has edited Thomas Carlyle's *Selected Writings* and Mrs Gaskell's *The Life of Charlotte Brontë*.

CONTENTS

CONTENTS

INTRODUCTION

I

Ruth, published in three volumes in 1853, was Elizabeth Gaskell's second full-length novel. *Mary Barton* (1848), her 'tale of Manchester Life', had brought her both criticism and success: it had given her also the confidence and the freedom to experiment. The immediate result was a series of stories and occasional pieces, mostly with a provincial setting, that culminated in the episodes she collected together as *Cranford*. By its choice of setting, and by its general tenor, *Ruth* would seem to confirm this movement on the part of its author away from the Manchester setting of the novel that had made her famous. *Ruth*, however, like *Mary Barton*, was explicitly conceived as a social-problem novel; furthermore, and again like its predecessor, it drew upon its author's direct experience of the issues it sought to bring to public attention.

The sufferings of the unmarried mother, like the hardships of the industrially oppressed that formed the subject of *Mary Barton*, were familiar to Mrs Gaskell from her charitable work in Manchester. In 1850 she took up the cause of a girl called Pasley whom she had come across in the New Bayley prison. In a long letter to Dickens, at that time involved in his emigration project for fallen women, she gives details of the case. Pasley's career exemplifies the dangers facing even a girl of respectable parentage who was neglected. The daughter of an Irish clergyman who had died when she was two, she had been neglected by an indifferent mother, and then placed in an orphanage, before becoming a dressmaker's apprentice. Following a series of misfortunes for which she had not herself been responsible she had been seduced by her own doctor. The consequence had been first the Penitentiary and then a career of petty crime; finally, by an appalling stroke of coincidence, the poor girl had been confronted when in prison by her very seducer, now acting as prison surgeon.[1]

The Pasley case obviously anticipates *Ruth* in many of its details—in the social class of Pasley herself (Ruth Hilton is the daughter of 'a respectable farmer' and the grand-daughter of a clergyman), in the choice of dressmaking as a trade whose apprentices were easily exposed to moral temptation, and in the dramatic detail of the reappearance of the seducer, a man whose superior social position served to reinforce both his own irresponsibility and the double standard generally associated with his behaviour. Having secured her objective of salvation by emigration for Pasley, Mrs Gaskell made no further reference to the case, and the fact that she was to wait another two years before apparently reproducing its details in *Ruth* suggests that the relationship between them and her novel is as much as anything coincidental. In fact several of the fictional situations to be found in Mrs Gaskell's early work refer to the issue of the sexual vulnerability of young girls. In *Mary Barton* the heroine, herself for a time a dressmaker's apprentice, is exposed to the attentions of a rich mill-owner's son; even more to the point she has an aunt who has taken to the streets as a result of her own sexual lapse. In *Lizzie Leigh* (1850), a short story of Manchester life, Mrs Gaskell approached the topic again, this time making it the centre of her narrative. Others amongst these early stories deal with the wider theme of betrayed love and its concomitant unhappiness. *Ruth*, then, by its consideration of what Mrs Gaskell herself conceded would be regarded as 'a subject unfit for fiction' (*Letters*, p. 220), is not so much a special case as the logical outcome of her interest in its theme.

Although Mrs Gaskell's earlier approaches to the sexual theme had passed without remark she came to it again in *Ruth* with considerable foreboding. Even while working on the novel she feared its publication, recording that she had lost 'my own power of judging', and that she could not tell 'whether I had done it well or ill'. On its appearance it

[1] See *The Letters of Mrs Gaskell*, ed. J. A. V. Chapple and Arthur Pollard (Manchester, 1966), pp. 98–100.

immediately became 'a prohibited book' (by her husband, presumably) in her own household, and 'not a book for young people, unless read with somebody older'. The reactions of acquaintances served to confirm her worst fears: '"Deep regret" is what my friends here feel and express'; two men, she knew, had 'burnt the 1st vol. of *Ruth* as so very bad' (*Letters*, pp. 203–26, *passim*). As the wife of the minister to the Manchester Unitarian community, a group which included powerful middle-class interests, and which she may well have drawn on for her portrait of the Bradshaw family in the novel itself, Mrs Gaskell was exposed to articulate personal criticism. As had been the case with *Mary Barton*, frankness on an issue of public morality was met by the pointed objections of those amongst her direct acquaintance who took a different point of view.

Experienced reviewers, however, were markedly more sympathetic. Mrs Gaskell may refer in her correspondence to instances of reviews whose comments had distressed her, but in fact on its publication *Ruth* was reviewed both extensively and for the most part generously. Seduction and illegitimacy were prominent topics in the fiction of the early 1850s: the examples of *David Copperfield*, with the story of Little Emily at its heart, and *Bleak House*, with its heroine whose birth out of wedlock is the trigger of its mystery plot, show that whatever may have obtained in the Gaskell household such subjects were in themselves generally acceptable as family reading. On the whole *Ruth* was received as a proper and valuable commentary on a subject of public concern. If few reviewers were prepared to go as far as the anonymous contributor to *Tait's Edinburgh Magazine* who, in the course of an attack on the double standard involved in conventional attitudes to sexual morality, concluded that condemnation of the heroine could only be based upon 'a superstitious and exaggerated estimate of physical virginity', only a minority were directly hostile.

Mrs Gaskell's anxieties about *Ruth*, therefore, would seem to have been exaggerated if we consider them in the light of contemporary reactions. Nevertheless it is fair to

say that by devoting her novel explicitly and exclusively to
the issue of the fallen woman she was challenging her
readership in a distinctly provocative way. When mid-
Victorian fiction draws attention to sexual frailty it invariably does so in ways that confirm the existing stereo-
types of feminine behaviour: this is as true of George Eliot's
Adam Bede (1859), for example, as it is of Dickens's more
theatrical considerations of the topic. What was new about
Ruth was not only that it confronted the issue head-on, but
that in doing so—however awkwardly—it presented the
reader with a woman whose psychology as well as whose
situation demanded more than conventional sympathy and
understanding. The only real equivalent in its own time is
the somewhat special case of Hawthorne's *The Scarlet
Letter* (1850), a novel which Mrs Gaskell is likely to have
read, and which we may legitimately expect to have influenced her thinking. Not until Hardy's Tess—like Ruth
Hilton, 'a pure woman, faithfully presented'—do we have a
heroine who challenges the reader in the same way as does
the heroine of *Ruth*.

II

In the Preface to *Mary Barton* Mrs Gaskell had described
how, 'living in Manchester but with a deep relish and fond
admiration for the country', her first thought had been 'to
find a frame-work for my story in some rural scene'. This,
she says, she abandoned for an account of 'the lives of some
of those who elbowed me daily in the busy streets of the
town in which I resided'. In *Ruth*, again dealing with an
issue arising out of her Manchester experience, her chosen
'frame-work' was one that would allow her to express her
affection for country life.

The change of scene is an important one. In the first
place, provincialism in the Victorian novel invariably
implies the backward glance. The rhythms and pace of rural
society always carried for Victorian authors the implications
of rest and release. In a story which was to be devoted to
the redemption of its heroine from a disaster which marks
her for life the tranquillity of country life is the most potent

of restoratives. In such a context the symbolism of nature can play its part to the full: the flowers of field and garden suggest natural freshness and growth, while the vaster landscapes of nature evoke a permanence that provides fit setting for the moments of individual crisis. In a novel in which the healing power of time redeems the errors of a moment the passage of the seasons and of the years carries its own therapeutic force. But the choice of setting is significant in other ways. It allows Mrs Gaskell, for example, to indulge her enthusiasm for country manners and country ways, for the curiosities of dialect and of behavioural detail, in a way which somehow invests them with a moral weight of their own. The minor characters, like the Welsh inn-keeper, and notably the servant Sally, are somehow worthy *because* of the limiting nature of their provincialism: just as country recipes and country air are invested not only with physical but with moral quality. Mrs Gaskell deliberately chose for her action settings which had explicit personal significance for her and throughout *Ruth* we have a sense of the author's own presence in the novel that is generated as much by her attachment to her chosen scene as by her direct—and frequent—authorial inter-polations. Authorial intrusiveness is one of the dominant characteristics of Mrs Gaskell's fiction, based as it in-variably is upon personal commitment and remembered experience. *Ruth*, however, is a novel about which, as we have seen, she had serious misgivings, and the effect of her personal involvement in this case can be ambivalent. If at one level we sense her very real affection for the person-alities and the places she describes, at another the effect is one of uncertainty and reserve.

An examination of Mrs Gaskell's choice of settings in closer detail will indicate the kind of uncertainty to which I refer. As I suggest in detail in my notes to this edition, each of the four locational settings of the novel—Fordham, where Ruth is an apprentice; North Wales, where she is taken by Bellingham; Eccleston, where she lives out her life of repentance; and Abermouth, where she undergoes the traumatic experience of Bellingham's reappearance—can be associated fairly readily with places that Mrs Gaskell knew

well and which, in three of those four cases, had powerful
emotional associations for her. In each case, however, she
superimposes a kind of fictional disguise, as if reluctant to
allow the direct association to be made. Embarrassment like
this is perhaps not unusual in a novelist still learning her
trade. (*Jane Eyre* might offer a somewhat similar example:
any reader of that novel will find its geography awkwardly
contrived.) In *Ruth*, though, Mrs Gaskell seems both positively to want her story to embody the emotional associations these locations had for her while insisting all the time
that it is all only a fiction. All too conscious of the boundaries
between fiction and reality, in a work that deals fictionally
with a real-life issue she lacks the sophistication as a
novelist to conceal them.

Similar uncertainty can be seen to arise over the period in
which the novel is set. After the birth of Ruth's baby
concludes the first part of the novel, leaving her established
with the Bensons, we are given a chapter (Chapter 19) in
which, as Mrs Gaskell says, 'the quiet days grew into weeks
and months, and even years, without any event to startle
the little circle into the consciousness of the lapse of time'.
Later in the same chapter we are told that the child,
Leonard, is now 'a noble boy of six'. It is at this point that
we are introduced to the Bradshaw family, with Ruth's
appointment as a governess, and there is then the rapid
movement to the events of the election that will reintroduce
Ruth's lover Bellingham, now the Parliamentary candidate,
Mr Donne. It is quite clear, from the references to railway
travel alone, that these events, even if the geography is
entirely fictional, cannot take place earlier than the late
1830s. But at the outset of the novel we are told that Ruth's
apprenticeship was served in a 'country town many years
ago', and while 'many years ago' in a novel written in 1852
might legitimately be said to allow for the passage of less
than a quarter of a century—the longest period consistent
with the later events—the sense of the phrase in context
certainly seems to imply a date rather further in the past.
The point may seem a small one, but what I think it
suggests is that *Ruth*, not unlike *Cranford*, is at one and the
same time a contemporary novel and a retrospective novel.

In the same way, by the deliberate choice for her principal setting of a manufacturing town that is also a country town, Mrs Gaskell provides for the presentation of what came to her primarily as an urban issue within a provincial context. This is not to imply, of course, that there was no illegitimacy in provincial towns, or that unmarried mothers who lived in them were not at a social disadvantage. From the outset, however, critics have detected a problem at the heart of Mrs Gaskell's treatment of her theme, and while the root of that problem lies in her conception of her heroine, a contributory factor is that she brings to it what often seems to be an exaggerated sense of the shame attaching to Ruth's situation. Every reader of *Ruth* is likely to feel that the heroine's own sense of shame is painfully over-intense, even more so the reaction of her child to the discovery of his bastardy. Partly, at least, this must be because attitudes that have been formed by a Mancunian middle-class sensibility, and which apply within the context of urban domesticity, are brought to bear upon an issue that is formulated in terms of an earlier and different tradition.

Undoubtedly the uncertainties that reveal themselves in this way reflect Mrs Gaskell's deeper misgivings about *Ruth*; moreover, they are symptomatic of confusions that lie at the heart of the novel. If, as I have indicated, contemporary reviewers reacted on the whole favourably to *Ruth* they invariably pointed out that, far from over-stating her case, Mrs Gaskell had compromised it by the way in which she had presented her heroine. In particular they drew attention to Ruth Hilton's faultlessness, represented as it is by her unworldly innocence in matters of sexual relationships before her fall and by her acquiescence in the life of self-denial she is required to lead after it. Thus the reviewer in *Sharpe's London Magazine* (15 January 1853), while acknowledging the novel's 'tenderness' and 'delicious scenic descriptions', objected to Ruth herself as 'childlike': his counterpart in *The Gentleman's Magazine* (July 1853) felt that she should have been portrayed as 'more alive and less simple', and shown as 'less passive, more enthralled'—more subject, that is, to the pressure of her own sexual feeling. Fuller expression of these, and similar objections, was given in George Henry Lewes's expressly generous assessment in *The Westminster Review* (April 1853), where he argued that Ruth's fall was so qualified by 'extenuating circumstances' that 'the question of "guilt" is reduced to a point of casuistry'. Such criticism was taken to its logical conclusion by W. R. Greg, a Unitarian intellectual and businessman known personally to Mrs Gaskell, who had previously taken issue with her over the social philosophy of *Mary Barton*. In a long article entitled 'The False Morality of Lady Novelists', published in *The National Review* in January 1859, Greg wrote retrospectively of Mrs Gaskell's treatment of her heroine:

She has first imagined a character as pure, pious, and unselfish as poet ever fancied; and described a lapse from chastity as faultless as such a fault can be; and then, with damaging and unfaithful inconsistency, has given in to the world's estimate in such matters, by affirming that the sin committed was of so deep a dye that only a life of atoning and enduring persistence could wipe it out.

Greg goes on to point out that such a conception inevitably invalidates Ruth's representative status: she simply cannot be considered as one of 'the ordinary class of betrayed and deserted Magdalens'.

Criticism of this kind, from predominantly sympathetic commentators, is an interesting endorsement of the suggestion that Mrs Gaskell's anxieties about the propriety of her subject were exaggerated: what these critics are calling for is a more open examination of the realities of the case. And in terms of the novel itself their objections, as more recent assessments of *Ruth* have confirmed, are unanswerable. From the outset it is clear that Ruth Hilton is no ordinary sinner, nor even an ordinary dressmaker's apprentice. In a way that anticipates Hardy's account of Tess in *Tess of the d'Urbervilles*, Ruth is given qualities that distinguish her from her workmates, and which they themselves instinctively recognize; again, like Tess, her sexual ignorance—'she was too young', we are told, 'when her mother died to have received any cautions or words of advice respecting *the* subject of a woman's life', though it is difficult to believe that her workmates would not have

enlightened her—becomes not simply the instrument of her
downfall but a feature that contributes to the sense of her
fragile distinction. 'Remember', Mrs Gaskell insists, 'how
young and innocent, and motherless she was'—as if in some
way there could be degrees of motherlessness. Crucially
Mrs Gaskell turns her back on the period when Ruth must
have become Bellingham's physical lover, intimating only
that they had lived together for a while in London: when we
first see Ruth after she has run away with Bellingham it is
in the North Wales setting that is to be the scene of love
betrayed. The effect of all this—and of the manipulation of a
pattern of imagery that presents Ruth as a child of nature—
must be to deflect criticism from her, and it leaves the
reader with two problems. If we ask too many questions we
will find Ruth incredible; and if we accept her on Mrs
Gaskell's terms we will find it difficult to concede that she
must spend a lifetime in redemption of her guilt. For while
the history of Ruth's life with her benefactors, the Bensons,
is clearly meant to show us the way in which the world
should respond to cases like hers, as distinct from the way in
which it all too often does, her guilt is never questioned in
radical terms. Indeed, no one accepts it more completely
than she does herself: her sense of shame contributes as
much to her 'specialness' after her rescue as does her sexual
ignorance before her fall.

   Clearly Mrs Gaskell's first critics were right: over-
conscious of the hostility that might be aroused by her
theme, she compromises the issue by giving us a heroine to
whom no one could conceivably object. The fact that Hardy
should have felt the need to devise similar strategies in the
case of Tess is in itself interesting: determined that no one
should doubt the impeccable credentials of their heroines,
both authors undermine their representative credibility.
But comparison with Hardy reminds us of a simple and
central fact that we need to keep in mind where *Ruth* is
concerned. If Mrs Gaskell burdens her heroine with guilt it
is because she, unlike Hardy, has absolutely no doubt that
what she did, whatever the circumstances, was wrong.
Ruth Hilton is not, in her final analysis, innocent, and it
would have been inconceivable for Mrs Gaskell to have

regarded sexual relationships outside marriage as other than explicitly forbidden. Her novel is not a plea for sexual permissiveness, but for sympathy on society's part for those who have sinned: its criticisms are against the double standard that would absolve Bellingham and the inflexible moralism that would reject the sinner as does the obdurate Mr Bradshaw. Seen in this light the projection of Ruth as perfect beyond criticism has a logic of its own. If society can reject a sinner such as she, how will it react to the many less unexceptionable cases that are part of its daily experience?

Only when we have accepted Ruth Hilton on Mrs Gaskell's own terms is it possible to see what insight she offers into her situation. For Ruth's distinctiveness is not simply a matter of innocence and resignation; it embraces a sensitivity and depth of feeling that intensify the suffering involved in her tragedy. She has a receptivity to experience that is always at odds with the experiences that are forced upon her: our sense throughout is of what is lost to her in her enforced withdrawal from life. In the first chapter we are shown her at work in the apprentices' attic: 'Ruth pressed her hot forehead against the cold glass, and strained her aching eyes in gazing out on the lovely sky of a winter's night.' The scene is prophetic: throughout the novel we are to see the constraints imposed upon a heroine whose natural instincts are those of impulse and freedom. In Wales her response to the beauty around her defines both her inherent goodness and the unnaturalness of the relationship into which she has been coerced by Bellingham, and when he returns to her life at Abermouth the trauma of the situation is conveyed through an evocation of the power of a landscape to which we feel she, above all, responds. If Ruth, more than anyone, feels her own shame, so it is implicit in her suffering that she most of all should feel its intensity. And part of that suffering is that she *has* loved Bellingham, so much so that, when he returns, she fears the effect of the memories that he brings:

She dared not look round to see the figure of him who spoke, dark as it was. She knew he was there—she heard him speak in the manner in which he used to address strangers years ago; perhaps she answered him, perhaps she did not—God knew. It seemed as if weights were tied to her feet—as if time stood still,—it was so long, so terrible, that path across the reeling sand. [Chapter 23]

Inevitably in such a situation Mrs Gaskell overwrites, but the melodrama does not invalidate the feeling. Regardless of the reservations that can logically be held about Mrs Gaskell's presentation of her heroine in the context of her public theme, our reading experience, at central moments of the novel, is that she is determined to do justice to the expression of her inner life.

III

Inevitably discussion of *Ruth* must focus upon its heroine. But in this second novel Mrs Gaskell also reveals very real accomplishment in her account of the situations in which Ruth's drama is played out. Her presentation of the Benson household is an example of the tactful domestic quietism that had expressed itself in *Cranford* and was to be seen at its finest in her later story, *Cousin Phillis*, and it is underpinned in this case by her very firm grasp of the morality on which such a habit of life is based. The example of George Eliot was to show how provincial religious practice—particularly that of Dissent, with its emphasis on the claims of the individual conscience—could provide fertile soil for the novelist committed to the working out of a humane social morality: that is indeed what the Bensons themselves have to do, confronted by Ruth's plight. 'We are not to do evil that good may come,' Benson says, in response to the prospect of bribery in the Eccleston election: as he says it he recognizes immediately how the words reflect on the lie he has told to protect Ruth from public blame. Later Mrs Gaskell reverts to this issue, in an unresolved discussion between Benson and his sister in which his claim that 'God's omnipotence did not need our sin' is followed by an enigmatic silence. Criticism has made much of Benson's lie and Mrs Gaskell has been censured for failing to resolve the issue: the point surely is that it cannot be satisfactorily resolved. Benson's code is one of what might be called sympathetic morality, as opposed to the absolutism embodied in Mr Bradshaw, and sympathetic morality is of its essence a complex and uncertain affair.

The make-up of the Benson household is a simple one, its appeal lying in the deftness with which Mrs Gaskell juxtaposes the contrasting and complementary person-alities of the minister himself, his sister, and the servant, Sally. The Bensons represent, as I have suggested, the humanity of the Dissenting conscience: Sally's 'church' background is a detail which places them nicely. The Bradshaw *ménage*, by contrast, involves a much more complicated grouping. In the father is expressed the inflexibility of nonconformist morality, reinforced as it is by a utilitarian business ethic, while in his family we see the consequences of the rigorous application of his principles: the submissive ineffectiveness of the mother and the rebel-liousness of both daughter and son. If *Ruth* generally can be said to look forward to the provincial novels of George Eliot, in the specific instance of the Bradshaw family—from the overall conception down to the details of the criminality of the son and heir—we have a clear anticipation of the Gradgrinds of Dickens's *Hard Times*. (Dickens, it should be recorded, was much involved with Mrs Gaskell in the early 1850s; he expressed his admiration of *Ruth* when it first appeared in 1853, and began work on *Hard Times* in January 1854.) Where Dickens for the most part gives us the broad outlines of comic characterization and incident Mrs Gaskell offers a more sober analysis of the situation that has its own strengths. Ruth's assimilation into the Bradshaw family allows for the extension of the issue of her redemption from within the purely private sanctuary offered by the Bensons: at the same time it is the catalyst of a sequence of events that involves the Bradshaws themselves in a reconsideration of their own moral premises. As Mrs Gaskell says of Jemima, when she learns of Ruth's past, 'she had never imagined that she should ever come in contact with anyone who had committed open sin'. The interaction between Ruth and Jemima, with the insight it offers into Victorian conceptions of the role of women both within and without marriage, is only one aspect of the way in which the novel as a whole extends its terms of reference as the

Bradshaw context is developed. If much of the action
involving the election, with the reintroduction of
Bellingham as the candidate, seems contrived, the understanding Mrs Gaskell reveals of the pressures to be found
within a particular kind of Victorian family life is both
sympathetic and acute.

'Why should she die? Why are we to shut up the book
weeping?' Charlotte Brontë asked of the conclusion Mrs
Gaskell contrived for *Ruth*. In his turn, A. W. Ward, editor
of the 'Knutsford' edition, observed that 'the last chapters
of *Ruth* cannot very easily be treated from a purely literary
point of view'. In Charlotte Brontë's novels, of course, it is
the men who suffer in the end; it can fairly be said that Mrs
Gaskell's sense of realism would have saved her from
showing us Ruth triumphant. But even the most generous
criticism is bound to feel that the ultimate irony of her death
as a consequence of nursing her erstwhile seducer is ill
judged. *Ruth* is at best an uneven novel, its positive virtues
of honesty and insight going hand in hand with uncertainties
of focus and awkwardness of narrative contrivance.
Furthermore the whole story is coloured by its author's
overt and often embarrassing religiosity, and these limitations are never more in evidence than in the concluding
pages, where Mrs Gaskell contrives martyrdom for a
heroine who has at least earned the right to be accepted
amongst the living rather than glorified with the dead. That
Ruth should find her ultimate calling fulfilling a need within
the wider community is in itself appropriate, and in this
respect it is interesting that Mrs Gaskell should later have
found herself attracted to Florence Nightingale, whom she
described as 'like a Saint' and of whose hospital work she
was to write: 'it makes one feel the livingness of God more
than ever to think how straight He is sending his spirit
down into her, as into the prophets & saints of old' (*Letters*,
p. 307). In this instance, life would seem to have imitated
art. But Florence Nightingale was not a fallen woman. It
was ultimately impossible for Mrs Gaskell to conceive of
Ruth in other than tragic terms: the convention that the
social problem she represented was a tragedy in itself
ensured that the conventions of literary tragedy were the

only ones appropriate to the case. Hence Bellingham's last, and surely most unnecessary, reappearance; hence the death scene, appropriately solemnized by a Shakespearian text. The range of feeling embodied in *Ruth* as a whole, however, is far greater than that suggested by its conclusion alone. At its best a genuinely poetic novel, it examines its central issue with a deeply felt moral conviction. At the same time it never loses its sense of the way in which human beings behave, of their limitations and frailties, and of the potential that lies within them.

ALAN SHELSTON

NOTE ON THE TEXT

FOUR editions of *Ruth* were published in England in Mrs Gaskell's lifetime: the first edition, published in three volumes by Chapman and Hall in January 1853; the one-volume 'Cheap Edition', also published by Chapman and Hall, of 1855; the edition in two volumes published by Smith, Elder in 1857; and the 'new edition' published in the 'Parlour Library' in 1861. We have no record of Mrs Gaskell's involvement in corrections to her text, although we know that she altered it in one instance in response to a suggestion by Dickens (see note to page 64 in this edition). All editions after the first incorporate this amendment, together with minor textual corrections. *Ruth* was first published in The World's Classics in 1906, with an Introduction by Clement K. Shorter. The text used was based on the first edition, and it has been retained on this occasion.

SELECT BIBLIOGRAPHY

As well as the editions referred to in the Note on the Text there was a Tauchnitz edition of *Ruth* in two volumes, published in Leipzig in 1853, an American edition (Boston, 1855), and a French translation in the Bibliothèque des Chemins de Fer (1856). In the years following Mrs Gaskell's death *Ruth* retained its popularity, and there were various reprints in the later years of the nineteenth century. A second French translation, published in 1866, was reprinted six times in the same period. In this century, however, the popularity of this novel has declined: it appears only in The World's Classics edition of 1906, the Knutsford edition of the same year, reprinted in 1925, and in the Everyman's Library edition, with an Introduction by Margaret Lane (1967).

COLLECTED EDITIONS: The Knutsford edition (8 vols), with Introductions by A. W. Ward (Smith, Elder and Co., 1906), has generally taken precedence: its Introductions are sensitive and informative, but its text has been shown to be unreliable on occasion. It was reprinted under the imprint of John Murray in 1925. The other principal collected editions are *The Novels and Tales of Mrs Gaskell*, 8 vols (Smith, Elder, 1872–3) and the eleven separate volumes which appeared in The World's Classics between 1906 and 1919, each with an Introduction by Clement K. Shorter.

BIBLIOGRAPHIES: William E. A. and Ernest Axon, 'Bibliography of the Writings of Mrs Elizabeth Cleghorn Gaskell, Author of "Mary Barton", and of her husband, the Rev. William Gaskell, M.A.', in *Papers of the Manchester Literary Club* (1895); J. A. Green, *A Bibliographical Guide to the Gaskell Collection in the Moss Side Library* (1911); Clark S. Northup, 'Bibliographies' in G. DeWitt Sanders, *Elizabeth Gaskell* (1929); Robert L. Selig, *Elizabeth Gaskell: A Reference Guide* (1977); Jeffrey Welch, *Elizabeth Gaskell: An Annotated Bibliography 1929-1975* (1977).

BIOGRAPHY AND CRITICISM: The most valuable single source is *The Letters of Mrs Gaskell*, ed. J. A. V. Chapple and Arthur

Pollard (1966). Mrs Gaskell has attracted the attention of biographers from early days: amongst the more useful earlier biographical sources are Ward's Introductions to the Knutsford edition; Mrs Ellis H. Chadwick, *Mrs Gaskell, Haunts, Homes, and Stories* (1910, revised edn. 1913); Elizabeth Haldane, *Mrs Gaskell and her Friends* (1930); 'Letters addressed to Mrs Gaskell by Celebrated Contemporaries, Now in the Possession of the John Rylands Library', *Bulletin of the John Rylands Library*, XIX (1935). More substantial are the biographies by G. DeWitt Sanders (1929), Annette B. Hopkins (1952) and the most recent and comprehensive biography, *Elizabeth Gaskell* by Winifred Gérin (1976). J. G. Sharps, *Mrs Gaskell's Observation and Invention* (1970) is valuable primarily for its biographical detail and literary chronology; J. A. V. Chapple and J. G. Sharps, *Elizabeth Gaskell: A Portrait in Letters* (1980), draws on the *Letters* of 1966, and on further material that has come to light since that date

Modern full-length critical studies embodying substantial discussion of *Ruth* include: Arthur Pollard, *Mrs Gaskell: Novelist and Biographer* (1965); Edgar Wright, *Mrs Gaskell: The Basis for Reassessment* (1965); Margaret Ganz, *Elizabeth Gaskell: The Artist in Conflict* (1969); W. A. Craik, *Elizabeth Gaskell and the English Provincial Novel* (1975); Coral Lansbury, *Elizabeth Gaskell: the Novel of Social Crisis* (1975); Angus Easson, *Elizabeth Gaskell* (1979). See also: Wanda Neff, *Victorian Working Women* (1929); Patricia Thompson, *The Victorian Heroine: A Changing Ideal 1837–1873* (1956); Valentine Cunningham, *Everywhere Spoken Against: Dissent in the Victorian Novel* (1975); Michael D. Wheeler, 'The Sinner as Heroine: A Study of *Ruth* and the Bible', *Durham University Journal*, New Series vol. 37 (no. 2, June 1976); Nina Auerbach, 'The Rise of the Fallen Woman', *Nineteenth-Century Fiction*, vol. 35, no. 1 (June 1980); George Watt, *The Fallen Woman in the Nineteenth-Century English Novel* (1984).

A CHRONOLOGY OF
ELIZABETH GASKELL

RUTH

Drop, drop, slow tears!
  And bathe those beauteous feet,
Which brought from heaven
  The news and Prince of peace.
Cease not, wet eyes,
  For mercy to entreat:
To cry for vengeance
  Sin doth never cease.
In your deep floods
  Drown all my faults and fears;
Nor let His eye
  See sin, but through my tears.

*Phineas Fletcher**

RUTH

CHAPTER I

THERE is an assize-town in one of the eastern counties*
which was much distinguished by the Tudor sovereigns,
and, in consequence of their favour and protection,
attained a degree of importance that surprises the
modern traveller.

A hundred years ago, its appearance was that of
picturesque grandeur. The old houses, which were
the temporary residences of such of the county-families
as contented themselves with the gaieties of a provincial town, crowded the streets and gave them the
irregular but noble appearance yet to be seen in the
cities of Belgium. The sides of the streets had a
quaint richness, from the effect of the gables, and the
stacks of chimneys which cut against the blue sky
above; while, if the eye fell lower down, the attention
was arrested by all kinds of projections in the shape of
balcony and oriel; and it was amusing to see the
infinite variety of windows that had been crammed into
the walls long before Mr Pitt's days of taxation.* The
streets below suffered from all these projections and
advanced stories above; they were dark, and ill-paved
with large, round, jolting pebbles, and with no side-
path protected by kerb-stones; there were no lamp-
posts for long winter nights; and no regard was paid
to the wants of the middle class, who neither drove
about in coaches of their own, nor were carried by their
own men in their own sedans into the very halls of
their friends. The professional men and their wives,
the shopkeepers and their spouses, and all such people,

walked about at considerable peril both night and day.
The broad unwieldly carriages hemmed them up against
the houses in the narrow streets.   The inhospitable
houses projected their flights of steps almost into the
carriageway, forcing pedestrians again into the danger
they had avoided for twenty or thirty paces.   Then,
at night, the only light was derived from the glaring,
flaring oil-lamps hung above the doors of the more
aristocratic mansions; just allowing space for the
passers-by to become visible, before they again disappeared into the darkness, where it was no uncommon
thing for robbers to be in waiting for their prey.

The traditions of those bygone times, even to the
smallest social particular, enable one to understand
more clearly the circumstances which contributed to
the formation of character.   The daily life into which
people are born, and into which they are absorbed
before they are well aware, forms chains which only one
in a hundred has moral strength enough to despise, and
to break when the right times comes—when an inward
necessity for independent individual action arises,
which is superior to all outward conventionalities.
Therefore it is well to know what were the chains of
daily domestic habit which were the natural leading-
strings of our forefathers before they learnt to go
alone.

The picturesqueness of those ancient streets has
departed now.   The Astleys, the Dunstans, the
Waverhams—names of power in that district—go up
duly to London in the season, and have sold their
residences in the county-town fifty years ago, or
more.   And when the county-town lost its attraction
for the Astleys, the Dunstans, the Waverhams, how
could it be supposed that the Domvilles, the Bextons,
and the Wildes would continue to go and winter there
in their second-rate houses, and with their increased
expenditure?   So the grand old houses stood empty
awhile; and then speculators ventured to purchase,
and to turn the deserted mansions into many smaller
dwellings, fitted for professional men, or even (bend

your ear lower, lest the shade of Marmaduke, first
Baron Waverham, hear) into shops !

Even that was not so very bad, compared with the
next innovation on the old glories. The shopkeepers
found out that the once fashionable street was dark,
and that the dingy light did not show off their goods
to advantage ; the surgeon could not see to draw his
patient's teeth ; the lawyer had to ring for candles an
hour earlier than he was accustomed to do when living
in a more plebeian street. In short, by mutual
consent, the whole front of one side of the street was
pulled down, and rebuilt in the flat, mean, unrelieved
style of George the Third. The body of the houses
was too solidly grand to submit to alteration ; so
people were occasionally surprised, after passing
through a commonplace-looking shop, to find themselves at the foot of a grand carved oaken staircase,
lighted by a window of stained glass, storied all over
with armorial bearings.

Up such a stair—past such a window (through which
the moonlight fell on her with a glory of many colours)
—Ruth Hilton passed wearily one January night, now
many years ago.* I call it night ; but, strictly speaking,
it was morning. Two o'clock in the morning chimed
forth the old bells of St Saviour's. And yet more than
a dozen girls still sat in the room into which Ruth
entered, stitching away as if for very life, not daring to
gape, or show any outward manifestation of sleepiness.
They only sighed a little when Ruth told Mrs Mason
the hour of the night, as the result of her errand ;
for they knew that, stay up as late as they might, the
work-hours of the next day must begin at eight, and
their young limbs were very weary.

Mrs Mason worked away as hard as any ot them ;
but she was older and tougher ; and, besides, the gains
were hers. But even she perceived that some rest was
needed. " Young ladies ! there will be an interval
allowed of half an hour. Ring the bell, Miss Sutton.
Martha shall bring you up some bread and cheese and
beer. You will be so good as to eat it standing—

away from the dresses—and to have your hands washed ready for work when I return. In half an hour," said she once more, very distinctly ; and then she left the room.

It was curious to watch the young girls as they instantaneously availed themselves of Mrs Mason's absence. One fat, particularly heavy-looking damsel, laid her head on her folded arms and was asleep in a moment ; refusing to be wakened for her share in the frugal supper, but springing up with a frightened look at the sound of Mrs Mason's returning footstep, even while it was still far off on the echoing stairs. Two or three others huddled over the scanty fireplace, which, with every possible economy of space, and no attempt whatever at anything of grace or ornament, was inserted in the slight, flat-looking wall, that had been run up by the present owner of the property to portion off this division of the grand old drawing-room of the mansion. Some employed the time in eating their bread and cheese, with as measured and incessant a motion of the jaws (and almost as stupidly placid an expression of countenance), as you may see in cows ruminating in the first meadow you happen to pass.

Some held up admiringly the beautiful ball-dress in progress, while others examined the effect, backing from the object to be criticized in the true artistic manner. Others stretched themselves into all sorts of postures to relieve the weary muscles ; one or two gave vent to all the yawns, coughs, and sneezes that had been pent up so long in the presence of Mrs Mason. But Ruth Hilton sprang to the large old window, and pressed against it as a bird presses against the bars of its cage. She put back the blind, and gazed into the quiet moonlight night. It was doubly light—almost as much so as day—for everything was covered with the deep snow which had been falling silently ever since the evening before. The window was in a square recess ; the old strange little panes of glass had been replaced by those which gave more light. A little distance off, the feathery branches of a larch waved softly to and fro in the scarcely perceptible night-breeze. Poor old larch! the time had been when it had stood in a pleasant lawn, with the tender grass creeping caressingly up to its very trunk; but now the lawn was divided into yards and squalid back premises, and the larch was pent up and girded about with flag-stones. The snow lay thick on its boughs, and now and then fell noiselessly down. The old stables had been added to, and altered into a dismal street of mean-looking houses, back to back with the ancient mansions. And over all these changes from grandeur to squalor, bent down the purple heavens with their unchanging splendour!

Ruth pressed her hot forehead against the cold glass, and strained her aching eyes in gazing out on the lovely sky of a winter's night. The impulse was strong upon her to snatch up a shawl, and wrapping it round her head, to sally forth and enjoy the glory; and time was when that impulse would have been instantly followed; but now, Ruth's eyes filled with tears, and she stood quite still, dreaming of the days that were gone. Some one touched her shoulder while her thoughts were far away, remembering past January nights, which had resembled this, and were yet so different.

"Ruth, love," whispered a girl who had unwillingly distinguished herself by a long hard fit of coughing, "come and have some supper. You don't know yet how it helps one through the night."

"One run—one blow of the fresh air would do me more good," said Ruth.

"Not such a night as this," replied the other, shivering at the very thought.

"And why not such a night as this, Jenny?" answered Ruth. "Oh! at home I have many a time run up the lane all the way to the mill, just to see the icicles hang on the great wheel, and when I was once out, I could hardly find in my heart to come in, even to mother, sitting by the fire;—even to mother," she added, in a low, melancholy tone, which had some-

thing of inexpressible sadness in it. "Why, Jenny!"
said she, rousing herself, but not before her eyes were
swimming with tears, "own, now, that you never saw
those dismal, hateful, tumble-down old houses there
look half so—what shall I call them? almost beautiful
—as they do now, with that soft, pure, exquisite
covering; and if they are so improved, think of what
trees, and grass, and ivy, must be on such a night as
this."

Jenny could not be persuaded into admiring the
winter's night, which to her came only as a cold and
dismal time, when her cough was more troublesome,
and the pain in her side worse than usual. But she
put her arm round Ruth's neck, and stood by her;
glad that the orphan apprentice, who was not yet in-
ured to the hardship of a dressmaker's workroom,
should find so much to give her pleasure in such a
common occurrence as a frosty night.

They remained deep in separate trains of thought
till Mrs Mason's step was heard, when each returned,
supperless but refreshed, to her seat.

Ruth's place was the coldest and the darkest in the
room, although she liked it the best; she had instinctively chosen it for the sake of the wall opposite to
her, on which was a remnant of the beauty of the old
drawing-room, which must once have been magnificent,
to judge from the faded specimen left. It was divided
into panels of pale sea-green, picked out with white
and gold; and on these panels were painted—were
thrown with the careless, triumphant hand of a master
—the most lovely wreaths of flowers, profuse and luxuriant beyond description, and so real-looking, that you
could almost fancy you smelt their fragrance, and heard
the south wind go softly rustling in and out among the
crimson roses—the branches of purple and white lilac
—the floating golden-tressed laburnum boughs. Besides these, there were stately white lilies, sacred to the
Virgin—hollyhocks, fraxinella, monk's-hood, pansies,
primroses; every flower which blooms profusely in
charming old-fashioned country-gardens was there,

depicted among its graceful foliage, but not in the wild disorder in which I have enumerated them. At the bottom of the panel lay a holly-branch, whose stiff straightness was ornamented by a twining drapery of English ivy and mistletoe and winter aconite; while down either side hung pendant garlands of spring and autumn flowers; and, crowning all, came gorgeous summer with the sweet musk-roses, and the rich-coloured flowers of June and July.

Surely Monnoyer,* or whoever the dead and gone artist might be, would have been gratified to know the pleasure his handiwork, even in its wane, had power to give to the heavy heart of a young girl; for they conjured up visions of other sister-flowers that grew, and blossomed, and withered away in her early home.

Mrs Mason was particularly desirous that her work-women should exert themselves to-night, for, on the next, the annual hunt-ball was to take place. It was the one gaiety of the town since the assize-balls had been discontinued. Many were the dresses she had promised should be sent home "without fail" the next morning; she had not let one slip through her fingers, for fear, if it did, it might fall into the hands of the rival dressmaker, who had just established herself in the very same street.

She determined to administer a gentle stimulant to the flagging spirits, and with a little preliminary cough to attract attention, she began:

"I may as well inform you, young ladies, that I have been requested this year, as on previous occasions, to allow some of my young people to attend in the ante-chamber of the assembly-room with sandal ribbon, pins, and such little matters, and to be ready to repair any accidental injury to the ladies' dresses. I shall send four—of the most diligent." She laid a marked emphasis on the last words, but without much effect; they were too sleepy to care for any of the pomps and vanities, or, indeed, for any of the comforts of this world, excepting one sole thing— their beds.

Mrs Mason was a very worthy woman, but, like
many other worthy women, she had her foibles; and
one (very natural to her calling) was to pay an extreme
regard to appearances. Accordingly, she had already
selected in her own mind the four girls who were most
likely to do credit to the "establishment"; and these
were secretly determined upon, although it was very
well to promise the reward to the most diligent.
She was really not aware of the falseness of this
conduct; being an adept in that species of sophistry
with which people persuade themselves that what they
wish to do is right.

At last there was no resisting the evidence of weariness. They were told to go to bed; but even that
welcome command was languidly obeyed. Slowly
they folded up their work, heavily they moved about,
until at length all was put away, and they trooped up
the wide, dark staircase.

"Oh! how shall I get through five years of these
terrible nights!* in that close room! and in that
oppressive stillness! which lets every sound of the
thread be heard as it goes eternally backwards and
forwards," sobbed out Ruth, as she threw herself on
her bed, without even undressing herself.

"Nay, Ruth, you know it won't be always as it has
been to-night. We often get to bed by ten o'clock;
and by and by you won't mind the closeness of the
room. You're worn out to-night, or you would not
have minded the sound of the needle; I never hear
it. Come, let me unfasten you," said Jenny.

"What is the use of undressing? We must be up
again and at work in three hours."

"And in those three hours you may get a great deal
of rest, if you will but undress yourself and fairly go
to bed. Come, love."

Jenny's advice was not resisted; but before Ruth
went to sleep, she said:

"Oh! I wish I was not so cross and impatient. I
don't think I used to be."

"No, I am sure not. Most new girls get impatient

at first ; but it goes off, and they don't care much for anything after awhile. Poor child ! she's asleep already," said Jenny to herself.

She could not sleep or rest. The tightness at her side was worse than usual. She almost thought she ought to mention it in her letters home ; but then she remembered the premium her father had struggled hard to pay, and the large family, younger than herself, that had to be cared for, and she determined to bear on, and trust that when the warm weather came both the pain and the cough would go away. She would be prudent about herself.

What was the matter with Ruth ? She was crying in her sleep as if her heart would break. Such agitated slumber could be no rest; so Jenny wakened her.

"Ruth ! Ruth !"

"Oh, Jenny !" said Ruth, sitting up in bed, and pushing back the masses of hair that were heating her forehead, "I thought I saw mamma by the side of the bed, coming, as she used to do, to see if I were asleep and comfortable ; and when I tried to take hold of her, she went away and left me alone—I don't know where ; so strange !"

"It was only a dream ; you know you'd been talking about her to me, and you're feverish with sitting up late. Go to sleep again, and I'll watch, and waken you if you seem uneasy."

"But you'll be so tired. Oh, dear ! dear !" Ruth was asleep again, even while she sighed.

Morning came, and though their rest had been short, the girls arose refreshed.

"Miss Sutton, Miss Jennings, Miss Booth, and Miss Hilton, you will see that you are ready to accompany me to the shire-hall by eight o'clock."

One or two of the girls looked astonished, but the majority having anticipated the selection, and knowing from experience the unexpressed rule by which it was made, received it with the sullen indifference which had become their feeling with regard to most events—

a deadened sense of life, consequent upon their unnatural mode of existence, their sedentary days, and
their frequent nights of late watching.

But to Ruth it was inexplicable. She had yawned,
and loitered, and looked off at the beautiful panel, and
lost herself in thoughts of home, until she fully expected the reprimand which at any other time she
would have been sure to receive, and now, to her surprise, she was singled out as one of the most diligent!

Much as she longed for the delight of seeing the
noble shire-hall—the boast of the county—and of
catching glimpses of the dancers, and hearing the
band; much as she longed for some variety to the dull
monotonous life she was leading, she could not feel
happy to accept a privilege, granted, as she believed,
in ignorance of the real state of the case; so she
startled her companions by rising abruptly and going
up to Mrs Mason, who was finishing a dress which
ought to have been sent home two hours before:

"If you please, Mrs Mason, I was not one of the
most diligent; I am afraid—I believe—I was not diligent at all. I was very tired; and I could not help
thinking, and when I think, I can't attend to my
work." She stopped, believing she had sufficiently
explained her meaning; but Mrs Mason would not
understand, and did not wish for any further
elucidation.

"Well, my dear, you must learn to think and work
too; or, if you can't do both, you must leave off thinking. Your guardian, you know, expects you to make
great progress in your business, and I am sure you
won't disappoint him."

But that was not to the point. Ruth stood still an
instant, although Mrs Mason resumed her employment
in a manner which any one but a "new girl" would
have known to be intelligible enough, that she did not
wish for any more conversation just then.

"But as I was not diligent I ought not to go, ma'am.
Miss Wood was far more industrious than I, and many
of the others."

"Tiresome girl!" muttered Mrs Mason; "I've half a mind to keep her at home for plaguing me so." But, looking up, she was struck afresh with the remarkable beauty which Ruth possessed; such a credit to the house, with her waving outline of figure, her striking face, with dark eyebrows and dark lashes, combined with auburn hair and a fair complexion. No! diligent or idle, Ruth Hilton must appear to-night.

"Miss Hilton," said Mrs Mason, with stiff dignity, "I am not accustomed (as these young ladies can tell you) to have my decisions questioned. What I say, I mean; and I have my reasons. So sit down, if you please, and take care and be ready by eight. Not a word more," as she fancied she saw Ruth again about to speak.

"Jenny! you ought to have gone, not me," said Ruth, in no low voice to Miss Wood, as she sat down by her.

"Hush! Ruth. I could not go if I might, because of my cough. I would rather give it up to you than any one, if it were mine to give. And suppose it is, and take the pleasure as my present, and tell me every bit about it when you come home to-night."

"Well! I shall take it in that way, and not as if I'd earned it, which I haven't. So thank you. You can't think how I shall enjoy it now. I did work diligently for five minutes last night, after I heard of it, I wanted to go so much. But I could not keep it up. Oh, dear! and I shall really hear a band! and see the inside of that beautiful shire-hall!"

CHAPTER II

In due time that evening, Mrs Mason collected "her young ladies" for an inspection of their appearance before proceeding to the shire-hall. Her eager, important, hurried manner of summoning them was not unlike that of a hen clucking her chickens together; and

to judge from the close investigation they had to un-
dergo, it might have been thought that their part in
the evening's performance was to be far more important
than that of temporary ladies'-maids.

"Is that your best frock, Miss Hilton?" asked Mrs
Mason, in a half-dissatisfied tone, turning Ruth about;
for it was only her Sunday black silk, and was somewhat worn and shabby.

"Yes, ma'am," answered Ruth, quietly.

"Oh! indeed. Then it will do" (still the half-
satisfied tone). "Dress, young ladies, you know is a
very secondary consideration. Conduct is everything.
Still, Miss Hilton, I think you should write and ask
your guardian to send you money for another gown.
I am sorry I did not think of it before."

"I do not think he would send any if I wrote,"
answered Ruth, in a low voice. "He was angry when
I wanted a shawl, when the cold weather set in."

Mrs Mason gave her a little push of dismissal, and
Ruth fell into the ranks by her friend, Miss Wood.

"Never mind, Ruthie; you're prettier than any of
them," said a merry, good-natured girl, whose plain-
ness excluded her from any of the envy of rivalry.

"Yes! I know I am pretty," said Ruth, sadly, "but
I am sorry I have no better gown, for this is very
shabby. I am ashamed of it myself, and I can see Mrs
Mason is twice as much ashamed. I wish I need not
go. I did not know we should have to think about our
own dress at all, or I should not have wished to go."

"Never mind, Ruth," said Jenny, "you've been
looked at now, and Mrs Mason will soon be too busy
to think about you and your gown."

"Did you hear Ruth Hilton say she knew she was
pretty?" whispered one girl to another, so loudly
that Ruth caught the words.

"I could not help knowing," answered she, simply,
"for many people have told me so."

At length these preliminaries were over, and they
were walking briskly through the frosty air; the free
motion was so inspiriting that Ruth almost danced

along, and quite forgot all about shabby gowns and
grumbling guardians. The shire-hall was even more
striking than she had expected. The sides of the staircase were painted with figures that showed ghostly in the
dim light, for only their faces looked out of the dark
dingy canvas, with strange fixed stare of expression.

The young milliners had to arrange their wares
on tables in the ante-room, and make all ready before
they could venture to peep into the ball-room, where
the musicians were already tuning their instruments,
and where one or two char-women (strange contrast!
with their dirty, loose attire, and their incessant
chatter, to the grand echoes of the vaulted room)
were completing the dusting of benches and chairs.

They quitted the place as Ruth and her companions
entered. They had talked lightly and merrily in the
ante-room, but now their voices were hushed, awed
by the old magnificence of the vast apartment. It
was so large, that objects showed dim at the further
end, as through mist. Full-length figures of county
worthies hung around, in all varieties of costume,
from the days of Holbein to the present time. The
lofty roof was indistinct for the lamps were not fully
lighted; yet while through the richly-painted Gothic
window at one end the moonbeams fell, many-tinted, on
the floor, and mocked with their vividness the struggles
of the artificial light to illuminate its little sphere.

High above sounded the musicians, fitfully trying
some strain of which they were not certain. Then
they stopped playing and talked, and their voices
sounded goblin-like in their dark recess, where candles
were carried about in an uncertain wavering manner,
reminding Ruth of the flickering zigzag motion of
the will-o'-the-wisp.

Suddenly the room sprang into the full blaze of
light, and Ruth felt less impressed with its appearance, and more willing to obey Mrs Mason's sharp
summons to her wandering flock, than she had been
when it was dim and mysterious. They had presently enough to do in rendering offices of assistance

to the ladies who thronged in, and whose voices
drowned all the muffled sound of the band Ruth
had longed so much to hear. Still, if one pleasure
was less, another was greater than she had anticipated.

"On condition" of such a number of little ob-
servances that Ruth thought Mrs Mason would never
have ended enumerating them, they were allowed
during the dances to stand at a side-door and watch.
And what a beautiful sight it was! Floating away
to that bounding music, now far away, like garlands
of fairies, now near, and showing as lovely women,
with every ornament of graceful dress, the élite of
the county danced on, little caring whose eyes gazed
and were dazzled. Outside all was cold, and colourless,
and uniform, one coating of snow over all. But inside
it was warm, and glowing, and vivid; flowers scented
the air, and wreathed the head, and rested on the
bosom, as if it were midsummer. Bright colours
flashed on the eye and were gone, and succeeded by
others as lovely in the rapid movement of the dance.
Smiles dimpled every face, and low tones of happiness
murmured indistinctly through the room in every pause
of the music.

Ruth did not care to separate the figures that formed
a joyous and brilliant whole; it was enough to gaze,
and dream of the happy smoothness of the lives in
which such music, and such profusion of flowers, of
jewels, elegance of every description, and beauty of
all shapes and hues, were everyday things. She did
not want to know who the people were; although to
hear a catalogue of names seemed to be the great
delight of most of her companions.

In fact, the enumeration rather disturbed her; and
to avoid the shock of too rapid a descent into the
commonplace world of Miss Smiths and Mr Thomsons,
she returned to her post in the ante-room. There
she stood thinking, or dreaming. She was startled
back to actual life by a voice close to her. One of
the dancing young ladies had met with a misfortune.
Her dress of some gossamer material, had been looped

up by nosegays of flowers, and one of these had fallen
off in the dance, leaving her gown to trail. To repair
this, she had begged her partner to bring her to the
room where the assistants should have been. None
were there but Ruth.

"Shall I leave you?" asked the gentleman. "Is
my absence necessary?"

"Oh, no!" replied the lady. "A few stitches
will set all to rights. Besides, I dare not enter that
room by myself." So far she spoke sweetly and
prettily. But now she addressed Ruth. "Make
haste. Don't keep me an hour." And her voice
became cold and authoritative.

She was very pretty, with long dark ringlets and
sparkling black eyes. These had struck Ruth in the
hasty glance she had taken, before she knelt down
to her task. She also saw that the gentleman was
young and elegant.

"Oh, that lovely galop! How I long to dance to
it! Will it never be done? What a frightful time
you are taking; and I'm dying to return in time for
this galop!"

By way of showing a pretty childlike impatience,
she began to beat time with her feet to the spirited air
the band was playing. Ruth could not darn the rent
in her dress with this continual motion, and she looked
up to remonstrate. As she threw her head back for
this purpose, she caught the eye of the gentleman who
was standing by; it was so expressive of amusement at
the airs and graces of his pretty partner, that Ruth
was infected by the feeling, and had to bend her face
down to conceal the smile that mantled there. But
not before he had seen it, and not before his attention
had been thereby drawn to consider the kneeling figure,
that, habited in black up to the throat, with the noble
head bent down to the occupation in which she was
engaged, formed such a contrast to the flippant, bright,
artificial girl who sat to be served with an air as haughty
as a queen on her throne.

"Oh, Mr Bellingham! I'm ashamed to detain you

so long. I had no idea any one could have spent so
much time over a little tear. No wonder Mrs Mason
charges so much for dress-making, if her work-women
are so slow."

It was meant to be witty, but Mr Bellingham looked
grave. He saw the scarlet colour of annoyance flush
to that beautiful cheek which was partially presented
to him. He took a candle from the table, and held
it so that Ruth had more light. She did not look up
to thank him, for she felt ashamed that he should have
seen the smile which she had caught from him.

"I am sorry I have been so long, ma'am," said she,
gently, as she finished her work. "I was afraid it
might tear out again if I did not do it carefully." She
rose.

"I would rather have had it torn than have missed
that charming galop," said the young lady shaking
out her dress as a bird shakes its plumage. "Shall
we go, Mr Bellingham?" looking up at him.

He was surprised that she gave no word or sign of
thanks to the assistant. He took up a camellia that
some one had left on the table.

"Allow me, Miss Duncombe, to give this in your
name to this young lady, as thanks for her dexterous
help."

"Oh—of course," said she.

Ruth received the flower silently, but with a grave,
modest motion of her head. They had gone, and she
was once more alone. Presently, her companions
returned.

"What was the matter with Miss Duncombe? Did
she come here?" asked they.

"Only her lace dress was torn, and I mended it,"
answered Ruth, quietly.

"Did Mr Bellingham come with her? They say
he's going to be married to her; did he come
Ruth?"

"Yes," said Ruth, and relapsed into silence.

Mr Bellingham danced on gaily and merrily through
the night, and flirted with Miss Duncombe, as he

thought good. But he looked often to the side-door
where the milliner's apprentices stood ; and once he
recognised the tall, slight figure, and the rich auburn
hair of the girl in black ; and then his eye sought for
the camellia. It was there, snowy white in her bosom.
And he danced on more gaily than ever.

The cold grey dawn was drearily lighting up the
streets when Mrs Mason and her company returned
home. The lamps were extinguished, yet the shutters
of the shops and dwelling-houses were not opened.
All sounds had an echo unheard by day. One or two
houseless beggars sat on doorsteps, and, shivering,
slept, with heads bowed on their knees, or resting
against the cold hard support afforded by the wall.

Ruth felt as if a dream had melted away, and she
were once more in the actual world. How long it
would be, even in the most favourable chance, before
she should again enter the shire-hall ! or hear a band
of music ! or even see again those bright happy people
—as much without any semblance of care or woe as if
they belonged to another race of beings. Had they
ever to deny themselves a wish, much less a want ?
Literally and figuratively, there lives seemed to wander
through flowery pleasure-paths. Here was cold, biting
mid-winter for her, and such as her—for those poor
beggars almost a season of death ; but to Miss
Duncombe and her companions, a happy, merry time,
when flowers still bloomed, and fires crackled, and
comforts and luxuries were piled around them like
fairy gifts. What did they know of the meaning of
the word, so terrific to the poor ? What was winter
to them ? But Ruth fancied that Mr Bellingham
looked as if he could understand the feelings of those
removed from him by circumstance and station. He
had drawn up the windows of his carriage, it is true,
with a shudder.

Ruth, then, had been watching him.

Yet she had no idea that any association made her
camellia precious to her. She believed it was solely on
account of its exquisite beauty that she tended it so

carefully. She told Jenny every particular of its
presentation, with open, straight-looking eye, and
without the deepening of a shade of colour.

"Was it not kind of him? You can't think how
nicely he did it, just when I was a little bit mortified
by her ungracious ways."

"It was very nice, indeed," replied Jenny. "Such
a beautiful flower! I wish it had some scent."

"I wish it to be exactly as it is; it is perfect. So
pure!" said Ruth, almost clasping her treasure as she
placed it in water. "Who is Mr Bellingham?"

"He is son to that Mrs Bellingham of the Priory,
for whom we made the grey satin pelisse," answered
Jenny, sleepily.

"That was before my time," said Ruth. But there
was no answer. Jenny was asleep.

It was long before Ruth followed her example.
Even on a winter day, it was clear morning light that
fell upon her face as she smiled in her slumber.
Jenny would not waken her, but watched her face with
admiration; it was so lovely in its happiness.

"She is dreaming of last night," thought Jenny.

It was true she was; but one figure flitted more
than all the rest through her visions. He presented
flower after flower to her in that baseless morning
dream, which was all too quickly ended. The night
before, she had seen her dead mother in her sleep, and
she wakened, weeping. And now she dreamed of Mr
Bellingham, and smiled.

And yet, was this a more evil dream than the
other?

The realities of life seemed to cut more sharply
against her heart than usual that morning. The late
hours of the preceding nights, and perhaps the excitement of the evening before, had indisposed her to bear
calmly the rubs and crosses which beset all Mrs Mason's
young ladies at times.

For Mrs Mason, though the first dressmaker in the
county, was human after all; and suffered, like her
apprentices, from the same causes that affected them.

This morning she was disposed to find fault with everything, and everybody. She seemed to have risen with the determination of putting the world and all that it contained (her world, at least) to rights before night; and abuses and negligences, which had long passed unreproved, or winked at, were to-day to be dragged to light, and sharply reprimanded. Nothing less than perfection would satisfy Mrs Mason at such times.

She had her ideas of justice, too; but they were not divinely beautiful and true ideas; they were something more resembling a grocer's, or tea-dealer's ideas of equal right. A little over-indulgence last night was to be balanced by a good deal of over-severity to-day; and this manner of rectifying previous errors fully satisfied her conscience.

Ruth was not inclined for, or capable of, much extra exertion; and it would have tasked all her powers to have pleased her superior. The work-room seemed filled with sharp calls. "Miss Hilton! where have you put the blue Persian? Whenever things are mislaid, I know it has been Miss Hilton's evening for siding away!"

"Miss Hilton was going out last night, so I offered to clear the workroom for her. I will find it directly, ma'am," answered one of the girls.

"Oh, I am well aware of Miss Hilton's custom of shuffling off her duties upon any one who can be induced to relieve her," replied Mrs Mason.

Ruth reddened, and tears sprang to her eyes; but she was so conscious of the falsity of the accusation, that she rebuked herself for being moved by it, and, raising her head, gave a proud look round, as if in appeal to her companions.

"Where is the skirt of Lady Farnham's dress? The flounces not put on! I am surprised. May I ask to whom this work was entrusted yesterday?" inquired Mrs Mason, fixing her eyes on Ruth.

"I was to have done it, but I made a mistake, and had to undo it. I am very sorry."

"I might have guessed, certainly. There is little difficulty, to be sure, in discovering, when work has been neglected or spoilt, into whose hands it has fallen."

Such were the speeches which fell to Ruth's share on this day of all days, when she was least fitted to bear them with equanimity.

In the afternoon it was necessary for Mrs Mason to go a few miles into the country. She left injunctions, and orders, and directions, and prohibitions without end; but at last she was gone, and in the relief of her absence, Ruth laid her arms on the table, and, burying her head, began to cry aloud, with weak, unchecked sobs.

"Don't cry, Miss Hilton,"—"Ruthie, never mind the old dragon,"—"How will you bear on for five years, if you don't spirit yourself up not to care a straw for what she says?"—were some of the modes of comfort and sympathy administered by the young workwomen.

Jenny, with a wiser insight into the grievance and its remedy, said:

"Suppose Ruth goes out instead of you, Fanny Barton, to do the errands. The fresh air will do her good; and you know you dislike the cold east winds, while Ruth says she enjoys frost and snow, and all kinds of shivery weather."

Fanny Barton was a great sleepy-looking girl, huddling over the fire. No one so willing as she to relinquish the walk on this bleak afternoon, when the east wind blew keenly down the street, drying up the very snow itself. There was no temptation to come abroad, for those who were not absolutely obliged to leave their warm rooms; indeed, the dusk hour showed that it was the usual tea-time for the humble inhabitants of that part of the town through which Ruth had to pass on her shopping expedition. As she came to the high ground just above the river, where the street sloped rapidly down to the bridge, she saw the flat country beyond all covered with snow, making the black dome of the cloud-laden sky appear yet blacker; as if the winter's night had never fairly gone away, but had hovered on the edge of the world all through the short bleak day. Down by the bridge (where there was a little shelving bank, used as a landing-place for any pleasure-boats that could float on that shallow stream) some children were playing, and defying the cold; one of them had got a large washing-tub, and with the use of a broken oar kept steering and pushing himself hither and thither in the little creek, much to the admiration of his companions, who stood gravely looking on, immovable in their attentive observation of the hero, although their faces were blue with cold, and their hands crammed deep into their pockets with some faint hope of finding warmth there. Perhaps they feared that, if they unpacked themselves from their lumpy attitudes and began to move about, the cruel wind would find its way into every cranny of their tattered dress. They were all huddled up, and still; with eyes intent on the embryo sailor. At last, one little man, envious of the reputation that his playfellow was acquiring by his daring, called out:

"I'll set thee a craddy,* Tom! Thou dar'n't go over yon black line in the water, out into the real river."

Of course the challenge was not to be refused, and Tom paddled away towards the dark line, beyond which the river swept with smooth, steady current. Ruth (a child in years herself) stood at the top of the declivity watching the adventurer, but as unconscious of any danger as the group of children below. At their playfellow's success, they broke through the calm gravity of observation into boisterous marks of applause, clapping their hands, and stamping their impatient little feet, and shouting, "Well done, Tom; thou hast done it rarely!"

Tom stood in childish dignity for a moment, facing his admirers; then, in an instant, his washing-tub boat was whirled round, and he lost his balance, and

fell out; and both he and his boat were carried away
slowly, but surely, by the strong full river which
eternally moved onwards to the sea.

The children shrieked aloud with terror; and Ruth
flew down to the little bay, and far into its shallow
waters, before she felt how useless such an action was,
and that the sensible plan would have been to seek for
efficient help.   Hardly had this thought struck her,
when, louder and sharper than the sullen roar of the
stream that was ceaselessly and unrelentingly flowing
on, came the splash of a horse galloping through the
water in which she was standing.   Passed her like
lightning—down in the stream, swimming along with
the current—a stooping rider—an outstretched, grasping arm—a little life redeemed, and a child saved to
those who loved it!   Ruth stood dizzy and sick with
emotion while all this took place; and when the rider
turned his swimming horse, and slowly breasted up
the river to the landing-place, she recognised him as
the Mr Bellingham of the night before.   He carried
the unconscious child across his horse; the body hung
in so lifeless a manner that Ruth believed it was dead,
and her eyes were suddenly blinded with tears.   She
waded back to the beach, to the point towards which
Mr Bellingham was directing his horse.

"Is he dead?" asked she, stretching out her arms
to receive the little fellow; for she instinctively felt
that the position in which he hung was not the most
conducive to returning consciousness, if, indeed, it
would ever return.

"I think not," answered Mr Bellingham, as he gave
the child to her, before springing off his horse.   "Is
he your brother?   Do you know who he is?"

"Look!" said Ruth, who had sat down upon the
ground, the better to prop the poor lad, "his hand
twitches! he lives! oh, sir, he lives!   Whose boy is
he?" (to the people, who came hurrying and gathering
to the spot at the rumour of an accident).

"He's old Nelly Brownson's," said they.   "Her
grandson."

"We must take him into a house directly," said she. "Is his home far off?"

"No, no; it's just close by."

"One of you go for a doctor at once," said Mr Bellingham, authoritatively, "and bring him to the old woman's without delay. You must not hold him any longer," he continued, speaking to Ruth, and remembering her face now for the first time; "your dress is dripping wet already. Here! you fellow, take him up, d'ye see!"

But the child's hand had nervously clenched Ruth's dress, and she would not have him disturbed. She carried her heavy burden very tenderly towards a mean little cottage indicated by the neighbours; an old crippled woman was coming out of the door, shaking all over with agitation.

"Dear heart?" said she, "he's the last of 'em all, and he's gone afore me."

"Nonsense," said Mr Bellingham, "the boy is alive, and likely to live."

But the old woman was helpless and hopeless, and insisted on believing that her grandson was dead; and dead he would have been if it had not been for Ruth, and one or two of the more sensible neighbours, who, under Mr Bellingham's directions, bustled about, and did all that was necessary until animation was restored.

"What a confounded time these people are in fetching the doctor," said Mr Bellingham to Ruth, between whom and himself a sort of silent understanding had sprung up from the circumstance of their having been the only two (besides mere children) who had witnessed the accident, and also the only two to whom a certain degree of cultivation had given the power of understanding each other's thoughts and even each other's words.

"It takes so much to knock an idea into such stupid people's heads. They stood gaping and asking which doctor they were to go for, as if it signified whether it was Brown or Smith, so long as he had his

wits about him. I have no more time to waste here
either; I was on the gallop when I caught sight of the
lad; and now he has fairly sobbed and opened his
eyes, I see no use in my staying in this stifling atmosphere. May I trouble you with one thing? Will
you be so good as to see that the little fellow has all
that he wants? If you'll allow me, I'll leave you my
purse," continued he, giving it to Ruth, who was only
too glad to have this power entrusted to her of procuring one or two requisites which she had perceived to
be wanted. But she saw some gold between the
net-work; she did not like the charge of such
riches.

"I shall not want so much, really, sir, One
sovereign will be plenty—more than enough. May I
take that out, and I will give you back what is left of
it when I see you again? or, perhaps I had better send
it to you, sir?"

"I think you had better keep it all at present.
Oh! what a horrid dirty place this is; insufferable
two minutes longer. You must not stay here; you'll
be poisoned with this abominable air. Come towards
the door, I beg. Well, if you think one sovereign
will be enough, I will take my purse; only, remember
you apply to me if you think they want more."

They were standing at the door, where some one was
holding Mr Bellingham's horse. Ruth was looking at
him with her earnest eyes (Mrs Mason and her errands
quite forgotten in the interest of the afternoon's event),
her whole thoughts bent upon rightly understanding
and following out his wishes for the little boy's welfare;
and until now this had been the first object in his own
mind. But at this moment the strong perception of
Ruth's exceeding beauty came again upon him. He
almost lost the sense of what he was saying, he was so
startled into admiration. The night before, he had
not seen her eyes; and now they looked straight and
innocently full at him, grave, earnest, and deep. But
when she instinctively read the change in the expression of his countenance, she dropped her large white

veiling lids; and he thought her face was lovelier still.

The irresistible impulse seized him to arrange matters so that he might see her again before long.

"No!" said he. "I see it would be better that you should keep the purse. Many things may be wanted for the lad which we cannot calculate upon now. If I remember rightly, there are three sovereigns and some loose change; I shall, perhaps, see you again in a few days, when, if there be any money left in the purse, you can restore it to me."

"Oh, yes, sir," said Ruth, alive to the magnitude of the wants to which she might have to administer, and yet rather afraid of the responsibility implied in the possession of so much money.

"Is there any chance of my meeting you again in this house?" asked he.

"I hope to come whenever I can, sir; but I must run in errand-times, and I don't know when my turn may be."

"Oh"—he did not fully understand this answer— "I should like to know how you think the boy is going on, if it is not giving you too much trouble; do you ever take walks?"

"Not for walking's sake, sir."

"Well!" said he, "you go to church, I suppose? Mrs Mason does not keep you at work on Sundays, I trust?"

"Oh, no, sir. I go to church regularly."

"Then, perhaps, you will be so good as to tell me what church you go to, and I will meet you there next Sunday afternoon?"

"I go to St Nicholas', sir. I will take care and bring you word how the boy is, and what doctor they get; and I will keep an account of the money I spend."

"Very well; thank you. Remember, I trust to you."

He meant that he relied on her promise to meet him; but Ruth thought that he was referring to the

responsibility of doing the best she could for the child.
He was going away, when a fresh thought struck him,
and he turned back into the cottage once more, and
addressed Ruth, with a half smile on his countenance :

"It seems rather strange, but we have no one to
introduce us ; my name is Bellingham—yours is——?"

"Ruth Hilton, sir," she answered, in a low voice,
for now that the conversation no longer related to the
boy, she felt shy and restrained.

He held out his hand to shake hers, and just as she
gave it to him, the old grandmother came tottering up
to ask some question. The interruption jarred upon
him, and made him once more keenly alive to the
closeness of the air, and the squalor and dirt by which
he was surrounded.

"My good woman," said he to Nelly Brownson,
"could you not keep your place a little neater and
cleaner? It is more fit for pigs than human beings.
The air in this room is quite offensive, and the dirt and
filth is really disgraceful."

By this time he was mounted, and, bowing to Ruth,
he rode away.

Then the old woman's wrath broke out.

"Who may you be, that knows no better manners
than to come into a poor woman's house to abuse it?—
fit for pigs, indeed ! What d'ye call yon fellow?"

"He is Mr Bellingham," said Ruth, shocked at the
old woman's apparent ingratitude. "It was he that
rode into the water to save your grandson. He would
have been drowned but for Mr Bellingham. I thought
once they would both have been swept away by the
current, it was so strong."

"The river is none so deep, either," the old woman
said, anxious to diminish as much as possible the
obligation she was under to one who had offended her.
"Some one else would have saved him, if this fine
young spark had never been near. He's an orphan,
and God watches over orphans, they say. I'd rather
it had been any one else as had picked him out, than

one who comes into a poor body's house only to abuse it."

"He did not come in only to abuse it," said Ruth, gently. "He came with little Tom; he only said it was not quite so clean as it might be."

"What! you're taking up the cry, are you? Wait till you are an old woman like me, crippled with rheumatiz, and a lad to see after like Tom, who is always in mud when he isn't in water; and his food and mine to scrape together (God knows we're often short, and do the best I can), and water to fetch up that steep brow."

She stopped to cough; and Ruth judiciously changed the subject, and began to consult the old woman as to the wants of her grandson, in which consultation they were soon assisted by the medical man.

When Ruth had made one or two arrangements with a neighbour, whom she asked to procure the most necessary things, and had heard from the doctor that all would be right in a day or two, she began to quake at the recollection of the length of time she had spent at Nelly Brownson's, and to remember, with some affright, the strict watch kept by Mrs Mason over her apprentices' out-goings and in-comings on working days. She hurried off to the shops, and tried to recal her wandering thoughts to the respective merits of pink and blue as a match to lilac, found she had lost her patterns, and went home with ill-chosen things, and in a fit of despair at her own stupidity.

The truth was, that the afternoon's adventure filled her mind; only, the figure of Tom (who was now safe, and likely to do well) was receding into the background, and that of Mr Bellingham becoming more prominent than it had been. His spirited and natural action of galloping into the water to save the child, was magnified by Ruth into the most heroic deed of daring; his interest about the boy was tender, thoughtful benevolence in her eyes, and his careless liberality of money was fine generosity; for she forgot that generosity implies some degree of

self-denial. She was gratified, too, by the power of
dispensing comfort he had entrusted to her, and was
busy with Alnaschar visions*of wise expenditure, when
the necessity of opening Mrs Mason's house-door summoned her back into actual present life, and the dread
of an immediate scolding.

For this time, however, she was spared ; but spared
for such a reason that she would have been thankful
for some blame in preference to her impunity. During
her absence, Jenny's difficulty of breathing had suddenly become worse, and the girls had, on their own
responsibility, put her to bed, and were standing round
her in dismay, when Mrs Mason's return home (only a
few minutes before Ruth arrived) fluttered them back
into the workroom.

And now, all was confusion and hurry ; a doctor to
be sent for ; a mind to be unburdened of directions
for a dress to a forewoman, who was too ill to
understand ; scoldings to be scattered with no illiberal
hand amongst a group of frightened girls, hardly
sparing the poor invalid herself for her inopportune
illness. In the middle of all this turmoil, Ruth
crept quietly to her place, with a heavy saddened
heart at the indisposition of the gentle forewoman.
She would gladly have nursed Jenny herself, and
often longed to do it, but she could not be spared.
Hands, unskilful in fine and delicate work, would be
well enough qualified to tend the sick, until the
mother arrived from home. Meanwhile, extra diligence was required in the workroom ; and Ruth found
no opportunity of going to see little Tom, or to fulfil the
plans for making him and his grandmother more
comfortable, which she had proposed to herself. She
regretted her rash promise to Mr Bellingham, of
attending to the little boy's welfare ; all that she could
do, was done by means of Mrs Mason's servant, through
whom she made inquiries, and sent the necessary
help.

The subject of Jenny's illness was the prominent one
in the house. Ruth told of her own adventure, to be

sure, but when she was at the very crisis of the boy's
fall into the river, the more fresh and vivid interest of
some tidings of Jenny was brought into the room, and
Ruth ceased, almost blaming herself for caring for
anything besides the question of life or death to be
decided in that very house.

Then a pale, gentle-looking woman was seen moving
softly about; and it was whispered that this was the
mother come to nurse her child. Everybody liked
her, she was so sweet-looking, and gave so little
trouble, and seemed so patient, and so thankful for
any inquiries about her daughter, whose illness, it was
understood, although its severity was mitigated, was
likely to be long and tedious. While all the feelings
and thoughts relating to Jenny were predominant,
Sunday arrived. Mrs Mason went the accustomed
visit to her father's, making some little show of
apology to Mrs Wood for leaving her and her
daughter; the apprentices dispersed to the various
friends with whom they were in the habit of spending the day; and Ruth went to St Nicholas', with a
sorrowful heart, depressed on account of Jenny, and
self-reproachful at having rashly undertaken what she
had been unable to perform.

As she came out of church, she was joined by Mr
Bellingham. She had half hoped that he might have
forgotten the arrangement, and yet she wished to
relieve herself of her responsibility. She knew his
step behind her, and the contending feelings made her
heart beat hard, and she longed to run away.

"Miss Hilton, I believe," said he, overtaking her,
and bowing forward, so as to catch a sight of her rose-
red face. "How is our little sailor going on? Well,
I trust, from the symptoms the other day."

"I believe, sir, he is quite well now. I am very
sorry, but I have not been able to go and see him. I
am so sorry—I could not help it. But I have got one
or two things through another person. I have put
them down on this slip of paper; and here is your
purse, sir, for I am afraid I can do nothing more for

him. We have illness in the house, and it makes us
very busy."

Ruth had been so much accustomed to blame of
late, that she almost anticipated some remonstrance
or reproach now, for not having fulfilled her promise
better. She little guessed that Mr Bellingham was
far more busy trying to devise some excuse for meeting
her again, during the silence that succeeded her
speech, than displeased with her for not bringing a
more particular account of the little boy, in whom he
had ceased to feel any interest.

She repeated, after a minute's pause :

" I am very sorry I have done so little, sir."

" Oh, yes, I am sure you have done all you could.
It was thoughtless in me to add to your engage-
ments."

" He is displeased with me," thought Ruth, " for
what he believes to have been neglect of the boy,
whose life he risked his own to save. If I told all,
he would see that I could not do more ; but I cannot
tell him all the sorrows and worries that have taken
up my time."

" And yet I am tempted to give you another little
commission, if it is not taking up too much of your
time, and presuming too much on your good-nature,"
said he, a bright idea having just struck him. " Mrs
Mason lives in Heneage Place, does not she ? My
mother's ancestors lived there ; and once, when the
house was being repaired, she took me in to show me
the old place. There was an old hunting-piece painted
on a panel over one of the chimney-pieces ; the figures
were portraits of my ancestors. I have often thought
I should like to purchase it, if it still remained there.
Can you ascertain this for me, and bring me word next
Sunday ?"

" Oh, yes, sir," said Ruth, glad that this commission was completely within her power to execute, and
anxious to make up for her previous seeming neglect.
" I'll look directly I get home, and ask Mrs Mason to
write and let you know."

"Thank you," said he, only half satisfied; "I think perhaps, however, it might be as well not to trouble Mrs Mason about it; you see, it would compromise me, and I am not quite determined to purchase the picture; if you would ascertain whether the painting is there, and tell me, I would take a little time to reflect, and afterwards I could apply to Mrs Mason myself."

"Very well, sir, I will see about it." So they parted.

Before the next Sunday, Mrs Wood had taken her daughter to her distant home, to recruit* in that quiet place. Ruth watched her down the street from an upper window, and, sighing deep and long, returned to the workroom, whence the warning voice and the gentle wisdom had departed.

CHAPTER III

MR BELLINGHAM attended afternoon service at St Nicholas' church the next Sunday. His thoughts had been far more occupied by Ruth than hers by him, although his appearance upon the scene of her life was more an event to her than it was to him. He was puzzled by the impression she had produced on him, though he did not in general analyse the nature of his feelings, but simply enjoyed them with the delight which youth takes in experiencing new and strong emotion.

He was old compared to Ruth, but young as a man; hardly three-and-twenty. The fact of his being an only child had given him, as it does to many, a sort of inequality in those parts of the character which are usually formed by the number of years that a person has lived.

The unevenness of discipline to which only children are subjected; the thwarting, resulting from over-anxiety; the indiscreet indulgence, arising from a love centred all in one object; had been exaggerated in his education, probably from the circumstance that his mother (his only surviving parent) had been similarly situated to himself.

He was already in possession of the comparatively small property he inherited from his father. The estate on which his mother lived was her own; and her income gave her the means of indulging or controlling him, after he had grown to man's estate, as her wayward disposition and her love of power prompted her.

Had he been double-dealing in his conduct towards her, had he condescended to humour her in the least, her passionate love for him would have induced her to strip herself of all her possessions to add to his dignity or happiness. But although he felt the warmest affection for her, the regardlessness which she had taught him (by example, perhaps, more than by precept) of the feelings of others, was continually prompting him to do things that she, for the time being, resented as mortal affronts. He would mimic the clergyman she specially esteemed, even to his very face; he would refuse to visit her schools for months and months, and, when wearied into going at last, revenge himself by puzzling the children with the most ridiculous questions (gravely put) that he could imagine.

All these boyish tricks annoyed and irritated her far more than the accounts which reached her of more serious misdoings at college and in town. Of these grave offences she never spoke; of the smaller misdeeds she hardly ever ceased speaking.

Still, at times, she had great influence over him, and nothing delighted her more than to exercise it. The submission of his will to hers was sure to be liberally rewarded; for it gave her great happiness to extort, from his indifference or his affection, the concessions which she never sought by force of reason, or by appeals to principle—concessions which he frequently withheld, solely for the sake of asserting his independence of her control.

She was anxious for him to marry Miss Duncombe. He cared little or nothing about it—it was time enough to be married ten years hence; and so he was dawdling through some months of his life—sometimes flirting with the nothing-loath Miss Duncombe, sometimes plaguing, and sometimes delighting his mother, at all times taking care to please himself—when he first saw Ruth Hilton, and a new, passionate, hearty feeling shot through his whole being. He did not know why he was so fascinated by her. She was very beautiful, but he had seen others equally beautiful, and with many more *agaceries* *calculated to set off the effect of their charms.

There was, perhaps, something bewitching in the union of the grace and loveliness of womanhood with the *naïveté*, simplicity, and innocence of an intelligent child. There was a spell in the shyness, which made her avoid and shun all admiring approaches to acquaintance. It would be an exquisite delight to attract and tame her wildness, just as he had often allured and tamed the timid fawns in his mother's park.

By no over-bold admiration, or rash, passionate word, would he startle her; and, surely, in time she might be induced to look upon him as a friend, if not something nearer and dearer still.

In accordance with this determination, he resisted the strong temptation of walking by her side the whole distance home after church. He only received the intelligence she brought respecting the panel with thanks, spoke a few words about the weather, bowed, and was gone. Ruth believed she should never see him again; and, in spite of sundry self-upbraidings for her folly, she could not help feeling as if a shadow were drawn over her existence for several days to come.

Mrs Mason was a widow, and had to struggle for the sake of the six or seven children left dependent on her exertions; thus there was some reason, and great excuse, for the pinching economy which regulated her household affairs.

On Sundays she chose to conclude that all her apprentices had friends who would be glad to see them to dinner, and give them a welcome reception for the remainder of the day; while she, and those of her children who were not at school, went to spend the day at her father's house, several miles out of the town. Accordingly, no dinner was cooked on Sundays for the young workwomen; no fires were lighted in any rooms to which they had access. On this morning they breakfasted in Mrs Mason's own parlour, after which the room was closed against them through the day by some understood, though unspoken prohibition.

What became of such as Ruth, who had no home and no friends in that large populous desolate town? She had hitherto commissioned the servant, who went to market on Saturdays for the family, to buy her a bun or biscuit, whereon she made her fasting dinner in the deserted workroom; sitting in her walking-dress to keep off the cold, which clung to her in spite of shawl and bonnet. Then she would sit at the window, looking out on the dreary prospect till her eyes were often blinded by tears; and partly to shake off thoughts and recollections, the indulgence in which she felt to be productive of no good, and partly to have some ideas to dwell upon during the coming week beyond those suggested by the constant view of the same room, she would carry her Bible, and place herself in the window-seat on the wide landing, which commanded the street in front of the house. From thence she could see the irregular grandeur of the place; she caught a view of the grey church-tower, rising hoary and massive into mid-air; she saw one or two figures loiter along on the sunny side of the street, in all the enjoyment of their fine clothes and Sunday leisure; and she imagined histories for them, and tried to picture to herself their homes and their daily doings.

And before long, the bells swung heavily in the church-tower, and struck out with musical clang the first summons to afternoon church.

After church was over, she used to return home to
the same window-seat, and watch till the winter
twilight was over and gone, and the stars came out
over the black masses of houses.   And then she would
steal down to ask for a candle, as a companion to her
in the deserted workroom.   Occasionally the servant
would bring her up some tea ; but of late Ruth had
declined taking any, as she had discovered she was
robbing the kind-hearted creature of part of the small
provision left out for her by Mrs Mason.   She sat on,
hungry and cold, trying to read her Bible, and to think
the old holy thoughts which had been her childish
meditations at her mother's knee, until one after
another the apprentices returned, weary with their
day's enjoyment, and their week's late watching ; too
weary to make her in any way a partaker of their
pleasure by entering into details of the manner in
which they had spent their day.

And last of all, Mrs Mason returned ; and, summoning her " young people " once more into the parlour,
she read a prayer before dismissing them to bed.   She
always expected to find them all in the house when
she came home, but asked no questions as to their
proceedings through the day ; perhaps, because she
dreaded to hear that one or two had occasionally
nowhere to go, and that it would be sometimes necessary to order a Sunday's dinner, and leave a lighted
fire on that day.

For five months Ruth had been an inmate at Mrs
Mason's, and such had been the regular order of the
Sundays.   While the forewoman stayed there, it is
true, she was ever ready to give Ruth the little variety
of hearing of recreations in which she was no partaker ;
and however tired Jenny might be at night, she had
ever some sympathy to bestow on Ruth for the dull
length of day she had passed.   After her departure,
the monotonous idleness of the Sunday seemed worse
to bear than the incessant labour of the work-days ;
until the time came when it seemed to be a recognized
hope in her mind, that on Sunday afternoons she

should see Mr Bellingham, and hear a few words from
him, as from a friend who took an interest in her
thoughts and proceedings during the past week.

Ruth's mother had been the daughter of a poor
curate in Norfolk, and, early left without parents or
home, she was thankful to marry a respectable farmer,
a good deal older than herself. After their marriage,
however, everything seemed to go wrong. Mrs Hilton
fell into a delicate state of health, and was unable to
bestow the ever-watchful attention to domestic affairs,
so requisite in a farmer's wife. Her husband had a
series of misfortunes—of a more important kind than
the death of a whole brood of turkeys from getting
among the nettles, or the year of bad cheeses spoilt by
a careless dairymaid—which were the consequences
(so the neighbours said) of Mr Hilton's mistake in
marrying a delicate, fine lady. His crops failed ; his
horses died ; his barn took fire ; in short, if he had
been in any way a remarkable character, one might
have supposed him to be the object of an avenging fate,
so successive were the evils which pursued him ; but
as he was only a somewhat commonplace farmer, I
believe we must attribute his calamities to some want
in his character of the one quality required to act as
keystone to many excellences. While his wife lived,
all worldly misfortunes seemed as nothing to him ; her
strong sense and lively faculty of hope upheld him
from despair ; her sympathy was always ready, and the
invalid's room had an atmosphere of peace and encouragement, which affected all who entered it. But when
Ruth was about twelve, one morning in the busy hay-
time, Mrs Hilton was left alone for some hours. This
had often happened before, nor had she seemed weaker
than usual when they had gone forth to the field ; but
on their return, with merry voices, to fetch the dinner
prepared for the haymakers, they found an unusual
silence brooding over the house ; no low voice called
out gently to welcome them, and ask after the day's
progress ; and, on entering the little parlour, which
was called Mrs Hilton's, and was sacred to her, they

found her lying dead on her accustomed sofa. Quite
calm and peaceful she lay ; there had been no struggle
at last ; the struggle was for the survivors, and one
sank under it. Her husband did not make much ado
at first, at least, not in outward show ; her memory
seemed to keep in check all external violence of grief ;
but, day by day, dating from his wife's death, his mental
powers decreased. He was still a hale-looking elderly
man, and his bodily health appeared as good as ever ;
but he sat for hours in his easy chair, looking into the
fire, not moving, nor speaking unless when it was absolutely necessary to answer repeated questions. If
Ruth, with coaxings and draggings, induced him to
come out with her, he went with measured steps around
his fields, his head bent to the ground with the same
abstracted, unseeing look ; never smiling—never changing the expression of his face, not even to one of deeper
sadness, when anything occurred which might be supposed to remind him of his dead wife. But in this abstraction from all outward things, his worldly affairs
went ever lower down. He paid money away, or
received it, as if it had been so much water ; the gold
mines of Potosi*could not have touched the deep grief
of his soul ; but God in His mercy knew the sure balm,
and sent the Beautiful Messenger to take the weary
one home.

After his death, the creditors were the chief people
who appeared to take any interest in the affairs ; and
it seemed strange to Ruth to see people, whom she
scarcely knew, examining and touching all that she
had been accustomed to consider as precious and sacred.
Her father had made his will at her birth. With the
pride of newly and late-acquired paternity, he had considered the office of guardian to his little darling as one
which would have been an additional honour to the
lord-lieutenant of the county ; but as he had not the
pleasure of his lordship's acquaintance, he selected the
person of most consequence amongst those whom he
did know ; not any very ambitious appointment, in
those days of comparative prosperity ; but certainly

the flourishing maltster of Skelton was a little surprised, when, fifteen years later, he learnt that he was
executor to a will bequeathing many vanished hundreds
of pounds, and guardian to a young girl whom he could
not remember ever to have seen.

He was a sensible, hard-headed man of the world ;
having a very fair proportion of conscience as con-
sciences go ; indeed, perhaps more than many people ;
for he had some ideas of duty extending to the circle
beyond his own family ; and did not, as some would
have done, decline acting altogether, but speedily summoned the creditors, examined into the accounts, sold
up the farming-stock, and discharged all the debts ;
paid about £80 into the Skelton bank for a week, while
he inquired for a situation or apprenticeship of some
kind for poor heart-broken Ruth ; heard of Mrs Mason's,
arranged all with her in two short conversations ; drove
over for Ruth in his gig ; waited while she and the old
servant packed up her clothes, and grew very impatient while she ran, with her eyes streaming with
tears, round the garden, tearing off in a passion of love
whole boughs of favourite China and damask roses, late
flowering against the casement-window of what had
been her mother's room. When she took her seat in
the gig, she was little able, even if she had been inclined,
to profit by her guardian's lectures on economy and
self-reliance ; but she was quiet and silent, looking
forward with longing to the night-time, when, in her
bedroom, she might give way to all her passionate
sorrow at being wrenched from the home where she
had lived with her parents, in that utter absence of
any anticipation of change, which is either the blessing
or the curse of childhood. But at night there were
four other girls in her room, and she could not cry
before them. She watched and waited till one by one
dropped off to sleep, and then she buried her face in
the pillow, and shook with sobbing grief ; and then
she paused to conjure up, with fond luxuriance, every
recollection of the happy days, so little valued in their
uneventful peace while they lasted, so passionately

regretted when once gone for ever ; to remember every
look and word of the dear mother, and to moan afresh
over the change caused by her death ;—the first clouding in of Ruth's day of life. It was Jenny's sympathy
on this first night, when awakened by Ruth's irrepressible agony, that had made the bond between them.
But Ruth's loving disposition, continually sending
forth fibres in search of nutriment, found no other
object for regard among those of her daily life to com-
pensate for the want of natural ties.

But, almost insensibly, Jenny's place in Ruth's
heart was filled up ; there was some one who listened
with tender interest to all her little revelations ; who
questioned her about her early days of happiness, and,
in return, spoke of his own childhood—not so golden
in reality as Ruth's, but more dazzling, when re-
counted with stories of the beautiful cream-coloured
Arabian pony, and the old picture gallery in the house,
and avenues, and terraces, and fountains in the garden,
for Ruth to paint, with all the vividness of imagination,
as scenery and background for the figure which was
growing by slow degrees most prominent in her
thoughts.

It must not be supposed that this was effected all at
once, though the intermediate stages have been passed
over. On Sunday, Mr Bellingham only spoke to her
to receive the information about the panel ; nor did he
come to St Nicholas' the next, nor yet the following
Sunday. But the third he walked by her side a little
way, and, seeing her annoyance, he left her ; and then
she wished for him back again, and found the day very
dreary, and wondered why a strange undefined feeling
had made her imagine she was doing wrong in walking
alongside of one so kind and good as Mr Bellingham ;
it had been very foolish of her to be self-conscious all
the time, and if ever he spoke to her again she would
not think of what people might say, but enjoy the
pleasure which his kind words and evident interest in
her might give. Then she thought it was very likely
he never would notice her again, for she knew she had

been very rude with her short answers; it was very
provoking that she had behaved so rudely. She should
be sixteen in another month, and she was still childish
and awkward. Thus she lectured herself, after parting
with Mr Bellingham; and the consequence was, that
on the following Sunday she was ten times as blushing
and conscious, and (Mr Bellingham thought) ten times
more beautiful than ever. He suggested, that instead
of going straight home through High-street, she should
take the round by the Leasowes;* at first she declined,
but then, suddenly wondering and questioning herself
why she refused a thing which was, as far as reason
and knowledge (*her* knowledge) went, so innocent,
and which was certainly so tempting and pleasant, she
agreed to go the round; and when she was once in
the meadows that skirted the town, she forgot all
doubt and awkwardness—nay, almost forgot the presence of Mr Bellingham—in her delight at the new
tender beauty of an early spring day in February.
Among the last year's brown ruins, heaped together
by the wind in the hedgerows, she found the fresh
green crinkled leaves and pale star-like flowers of the
primroses. Here and there a golden celandine made
brilliant the sides of the little brook that (full of
water in "February fill-dyke")* bubbled along by the
side of the path; the sun was low in the horizon, and
once, when they came to a higher part of the Leasowes,
Ruth burst into an exclamation of delight at the
evening glory of mellow light which was in the sky
behind the purple distance, while the brown leafless
woods in the foreground derived an almost metallic
lustre from the golden mist and haze of the sunset.
It was but three-quarters of a mile round by the
meadows, but somehow it took them an hour to walk it.
Ruth turned to thank Mr Bellingham for his kindness in taking her home by this beautiful way, but his
look of admiration at her glowing, animated face, made
her suddenly silent; and, hardly wishing him good-bye,
she quickly entered the house with a beating, happy,
agitated heart.

"How strange it is," she thought that evening, "that I should feel as if this charming afternoon's walk were, somehow, not exactly wrong, but yet as if it were not right. Why can it be? I am not defrauding Mrs Mason of any of her time ; that I know would be wrong ; I am left to go where I like on Sundays ; I have been to church, so it can't be because I have missed doing my duty. If I had gone this walk with Jenny, I wonder whether I should have felt as I do now. There must be something wrong in me, myself, to feel so guilty when I have done nothing which is not right ; and yet I can thank God for the happiness I have had in this charming spring walk, which dear mamma used to say was a sign when pleasures were innocent and good for us."

She was not conscious, as yet, that Mr Bellingham's presence had added any charm to the ramble ; and when she might have become aware of this, as, week after week, Sunday after Sunday, loitering ramble after loitering ramble succeeded each other, she was too much absorbed with one set of thoughts to have much inclination for self-questioning.

"Tell me everything, Ruth, as you would to a brother ; let me help you, if I can, in your difficulties," he said to her one afternoon. And he really did try to understand, and to realise, how an insignificant and paltry person like Mason the dressmaker could be an object of dread, and regarded as a person having authority, by Ruth. He flamed up with indignation when, by way of impressing him with Mrs Mason's power and consequence, Ruth spoke of some instance of the effects of her employer's displeasure. He declared his mother should never have a gown made again by such a tyrant—such a Mrs Brownrigg ;*that he would prevent all his acquaintances from going to such a cruel dressmaker ; till Ruth was alarmed at the threatened consequences of her one-sided account, and pleaded for Mrs Mason as earnestly as if a young man's menace of this description were likely to be literally fulfilled.

"Indeed, sir, I have been very wrong; if you please,
sir, don't be so angry. She is often very good to us;
it is only sometimes she goes into a passion; and we
are very provoking, I dare say. I know I am for one.
I have often to undo my work, and you can't think how
it spoils anything (particularly silk) to be unpicked;
and Mrs Mason has to bear all the blame. Oh! I am
sorry I said anything about it. Don't speak to your
mother about it, pray, sir. Mrs Mason thinks so much
of Mrs Bellingham's custom."

"Well, I won't this time"—recollecting that there
might be some awkwardness in accounting to his
mother for the means by which he had obtained his
very correct information as to what passed in Mrs
Mason's workroom—"but if ever she does so again,
I'll not answer for myself."

"I will take care and not tell again, sir," said Ruth,
in a low voice.

"Nay, Ruth, you are not going to have secrets from
me, are you? Don't you remember your promise to
consider me as a brother? Go on, telling me everything that happens to you, pray; you cannot think
how much interest I take in all your interests. I can
quite fancy that charming home at Milham you told
me about last Sunday. I can almost fancy Mrs Mason's
workroom; and that, surely, is a proof either of the
strength of my imagination, or of your powers of
description."

Ruth smiled. "It is, indeed, sir. Our workroom
must be so different to anything you ever saw. I think
you must have passed through Milham often on your
way to Lowford."

"Then you don't think it is any stretch of fancy
to have so clear an idea as I have of Milham Grange?
On the left hand of the road, is it, Ruth?"

"Yes, sir, just over the bridge, and up the hill
where the elm-trees meet overhead and make a green
shade; and then comes the dear old Grange, that I
shall never see again."

"Never! Nonsense, Ruthie; it is only six miles

off; you may see it any day. It is not an hour's ride."

"Perhaps I may see it again when I am grown old; I did not think exactly what 'never' meant; it is so very long since I was there, and I don't see any chance of my going for years and years, at any rate."

"Why, Ruth, you—we may go next Sunday afternoon, if you like."

She looked up at him with a lovely light of pleasure in her face at the idea. "How, sir? Can I walk it between afternoon service and the time Mrs Mason comes home? I would go for only one glimpse; but if I could get into the house—oh, sir! if I could just see mamma's room again!"

He was revolving plans in his head for giving her this pleasure, and he had also his own in view. If they went in any of his carriages, the loitering charm of the walk would be lost; and they must, to a certain degree, be encumbered by, and exposed to, the notice of servants.

"Are you a good walker, Ruth? Do you think you can manage six miles? If we set off at two o'clock, we shall be there by four, without hurrying; or say half-past four. Then we might stay two hours, and you could show me all the old walks and old places you love, and we could still come leisurely home. Oh, it's all arranged directly!"

"But do you think it would be right, sir? It seems as if it would be such a great pleasure, that it must be in some way wrong."

"Why, you little goose, what can be wrong in it?"

"In the first place, I miss going to church by setting out at two," said Ruth, a little gravely.

"Only for once. Surely you don't see any harm in missing church for once? You will go in the morning, you know."

"I wonder if Mrs Mason would think it right—if she would allow it?"

"No, I dare say not. But you don't mean to be governed by Mrs Mason's notions of right and wrong.

She thought it right to treat that poor girl Palmer in the way you told me about. You would think that wrong, you know, and so would every one of sense and feeling. Come, Ruth, don't pin your faith on any one, but judge for yourself. The pleasure is perfectly innocent; it is not a selfish pleasure either, for I shall enjoy it to the full as much as you will. I shall like to see the places where you spent your childhood; I shall almost love them as much as you do." He had dropped his voice; and spoke in low, persuasive tones. Ruth hung down her head, and blushed with exceeding happiness; but she could not speak, even to urge her doubts afresh. Thus it was in a manner settled.

How delightfully happy the plan made her through the coming week! She was too young when her mother died to have received any cautions or words of advice respecting *the* subject of a woman's life—if, indeed, wise parents ever directly speak of what, in its depth and power, cannot be put into words—which is a brooding spirit with no definite form or shape that men should know it, but which is there, and present before we have recognized and realized its existence. Ruth was innocent and snow-pure. She had heard of falling in love, but did not know the signs and symptoms thereof; nor, indeed, had she troubled her head much about them. Sorrow had filled up her days, to the exclusion of all lighter thoughts than the consideration of present duties, and the remembrance of the happy time which had been. But the interval of blank, after the loss of her mother and during her father's life-in-death, had made her all the more ready to value and cling to sympathy—first from Jenny, and now from Mr Bellingham. To see her home again, and to see it with him; to show him (secure of his interest) the haunts of former times, each with its little tale of the past—of dead and gone events!—No coming shadow threw its gloom over this week's dream of happiness—a dream which was too bright to be spoken about, to common and indifferent ears.

CHAPTER IV

SUNDAY came, as brilliant as if there were no sorrow,
or death, or guilt in the world ; a day or two of rain
had made the earth fresh and brave as the blue
heavens above. Ruth thought it was too strong a
realization of her hopes, and looked for an over-
clouding at noon ; but the glory endured, and at two
o'clock she was in the Leasowes, with a beating heart
full of joy, longing to stop the hours, which would
pass too quickly through the afternoon.

They sauntered through the fragrant lanes, as if
their loitering would prolong the time, and check the
fiery-footed steeds galloping apace towards the close of
the happy day. It was past five o'clock before they
came to the great mill-wheel, which stood in Sabbath
idleness, motionless in a brown mass of shade, and
still wet with yesterday's immersion in the deep
transparent water beneath. They clambered the little
hill, not yet fully shaded by the overarching elms ;
and then Ruth checked Mr Bellingham, by a slight
motion of the hand which lay within his arm, and
glanced up into his face to see what that face should
express as it looked on Milham Grange, now lying
still and peaceful in its afternoon shadows. It was a
house of afterthoughts ; building materials were plen-
tiful in the neighbourhood, and every successive owner
had found a necessity for some addition or projection,
till it was a picturesque mass of irregularity—of broken
light and shadow—which, as a whole, gave a full and
complete idea of a "Home." All its gables and nooks
were blended and held together by the tender green
of the climbing roses and young creepers. An old
couple were living in the house until it should be let,
but they dwelt in the back part, and never used the
front door ; so the little birds had grown tame and
familiar, and perched upon the window-sills and porch,
and on the old stone cistern which caught the water
from the roof.

They went silently through the untrimmed garden, full of the pale-coloured flowers of spring. A spider had spread her web over the front door. The sight of this conveyed a sense of desolation to Ruth's heart; she thought it was possible the state entrance had never been used since her father's dead body had been borne forth, and, without speaking a word, she turned abruptly away, and went round the house to another door. Mr Bellingham followed without questioning, little understanding her feelings, but full of admiration for the varying expression called out upon her face.

The old woman had not yet returned from church, or from the weekly gossip or neighbourly tea which succeeded. The husband sat in the kitchen, spelling the psalms for the day in his Prayer Book, and reading the words out aloud—a habit he had acquired from the double solitude of his life, for he was deaf. He did not hear the quiet entrance of the pair, and they were struck with the sort of ghostly echo which seems to haunt half-furnished and uninhabited houses. The verses he was reading were the following:

"Why art thou so vexed, O my soul: and why art thou so disquieted within me?

"O put thy trust in God :* for I will yet thank him, which is the help of my countenance, and my God."

And when he had finished he shut the book, and sighed with the satisfaction of having done his duty. The words of holy trust, though perhaps they were not fully understood, carried a faithful peace down into the depths of his soul. As he looked up, he saw the young couple standing on the middle of the floor. He pushed his iron rimmed spectacles on to his forehead, and rose to greet the daughter of his old master and ever-honoured mistress.

"God bless thee, lass; God bless thee! My old eyes are glad to see thee again."

Ruth sprang forward to shake the horny hand stretched forward in the action of blessing. She pressed it between both of hers, as she rapidly poured out questions. Mr Bellingham was not altogether

comfortable at seeing one whom he had already begun
to appropriate as his own, so tenderly familiar with a
hard-featured, meanly-dressed day-labourer. He sauntered to the window, and looked out into the grass-
grown farm-yard; but he could not help overhearing
some of the conversation, which seemed to him carried
on too much in the tone of equality. "And who's
yon?" asked the old labourer at last. "Is he your
sweetheart? Your missis's son, I reckon. He's a
spruce young chap, anyhow."

Mr Bellingham's "blood of all the Howards"*rose
and tingled about his ears, so that he could not hear
Ruth's answer. It began by "Hush, Thomas; pray
hush!" but how it went on he did not catch. The
idea of his being Mrs Mason's son! It was really
too ridiculous; but, like most things which are "too
ridiculous," it made him very angry. He was hardly
himself again when Ruth shyly came to the window-
recess and asked him if he would like to see the house-
place, into which the front door entered; many people
thought it very pretty, she said, half timidly, for his
face had unconsciously assumed a hard and haughty
expression, which he could not instantly soften
down. He followed her, however; but before he
left the kitchen he saw the old man standing,
looking at Ruth's companion with a strange, grave
air of dissatisfaction.

They went along one or two zigzag, damp-smelling
stone passages, and then entered the house-place, or
common sitting-room for a farmer's family in that part
of the country. The front door opened into it, and
several other apartments issued out of it, such as the
dairy, the state bedroom (which was half-parlour as
well), and a small room which had been appropriated
to the late Mrs Hilton, where she sat, or more frequently lay, commanding through the open door the
comings and goings of her household. In those days
the house-place had been a cheerful room, full of life,
with the passing to and fro of husband, child, and
servants; with a great merry wood fire crackling and

blazing away every evening, and hardly let out in the
very heat of summer ; for with the thick stone walls,
and the deep window-seats, and the drapery of vine-
leaves and ivy, that room, with its flag-floor, seemed
always to want the sparkle and cheery warmth of a
fire. But now the green shadows from without seemed
to have become black in the uninhabited desolation.
The oaken shovel-board,* the heavy dresser, and the
carved cupboards, were now dull and damp, which
were formerly polished up to the brightness of a
looking-glass, where the fire-blaze was for ever
glinting ; they only added to the oppressive gloom ;
the flag-floor was wet with heavy moisture. Ruth
stood gazing into the room, seeing nothing of what
was present. She saw a vision of former days—an
evening in the days of her childhood ; her father
sitting in the "master's corner" near the fire, sedately
smoking his pipe, while he dreamily watched his wife
and child ; her mother reading to her, as she sat on a
little stool at her feet. It was gone—all gone into
the land of shadows ; but for the moment it seemed so
present in the old room, that Ruth believed her actual
life to be the dream. Then, still silent, she went on
into her mother's parlour. But there, the bleak look
of what had once been full of peace and mother's love,
struck cold on her heart. She uttered a cry, and
threw herself down by the sofa, hiding her face in her
hands, while her frame quivered with her repressed
sobs.

"Dearest Ruth, don't give way so. It can do no
good ; it cannot bring back the dead," said Mr Bellingham, distressed at witnessing her distress.

"I know it cannot," murmured Ruth ; "and that
is why I cry. I cry because nothing will ever bring
them back again." She sobbed afresh, but more
gently, for his kind words soothed her, and softened,
if they could not take away, her sense of desolation.

"Come away ; I cannot have you stay here, full of
painful associations as these rooms must be. Come"
—raising her with gentle violence—"show me your

little garden you have often told me about. Near the window of this very room, is it not? See how well I remember everything you tell me."

He led her round through the back part of the house into the pretty old-fashioned garden. There was a sunny border just under the windows, and clipped box and yew-trees by the grass-plat, further away from the house; and she prattled again of her childish adventures and solitary plays. When they turned round they saw the old man, who had hobbled out with the help of his stick, and was looking at them with the same grave, sad look of anxiety.

Mr Bellingham spoke rather sharply.

"Why does that old man follow us about in that way? It is excessively impertinent of him, I think."

"Oh, don't call old Thomas impertinent. He is so good and kind, he is like a father to me. I remember sitting on his knee many and many a time when I was a child, whilst he told me stories out of the 'Pilgrim's Progress.' He taught me to suck up milk through a straw. Mamma was very fond of him too. He used to sit with us always in the evenings when papa was away at market, for mamma was rather afraid of having no man in the house, and used to beg old Thomas to stay; and he would take me on his knee, and listen just as attentively as I did while mamma read aloud."

"You don't mean to say you have sat upon that old fellow's knee?"

"Oh, yes! many and many a time."

Mr Bellingham looked graver than he had done while witnessing Ruth's passionate emotion in her mother's room. But he lost his sense of indignity in admiration of his companion as she wandered among the flowers, seeking for favourite bushes or plants, to which some history or remembrance was attached. She wound in and out in natural, graceful, wavy lines between the luxuriant and overgrown shrubs, which were fragrant with a leafy smell of spring growth; she went on, careless of watching eyes, indeed unconscious, for the time, of their existence. Once she stopped to take hold of a spray of jessamine, and softly kiss it; it had been her mother's favourite flower.

Old Thomas was standing by the horsemount, and was also an observer of all her goings on. But, while Mr Bellingham's feeling was that of passionate admiration mingled with a selfish kind of love, the old man gazed with tender anxiety, and his lips moved in words of blessing:

"She's a pretty creature, with a glint of her mother about her; and she's the same kind lass as ever. Not a bit set up with yon fine manty-maker's* shop she's in. I misdoubt that young fellow though, for all she called him a real gentleman, and checked me when I asked if he was her sweetheart. If his are not sweetheart's looks, I've forgotten all my young days. Here! they're going, I suppose. Look! he wants her to go without a word to the old man; but she is none so changed as that, I reckon."

Not Ruth, indeed! She never perceived the dissatisfied expression of Mr Bellingham's countenance, visible to the old man's keen eye; but came running up to Thomas to send her love to his wife, and to shake him many times by the hand.

"Tell Mary I'll make her such a fine gown, as soon as ever I set up for myself; it shall be all in the fashion, big gigot sleeves, that she shall not know herself in them! Mind you tell her that, Thomas, will you?"

"Aye, that I will, lass; and I reckon she'll be pleased to hear thou hast not forgotten thy old merry ways. The Lord bless thee—the Lord lift up the light of His countenance upon thee."

Ruth was half-way towards the impatient Mr Bellingham when her old friend called her back. He longed to give her a warning of the danger that he thought she was in, and yet he did not know how. When she came up, all he could think of to say was a text; indeed, the language of the Bible was the language in which he thought, whenever his ideas went beyond practical everyday life into expressions of emotion or feeling. "My dear, remember the devil goeth about as a roaring lion,* seeking whom he may devour ; remember that, Ruth."

The words fell on her ear, but gave no definite idea. The utmost they suggested was the remembrance of the dread she felt as a child when this verse came into her mind, and how she used to imagine a lion's head with glaring eyes peering out of the bushes in a dark shady part of the wood, which, for this reason, she had always avoided, and even now could hardly think of without a shudder. She never imagined that the grim warning related to the handsome young man who awaited her with a countenance beaming with love, and tenderly drew her hand within his arm.

The old man sighed as he watched them away. "The Lord may help her to guide her steps aright. He may. But I'm afeard she's treading in perilous places. I'll put my missis up to going to the town and getting speech of her, and telling her a bit of her danger. An old motherly woman like our Mary will set about it better nor a stupid fellow like me."

The poor old labourer prayed long and earnestly that night for Ruth. He called it "wrestling for her soul" ; and I think his prayers were heard, for "God judgeth not as man judgeth."*

Ruth went on her way, all unconscious of the dark phantoms of the future that were gathering around her ; her melancholy turned, with the pliancy of childish years, at sixteen not yet lost, into a softened manner which was infinitely charming. By and by she cleared up into sunny happiness. The evening was still and full of mellow light, and the new-born summer was so delicious that, in common with all young creatures, she shared its influence and was glad.

They stood together at the top of a steep ascent, "the hill" of the hundred.* At the summit there was a level space, sixty or seventy yards square, of unen-closed and broken ground, over which the golden

bloom of the gorse cast a rich hue, while its delicious
scent perfumed the fresh and nimble air.   On one
side of this common, the ground sloped down to a
clear bright pond, in which were mirrored the rough
sand-cliffs that rose abrupt on the opposite bank ;
hundreds of martens found a home there, and were
now wheeling over the transparent water, and dip-
ping in their wings in their evening sport. Indeed,
all sorts of birds seemed to haunt the lonely pool ;
the water wagtails were scattered around its margin,
the linnets perched on the topmost sprays of the gorse-
bushes, and other hidden warblers sang their vespers
on the uneven ground beyond. On the far side of the
green waste, close by the road, and well placed for the
requirements of horses or their riders who might be
weary with the ascent of the hill, there was a public-
house, which was more of a farm than an inn.   It was
a long, low building, rich in dormer windows on the
weather side, which were necessary in such an exposed
situation, and with odd projections and unlooked-for
gables on every side ; there was a deep porch in front,
on whose hospitable benches a dozen persons might sit
and enjoy the balmy air.   A noble sycamore grew
right before the house, with seats all round it
("such tents the patriarchs loved") ;* and a nonde-
script sign hung from a branch on the side next to the
road, which, being wisely furnished with an interpre-
tation, was found to mean King Charles in the oak.*

Near this comfortable, quiet, unfrequented inn,
there was another pond, for household and farm-
yard purposes, from which the cattle were drinking,
before returning to the fields after they had been
milked.   Their very motions were so lazy and slow,
that they served to fill up the mind with the sensation
of dreamy rest. Ruth and Mr Bellingham plunged
through the broken ground to regain the road near
the wayside inn.   Hand-in-hand, now pricked by
the far-spreading gorse, now ankle-deep in sand ;
now pressing the soft, thick heath, which should
make so brave an autumn show ; and now over wild

thyme and other fragrant herbs, they made their way, with many a merry laugh. Once on the road, at the summit, Ruth stood silent, in breathless delight at the view before her. The hill fell suddenly down into the plain, extending for a dozen miles or more. There was a clump of dark Scotch firs close to them, which cut clear against the western sky, and threw back the nearest levels into distance. The plain below them was richly wooded, and was tinted by the young tender hues of the earliest summer, for all the trees of the wood had donned their leaves except the cautious ash, which here and there gave a soft, pleasant greyness to the landscape. Far away in the champaign were spires, and towers, and stacks of chimneys belonging to some distant hidden farm-house, which were traced downwards through the golden air by the thin columns of blue smoke sent up from the evening fires. The view was bounded by some rising ground in deep purple shadow against the sunset sky.

When first they stopped, silent with sighing pleasure, the air seemed full of pleasant noises ; distant church-bells made harmonious music with the little singing-birds near at hand ; nor were the lowings of the cattle, nor the calls of the farm-servants discordant, for the voices seemed to be hushed by the brooding con-sciousness of the Sabbath. They stood loitering before the house, quietly enjoying the view. The clock in the little inn struck eight, and it sounded clear and sharp in the stillness.

"Can it be so late?" asked Ruth.

"I should not have thought it possible," answered Mr Bellingham. "But, never mind, you will be at home long before nine. Stay, there is a shorter road, I know, through the fields ; just wait a moment, while I go in and ask the exact way." He dropped Ruth's arm, and went into the public-house.

A gig had been slowly toiling up the sandy hill behind, unperceived by the young couple, and now it reached the table-land, and was close upon them as

they separated.   Ruth turned round, when the sound
of the horse's footsteps came distinctly as he reached
the level.   She faced Mrs Mason !

They were not ten—no, not five yards apart.   At
the same moment they recognized each other, and,
what was worse, Mrs Mason had clearly seen, with her
sharp, needle-like eyes, the attitude in which Ruth
had stood with the young man who had just quitted
her.   Ruth's hand had been lying in his arm, and
fondly held there by his other hand.

Mrs Mason was careless about the circumstances of
temptation into which the girls entrusted to her as
apprentices were thrown, but severely intolerant if
their conduct was in any degree influenced by the
force of these temptations.   She called this intoler-
ance " keeping up the character of her establishment."
It would have been a better and more Christian thing,
if she had kept up the character of her girls by tender
vigilance and maternal care.

This evening, too, she was in an irritated state of
temper.   Her brother had undertaken to drive her
round by Henbury, in order to give her the unpleasant
information of the misbehaviour of her eldest son, who
was an assistant in a draper's shop in a neighbouring
town.   She was full of indignation against want of
steadiness, though not willing to direct her indignation
against the right object—her ne'er-do-well darling.
While she was thus charged with anger (for her
brother justly defended her son's master and companions from her attacks), she saw Ruth standing
with a lover, far away from home, at such a time
in the evening, and she boiled over with intemperate
displeasure.

" Come here directly, Miss Hilton," she exclaimed,
sharply.   Then, dropping her voice to low, bitter
tones of concentrated wrath, she said to the trembling,
guilty Ruth :

" Don't attempt to show your face at my house
again after this conduct.   I saw you, and your spark
too.   I'll have no slurs on the character of my

apprentices. Don't say a word. I saw enough. I shall write and tell your guardian to-morrow."

The horse started away, for he was impatient to be off, and Ruth was left standing there, stony, sick, and pale, as if the lightning had torn up the ground beneath her feet. She could not go on standing, she was so sick and faint; she staggered back to the broken sand-bank, and sank down, and covered her face with her hands.

"My dearest Ruth! are you ill? Speak, darling! My love, my love, do speak to me!"

What tender words after such harsh ones! They loosened the fountain of Ruth's tears, and she cried bitterly.

"Oh! did you see her—did you hear what she said?"

"She! Who, my darling? Don't sob so, Ruth; tell me what it is. Who has been near you?—who has been speaking to you to make you cry so?"

"Oh, Mrs Mason." And there was a fresh burst of sorrow.

"You don't say so; are you sure? I was not away five minutes."

"Oh, yes, sir, I'm quite sure. She was so angry; she said I must never show my face there again. Oh, dear! what shall I do?"

It seemed to the poor child as if Mrs Mason's words were irrevocable, and that, being so, she was shut out from every house. She saw how much she had done that was deserving of blame, now when it was too late to undo it. She knew with what severity and taunts Mrs Mason had often treated her for involuntary failings, of which she had been quite unconscious; and now she had really done wrong, and shrank with terror from the consequences. Her eyes were so blinded by the fast-falling tears, she did not see (nor had she seen would she have been able to interpret) the change in Mr Bellingham's countenance, as he stood silently watching her. He was silent so long, that even in her sorrow she began to wonder that he

did not speak, and to wish to hear his soothing words
once more.

"It is very unfortunate," he began, at last ; and
then he stopped ; then he began again : "It is very
unfortunate ; for, you see, I did not like to name it to
you before, but, I believe—I have business, in fact,
which obliges me to go to town to-morrow—to London,
I mean ; and I don't know when I shall be able to
return."

"To London !" cried Ruth ; "are you going away?
Oh, Mr Bellingham !" She wept afresh, giving
herself up to the desolate feeling of sorrow, which
absorbed all the terror she had been experiencing at
the idea of Mrs Mason's anger. It seemed to her at
this moment as though she could have borne everything but his departure ; but she did not speak again ;
and after two or three minutes had elapsed, he spoke
—not in his natural careless voice, but in a sort of
constrained agitated tone.

"I can hardly bear the idea of leaving you, my own
Ruth. In such distress, too ; for where you can go I
do not know at all. From all you have told me of
Mrs Mason, I don't think she is likely to mitigate her
severity in your case."

No answer, but tears quietly, incessantly flowing.
Mrs Mason's displeasure seemed a distant thing ; his
going away was the present distress. He went on :

"Ruth, would you go with me to London? My
darling, I cannot leave you here without a home ; the
thought of leaving you at all is pain enough, but in
these circumstances—so friendless, so homeless—it is
impossible. You must come with me, love, and trust
to me."

Still, she did not speak. Remember how young,
and innocent, and motherless she was ! It seemed to
her as if it would be happiness enough to be with him ;
and as for the future, he would arrange and decide for
that. The future lay wrapped in a golden mist, which
she did not care to penetrate ; but if he, her sun, was
out of sight, and gone, the golden mist became dark

heavy gloom, through which no hope could come. He took her hand.

"Will you not come with me? Do you not love me enough to trust me? Oh, Ruth" (reproachfully), "can you not trust me?"

She had stopped crying, but was sobbing sadly.

"I cannot bear this, love. Your sorrow is absolute pain to me; but it is worse to feel how indifferent you are—how little you care about our separation."

He dropped her hand. She burst into a fresh fit of crying.

"I may have to join my mother in Paris; I don't know when I shall see you again. Oh, Ruth!" said he, vehemently, "do you love me at all?"

She said something in a very low voice; he could not hear it, though he bent down his head—but he took her hand again.

"What was it you said, love? Was it not that you did love me? My darling, you do! I can tell it by the trembling of this little hand; then, you will not suffer me to go away alone and unhappy, most anxious about you? There is no other course open to you; my poor girl has no friends to receive her. I will go home directly, and return in an hour with a carriage. You make me too happy by your silence, Ruth."

"Oh, what can I do!" exclaimed Ruth. "Mr Bellingham, you should help me, and instead of that you only bewilder me."

"How, my dearest Ruth? Bewilder you! It seems so clear to me. Look at the case fairly! Here you are, an orphan, with only one person to love you, poor child!—thrown off, for no fault of yours, by the only creature on whom you have a claim, that creature a tyrannical, inflexible woman; what is more natural (and, being natural, more right) than that you should throw yourself upon the care of the one who loves you dearly—who would go through fire and water for you— who would shelter you from all harm? Unless, indeed, as I suspect, you do not care for him. If so, Ruth! if you do not care for me, we had better part—I will

leave you at once; it will be better for me to go, if
you do not care for me."

He said this very sadly (it seemed so to Ruth, at
least), and made as though he would have drawn his
hand from hers, but now she held it with soft
force.

"Don't leave me, please, sir. It is very true I have
no friend but you. Don't leave me, please. But, oh!
do tell me what I must do!"

"Will you do it if I tell you? If you will trust me,
I will do my very best for you. I will give you my
best advice. You see your position; Mrs Mason writes
and gives her own exaggerated account to your
guardian; he is bound by no great love to you, from
what I have heard you say, and throws you off; I, who
might be able to befriend you—through my mother,
perhaps—I, who could at least comfort you a little
(could not I, Ruth?) am away, far away, for an indefinite time; that is your position at present. Now,
what I advise is this. Come with me into this little
inn; I will order tea for you—(I am sure you require
it sadly)—and I will leave you there, and go home for
the carriage. I will return in an hour at the latest.
Then we are together, come what may; that is enough
for me, is it not for you, Ruth? Say, yes—say it ever
so low, but give me the delight of hearing it. Ruth,
say yes."

Low and soft, with much hesitation, came the
"Yes"; the fatal word of which she so little imagined
the infinite consequences. The thought of being with
him was all and everything.

"How you tremble, my darling! You are cold,
love! Come into the house, and I'll order tea directly
and be off."

She rose, and, leaning on his arm, went into the
house. She was shaking and dizzy with the agitation
of the last hour. He spoke to the civil farmer-land-
lord, who conducted them into a neat parlour, with
windows opening into the garden at the back of the
house. They had admitted much of the evening's

fragrance through their open casements, before they were hastily closed by the attentive host.

"Tea, directly, for this lady!" The landlord vanished.

"Dearest Ruth, I must go; there is not an instant to be lost; promise me to take some tea, for you are shivering all over, and deadly pale with the fright that abominable woman has given you. I must go; I shall be back in half an hour—and then no more partings, darling."

He kissed her pale cold face, and went away. The room whirled round before Ruth; it was a dream—a strange, varying, shifting dream—with the old home of her childhood for one scene, with the terror of Mrs Mason's unexpected appearance for another; and then, strangest, dizziest, happiest of all, there was the consciousness of his love, who was all the world to her; and the remembrance of the tender words, which still kept up their low soft echo in her heart.

Her head ached so much that she could hardly see; even the dusky twilight was a dazzling glare to her poor eyes; and when the daughter of the house brought in the sharp light of the candles, preparatory for tea, Ruth hid her face in the sofa pillows with a low exclamation of pain.

"Does your head ache, miss?" asked the girl, in a gentle, sympathizing voice. "Let me make you some tea, miss, it will do you good. Many's the time poor mother's headaches were cured by good strong tea."

Ruth murmured acquiescence; the young girl (about Ruth's own age, but who was the mistress of the little establishment, owing to her mother's death) made tea, and brought Ruth a cup to the sofa where she lay. Ruth was feverish and thirsty, and eagerly drank it off, although she could not touch the bread and butter which the girl offered her. She felt better and fresher, though she was still faint and weak.

"Thank you," said Ruth. "Don't let me keep you; perhaps you are busy. You have been very kind, and the tea has done me a great deal of good."

The girl left the room.   Ruth became as hot as she
had previously been cold, and went and opened the
window, and leant out into the still, sweet, evening
air.   The bush of sweetbrier, underneath the window,
scented the place, and the delicious fragrance reminded
her of her old home.   I think scents affect and quicken
the memory more than either sights or sounds; for
Ruth had instantly before her eyes the little garden
beneath the window of her mother's room, with the old
man leaning on his stick, watching her, just as he had
done, not three hours before, on that very afternoon.

"Dear old Thomas!   He and Mary would take me
in, I think; they would love me all the more if I were
cast off.   And Mr Bellingham would, perhaps, not be
so very long away; and he would know where to find
me if I stayed at Milham Grange.   Oh, would it not
be better to go to them?   I wonder if he would be
very sorry!   I could not bear to make him sorry, so
kind as he has been to me; but I do believe it would
be better to go to them, and ask their advice, at any
rate.   He would follow me there; and I could talk
over what I had better do, with the three best friends
I have in the world—the only friends I have."

She put on her bonnet, and opened the parlour door;
but then she saw the square figure of the landlord
standing at the open house-door, smoking his evening
pipe, and looming large and distinct against the dark
air and landscape beyond.   Ruth remembered the cup
of tea that she had drank; it must be paid for, and she
had no money with her.   She feared that he would not
let her quit the house without paying.   She thought
that she would leave a note for Mr Bellingham, saying
where she was gone, and how she had left the house in
debt, for (like a child) all dilemmas appeared of equal
magnitude to her; and the difficulty of passing the
landlord while he stood there, and of giving him an
explanation of the circumstances (as far as such explanation was due to him), appeared insuperable, and as
awkward, and fraught with inconvenience, as far more
serious situations.   She kept peeping out of her room,

after she had written her little pencil note, to see if
the outer door was still obstructed. There he stood,
motionless, enjoying his pipe, and looking out into the
darkness which gathered thick with the coming night.
The fumes of the tobacco were carried by the air into
the house, and brought back Ruth's sick headache.
Her energy left her ; she became stupid and languid,
and incapable of spirited exertion ; she modified her
plan of action, to the determination of asking Mr Bellingham to take her to Milham Grange, to the care of
her humble friends, instead of to London. And she
thought, in her simplicity, that he would instantly
consent when he had heard her reasons.

She started up. A carriage dashed up to the door.
She hushed her beating heart, and tried to stop her
throbbing head to listen. She heard him speaking to
the landlord, though she could not distinguish what
he said ; heard the jingling of money, and, in another
moment, he was in the room, and had taken her arm
to lead her to the carriage.

"Oh, sir ! I want you to take me to Milham Grange,"
said she, holding back. "Old Thomas would give me
a home."

"Well, dearest, we'll talk of all that in the carriage ;
I am sure you will listen to reason. Nay, if you will
go to Milham you must go in the carriage," said he,
hurriedly. She was little accustomed to oppose the
wishes of any one—obedient and docile by nature, and
unsuspicious and innocent of any harmful consequences.
She entered the carriage, and drove towards London.

CHAPTER V

The June of 18— had been glorious and sunny, and
full of flowers ; but July came in with pouring rain,
and it was a gloomy time for travellers and for weather-
bound tourists, who lounged away the days in touching
up sketches, dressing flies, and reading over again for

the twentieth time the few volumes they had brought
with them. A number of the *Times*, five days old, had
been in constant demand, in all the sitting-rooms of a
certain inn in a little mountain village of North Wales,
through a long July morning. The valleys around
were filled with thick cold mist, which had crept up
the hillsides till the hamlet itself was folded in its
white dense curtain, and from the inn windows nothing
was seen of the beautiful scenery around. The tourists
who thronged the rooms might as well have been " wi'
their dear little bairnies at hame "; and so some of
them seemed to think, as they stood, with their faces
flattened against the window-panes, looking abroad in
search of an event to fill up the dreary time. How
many dinners were hastened that day, by way of getting
through the morning, let the poor Welsh kitchen-maid
say ! The very village children kept indoors; or if
one or two more adventurous stole out into the land of
temptation and puddles, they were soon clutched back
by angry and busy mothers.

It was only four o'clock, but most of the inmates of
the inn thought it must be between six and seven, the
morning had seemed so long—so many hours had
passed since dinner—when a Welsh car, drawn by two
horses, rattled briskly up to the door. Every window
of the ark was crowded with faces at the sound ; the
leathern curtains were undrawn to their curious eyes,
and out sprang a gentleman, who carefully assisted a
well-cloaked-up lady into the little inn, despite the
landlady's assurances of not having a room to spare.

The gentleman (it was Mr Bellingham) paid no
attention to the speeches of the hostess, but quietly
superintended the unpacking of the carriage, and paid
the postilion ; then, turning round with his face to
the light, he spoke to the landlady, whose voice had
been rising during the last five minutes :

"Nay, Jenny, you're strangely altered, if you can
turn out an old friend on such an evening as this. If
I remember right, Pen trê Voelas* is twenty miles
across the bleakest mountain road I ever saw."

"Indeed, sir, and I did not know you ; Mr Bellingham, I believe. Indeed, sir, Pen trê Voelas is not
above eighteen miles—we only charge for eighteen ;
it may not be much above seventeen ; and we're quite
full, indeed, more's the pity."

"Well, but Jenny, to oblige me, an old friend,
you can find lodgings out for some of your people—
the house across, for instance."

"Indeed, sir, and it's at liberty ; perhaps you
would not mind lodging there yourself ; I could
get you the best rooms, and send over a trifle or
so of furniture, if they wern't as you'd wish them
to be."

"No, Jenny ! here I stay. You'll not induce me
to venture over into those rooms, whose dirt I know
of old. Can't you persuade some one who is not an
old friend to move across ? Say, if you like, that I
had written beforehand to bespeak the rooms. Oh ! I
know you can manage it—I know your good-natured
ways."

"Indeed, sir—well ! I'll see, if you and the lady
will just step into the back parlour, sir—there's no
one there just now — the lady is keeping her bed
to-day for a cold, and the gentleman is having a
rubber at whist in number three. I'll see what I
can do."

"Thank you, thank you. Is there a fire? if not,
one must be lighted. Come, Ruthie, come."

He led the way into a large, bow-windowed room,
which looked gloomy enough that afternoon, but
which I have seen bright and buoyant with youth and
hope within, and sunny lights creeping down the
purple mountain slope, and stealing over the green,
soft meadows, till they reached the little garden, full
of roses and lavender bushes, lying close under the
window. I have seen—but I shall see no more.

"I did not know you had been here before," said
Ruth, as Mr Bellingham helped her off with her
cloak.

"Oh, yes ; three years ago I was here on a reading

party. We were here above two months, attracted by
Jenny's kind heart and oddities; but driven away
finally by the insufferable dirt. However, for a week
or two it won't much signify."

"But can she take us in, sir?" I thought I heard
her saying her house was full."

"Oh, yes—I dare say it is; but I shall pay her
well; she can easily make excuses to some poor devil,
and send him over to the other side; and, for a day
or two, so that we have shelter, it does not much
signify."

"Could not we go to the house on the other side,
sir?"

"And have our meals carried across to us in a half-
warm state, to say nothing of having no one to scold
for bad cooking! You don't know these out-of-the-
way Welsh inns yet, Ruthie."

"No! I only thought it seemed rather unfair—"
said Ruth, gently; but she did not end her sentence,
for Mr Bellingham formed his lips into a whistle, and
walked to the window to survey the rain.

The remembrance of his former good payment
prompted many little lies of which Mrs Morgan was
guilty that afternoon, before she succeeded in turning
out a gentleman and lady, who were only planning to
remain till the ensuing Saturday at the outside, so, if
they did fulfil their threat, and leave on the next day,
she would be no very great loser.

These household arrangements complete, she solaced
herself with tea in her own little parlour, and
shrewdly reviewed the circumstances of Mr Bellingham's arrival.

"Indeed! and she's not his wife," thought Jenny,
"that's clear as day. His wife would have brought
her maid, and given herself twice as many airs about
the sitting-rooms; while this poor miss never spoke,
but kept as still as a mouse. Indeed, and young men
will be young men; and, as long as their fathers and
mothers shut their eyes, it's none of my business to go
about asking questions."

In this manner they settled down to a week's enjoyment of that Alpine country. It was most true
enjoyment to Ruth. It was opening a new sense;
vast ideas of beauty and grandeur filled her mind at
the sight of the mountains now first beheld in full
majesty. She was almost overpowered by the vague
and solemn delight; but by and by her love for them
equalled her awe, and in the night-time she would
softly rise, and steal to the window to see the white
moonlight, which gave a new aspect to the everlasting
hills that girdle the mountain village.

Their breakfast-hour was late, in accordance with
Mr Bellingham's tastes and habits; but Ruth was up
betimes, and out and away, brushing the dew-drops
from the short crisp grass; the lark sung high above
her head, and she knew not if she moved or stood still,
for the grandeur of this beautiful earth absorbed all
idea of separate and individual existence. Even rain
was a pleasure to her. She sat in the window-seat of
their parlour (she would have gone out gladly, but
that such a proceeding annoyed Mr Bellingham, who
usually at such times lounged away the listless hours
on a sofa, and relieved himself by abusing the weather);
she saw the swift fleeting showers come athwart the
sunlight like a rush of silver arrows; she watched the
purple darkness on the heathery mountain side, and
then the pale golden gleam which succeeded. There
was no change or alteration of nature that had not its
own peculiar beauty in the eyes of Ruth; but if she
had complained of the changeable climate, she would
have pleased Mr Bellingham more; her admiration
and her content made him angry, until her pretty
motions and loving eyes soothed down his impatience.

" Really, Ruth," he exclaimed one day, when they
had been imprisoned by rain a whole morning, " one
would think you had never seen a shower of rain
before; it quite wearies me to see you sitting there
watching this detestable weather with such a placid
countenance; and for the last two hours you have
said nothing more amusing or interesting than—

'Oh, how beautiful!' or, 'There's another cloud coming across Moel Wynn.'"

Ruth left her seat very gently, and took up her work. She wished she had the gift of being amusing; it must be dull for a man accustomed to all kinds of active employments to be shut up in the house. She was recalled from her absolute self-forgetfulness. What could she say to interest Mr Bellingham? While she thought, he spoke again:

"I remember when we were reading here three years ago, we had a week of just such weather as this; but Howard and Johnson were capital whist players, and Wilbraham not bad, so we got through the days famously. Can you play *écarté*, Ruth, or picquet?"

"No, sir; I have sometimes played at beggar-my-neighbour," answered Ruth, humbly, regretting her own deficiencies.

He murmured impatiently, and there was silence for another half hour. Then he sprang up, and rung the bell violently. "Ask Mrs Morgan for a pack of cards. Ruthie, I'll teach you *écarté*," said he.

But Ruth was stupid, not so good as a dummy, he said; and it was no fun betting against himself. So the cards were flung across the table—on the floor—anywhere. Ruth picked them up. As she rose, she sighed a little with the depression of spirits consequent upon her own want of power to amuse and occupy him she loved.

"You're pale, love!" said he, half repenting of his anger at her blunders over the cards. "Go out, before dinner; you know you don't mind this cursed weather; and see that you come home full of adventures to relate. Come, little blockhead! give me a kiss, and begone."

She left the room with a feeling of relief; for if he were dull without her, she should not feel responsible, and unhappy at her own stupidity. The open air, that kind soothing balm which gentle mother Nature offers to us all in our seasons of depression, relieved her. The

rain had ceased, though every leaf and blade was
loaded with trembling glittering drops.   Ruth went
down to the circular dale, into which the brown-
foaming mountain river fell and made a deep pool,
and, after resting there for a while, ran on between
broken rocks down to the valley below.   The water-
fall was magnificent, as she had anticipated ; she
longed to extend her walk to the other side of the
stream, so she sought the stepping-stones, the usual
crossing-place, which were over-shadowed by trees, a
few yards from the pool.   The waters ran high and
rapidly, as busy as life, between the pieces of grey
rock ; but Ruth had no fear, and went lightly and
steadily on.   About the middle, however, there was
a great gap ; either one of the stones was so covered
with water as to be invisible, or it had been washed
lower down ; at any rate, the spring from stone to
stone was long, and Ruth hesitated for a moment
before taking it.   The sound of rushing waters was
in her ears to the exclusion of every other noise ;
her eyes were on the current running swiftly below her
feet ; and thus she was startled to see a figure close
before her on one of the stones, and to hear a voice
offering help.

She looked up and saw a man, who was apparently
long past middle life, and of the stature of a dwarf ;
a second glance accounted for the low height of the
speaker, for then she saw he was deformed.   As the
consciousness of this infirmity came into her mind, it
must have told itself in her softened eyes, for a faint
flush of colour came into the pale face of the deformed
gentleman, as he repeated his words :

"The water is very rapid ; will you take my hand ?
Perhaps I can help you."

Ruth accepted the offer, and with this assistance she
was across in a moment.   He made way for her to
precede him in the narrow wood path, and then
silently followed her up the glen.

When they had passed out of the wood into the
pasture-land beyond, Ruth once more turned to mark

him. She was struck afresh with the mild beauty of
the face, though there was something in the countenance which told of the body's deformity, something more and beyond the pallor of habitual ill-
health, something of a quick spiritual light in the
deep set eyes, a sensibility about the mouth; but
altogether, though a peculiar, it was a most attractive
face.

"Will you allow me to accompany you if you are
going the round by Cwm Dhu, as I imagine you are?
The hand-rail is blown away from the little wooden
bridge by the storm last night, and the rush of waters
below may make you dizzy; and it is really dangerous
to fall there, the stream is so deep."

They walked on without much speech. She wondered who her companion might be. She should
have known him, if she had seen him among the
strangers at the inn; and yet he spoke English
too well to be a Welshman; he knew the country
and the paths so perfectly, he must be a resident; and
so she tossed him from England to Wales and back
again in her imagination.

"I only came here yesterday," said he, as a widen-
ing in the path permitted them to walk abreast.
"Last night I went to the higher waterfalls; they are
most splendid."

"Did you go out in all that rain?" asked Ruth,
timidly.

"Oh, yes. Rain never hinders me from walking.
Indeed, it gives a new beauty to such a country as
this. Besides, my time for my excursion is so short, I
cannot afford to waste a day."

"Then, you do not live here?" asked Ruth.

"No! my home is in a very different place. I live
in a busy town, where at times it is difficult to feel the
truth that

> There are in this loud stunning tide
>   Of human care and crime,
> With whom the melodies abide
>   Of th' everlasting chime.

Who carry music in their heart
Through dusky lane and crowded mart,
Plying their task with busier feet,
Because their secret souls a holy strain repeat.*

I have an annual holiday, which I generally spend in Wales; and often in this immediate neighbourhood."

"I do not wonder at your choice," replied Ruth. "It is a beautiful country."

"It is, indeed; and I have been inoculated by an old innkeeper at Conway with a love for its people, and history, and traditions. I have picked up enough of the language to understand many of their legends; and some are very fine and awe-inspiring, others very poetic and fanciful."

Ruth was too shy to keep up the conversation by any remark of her own, although his gentle, pensive manner was very winning.

"For instance," said he, touching a long bud-laden stem of fox-glove in the hedge-side, at the bottom of which one or two crimson speckled flowers were bursting from their green sheaths, "I dare say, you don't know what makes this fox-glove bend and sway so gracefully. You think it is blown by the wind, don't you?" He looked at her with a grave smile, which did not enliven his thoughtful eyes, but gave an inexpressible sweetness to his face.

"I always thought it was the wind. What is it?" asked Ruth, innocently.

"Oh, the Welsh tell you that this flower is sacred to the fairies, and that it has the power of recognising them, and all spiritual beings who pass by, and that it bows in deference to them as they waft along. Its Welsh name is Maneg Ellyllyn*—the good people's glove; and hence, I imagine, our folk's-glove or fox-glove."

"It's a very pretty fancy," said Ruth, much interested, and wishing that he would go on, without expecting her to reply.

But they were already at the wooden bridge; he led her across, and then, bowing his adieu, he had taken a

different path even before Ruth had thanked him for
his attention.

It was an adventure to tell Mr Bellingham, however; and it roused and amused him till dinner-time
came, after which he sauntered forth with a cigar.

"Ruth," said he, when he returned, " I've seen
your little hunchback. He looks like Riquet-with-
the-Tuft.* He's not a gentleman, though. If it had
not been for his deformity, I should not have made
him out from your description; you called him a
gentleman."

"And don't you, sir?" asked Ruth, surprised.

"Oh, no! he's regularly shabby and seedy in his
appearance; lodging, too, the ostler told me, over
that horrible candle and cheese shop, the smell of
which is insufferable twenty yards off—no gentleman
could endure it; he must be a traveller or artist, or
something of that kind."

"Did you see his face, sir?" asked Ruth.

"No; but a man's back—his *tout ensemble** has
character enough in it to decide his rank."

"His face was very singular; quite beautiful!"
said she, softly; but the subject did not interest Mr
Bellingham, and he let it drop.

CHAPTER VI

THE next day the weather was brave and glorious; a
perfect " bridal of the earth and sky";*and every one
turned out of the inn to enjoy the fresh beauty of
nature. Ruth was quite unconscious of being the
object of remark, and, in her light rapid passings to
and fro, had never looked at the doors and windows,
where many watchers stood observing her, and com-
menting upon her situation or her appearance.

"She's a very lovely creature," said one gentleman,
rising from the breakfast-table to catch a glimpse of
her. as she entered from her morning's ramble.

"Not above sixteen, I should think. Very modest
and innocent-looking in her white gown!"

His wife, busy administering to the wants of a fine
little boy, could only say (without seeing the young
girl's modest ways, and gentle, downcast countenance):

"Well! I do think it's a shame such people should
be allowed to come here. To think of such wickedness under the same roof! Do come away, my dear,
and don't flatter her by such notice."

The husband returned to the breakfast-table; he
smelt the broiled ham and eggs, and he heard his
wife's commands. Whether smelling or hearing had
most to do in causing his obedience, I cannot tell;
perhaps you can.

"Now, Harry, go and see if nurse and baby are
ready to go out with you. You must lose no time this
beautiful morning."

Ruth found Mr Bellingham was not yet come down;
so she sallied out for an additional half-hour's ramble.
Flitting about through the village, trying to catch all
the beautiful sunny peeps at the scenery between the
cold stone houses, which threw the radiant distance
into aerial perspective far away, she passed by the
little shop; and, just issuing from it, came the nurse
and baby, and little boy. The baby sat in placid
dignity in her nurse's arms, with a face of queenly
calm. Her fresh, soft, peachy complexion was really
tempting; and Ruth, who was always fond of children,
went up to coo and to smile at the little thing, and,
after some "peep-boing," she was about to snatch a
kiss, when Harry, whose face had been reddening ever
since the play began, lifted up his sturdy little right
arm and hit Ruth a great blow on the face.

"Oh, for shame, sir!" said the nurse, snatching
back his hand; "how dare you do that to the lady
who is so kind as to speak to Sissy."

"She's not a lady!" said he, indignantly. "She's
a bad naughty girl—mamma said so, she did; and she
shan't kiss our baby."

The nurse reddened in her turn. She knew what he must have heard; but it was awkward to bring it out, standing face to face with the elegant young lady. "Children pick up such notions, ma'am," said she at last, apologetically to Ruth, who stood, white and still, with a new idea running through her mind.

"It's no notion; it's true, nurse; and I heard you say it yourself. Go away, naughty woman!" said the boy, in infantile vehemence of passion to Ruth.

To the nurse's infinite relief, Ruth turned away, humbly and meekly, with bent head, and slow, uncertain steps. But as she turned, she saw the mild sad face of the deformed gentleman, who was sitting at the open window above the shop; he looked sadder and graver than ever; and his eyes met her glance with an expression of deep sorrow. And so, condemned alike by youth and age, she stole with timid step into the house. Mr Bellingham was awaiting her coming in the sitting-room. The glorious day restored all his buoyancy of spirits. He talked gaily away, without pausing for a reply; while Ruth made tea, and tried to calm her heart, which was yet beating with the agitation of the new ideas she had received from the occurrence of the morning. Luckily for her, the only answers required for some time were monosyllables; but those few words were uttered in so depressed and mournful a tone, that at last they struck Mr Bellingham with surprise and displeasure, as the condition of mind they unconsciously implied did not harmonize with his own.

"Ruth, what is the matter this morning? You really are very provoking. Yesterday, when everything was gloomy, and you might have been aware that I was out of spirits, I heard nothing but expressions of delight; to-day, when every creature under heaven is rejoicing, you look most deplorable and woe-begone. You really should learn to have a little sympathy."

The tears fell quickly down Ruth's cheeks, but she did not speak. She could not put into words the sense she was just beginning to entertain of the estimation in which she was henceforward to be held. She thought he would be as much grieved as she was at what had taken place that morning; she fancied she should sink in his opinion if she told him how others regarded her; besides, it seemed ungenerous to dilate upon the suffering of which he was the cause.

"I will not," thought she, "embitter his life; I will try and be cheerful. I must not think of myself so much. If I can but make him happy, what need I care for chance speeches?"

Accordingly, she made every effort possible to be as light-hearted as he was; but, somehow, the moment she relaxed, thoughts would intrude, and wonders would force themselves upon her mind; so that altogether she was not the gay and bewitching companion Mr Bellingham had previously found her.

They sauntered out for a walk. The path they chose led to a wood on the side of a hill, and they entered, glad of the shade of the trees. At first it appeared like any common grove, but they soon came to a deep descent, on the summit of which they stood, looking down on the tree-tops, which were softly waving far beneath their feet. There was a path leading sharp down, and they followed it; the ledge of rock made it almost like going down steps, and their walk grew into a bounding, and their bounding into a run, before they reached the lowest plane. A green gloom reigned there; it was the still hour of noon; the little birds were quiet in some leafy shade. They went on a few yards, and then they came to a circular pool overshadowed by the trees, whose highest boughs had been beneath their feet a few minutes before. The pond was hardly below the surface of the ground, and there was nothing like a bank on any side. A heron was standing there motionless, but when he saw them he flapped his wings and slowly rose, and soared above the green heights of the wood up into the very sky itself, for at that depth the trees appeared to touch the round white clouds which brooded over the earth.

The speed-well grew in the shallowest water or the pool, and all around its margin, but the flowers were hardly seen at first, so deep was the green shadow cast by the trees. In the very middle of the pond the sky was mirrored clear and dark, a blue which looked as if a black void lay behind.

"Oh, there are water-lilies," said Ruth, her eye catching on the farther side. "I must go and get some."

"No; I will get them for you. The ground is spongy all round there. Sit still, Ruth; this heap of grass will make a capital seat."

He went round, and she waited quietly for his return. When he came back he took off her bonnet, without speaking, and began to place his flowers in her hair. She was quite still while he arranged her coronet, looking up in his face with loving eyes, with a peaceful composure. She knew that he was pleased from his manner, which had the joyousness of a child playing with a new toy, and she did not think twice of his occupation. It was pleasant to forget everything except his pleasure. When he had decked her out, he said:

"There, Ruth! now you'll do. Come and look at yourself in the pond. Here, where there are no weeds. Come."

She obeyed, and could not help seeing her own loveliness; it gave her a sense of satisfaction for an instant, as the sight of any other beautiful object would have done, but she never thought of associating it with herself. She knew that she was beautiful; but that seemed abstract, and removed from herself. Her existence was in feeling, and thinking, and loving.

Down in that green hollow they were quite in harmony. Her beauty was all that Mr Bellingham cared for, and it was supreme. It was all he recognised of her, and he was proud of it. She stood in her white dress against the trees which grew around; her face was flushed into a brilliancy of colour which resembled that of a rose in June; the great heavy white

flowers drooped on either side of her beautiful head,
and if her brown hair was a little disordered, the very
disorder only seemed to add a grace. She pleased
him more by looking so lovely than by all her tender
endeavours to fall in with his varying humour.

But when they left the wood, and Ruth had
taken out her flowers, and resumed her bonnet, as
they came near the inn, the simple thought of
giving him pleasure was not enough to secure Ruth's
peace. She became pensive and sad, and could not
rally into gaiety.

"Really, Ruth," said he, that evening, "you must
not encourage yourself in this habit of falling into
melancholy reveries without any cause. You have
been sighing twenty times during the last half hour.
Do be a little cheerful. Remember, I have no
companion but you in this out-of-the-way place."

"I am very sorry, sir," said Ruth, her eyes filling
with tears ; and then she remembered that it was very
dull for him to be alone with her, heavy hearted as
she had been all day. She said in a sweet penitent
tone :

"Would you be so kind as to teach me one of those
games at cards you were speaking about yesterday, sir ?
I would do my best to learn."

Her soft, murmuring voice won its way. They rang
for the cards, and he soon forgot that there was such a
thing as depression or gloom in the world, in the
pleasure of teaching such a beautiful ignoramus the
mysteries of card-playing.

"There !" said he, at last, "that's enough for one
lesson. Do you know, little goose, your blunders
have made me laugh myself into one of the worst
headaches I have had for years."

He threw himself on the sofa, and in an instant she
was by his side.

"Let me put my cool hands on your forehead," she
begged ; "that used to do mamma good."

He lay still, his face away from the light, and not
speaking. Presently he fell asleep. Ruth put out

the candles, and sat patiently by him for a long time, fancying he would awaken refreshed. The room grew cool in the night air; but Ruth dare not rouse him from what appeared to be sound, restoring slumber. She covered him with her shawl, which she had thrown over a chair on coming in from their twilight ramble. She had ample time to think; but she tried to banish thought. At last, his breathing became quick and oppressed, and, after listening to it for some minutes with increasing affright, Ruth ventured to waken him. He seemed stupified and shivery. Ruth became more and more terrified; all the household were asleep except one servant-girl, who was wearied out of what little English she had knowledge of in more waking hours, she could only answer, "Iss, indeed, ma'am," to any question put to her by Ruth.

She sat by the bedside all night long. He moaned and tossed, but never spoke sensibly. It was a new form of illness to the miserable Ruth. Her yesterday's suffering went into the black distance of long-past years. The present was all-in-all. When she heard people stirring, she went in search of Mrs Morgan, whose shrewd sharp manners, unsoftened by inward respect for the poor girl, had awed Ruth even when Mr Bellingham was by to protect her.

"Mrs Morgan," said she, sitting down in the little parlour appropriated to the landlady, for she felt her strength suddenly desert her—"Mrs Morgan, I'm afraid Mr Bellingham is very ill;"—here she burst into tears, but instantly checking herself, "Oh, what must I do?" continued she; "I don't think he has known anything all through the night, and he looks so strange and wild this morning."

She gazed up into Mrs Morgan's face, as if reading an oracle.

"Indeed, miss, ma'am, and it's a very awkward thing. But don't cry, that can do no good, 'deed it can't. I'll go and see the poor young man myself, and then I can judge if a doctor is wanting."

Ruth followed Mrs Morgan upstairs. When they

entered the sick-room Mr Bellingham was sitting up
in bed, looking wildly about him, and as he saw them,
he exclaimed:

"Ruth! Ruth! come here; I won't be left alone!"
and then he fell down exhausted on the pillow. Mrs
Morgan went up and spoke to him, but he did not
answer or take any notice.

"I'll send for Mr Jones, my dear, 'deed and I will;
we'll have him here in a couple of hours, please
God."

"Oh, can't he come sooner?" asked Ruth, wild with
terror.

"'Deed no; he lives at Llanglâs when he's at home,
and that's seven mile away, and he may be gone a
round eight or nine mile on the other side Llanglâs;*
but I'll send a boy on the pony directly."

Saying this, Mrs Morgan left Ruth alone. There
was nothing to be done, for Mr Bellingham had again
fallen into a heavy sleep. Sounds of daily life began,
bells rang, breakfast-services clattered up and down
the passages, and Ruth sat on shivering by the bedside
in that darkened room. Mrs Morgan sent her breakfast
upstairs by a chambermaid, but Ruth motioned it
away in her sick agony, and the girl had no right to
urge her to partake of it. That alone broke the monotony of the long morning. She heard the sound of
merry parties setting out on excursions, on horseback
or in carriages; and once, stiff and wearied, she stole
to the window, and looked out on one side of the blind;
but the day looked bright and discordant to her aching,
anxious heart. The gloom of the darkened room was
better and more befitting.

It was some hours after he was summoned before
the doctor made his appearance. He questioned his
patient, and, receiving no coherent answers, he asked
Ruth concerning the symptoms, but when she questioned him in turn he only shook his head and looked
grave. He made a sign to Mrs Morgan to follow him
out of the room, and they went down to her parlour,
leaving Ruth in a depth of despair, lower than she

could have thought it possible there remained for her
to experience, an hour before.

"I am afraid this is a bad case," said Mr Jones
to Mrs Morgan in Welsh.   "A brain-fever has
evidently set in."

"Poor young gentleman! poor young man!   He
looked the very picture of health!"

"That very appearance of robustness will, in all
probability, make his disorder more violent.   However, we must hope for the best, Mrs Morgan.   Who
is to attend upon him?   He will require careful
nursing.   Is that young lady his sister?   She looks
too young to be his wife?"

"No, indeed!   Gentlemen like you must know, Mr
Jones, that we can't always look too closely into the
ways of young men who come to our houses.   Not but
what I'm sorry for her, for she's an innocent, in-
offensive young creature.   I always think it right, for
my own morals, to put a little scorn into my manners
when such as her come to stay here; but, indeed, she's
so gentle, I've found it hard work to show the proper
contempt."

She would have gone on to her inattentive listener
if she had not heard a low tap at the door, which
recalled her from her morality, and Mr Jones from
his consideration of the necessary prescriptions.

"Come in!" said Mrs Morgan, sharply.   And Ruth
came in.   She was white and trembling; but she
stood in that dignity which strong feeling, kept down
by self-command, always imparts.

"I wish you, sir, to be so kind as to tell me, clearly
and distinctly, what I must do for Mr Bellingham.
Every direction you give me shall be most carefully
attended to.   You spoke about leeches—I can put
them on, and see about them.   Tell me everything,
sir, that you wish to have done!"

Her manner was calm and serious, and her countenance and deportment showed that the occasion was
calling out strength sufficient to meet it.   Mr Jones
spoke with a deference which he had not thought of

using upstairs, even while he supposed her to be the sister of the invalid. Ruth listened gravely; she repeated some of the injunctions, in order that she might be sure that she fully comprehended them, and then, bowing, left the room.

"She is no common person," said Mr Jones. "Still she is too young to have the responsibility of such a serious case. Have you any idea where his friends live, Mrs Morgan?"

"Indeed and I have. His mother, as haughty a lady as you would wish to see, came travelling through Wales last year; she stopped here, and, I warrant you, nothing was good enough for her; she was real quality. She left some clothes and books behind her (for the maid was almost as fine as the mistress, and little thought of seeing after her lady's clothes, having a taste for going to see scenery along with the man-servant), and we had several letters from her. I have them locked in the drawers in the bar, where I keep such things."

"Well! I should recommend your writing to the lady, and telling her her son's state."

"It would be a favour, Mr Jones, if you would just write it yourself. English writing comes so strange to my pen."

The letter was written, and, in order to save time, Mr Jones took it to the Llanglâs post office.

CHAPTER VII

Ruth put away every thought of the past or future; everything that could unfit her for the duties of the present. Exceeding love supplied the place of ex-perience. She never left the room after the first day; she forced herself to eat, because his service needed her strength. She did not indulge in any tears, because the weeping she longed for would make her less able to attend upon him. She watched, and waited, and

prayed : prayed with an utter forgetfulness of self,
only with a consciousness that God was all powerful,
and that he, whom she loved so much, needed the aid
of the Mighty One.

Day and night, the summer night, seemed merged
into one. She lost count of time in the hushed and
darkened room. One morning Mrs Morgan beckoned
her out ; and she stole on tiptoe into the dazzling
gallery, on one side of which the bedrooms opened.

"She's come," whispered Mrs Morgan, looking very
much excited, and forgetting that Ruth had never
heard that Mrs Bellingham had been summoned.

"Who is come?" asked Ruth. The idea of Mrs
Mason flashed through her mind—but with a more
terrible, because a more vague dread, she heard that it
was his mother ; the mother of whom he had always
spoken as a person whose opinion was to be regarded
more than that of any other individual.

"What must I do? Will she be angry with me?"
said she, relapsing into her childlike dependence on
others ; and feeling that even Mrs Morgan was some
one to stand between her and Mrs Bellingham.

Mrs Morgan herself was a little perplexed. Her
morality was rather shocked at the idea of a proper
real lady like Mrs Bellingham discovering that she had
winked at the connexion between her son and Ruth.
She was quite inclined to encourage Ruth in her inclination to shrink out of Mrs Bellingham's observation,
an inclination which arose from no definite consciousness
of having done wrong, but principally from the repre-
sentations she had always heard of the lady's awful-
ness. Mrs Bellingham swept into her son's room as if
she were unconscious what poor young creature had
lately haunted it ; while Ruth hurried into some
unoccupied bedroom, and, alone there, she felt her
self-restraint suddenly give way, and burst into the
saddest, most utterly wretched weeping she had ever
known. She was worn out with watching, and exhausted by passionate crying, and she lay down on the
bed and fell asleep. The day passed on ; she slumbered

unnoticed and unregarded; she awoke late in the evening with a sense of having done wrong in sleeping so long; the strain upon her responsibility had not yet left her. Twilight was closing fast around; she waited until it had become night, and then she stole down to Mrs Morgan's parlour.

"If you please may I come in?" asked she.

Jenny Morgan was doing up the hieroglyphics which she called her accounts; she answered sharply enough, but it was a permission to enter, and Ruth was thankful for it.

"Will you tell me how he is? Do you think I may go back to him?"

"No, indeed, that you may not. Nest, who has made his room tidy these many days, is not fit to go in now. Mrs Bellingham has brought her own maid, and the family nurse, and Mr Bellingham's man; such a tribe of servants and no end to packages; water-beds coming by the carrier, and a doctor from London coming down to-morrow, as if feather beds and Mr Jones was not good enough. Why, she won't let a soul of us into the room; there's no chance for you!"

Ruth sighed. "How is he?" she inquired, after a pause.

"How can I tell indeed, when I'm not allowed to go near him. Mr Jones said to-night was a turning point; but I doubt it, for it is four days since he was taken ill, and who ever heard of a sick person taking a turn on an even number of days; it's always on the third, or the fifth, or seventh, or so on. He'll not turn till to-morrow night, take my word for it, and their fine London doctor will get all the credit, and honest Mr Jones will be thrown aside. I don't think he will get better myself, though—Gelert* does not howl for nothing. My patience! what's the matter with the girl—lord, child, you're never going to faint, and be ill on my hands." Her sharp voice recalled Ruth from the sick unconsciousness that had been creeping over her as she listened to the latter part of this speech. She sat down and could not speak—the room whirled

round and round—her white reebleness touched Mrs
Morgan's heart.

"You've had no tea, I guess. Indeed, and the
girls are very careless." She rang the bell with
energy, and seconded her pull by going to the door
and shouting out sharp directions, in Welsh, to Nest
and Gwen, and three or four other rough, kind,
slatternly servants.

They brought her tea, which was comfortable,
according to the idea of comfort prevalent in that
rude, hospitable place; there was plenty to eat, too
much, indeed, for it revolted the appetite it was intended to provoke. But the heartiness with which the
kind, rosy waiter pressed her to eat, and the scolding
Mrs Morgan gave her, when she found the buttered
toast untouched (toast on which she had herself desired
that the butter might not be spared), did Ruth more
good than the tea. She began to hope, and to long for
the morning when hope might have become certainty.
It was all in vain that she was told that the room she
had been in all day was at her service; she did not say
a word, but she was not going to bed that night, of all
nights in the year, when life or death hung trembling
in the balance. She went into the sick room till the
bustling house was still, and heard busy feet passing to
and fro in the room she might not enter; and voices,
imperious, though hushed down to a whisper, ask for
innumerable things. Then there was silence; and
when she thought that all were dead asleep, except the
watchers, she stole out into the gallery. On the other
side were two windows, cut into the thick stone wall,
and flower pots were placed on the shelves thus formed,
where great, untrimmed, straggling geraniums grew,
and strove to reach the light. The window near Mr
Bellingham's door was open; the soft, warm-scented
night air came sighing in in faint gusts, and then was
still. It was summer; there was no black darkness in
the twenty-four hours; only the light grew dusky, and
colour disappeared from objects, of which the shape
and form remained distinct. A soft grey oblong of

barred light fell on the flat wall opposite to the windows, and deeper grey shadows marked out the tracery of the plants, more graceful thus than in reality. Ruth crouched where no light fell. She sat on the ground close by the door; her whole existence was absorbed in listening; all was still; it was only her heart beating with the strong, heavy, regular sound of a hammer. She wished she could stop its rushing, incessant clang. She heard a rustle of a silken gown, and knew it ought not to have been worn in a sick room; for her senses seemed to have passed into the keeping of the invalid, and to feel only as he felt. The noise was probably occasioned by some change of posture in the watcher inside, for it was once more dead still. The soft wind outside sank with a low, long, distant moan among the windings of the hills, and lost itself there, and came no more again. But Ruth's heart beat loud. She rose with as little noise as if she were a vision, and crept to the open window to try and lose the nervous listening for the ever-recurring sound. Out beyond, under the calm sky, veiled with a mist rather than with a cloud, rose the high, dark outlines of the mountains, shutting in that village as if it lay in a nest. They stood, like giants, solemnly watching for the end of Earth and Time. Here and there a black round shadow reminded Ruth of some "Cwm," or hollow, where she and her lover had rambled in sun and in gladness. She then thought the land enchanted into everlasting brightness and happiness; she fancied, then, that into a region so lovely no bale or woe could enter, but would be charmed away and disappear before the sight of the glorious guardian mountains. Now she knew the truth, that earth has no barrier which avails against agony. It comes lightning-like down from heaven, into the mountain house and the town garret; into the palace and into the cottage. The garden lay close under the house; a bright spot enough by day; for in that soil, whatever was planted grew and blossomed in spite of neglect. The white roses glimmered out in the dusk all the night through; the red were lost in shadow. Between the low boundary of the garden and the hills swept one or two green meadows; Ruth looked into the grey darkness till she traced each separate wave of outline. Then she heard a little restless bird chirp out its wakefulness from a nest in the ivy round the walls of the house. But the mother-bird spread her soft feathers, and hushed it into silence. Presently, however, many little birds began to scent the coming dawn, and rustled among the leaves, and chirruped loud and clear. Just above the horizon, too, the mist became a silvery grey cloud hanging on the edge of the world; presently it turned shimmering white; and then, in an instant, it flushed into rose, and the mountain tops sprang into heaven, and bathed in the presence of the shadow of God. With a bound, the sun of a molten fiery red came above the horizon, and immediately thousands of little birds sang out for joy, and a soft chorus of mysterious, glad murmurs came forth from the earth; the low whispering wind left its hiding-place among the clefts and hollows of the hills, and wandered among the rustling herbs and trees, waking the flower-buds to the life of another day. Ruth gave a sigh of relief that the night was over and gone; for she knew that soon suspense would be ended, and the verdict known, whether for life or for death. She grew faint and sick with anxiety; it almost seemed as if she must go into the room and learn the truth. Then she heard movements, but they were not sharp or rapid, as if prompted by any emergency; then, again, it was still. She sat curled up upon the floor, with her head thrown back against the wall, and her hands clasped round her knees. She had yet to wait. Meanwhile, the invalid was slowly rousing himself from a long, deep, sound, health-giving sleep. His mother had sat by him the night through, and was now daring to change her position for the first time; she was even venturing to give directions in a low voice to the old nurse, who had dozed away in an arm-chair, ready to obey any sum-

mons of her mistress. Mrs Bellingham went on tiptoe
towards the door, and chiding herself because her stiff,
weary limbs made some slight noise. She had an
irrepressible longing for a few minutes' change of
scene after her night of watching. She felt that the
crisis was over; and the relief to her mind made her
conscious of every bodily feeling and irritation, which
had passed unheeded as long as she had been in
suspense.

She slowly opened the door. Ruth sprang upright
at the first sound of the creaking handle. Her very
lips were stiff and unpliable with the force of the blood
which rushed to her head. It seemed as if she could
not form words. She stood right before Mrs Bellingham. "How is he, madam?"

Mrs Bellingham was for a moment surprised at the
white apparition which seemed to rise out of the
ground. But her quick, proud mind understood it all
in an instant. This was the girl, then, whose profligacy
had led her son astray; had raised up barriers in the
way of her favourite scheme of his marriage with Miss
Duncombe; nay, this was the real cause of his illness,
his mortal danger at this present time, and of her
bitter, keen anxiety. If, under any circumstances,
Mrs Bellingham could have been guilty of the ill-
breeding of not answering a question, it was now; and
for a moment she was tempted to pass on in silence.
Ruth could not wait; she spoke again:

"For the love of God, madam, speak! How is he?
Will he live?"

If she did not answer her, she thought the creature
was desperate enough to force her way into his room.
So she spoke.

"He has slept well: he is better."

"Oh! my God, I thank Thee," murmured Ruth,
sinking back against the wall.

It was too much to hear this wretched girl thanking
God for her son's life; as if, in fact, she had any lot
or part in him, and to dare to speak to the Almighty
on her son's behalf! Mrs Bellingham looked at her

with cold, contemptuous eyes, whose glances were like
ice-bolts, and made Ruth shiver up away from them.

"Young woman, if you have any propriety or
decency left, I trust that you will not dare to force
yourself into his room."

She stood for a moment as if awaiting an answer,
and half expecting it to be a defiance. But she did not
understand Ruth. She did not imagine the faithful
trustfulness of her heart. Ruth believed that if Mr
Bellingham was alive and likely to live, all was well.
When he wanted her, he would send for her, ask for
her, yearn for her, till every one would yield before
his steadfast will. At present she imagined that he
was probably too weak to care or know who was about
him; and though it would have been an infinite delight
to her to hover and brood around him, yet it was of
him she thought and not of herself. She gently drew
herself on one side to make way for Mrs Bellingham
to pass.

By and by Mrs Morgan came up. Ruth was still
near the door, from which it seemed as if she could not
tear herself away.

"Indeed, miss, and you must not hang about the
door in this way; it is not pretty manners. Mrs
Bellingham has been speaking very sharp and cross
about it, and I shall lose the character of my inn if
people take to talking as she does. Did not I give you
a room last night to keep in, and never be seen or
heard of; and did I not tell you what a particular lady
Mrs Bellingham was, but you must come out here
right in her way? Indeed, it was not pretty, nor
grateful to me, Jenny Morgan, and that I must say."

Ruth turned away like a chidden child. Mrs
Morgan followed her to her room, scolding as she
went; and then, having cleared her heart after her
wont by uttering hasty words, her real kindness made
her add, in a softened tone:

"You stop up here like a good girl. I'll send you
your breakfast by and by, and let you know from time
to time how he is; and you can go out for a walk,

you know; but if you do, I'll take it as a favour if
you'll go out by the side door. It will, maybe, save
scandal."

All that day long, Ruth kept herself close prisoner
in the room to which Mrs Morgan accorded her; all
that day, and many succeeding days. But at nights,
when the house was still, and even the little brown
mice had gathered up the crumbs, and darted again to
their holes, Ruth stole out, and crept to his door to
catch, if she could, the sound of his beloved voice.
She could tell by its tones how he felt, and how he was
getting on, as well as any of the watchers in the room.
She yearned and pined to see him once more; but she
had reasoned herself down into something like patience.
When he was well enough to leave his room, when he
had not always one of the nurses with him, then he
would send for her, and she would tell him how very
patient she had been for his dear sake. But it was
long to wait even with this thought of the manner in
which the waiting would end. Poor Ruth! her faith
was only building up vain castles in the air; they
towered up into heaven, it is true, but, after all, they
were but visions.

CHAPTER VIII

If Mr Bellingham did not get rapidly well, it was
more owing to the morbid querulous fancy attendant
on great weakness than from any unfavourable medical
symptom. But he turned away with peevish loathing
from the very sight of food, prepared in the slovenly
manner which had almost disgusted him when he was
well. It was of no use telling him that Simpson, his
mother's maid, had superintended the preparation at
every point. He offended her by detecting something
offensive and to be avoided in her daintiest messes, and
made Mrs Morgan mutter many a hasty speech, which,
however, Mrs Bellingham thought it better not to hear
until her son should be strong enough to travel.

"I think you are better to-day," said she, as his man wheeled his sofa to the bedroom window. "We shall get you downstairs to-morrow."

"If it were to get away from this abominable place, I could go down to-day; but I believe I'm to be kept prisoner here for ever. I shall never get well here, I'm sure."

He sank back on his sofa in impatient despair. The surgeon was announced, and eagerly questioned by Mrs Bellingham as to the possibility of her son's removal; and he, having heard the same anxiety for the same end expressed by Mrs Morgan in the regions below, threw no great obstacles in the way. After the doctor had taken his departure, Mrs Bellingham cleared her throat several times. Mr Bellingham knew the prelude of old, and winced with nervous annoyance.

"Henry, there is something I must speak to you about; an unpleasant subject, certainly, but one which has been forced upon me by the very girl herself; you must be aware to what I refer without giving me the pain of explaining myself."

Mr Bellingham turned himself sharply round to the wall, and prepared himself for a lecture by concealing his face from her notice; but she herself was in too nervous a state to be capable of observation.

"Of course," she continued, "it was my wish to be as blind to the whole affair as possible, though you can't imagine how Mrs Mason has blazoned it abroad; all Fordham rings with it; but of course it could not be pleasant, or, indeed, I may say correct, for me to be aware that a person of such improper character was under the same—I beg your pardon, dear Henry, what do you say?"

"Ruth is no improper character, mother; you do her injustice!"

"My dear boy, you don't mean to uphold her as a paragon of virtue!"

"No, mother, but I led her wrong; I——"

"We will let all discussions into the cause or duration of her present character drop, if you please," said Mrs

Bellingham, with the sort of dignified authority which
retained a certain power over her son—a power which
originated in childhood, and which he only defied when
he was roused into passion. He was too weak in body
to oppose himself to her, and fight the ground inch by
inch. "As I have implied, I do not wish to ascertain
your share of blame; from what I saw of her one morning, I am convinced of her forward, intrusive manners,
utterly without shame, or even common modesty."

"What are you referring to?" asked Mr Bellingham, sharply.

"Why, when you were at the worst, and I had been
watching you all night, and had just gone out in the
morning for a breath of fresh air, this girl pushed herself before me, and insisted upon speaking to me. I
really had to send Mrs Morgan to her before I could
return to your room. A more impudent, hardened
manner, I never saw."

"Ruth was neither impudent nor hardened; she
was ignorant enough, and might offend from knowing
no better."

He was getting weary of the discussion, and wished
it had never been begun. From the time he had
become conscious of his mother's presence, he had felt
the dilemma he was in in regard to Ruth, and various
plans had directly crossed his brain; but it had been
so troublesome to weigh and consider them all properly,
that they had been put aside to be settled when he
grew stronger. But this difficulty in which he was
placed by his connexion with Ruth, associated the idea
of her in his mind with annoyance and angry regret at
the whole affair. He wished, in the languid way in
which he wished and felt everything not immediately
relating to his daily comfort, that he had never seen
her. It was a most awkward, a most unfortunate
affair. Notwithstanding this annoyance connected
with and arising out of Ruth, he would not submit to
hear her abused; and something in his manner impressed this on his mother, for she immediately
changed her mode of attack.

"We may as well drop all dispute as to the young woman's manners ; but I suppose you do not mean to defend your connexion with her ; I suppose you are not so lost to all sense of propriety as to imagine it fit or desirable that your mother and this degraded girl should remain under the same roof, liable to meet at any hour of the day?" She waited for an answer, but no answer came.

"I ask you a simple question ; is it, or is it not desirable?"

"I suppose it is not," he replied, gloomily.

"And *I* suppose, from your manner, that you think the difficulty would be best solved by my taking my departure, and leaving you with your vicious companion?"

Again no answer, but inward and increasing annoyance, of which Mr Bellingham considered Ruth the cause. At length he spoke.

"Mother, you are not helping me in my difficulty. I have no desire to banish you, nor to hurt you, after all your care for me. Ruth has not been so much to blame as you imagine, that I must say ; but I do not wish to see her again, if you can tell me how to arrange it otherwise, without behaving unhandsomely. Only spare me all this worry while I am so weak. I put myself in your hands. Dismiss her, as you wish it ; but let it be done handsomely, and let me hear no more about it ; I cannot bear it ; let me have a quiet life, without being lectured while I am pent up here, and unable to shake off unpleasant thoughts."

"My dear Henry, rely upon me."

"No more, mother ; it's a bad business, and I can hardly avoid blaming myself in the matter ; I don't want to dwell upon it."

"Don't be too severe in your self-reproaches while you are so feeble, dear Henry ; it is right to repent, but I have no doubt in my own mind she led you wrong with her artifices. But, as you say, everything should be done handsomely. I confess I was deeply grieved when I first heard of the affair, but since I have seen

the girl——Well! I'll say no more about her, since I
see it displeases you; but I am thankful to God that
you see the error of your ways."

She sat silent, thinking for a little while, and then
sent for her writing-case, and began to write. Her
son became restless, and nervously irritated.

"Mother," he said, "this affair worries me to death.
I cannot shake off the thoughts of it."

"Leave it to me, I'll arrange it satisfactorily."

"Could we not leave to-night? I should not be so
haunted by this annoyance in another place. I dread
seeing her again, because I fear a scene; and yet I
believe I ought to see her, in order to explain."

"You must not think of such a thing, Henry," said
she, alarmed at the very idea. "Sooner than that, we
will leave in half an hour, and try to get to Pen trê
Voelas to-night. It is not yet three, and the evenings
are very long. Simpson should stay and finish the
packing; she could go straight to London and meet us
there. Macdonald and nurse could go with us. Could
you bear twenty miles, do you think?"

Anything to get rid of his uneasiness. He felt that
he was not behaving as he should do, to Ruth, though
the really right never entered his head. But it would
extricate him from his present dilemma, and save him
many lectures; he knew that his mother, always liberal
where money was concerned, would "do the thing
handsomely," and it would always be easy to write and
give Ruth what explanation he felt inclined, in a day
or two; so he consented, and soon lost some of his
uneasiness in watching the bustle of the preparation
for their departure.

All this time Ruth was quietly spending in her
room, beguiling the waiting, weary hours, with
pictures of the meeting at the end. Her room
looked to the back, and was in a side wing away
from the principal state apartments, consequently
she was not roused to suspicion by any of the commotion; but, indeed, if she had heard the banging
of doors, the sharp directions, the carriage wheels,

she would still not have suspected the truth ; her
own love was too faithful.

It was four o'clock and past, when some one knocked
at her door, and, on entering, gave her a note, which
Mrs Bellingham had left.   That lady had found some
difficulty in wording it, so as to satisfy herself, but it
was as follows :

" My son, on recovering from his illness, is, I thank
God, happily conscious of the sinful way in which he
has been living with you.   By his earnest desire, and
in order to avoid seeing you again, we are on the
point of leaving this place ; but before I go, I wish
to exhort you to repentance, and to remind you that
you will not have your own guilt alone upon your
head, but that of any young man whom you may
succeed in entrapping into vice.   I shall pray that
you may turn to an honest life, and I strongly
recommend you, if indeed you are not ' dead in
trespasses and sins,' to enter some penitentiary.*   In
accordance with my son's wishes, I forward you in this
envelope a bank-note of fifty pounds."
                                   " MARGARET BELLINGHAM."

Was this the end of all ?   Had he, indeed, gone ?
She started up, and asked this last question of the
servant, who, half guessing at the purport of the
note, had lingered about the room, curious to see
the effect produced.

"Iss, indeed, miss ; the carriage drove from the
door as I came upstairs.   You'll see it now on the
Yspytty road,* if you'll please to come to the window
of No. 24."

Ruth started up, and followed the chambermaid.
Aye, there it was, slowly winding up the steep
white road, on which it seemed to move at a snail's
pace.

She might overtake him—she might—she might
speak one farewell word to him, print his face on
her heart with a last look—nay, when he saw her

he might retract, and not utterly, for ever, leave her. Thus she thought; and she flew back to her room, and snatching up her bonnet, ran, tying the strings with her trembling hands as she went down the stairs, out at the nearest door, little heeding the angry words of Mrs Morgan; for the hostess, more irritated at Mrs Bellingham's severe upbraiding at parting, than mollified by her ample payment, was offended by the circumstance of Ruth, in her wild haste, passing through the prohibited front door.

But Ruth was away before Mrs Morgan had finished her speech, out and away, scudding along the road, thought-lost in the breathless rapidity of her motion. Though her heart and head beat almost to bursting, what did it signify if she could but overtake the carriage. It was a nightmare, constantly evading the most passionate wishes and endeavours, and constantly gaining ground. Every time it was visible it was in fact more distant, but Ruth would not believe it. If she could but gain the summit of that weary, everlasting hill, she believed that she could run again, and would soon be nigh upon the carriage. As she ran, she prayed with wild eagerness; she prayed that she might see his face once more, even if she died on the spot before him. It was one of those prayers which God is too merciful to grant; but despairing and wild. As it was, Ruth put her soul into it, and prayed it again, and yet again.

Wave above wave of the ever-rising hills were gained, were crossed, and at last Ruth struggled up to the very top and stood on the bare table of moor, brown and purple, stretching far away till it was lost in the haze of the summer afternoon; and the white road was all flat before her, but the carriage she sought and the figure she sought had disappeared. There was no human being there; a few wild, black-faced mountain sheep quietly grazing near the road, as if it were long since they had been disturbed by the passing of any vehicle, was all the life she saw on the bleak moorland.

She threw herself down on the ling* by the side of
the road in despair. Her only hope was to die, and
she believed she was dying. She could not think ;
she could believe anything. Surely life was a horrible
dream, and God would mercifully awaken her from it.
She had no penitence, no consciousness of error or
offence ; no knowledge of any one circumstance but
that he was gone. Yet afterwards, long afterwards,
she remembered the exact motion of a bright green
beetle busily meandering among the wild thyme near
her, and she recalled the musical, balanced, wavering
drop of a skylark into her nest near the heather-bed
where she lay. The sun was sinking low, the hot air
had ceased to quiver near the hotter earth, when she
bethought her once more of the note which she had
impatiently thrown down before half mastering its
contents. "Oh, perhaps," she thought, "I have been
too hasty. There may be some words of explanation
from him on the other side of the page, to which, in
my blind anguish, I never turned. I will go and
find it."

She lifted herself heavily and stiffly from the crushed
heather. She stood dizzy and confused with her
change of posture ; and was so unable to move at first,
that her walk was but slow and tottering ; but, by
and by, she was tasked and goaded by thoughts which
forced her into rapid motion, as if, by it, she could
escape from her agony. She came down on the level
ground, just as many gay or peaceful groups were
sauntering leisurely home with hearts at ease ; with
low laughs and quiet smiles, and many an exclamation
at the beauty of the summer evening.

Ever since her adventure with the little boy and his
sister, Ruth had habitually avoided encountering these
happy—innocents, may I call them?—these happy
fellow-mortals ! And even now, the habit grounded
on sorrowful humiliation had power over her ; she
paused, and then, on looking back, she saw more
people who had come into the main road from a side
path. She opened a gate into a pasture field, and crept

up to the hedge-bank until all should have passed by, and she could steal into the inn unseen. She sat down on the sloping turf by the roots of an old hawthorn-tree which grew in the hedge; she was still tearless with hot burning eyes; she heard the merry walkers pass by; she heard the footsteps of the village children, as they ran along to their evening play; she saw the small black cows come into the fields after being milked; and life seemed yet abroad. When would the world be still and dark, and fit for such a deserted, desolate creature as she was? Even in her hiding-place she was not long at peace. The little children, with their curious eyes peering here and there, had peeped through the hedge, and through the gate, and now they gathered from all the four corners of the hamlet, and crowded round the gate; and one more adventurous than the rest, had run into the field to cry, "Gi' me a halfpenny," which set the example to every little one, emulous of his boldness; and there, where she sat, low on the ground, and longing for the sure hiding-place earth gives to the weary, the children kept running in, and pushing one another forwards, and laughing. Poor things; their time had not come for understanding what sorrow is. Ruth would have begged them to leave her alone, and not madden her utterly; but they knew no English save the one eternal "Gi' me a halfpenny." She felt in her heart that there was no pity anywhere. Suddenly, while she thus doubted God, a shadow fell across her garments, on which her miserable eyes were bent. She looked up. The deformed gentleman she had twice before seen, stood there. He had been attracted by the noisy little crowd, and had questioned them in Welsh, but not understanding enough of the language to comprehend their answers, he had obeyed their signs, and entered the gate to which they pointed. There he saw the young girl whom he had noticed at first for her innocent beauty, and the second time for the idea he had gained respecting her situation; there he saw her, crouched up like some hunted creature,

with a wild, scared look of despair, which almost made
her lovely face seem fierce ; he saw her dress soiled
and dim, her bonnet crushed and battered with her
tossings to and fro on the moorland bed ; he saw the
poor, lost wanderer, and when he saw her, he had
compassion on her.

There was some look of heavenly pity in his eyes,
as gravely and sadly they met her upturned gaze,
which touched her stony heart. Still looking at him,
as if drawing some good influence from him, she said
low and mournfully, " He has left me, sir !—sir, he
has indeed—he has gone and left me ! "

Before he could speak a word to comfort her, she
had burst into the wildest, dreariest crying ever
mortal cried. The settled form of the event, when
put into words, went sharp to her heart ; her moans
and sobs wrung his soul ; but as no speech of his
could be heard, if he had been able to decide what
best to say, he stood by her in apparent calmness,
while she, wretched, wailed and uttered her woe. But
when she lay worn out, and stupefied into silence, she
heard him say to himself, in a low voice :

" Oh, my God ! for Christ's sake, pity her ! "

Ruth lifted up her eyes, and looked at him with a
dim perception of the meaning of his words. She
regarded him fixedly in a dreamy way, as if they
struck some chord in her heart, and she were listening to its echo ; and so it was. His pitiful look,
or his words, reminded her of the childish days
when she knelt at her mother's knee, and she was
only conscious of a straining, longing desire to recall
it all.

He let her take her time, partly because he was
powerfully affected himself by all the circumstances,
and by the sad pale face upturned to his ; and partly
by an instinctive consciousness that the softest patience
was required. But suddenly she startled him, as she
herself was startled into a keen sense of the suffering
agony of the present ; she sprang up and pushed him
aside, and went rapidly towards the gate of the field.

He could not move as quickly as most men, but he put forth his utmost speed. He followed across the road, on to the rocky common ; but as he went along, with his uncertain gait, in the dusk gloaming, he stumbled, and fell over some sharp projecting stone. The acute pain which shot up his back forced a short cry from him ; and, when bird and beast are hushed into rest and the stillness of the night is over all, a high-pitched sound, like the voice of pain, is carried far in the quiet air. Ruth, speeding on in her despair, heard the sharp utterance, and stopped suddenly short. It did what no remonstrance could have done ; it called her out of herself. The tender nature was in her still, in that hour when all good angels seemed to have abandoned her. In the old days she could never bear to hear or see bodily suffering in any of God's meanest creatures, without trying to succour them ; and now, in her rush to the awful death of the suicide, she stayed her wild steps, and turned to find from whom that sharp sound of anguish had issued.

He lay among the white stones, too faint with pain to move, but with an agony in his mind far keener than any bodily pain, as he thought that by his unfortunate fall he had lost all chance of saving her. He was almost overpowered by his intense thankfulness when he saw her white figure pause, and stand listening, and turn again with slow footsteps, as if searching for some lost thing. He could hardly speak, but he made a sound which, though his heart was inexpressibly glad, was like a groan. She came quickly towards him.

"I am hurt," said he ; "do not leave me ;" his disabled and tender frame was overcome by the accident and the previous emotions, and he fainted away. Ruth flew to the little mountain stream, the dashing sound of whose waters had been tempting her, but a moment before, to seek forgetfulness in the deep pool into which they fell. She made a basin of her joined hands, and carried enough of the cold fresh water

back to dash into his face and restore him to consciousness. While he still kept silence, uncertain
what to say best fitted to induce her to listen to him,
she said softly :

"Are you better, sir?—are you very much hurt?"

"Not very much ; I am better. Any quick movement is apt to cause me a sudden loss of power in my
back, and I believe I stumbled over some of these projecting stones. It will soon go off, and you will help
me to go home, I am sure."

"Oh, yes ! Can you go now? I am afraid of your
lying too long on this heather ; there is a heavy
dew."

He was so anxious to comply with her wish, and not
weary out her thought for him, and so turn her back
upon herself, that he tried to rise. The pain was acute,
and this she saw.

"Don't hurry yourself, sir ; I can wait."

Then came across her mind the recollection of the
business that was thus deferred, but the few homely
words which had been exchanged between them seemed
to have awakened her from her madness. She sat
down by him, and, covering her face with her hands,
cried mournfully and unceasingly. She forgot his
presence, and yet she had a consciousness that some
one looked for her kind offices, that she was wanted in
the world, and must not rush hastily out of it. The
consciousness did not take this definite form, it did
not become a thought, but it kept her still, and it was
gradually soothing her.

"Can you help me to rise now?" said he, after a
while. She did not speak, but she helped him up,
and then he took her arm, and she led him tenderly
through all the little velvet paths, where the turf grew
short and soft between the rugged stones. Once more
on the highway, they slowly passed along in the moonlight. He guided her by a slight motion of the arm,
through the more unfrequented lanes, to his lodgings
at the shop ; for he thought for her, and conceived the
pain she would have in seeing the lighted windows of

the inn. He leant more heavily on her arm, as they awaited the opening of the door.

"Come in," said he, not relaxing his hold, and yet dreading to tighten it, lest she should defy restraint, and once more rush away.

They went slowly into the little parlour behind the shop. The bonny-looking hostess, Mrs Hughes by name, made haste to light the candle, and then they saw each other, face to face. The deformed gentleman looked very pale, but Ruth looked as if the shadow of death was upon her.

CHAPTER IX

Mrs Hughes bustled about with many a sympathetic exclamation, now in pretty broken English, now in more fluent Welsh, which sounded as soft as Russian or Italian, in her musical voice. Mr Benson, for that was the name of the hunchback, lay on the sofa, thinking; while the tender Mrs Hughes made every arrangement for his relief from pain. He had lodged with her for three successive years, and she knew and loved him.

Ruth stood in the little bow-window, looking out. Across the moon, and over the deep blue heavens, large, torn, irregular-shaped clouds went hurrying, as if summoned by some storm-spirit. The work they were commanded to do was not here; the mighty gathering-place lay eastward, immeasurable leagues, and on they went, chasing each other over the silent earth, now black, now silver-white at one transparent edge, now with the moon shining like Hope through their darkest centre, now again with a silver lining; and now, utterly black, they sailed lower in the lift, and disappeared behind the immovable mountains; they were rushing in the very direction in which Ruth had striven and struggled to go that afternoon; they, in their wild career, would soon pass over the very

spot where he (her world's he) was lying sleeping, or
perhaps not sleeping, perhaps thinking of her. The
storm was in her mind, and rent and tore her purposes
into forms as wild and irregular as the heavenly shapes
she was looking at. If, like them, she could pass the
barrier horizon in the night, she might overtake
him.

Mr Benson saw her look, and read it partially. He
saw her longing gaze outwards upon the free, broad
world, and thought that the syren waters, whose
deadly music yet rang in her ears, were again tempting her. He called her to him, praying that his feeble
voice might have power.

"My dear young lady, I have much to say to you;
and God has taken my strength from me now when I
most need it.—Oh, I sin to speak so—but, for His sake,
I implore you to be patient here, if only till to-morrow
morning." He looked at her, but her face was immovable, and she did not speak. She could not give
up her hope, her chance, her liberty till to-morrow.

"God help me," said he, mournfully, "my words
do not touch her"; and, still holding her hand, he
sank back on the pillows. Indeed, it was true that his
words did not vibrate in her atmosphere. The storm-
spirit raged there, and filled her heart with the thought
that she was an outcast; and the holy words, "for
His sake," were answered by the demon, who held
possession, with a blasphemous defiance of the merciful
God:

"What have I to do with Thee?"*

He thought of every softening influence of religion
which over his own disciplined heart had power, but
put them aside as useless. Then the still small voice
whispered, and he spake:

"In your mother's name, whether she be dead or
alive, I command you to stay here until I am able to
speak to you."

She knelt down at the foot of the sofa, and shook it
with her sobs. Her heart was touched, and he hardly
dared to speak again. At length he said:

"I know you will not go—you could not—for her sake. You will not, will you?"

"No," whispered Ruth; and then there was a great blank in her heart. She had given up her chance. She was calm, in the utter absence of all hope.

"And now you will do what I tell you," said he, gently, but, unconsciously to himself, in the tone of one who has found the hidden spell by which to rule spirits.

She slowly said, "Yes." But she was subdued.

He called Mrs Hughes. She came from her adjoining shop.

"You have a bedroom within yours, where your daughter used to sleep, I think? I am sure you will oblige me, and I shall consider it as a great favour, if you will allow this young lady to sleep there to-night. Will you take her there now? Go, my dear. I have full trust in your promise not to leave until I can speak to you." His voice died away to silence; but as Ruth rose from her knees at his bidding, she looked at his face through her tears. His lips were moving in earnest, unspoken prayer, and she knew it was for her.

That night, although his pain was relieved by rest, he could not sleep; and, as in fever, the coming events kept unrolling themselves before him in every changing and fantastic form. He met Ruth in all possible places and ways, and addressed her in every manner he could imagine most calculated to move and affect her to penitence and virtue. Towards morning he fell asleep, but the same thoughts haunted his dreams; he spoke, but his voice refused to utter aloud; and she fled, relentless, to the deep, black pool.

But God works in His own way.

The visions melted into deep, unconscious sleep. He was awakened by a knock at the door, which seemed a repetition of what he had heard in his last sleeping moments.

It was Mrs Hughes. She stood at the first word of permission within the room.

"Please, sir, I think the young lady is very ill indeed, sir; perhaps you would please to come to her."

"How is she ill?" said he, much alarmed.

"Quite quiet-like, sir; but I think she is dying, that's all, indeed, sir!"

"Go away, I will be with you directly!" he replied, his heart sinking within him.

In a very short time he was standing with Mrs Hughes by Ruth's bedside. She lay as still as if she were dead, her eyes shut, her wan face numbed into a fixed anguish of expression. She did not speak when they spoke, though after a while they thought she strove to do so. But all power of motion and utterance had left her. She was dressed in everything, except her bonnet, as she had been the day before; although sweet, thoughtful Mrs Hughes, had provided her with nightgear, which lay on the little chest of drawers that served as a dressing-table. Mr Benson lifted up her arm to feel her feeble, fluttering pulse; and when he let go her hand, it fell upon the bed in a dull heavy way, as if she were already dead.

"You gave her some food," said he, anxiously, to Mrs Hughes.

"Indeed, and I offered her the best in the house, but she shook her poor pretty head, and only asked if I would please to get her a cup of water. I brought her some milk though, and 'deed, I think she'd rather have had the water; but not to seem sour and cross, she took some milk." By this time Mrs Hughes was fairly crying.

"When does the doctor come up here?"

"Indeed, sir, and he's up nearly every day now, the inn is so full."

"I'll go for him. And can you manage to undress her and lay her in bed? Open the window too, and let in the air; if her feet are cold, put bottles of hot water to them."

It was a proof of the true love, which was the nature of both, that it never crossed their minds to regret that this poor young creature had been thus thrown upon their hands. On the contrary, Mrs Hughes called it a " a blessing."

" It blesseth him that gives, and him that takes."*

CHAPTER X

AT the inn everything was life and bustle. Mr Benson had to wait long in Mrs Morgan's little parlour before she could come to him, and he kept growing more and more impatient. At last she made her appearance and heard his story.

People may talk as they will about the little respect that is paid to virtue, unaccompanied by the outward accidents of wealth or station; but I rather think it will be found that, in the long run, true and simple virtue always has its proportionate reward in the respect and reverence of every one whose esteem is worth having. To be sure, it is not rewarded after the way of the world as mere worldly possessions are, with low obeisance and lip-service; but all the better and more noble qualities in the hearts of others make ready and go forth to meet it on its approach, provided only it be pure, simple, and unconscious of its own existence.

Mr Benson had little thought for outward tokens of respect just then, nor had Mrs Morgan much time to spare; but she smoothed her ruffled brow, and calmed her bustling manner, as soon as ever she saw who it was that awaited her; for Mr Benson was well known in the village where he had taken up his summer holiday among the mountains year after year, always a resident at the shop, and seldom spending a shilling at the inn.

Mrs Morgan listened patiently—for her.

" Mr Jones will come this afternoon. But it is a shame you should be troubled with such as her. I had but little time yesterday, but I guessed there was something wrong, and Gwen has just been telling me her bed has not been slept in. They were in a pretty hurry to be gone yesterday, for all that the gentleman was not fit to travel, to my way of thinking; indeed, William Wynn, the postboy, said he was weary enough before he got to the end of that Yspytty road; and he thought they would have to rest there a day or two before they could go further than Pen trê Voelas. Indeed, and anyhow, the servant is to follow them with the baggage this very morning; and now I remember, William Wynn said they would wait for her. You'd better write a note, Mr Benson, and tell them her state."

It was good, though unpalatable advice. It came from one accustomed to bring excellent, if unrefined sense, to bear quickly upon any emergency, and to decide rapidly. She was, in truth, so little accustomed to have her authority questioned, that before Mr Benson had made up his mind, she had produced paper, pens, and ink from the drawer in her bureau, placed them before him, and was going to leave the room.

"Leave the note on this shelf, and trust me that it goes by the maid. The boy that drives her there in the car shall bring you an answer back."

She was gone before he could rally his scattered senses enough to remember that he had not the least idea of the name of the party to whom he was to write. The quiet leisure and peace of his little study at home favoured his habit of reverie and long deliberation, just as her position as mistress of an inn obliged her to quick, decisive ways.

Her advice, though good in some points, was un-palatable in others. It was true that Ruth's condition ought to be known by those who were her friends; but were these people to whom he was now going to write, friends? He knew there was a rich mother, and a handsome, elegant son; and he had also some idea of the circumstances which might a little extenuate their mode of quitting Ruth. He had wide enough sym-pathy to understand that it must have been a most painful position in which the mother had been placed, on finding herself under the same roof with a girl, who was living with her son as Ruth was. And yet he did not like to apply to her; to write to the son was still more out of the question, as it seemed like asking him to return. But through one or the other lay the only clue to her friends, who certainly ought to be made acquainted with her position. At length he wrote:

"Madam,—I write to tell you of the condition of the poor young woman"—(here came a long pause of deliberation)—"who accompanied your son on his arrival here, and who was left behind on your departure yesterday. She is lying (as it appears to me) in a very dangerous state at my lodgings; and, if I may suggest, it would be kind to allow your maid to return and attend upon her until she is sufficiently recovered to be restored to her friends, if, indeed, they could not come to take charge of her themselves.

"I remain, madam,
"Your obedient servant,
"Thurstan Benson."

The note was very unsatisfactory after all his consideration, but it was the best he could do. He made inquiry of a passing servant as to the lady's name, directed the note, and placed it on the indicated shelf. He then returned to his lodgings, to await the doctor's coming, and the postboy's return. There was no alteration in Ruth; she was as one stunned into unconsciousness; she did not move her posture, she hardly breathed. From time to time Mrs Hughes wetted her mouth with some liquid, and there was a little mechanical motion of the lips; that was the only sign of life she gave. The doctor came and shook his head,—"a thorough prostration of strength, occasioned by some great shock on the nerves,"—and prescribed care and quiet, and mysterious medicines, but acknowledged that the result was doubtful, very doubtful. After his departure, Mr Benson took his Welsh grammar and tried again to master the ever-puzzling rules for the mutations of letters; but it was of no use, for his thoughts were absorbed by the life-in-death condition of the young creature, who was lately bounding and joyous.

The maid and the luggage, the car and the driver, had arrived before noon at their journey's end, and the note had been delivered. It annoyed Mrs Bellingham exceedingly. It was the worst of these kind of connexions, there was no calculating the consequences; they were never ending. All sorts of claims seemed to be established, and all sorts of people to step in to their settlement. The idea of sending her maid! Why, Simpson would not go if she asked her. She soliloquized thus while reading the letter; and then, suddenly turning round to the favourite attendant, who had been listening to her mistress's remarks with no inattentive ear, she asked:

"Simpson, would you go and nurse this creature, as this——" she looked at the signature,—"Mr Benson, whoever he is, proposes?"

"Me! no, indeed, ma'am," said the maid, drawing herself up, stiff in her virtue. "I'm sure, ma'am, you would not expect it of me; I could never have the face to dress a lady of character again."

"Well, well! don't be alarmed; I cannot spare you; by the way, just attend to the strings on my dress, the chambermaid here pulled them into knots, and broke them terribly, last night. It is awkward though, very," said she, relapsing into a musing fit over the condition of Ruth.

"If you'll allow me, ma'am, I think I might say something that would alter the case. I believe, ma'am, you put a bank-note into the letter to the young woman yesterday?"

Mrs Bellingham bowed acquiescence, and the maid went on:

"Because, ma'am, when the little deformed man wrote that note (he's Mr Benson, ma'am), I have reason to believe neither he nor Mrs Morgan knew of any provision being made for the young woman. Me and the chambermaid found your letter and the bank-note lying quite promiscuous, like waste paper, on the floor of her room ; for I believe she rushed out like mad after you left."

"That, as you say, alters the case. This letter, then, is principally a sort of delicate hint that some provision ought to have been made, which is true enough, only it has been attended to already ; what became of the money ? "

"Law, ma'am ! do you ask ? Of course, as soon as I saw it, I picked it up and took it to Mrs Morgan, in trust for the young person."

"Oh, that's right. What friends has she ? Did you ever hear from Mason ?—perhaps they ought to know where she is."

"Mrs Mason did tell me, ma'am, she was an orphan ; with a guardian who was no-ways akin, and who washed his hands of her when she ran off ; but Mrs Mason was sadly put out, and went into hysterics, for fear you would think she had not seen after her enough, and that she might lose your custom ; she said it was no fault of hers, for the girl was always a forward creature, boasting of her beauty, and saying how pretty she was, and striving to get where her good looks could be seen and admired,—one night in particular, ma'am, at a county ball ; and how Mrs Mason had found out she used to meet Mr Bellingham at an old woman's house, who was a regular old witch, ma'am, and lives in the lowest part of the town, where all the bad characters haunt."

"There ! that's enough," said Mrs Bellingham, sharply, for the maid's chattering had outrun her tact ; and in her anxiety to vindicate the character of her friend Mrs Mason by blackening that of Ruth, she had forgotten that she a little implicated her mistress's son, whom his proud mother did not like to imagine as ever passing through a low and degraded part of the town.

"If she has no friends, and is the creature you describe (which is confirmed by my own observation),

the best place for her is, as I said before, the Penitentiary. Her fifty pounds will keep her for a week or so,
if she is really unable to travel, and pay for her journey ;
and if on her return to Fordham she will let me know,
I will undertake to obtain her admission immediately."

" I'm sure it's well for her she has to do with a lady
who will take any interest in her, after what has
happened."

Mrs Bellingham called for her writing-desk, and
wrote a few hasty lines to be sent back by the postboy,
who was on the point of starting :

" Mrs Bellingham presents her compliments to her
unknown correspondent, Mr Benson, and begs to
inform him of a circumstance of which she believes he
was ignorant when he wrote the letter with which she
has been favoured ; namely, that provision to the
amount of £50 was left for the unfortunate young
person who is the subject of Mr Benson's letter. This
sum is in the hands of Mrs Morgan, as well as a note
from Mrs Bellingham to the miserable girl, in which
she proposes to procure her admission into the Fordham Penitentiary,*the best place for such a character,
as by this profligate action she has forfeited the only
friend remaining to her in the world. This proposition,
Mrs Bellingham repeats ; and they are the young
woman's best friends who most urge her to comply
with the course now pointed out."

" Take care Mr Bellingham hears nothing of this
Mr Benson's note," said Mrs Bellingham, as she
delivered the answer to her maid ; " he is so sensitive
just now that it would annoy him sadly, I am sure."

CHAPTER XI

You have now seen the note which was delivered into
Mr Benson's hands, as the cool shades of evening stole
over the glowing summer sky. When he had read it,
he again prepared to write a few hasty lines before the

post went out. The postboy was even now sounding his horn through the village as a signal for letters to be ready; and it was well that Mr Benson, in his long morning's meditation, had decided upon the course to be pursued, in case of such an answer as that which he had received from Mrs Bellingham. His present note was as follows:

"DEAR FAITH,—You must come to this place directly, where I earnestly desire you and your advice. I am well myself, so do not be alarmed. I have no time for explanation, but I am sure you will not refuse me; let me trust that I shall see you on Saturday at the latest. You know the mode by which I came; it is the best for expedition and cheapness. Dear Faith, do not fail me.

                    "Your affectionate brother,
                              "THURSTAN BENSON.

"P.S.—I am afraid the money I left may be running short. Do not let this stop you. Take my Facciolati* to Johnson's, he will advance upon it; it is the third row, bottom shelf. Only come."

When this letter was despatched he had done all he could; and the next two days passed like a long monotonous dream of watching, thought, and care, undisturbed by any event, hardly by the change from day to night, which, now the harvest moon was at her full, was scarcely perceptible. On Saturday morning the answer came.

"DEAREST THURSTAN, — Your incomprehensible summons has just reached me, and I obey, thereby proving my right to my name of Faith. I shall be with you almost as soon as this letter. I cannot help feeling anxious, as well as curious. I have money enough, and it is well I have; for Sally, who guards your room like a dragon, would rather see me walk the whole way, than have any of your things disturbed.

                    "Your affectionate sister,
                              "FAITH BENSON."

It was a great relief to Mr Benson to think that his
sister would so soon be with him. He had been accustomed from childhood to rely on her prompt judgement
and excellent sense ; and to her care he felt that Ruth
ought to be consigned, as it was too much to go on
taxing good Mrs Hughes with night watching and sick
nursing, with all her other claims on her time. He
asked her once more to sit by Ruth, while he went to
meet his sister.

The coach passed by the foot of the steep ascent
which led up to Llan-dhu.* He took a boy to carry
his sister's luggage when she arrived ; they were
too soon at the bottom of the hill, and the boy began
to make ducks and drakes in the shallowest part of
the stream, which there flowed glassy and smooth,
while Mr Benson sat down on a great stone, under
the shadow of an alder bush which grew where the
green, flat meadow skirted the water. It was delightful to be once more in the open air, and away from
the scenes and thoughts which had been pressing on
him for the last three days. There was new beauty
in everything : from the blue mountains which glimmered in the distant sunlight, down to the flat, rich,
peaceful vale, with its calm round shadows, where he
sat. The very margin of white pebbles which lay on
the banks of the stream had a sort of cleanly beauty
about it. He felt calmer and more at ease than he
had done for some days ; and yet, when he began
to think, it was rather a strange story which he had
to tell his sister, in order to account for his urgent
summons. Here was he, sole friend and guardian
of a poor sick girl, whose very name he did not
know ; about whom all that he did know was, that
she had been the mistress of a man who had deserted
her, and that he feared—he believed—she had con-
templated suicide. The offence, too, was one for
which his sister, good kind as she was, had little
compassion. Well, he must appeal to her love for
him, which was a very unsatisfactory mode of proceeding, as he would far rather have had her interest

in the girl founded on reason, or some less personal
basis than showing it merely because her brother
wished it.

The coach came slowly rumbling over the stony
road.   His sister was outside, but got down in a
brisk active way, and greeted her brother heartily
and affectionately.   She was considerably taller than
he was, and must have been very handsome; her
black hair was parted plainly over her forehead, and
her dark, expressive eyes and straight nose still retained the beauty of her youth.   I do not know
whether she was older than her brother, but, probably owing to his infirmity requiring her care, she
had something of a mother's manner towards him.

"Thurstan, you are looking pale !   I do not believe you are well, whatever you may say.   Have you
had the old pain in your back?"

"No—a little—never mind that, dearest Faith.
Sit down here, while I send the boy up with your
box."   And then, with some little desire to show his
sister how well he was acquainted with the language,
he blundered out his directions in very grammatical
Welsh; so grammatical, in fact, and so badly pro-
nounced, that the boy, scratching his head, made
answer,

"Dim Saesoneg."*

So he had to repeat it in English.

"Well now, Thurstan, here I sit as you bid me.
But don't try me too long; tell me why you sent
for me."

Now came the difficulty, and oh! for a seraph's
tongue, and a seraph's powers of representation! but
there was no seraph at hand, only the soft running
waters singing a quiet tune, and predisposing Miss
Benson to listen with a soothed spirit to any tale,
not immediately involving her brother's welfare, which
had been the cause of her seeing that lovely vale.

"It is an awkward story to tell, Faith, but there
is a young woman lying ill at my lodgings whom
I wanted you to nurse."

He thought he saw a shadow on his sister's face, and detected a slight change in her voice as she spoke.

"Nothing very romantic, I hope, Thurstan. Remember, I cannot stand much romance; I always distrust it."

"I don't know what you mean by romance. The story is real enough, and not out of the common way, I'm afraid."

He paused; he did not get over the difficulty.

"Well, tell it me at once, Thurstan. I am afraid you have let some one, or perhaps only your own imagination, impose upon you; but don't try my patience too much; you know I've no great stock."

"Then I'll tell you. The young girl was brought to the inn here by a gentleman, who has left her; she is very ill, and has no one to see after her."

Miss Benson had some masculine tricks, and one was whistling a long low whistle, when surprised or displeased. She had often found it a useful vent for feelings, and she whistled now. Her brother would rather she had spoken.

"Have you sent for her friends?" she asked at last.

"She has none."

Another pause and another whistle, but rather softer and more wavering than the last.

"How is she ill?"

"Pretty nearly as quiet as if she were dead. She does not speak, or move, or even sigh."

"It would be better for her to die at once, I think."

"Faith!"

That one word put them right. It was spoken in the tone which had authority over her; it was so full of grieved surprise and mournful upbraiding. She was accustomed to exercise a sway over him, owing to her greater decision of character; and, probably, if everything were traced to its cause, to her superior vigour of constitution; but at times she was humbled before his pure, childlike nature, and felt where she was inferior. She was too good and true to conceal this feeling, or to resent its being forced upon her. After a time she said,

"Thurstan, dear, let us go to her."

She helped him with tender care, and gave him her arm up the long and tedious hill; but when they approached the village, without speaking a word on the subject, they changed their position, and she leant (apparently) on him. He stretched himself up into as vigorous a gait as he could, when they drew near to the abodes of men.

On the way they had spoken but little. He had asked after various members of his congregation, for he was a Dissenting minister in a country-town, and she had answered; but they neither of them spoke of Ruth, though their minds were full of her.

Mrs Hughes had tea ready for the traveller on her arrival. Mr Benson chafed a little internally, at the leisurely way in which his sister sipped and sipped, and paused to tell him some trifling particular respecting home affairs, which she had forgotten before.

"Mr Bradshaw has refused to let the children associate with the Dixons any longer, because one evening they played at acting charades."

"Indeed;—a little more bread and butter, Faith?"

"Thank you. This Welsh air does make one hungry. Mrs Bradshaw is paying poor old Maggie's rent, to save her from being sent into the workhouse."

"That's right. Won't you have another cup of tea?"

"I have had two. However, I think I'll take another."

Mr Benson could not refrain from a little sigh as he poured it out. He thought he had never seen his sister so deliberately hungry and thirsty before. He did not guess that she was feeling the meal rather a respite from a distasteful interview, which she was aware was awaiting her at its conclusion. But all things come to an end, and so did Miss Benson's tea.

"Now, will you go and see her?"

"Yes."

And so they went. Mrs Hughes had pinned up a piece of green calico, by way of a Venetian blind, to shut out the afternoon sun; and in the light thus shaded lay Ruth, still, and wan, and white. Even with her brother's account of Ruth's state, such death-like quietness startled Miss Benson—startled her into pity for the poor lovely creature who lay thus stricken and felled. When she saw her, she could no longer imagine her to be an impostor, or a hardened sinner; such prostration of woe belonged to neither. Mr Benson looked more at his sister's face than at Ruth's; he read her countenance as a book.

Mrs Hughes stood by, crying.

Mr Benson touched his sister, and they left the room together.

"Do you think she will live?" asked he.

"I cannot tell," said Miss Benson, in a softened voice. "But how young she looks! Quite a child, poor creature! When will the doctor come, Thurstan? Tell me all about her; you have never told me the particulars."

Mr Benson might have said, she had never cared to hear them before, and had rather avoided the subject; but he was too happy to see this awakening of interest in his sister's warm heart to say anything in the least reproachful. He told her the story as well as he could; and, as he felt it deeply, he told it with heart's eloquence; and, as he ended and looked at her, there were tears in the eyes of both.

"And what does the doctor say?" asked she, after a pause.

"He insists upon quiet; he orders medicines and strong broth. I cannot tell you all; Mrs Hughes can. She has been so truly good. 'Doing good, hoping for nothing again.'"

"She looks very sweet and gentle. I shall sit up to-night and watch her myself; and I shall send you and Mrs Hughes early to bed, for you have both a worn look about you I don't like. Are you sure the effect of that fall has gone off? Do you feel anything of it in your back still? After all, I owe her something for turning back to your help. Are you sure she was going to drown herself?"

"I cannot be sure, for I have not questioned her. She has not been in a state to be questioned; but I have no doubt whatever about it. But you must not think of sitting up after your journey, Faith."

"Answer me, Thurstan. Do you feel any bad effect from that fall?"

"No, hardly any. Don't sit up, Faith, to-night!"

"Thurstan, it's no use talking, for I shall; and, if you go on opposing me, I dare say I shall attack your back, and put a blister on it. Do tell me what that 'hardly any' means. Besides, to set you quite at ease, you know I have never seen mountains before, and they fill me and oppress me so much that I could not sleep; I must keep awake this first night, and see that they don't fall on the earth and overwhelm it. And now answer my questions about yourself."

Miss Benson had the power, which some people have, of carrying her wishes through to their fulfilment; her will was strong, her sense was excellent, and people yielded to her—they did not know why. Before ten o'clock she reigned sole power and potentate in Ruth's little chamber. Nothing could have been better devised for giving her an interest in the invalid. The very dependence of one so helpless upon her care inclined her heart towards her. She thought she perceived a slight improvement in the symptoms during the night, and she was a little pleased that this progress should have been made while she reigned monarch of the sick-room. Yes, certainly there was an improvement. There was more consciousness in the look of the eyes, although the whole countenance still retained its painful traces of acute suffering, manifested in an anxious, startled, uneasy aspect. It was broad morning light, though barely five o'clock, when Miss Benson caught the sight of Ruth's lips

moving, as if in speech. Miss Benson stooped down to
listen.

"Who are you?" asked Ruth, in the faintest of
whispers.

"Miss Benson—Mr Benson's sister," she replied.

The words conveyed no knowledge to Ruth; on the
contrary, weak as a babe in mind and body as she was,
her lip began to quiver, and her eyes to show a terror
similar to that of any little child who wakens in the
presence of a stranger, and sees no dear, familiar face
of mother or nurse to reassure its trembling heart.

Miss Benson took her hand in hers, and began to
stroke it caressingly.

"Don't be afraid, dear; I'm a friend come to take
care of you. Would you like some tea now, my
love?"

The very utterance of these gentle words was un-
locking Miss Benson's heart. Her brother was surprised to see her so full of interest, when he came to
inquire later on in the morning. It required Mrs
Hughes's persuasions, as well as his own, to induce her
to go to bed for an hour or two after breakfast; and,
before she went, she made them promise that she
should be called when the doctor came. He did not
come until late in the afternoon. The invalid was
rallying fast, though rallying to a consciousness of
sorrow, as was evinced by the tears which came slowly
rolling down her pale sad cheeks—tears which she had
not the power to wipe away.

Mr Benson had remained in the house all day to
hear the doctor's opinion; and now that he was
relieved from the charge of Ruth by his sister's
presence, he had the more time to dwell upon the
circumstances of her case—so far as they were known
to him. He remembered his first sight of her; her
little figure swaying to and fro as she balanced herself
on the slippery stones, half smiling at her own
dilemma, with a bright, happy light in the eyes that
seemed like a reflection from the glancing waters
sparkling below. Then he recalled the changed,

affrighted look of those eyes as they met his, after the
child's rebuff of her advances ;—how that little
incident filled up the tale at which Mrs Hughes had
hinted, in a kind of sorrowful way, as if loath (as a
Christian should be) to believe evil.   Then that fearful
evening, when he had only just saved her from
committing suicide, and that night-mare sleep !   And
now, lost, forsaken, and but just delivered from the
jaws of death, she lay dependent for everything on his
sister and him,—utter strangers a few weeks ago.
Where was her lover?   Could he be easy and happy?
Could he grow into perfect health, with these great
sins pressing on his conscience with a strong and hard
pain ?   Or had he a conscience?

Into whole labyrinths of social ethics Mr Benson's
thoughts wandered, when his sister entered suddenly
and abruptly.

"What does the doctor say?   Is she better?"

"Oh, yes ! she's better," answered Miss Benson,
sharp and short.   Her brother looked at her in dismay.
She bumped down into a chair in a cross, disconcerted
manner.   They were both silent for a few minutes ;
only Miss Benson whistled and clucked alternately.

"What is the matter, Faith?   You say she is
better."

"Why, Thurstan, there is something so shocking
the matter, that I cannot tell you."

Mr Benson changed colour with affright.   All things
possible and impossible crossed his mind, but the right
one.   I said "all things possible ;" I made a mistake.
He never believed Ruth to be more guilty than she
seemed.

"Faith, I wish you would tell me, and not bewilder
me with those noises of yours," said he, nervously.

"I beg your pardon ; but something so shocking
has just been discovered—I don't know how to word it
—She will have a child.   The doctor says so."

She was allowed to make noises unnoticed for a few
minutes.   Her brother did not speak.   At last she
wanted his sympathy.

"Isn't it shocking, Thurstan? You might have knocked me down with a straw when he told me."

"Does she know?"

"Yes; and I am not sure that that isn't the worst part of all."

"How?—what do you mean?"

"Oh! I was just beginning to have a good opinion of her, but I'm afraid she is very depraved. After the doctor was gone, she pulled the bed-curtain aside, and looked as if she wanted to speak to me. (I can't think how she heard, for we were close to the window, and spoke very low.) Well, I went to her, though I really had taken quite a turn against her. And she whispered, quite eagerly, 'Did he say I should have a baby?' Of course, I could not keep it from her; but I thought it my duty to look as cold and severe as I could. She did not seem to understand how it ought to be viewed, but took it just as if she had a right to have a baby. She said, 'Oh, my God, I thank Thee! Oh! I will be so good!' I had no patience with her then, so I left the room."

"Who is with her?"

"Mrs Hughes. She is not seeing the thing in a moral light, as I should have expected."

Mr Benson was silent again. After some time he began:

"Faith, I don't see this affair quite as you do. I believe I am right."

"You surprise me, brother! I don't understand you."

"Wait awhile! I want to make my feelings very clear to you, but I don't know where to begin, or how to express myself."

"It is, indeed, an extraordinary subject for us to have to talk about; but if once I get clear of this girl, I'll wash my hands of all such cases again."

Her brother was not attending to her; he was reducing his own ideas to form.

"Faith, do you know I rejoice in this child's advent."

'May God forgive you, Thurstan!—if you know

what you are saying. But, surely, it is a temptation, dear Thurstan."

"I do not think it is a delusion. The sin appears to me to be quite distinct from its consequences."

"Sophistry—and a temptation," said Miss Benson, decidedly.

"No, it is not," said her brother, with equal decision. "In the eye of God, she is exactly the same as if the life she has led had left no trace behind. We knew her errors before, Faith."

"Yes, but not this disgrace—this badge of her shame!"

"Faith, Faith! let me beg of you not to speak so of the little innocent babe, who may be God's messenger to lead her back to Him. Think again of her first words—the burst of nature from her heart! Did she not turn to God, and enter into a covenant with Him— 'I will be so good?' Why, it draws her out of herself! If her life has hitherto been self-seeking, and wickedly thoughtless, here is the very instrument to make her forget herself, and be thoughtful for another. Teach her (and God will teach her, if man does not come between) to reverence her child; and this reverence will shut out sin,—will be purification."

He was very much excited; he was even surprised at his own excitement; but his thoughts and meditations through the long afternoon had prepared his mind for this manner of viewing the subject.

"These are quite new ideas to me," said Miss Benson, coldly. "I think, you, Thurstan, are the first person I ever heard rejoicing over the birth of an illegitimate child. It appears to me, I must own, rather questionable morality."

"I do not rejoice. I have been all this afternoon mourning over the sin which has blighted this young creature; I have been dreading lest, as she recovered consciousness, there should be a return of her despair. I have been thinking of every holy word, every promise to the penitent—of the tenderness which led the Magdalen aright.* I have been feeling, severely and reproachfully, the timidity which has hitherto made me blink all encounter with evils of this particular kind. Oh, Faith! once for all, do not accuse me of questionable morality, when I am trying more than ever I did in my life to act as my blessed Lord would have done."

He was very much agitated. His sister hesitated, and then she spoke more softly than before.

"But, Thurstan, everything might have been done to 'lead her right' (as you call it), without this child, this miserable offspring of sin."

"The world has, indeed, made such children miserable, innocent as they are; but I doubt if this be according to the will of God, unless it be His punishment for the parents' guilt; and even then the world's way of treatment is too apt to harden the mother's natural love into something like hatred. Shame, and the terror of friends' displeasure, turn her mad—defile her holiest instincts; and, as for the fathers—God forgive them! I cannot—at least, not just now."

Miss Benson thought on what her brother said. At length she asked, "Thurstan (remember I'm not convinced), how would you have this girl treated according to your theory?"

"It will require some time, and much Christian love, to find out the best way. I know I'm not very wise; but the way I think it would be right to act in, would be this——" He thought for some time before he spoke, and then said:

"She has incurred a responsibility—that we both acknowledge. She is about to become a mother, and have the direction and guidance of a little tender life. I fancy such a responsibility must be serious and solemn enough, without making it into a heavy and oppressive burden, so that human nature recoils from bearing it. While we do all we can to strengthen her sense of responsibility, I would likewise do all we can to make her feel that it is responsibility for what may become a blessing."

"Whether the children are legitimate or illegitimate?" asked Miss Benson, drily.

"Yes!" said her brother, firmly. "The more I think, the more I believe I am right. No one," said he, blushing faintly as he spoke, "can have a greater recoil from profligacy than I have. You yourself have not greater sorrow over this young creature's sin than I have: the difference is this, you confuse the consequences with the sin."

"I don't understand metaphysics."

"I am not aware that I am talking metaphysics. I can imagine that if the present occasion be taken rightly, and used well, all that is good in her may be raised to a height unmeasured but by God; while all that is evil and dark may, by His blessing, fade and disappear in the pure light of her child's presence. Oh, Father! listen to my prayer, that her redemption may date from this time. Help us to speak to her in the loving spirit of thy Holy Son!"

The tears were full in his eyes; he almost trembled in his earnestness. He was faint with the strong power of his own conviction, and with his inability to move his sister. But she was shaken. She sat very still for a quarter of an hour or more, while he leaned back, exhausted by his own feelings.

"The poor child!" said she, at length—"the poor, poor child! what it will have to struggle through and endure! Do you remember Thomas Wilkins, and the way he threw the registry of his birth and baptism* back in your face? Why, he would not have the situation; he went to sea and was drowned, rather than present the record of his shame."

"I do remember it all. It has often haunted me. She must strengthen her child to look to God, rather than to man's opinion. It will be the discipline, the penance, she has incurred. She must teach it to be (humanly speaking) self-dependent."

"But after all," said Miss Benson (for she had known and esteemed poor Thomas Wilkins, and had mourned over his untimely death, and the recollection thereof softened her)—"after all, it might be concealed. The very child need never know its illegitimacy."

"How?" asked her brother.

"Why—we know so little about her yet; but in that letter, it said she had no friends;—now, could she not go into quite a fresh place, and be passed off as a widow?"

Ah, tempter! unconscious tempter! Here was a way of evading the trials for the poor little unborn child, of which Mr Benson had never thought. It was the decision—the pivot, on which the fate of years moved; and he turned it the wrong way. But it was not for his own sake. For himself, he was brave enough to tell the truth; for the little helpless baby, about to enter a cruel, biting world, he was tempted to evade the difficulty. He forgot what he had just said, of the discipline and penance to the mother consisting in strengthening her child to meet, trustfully and bravely, the consequences of her own weakness. He remembered more clearly the wild fierceness, the Cain-like look, of Thomas Wilkins, as the obnoxious word in the baptismal registry told him that he must go forth branded into the world, with his hand against every man's, and every man's against him.

"How could it be managed, Faith?"

"Nay, I must know much more, which she alone can tell us, before I can see how it is to be managed. It is certainly the best plan."

"Perhaps it is," said her brother, thoughtfully, but no longer clearly or decidedly; and so the conversation dropped.

Ruth moved the bed-curtain aside, in her soft manner, when Miss Benson re-entered the room; she did not speak, but she looked at her as if she wished her to come near. Miss Benson went and stood by her. Ruth took her hand in hers and kissed it; then, as if fatigued even by this slight movement, she feel asleep.

Miss Benson took up her work, and thought over her brother's speeches. She was not convinced, but she was softened and bewildered.

CHAPTER XII

Miss Benson continued in an undecided state of mind for the two next days; but on the third, as they sat at breakfast, she began to speak to her brother.

"That young creature's name is Ruth Hilton."

"Indeed! how did you find it out?"

"From herself, of course. She is much stronger. I slept with her last night, and I was aware she was awake long before I liked to speak, but at last I began. I don't know what I said, or how it went on, but I think it was a little relief to her to tell me something about herself. She sobbed and cried herself to sleep; I think she is asleep now."

"Tell me what she said about herself."

"Oh, it was really very little; it was evidently a most painful subject. She is an orphan, without brother or sister, and with a guardian, whom, I think she said, she never saw but once. He apprenticed her (after her father's death) to a dressmaker. This Mr Bellingham got acquainted with her, and they used to meet on Sunday afternoons. One day they were late, lingering on the road, when the dressmaker came up by accident. She seems to have been very angry, and not unnaturally so. The girl took fright at her threats, and the lover persuaded her to go off with him to London, there and then. Last May, I think it was. That's all."

"Did she express any sorrow for her error?"

"No, not in words, but her voice was broken with sobs, though she tried to make it steady. After a while she began to talk about her baby, but shyly, and with much hesitation. She asked me, how much I thought she could earn as a dressmaker, by working very, very hard; and that brought us round to her child. I thought of what you had said, Thurstan, and I tried to speak to her as you wished me. I am not sure if it was right; I am doubtful in my own mind still."

"Don't be doubtful, Faith! Dear Faith, I thank you for your kindness."

"There is really nothing to thank me for. It is almost impossible to help being kind to her; there is something so meek and gentle about her, so patient, and so grateful!"

"What does she think of doing?"

"Poor child! she thinks of taking lodgings—very cheap ones, she says; there she means to work night and day to earn enough for her child. For, she said to me, with such pretty earnestness, 'it must never know want, whatever I do. I have deserved suffering, but it will be such a little innocent darling!' Her utmost earnings would not be more than seven or eight shillings a week, I'm afraid; and then she is so young and so pretty!"

"There is that fifty pounds Mrs Morgan brought me, and those two letters. Does she know about them yet?"

"No; I did not like to tell her till she is a little stronger. Oh, Thurstan! I wish there was not this prospect of a child. I cannot help it. I do—I could see a way in which we might help her, if it were not for that."

"How do you mean?"

"Oh, it's no use thinking of it, as it is! Or else we might have taken her home with us, and kept her till she had got a little dress-making in the congregation, but for this meddlesome child; that spoils everything. You must let me grumble to you, Thurstan. I was very good to her, and spoke as tenderly and respectfully of the little thing as if it were the Queen's, and born in lawful matrimony."

"That's right, my dear Faith! Grumble away to me, if you like. I'll forgive you, for the kind thought of taking her home with us. But do you think her situation is an insuperable objection?"

"Why, Thurstan!—it's so insuperable, it puts it quite out of the question."

"How?—that's only repeating your objection. Why is it out of the question?"

"If there had been no child coming, we might have
called her by her right name—Miss Hilton ; that's one
thing. Then, another is, the baby in our house. Why,
Sally would go distraught !"

"Never mind Sally. If she were an orphan relation of our own, left widowed," said he, pausing, as if
in doubt. "You yourself suggested she should be
considered as a widow, for the child's sake. I'm only
taking up your ideas, dear Faith. I respect you for
thinking of taking her home ; it is just what we ought
to do. Thank you for reminding me of my duty."

"Nay, it was only a passing thought. Think of Mr
Bradshaw. Oh ! I tremble at the thought of his grim
displeasure."

"We must think of a higher than Mr Bradshaw. I
own I should be a very coward, if he knew. He is so
severe, so inflexible. But after all he sees so little of
us ; he never comes to tea, you know, but is always
engaged when Mrs Bradshaw comes. I don't think
he knows of what our household consists."

"Not know Sally? Oh yes, but he does. He
asked Mrs Bradshaw one day, if she knew what wages
we gave her, and said we might get a far more efficient
and younger servant for the money. And, speaking
about money, think what our expenses would be if we
took her home for the next six months."

That consideration was a puzzling one ; and both sat
silent and perplexed for a time. Miss Benson was as
sorrowful as her brother, for she was becoming as
anxious as he was to find it possible that her plan could
be carried out.

"There's the fifty pounds," said he, with a sigh of
reluctance at the idea.

"Yes, there's the fifty pounds," echoed his sister,
with the same sadness in her tone. "I suppose it is
hers."

"I suppose it is ; and being so, we must not think
who gave it to her. It will defray her expenses. I
am very sorry, but I think we must take it."

"It would never do to apply to him under the

present circumstances," said Miss Benson in a hesitating manner.

"No, that we won't," said her brother, decisively. "If she consents to let us take care of her, we will never let her stoop to request anything from him, even for his child. She can live on bread and water. We can all live on bread and water rather than that."

"Then I will speak to her and propose the plan. Oh, Thurstan! from a child you could persuade me to anything! I hope I am doing right. However much I oppose you at first, I am sure to yield; soon almost in proportion to my violence at first. I think I am very weak."

"No, not in this instance. We are both right; I, in the way in which the child ought to be viewed; you, dear good Faith, for thinking of taking her home with us. God bless you, dear, for it!"

When Ruth began to sit up (and the strange, new, delicious prospect of becoming a mother seemed to give her some mysterious source of strength, so that her recovery was rapid and swift from that time), Miss Benson brought her the letters and the bank-note.

"Do you recollect receiving this letter, Ruth?" asked she, with grave gentleness. Ruth changed colour, and took it and read it again without making any reply to Miss Benson. Then she sighed, and thought a while; and then took up and read the second note—the note which Mrs Bellingham had sent to Mr Benson in answer to his. After that she took up the bank-note and turned it round and round, but not as if she saw it. Miss Benson noticed that her fingers trembled sadly, and that her lips were quivering for some time before she spoke.

"If you please, Miss Benson, I should like to return this money."

"Why, my dear?"

"I have a strong feeling against taking it. While he," said she, deeply blushing, and letting her large white lids drop down and veil her eyes, "loved me, he gave me many things—my watch—oh, many things; and I took them from him gladly and thankfully because he loved me—for I would have given him anything—and I thought of them as signs of love. But this money pains my heart. He has left off loving me, and has gone away. This money seems —oh, Miss Benson—it seems as if he could comfort me, for being forsaken, by money." And at that word, the tears so long kept back and repressed, forced their way like rain.

She checked herself, however, in the violence of her emotion, for she thought of her child.

"So, will you take the trouble of sending it back to Mrs Bellingham?"

"That I will, my dear. I am glad of it, that I am! They don't deserve to have the power of giving: they don't deserve that you should take it."

Miss Benson went and enclosed it up, there, and then; simply writing these words in the envelope, "From Ruth Hilton."

"And now we wash our hands of these Bellinghams," said she, triumphantly. But Ruth looked tearful and sad; not about returning the note, but from the conviction that the reason she had given for the ground of her determination was true—he no longer loved her.

To cheer her, Miss Benson began to speak of the future. Miss Benson was one of those people who, the more she spoke of a plan in its details, and the more she realised it in her own mind, the more firmly she became a partisan of the project. Thus she grew warm and happy in the idea of taking Ruth home; but Ruth remained depressed and languid under the conviction that he no longer loved her. No home, no future, but the thought of her child, could wean her from this sorrow. Miss Benson was a little piqued; and this pique showed itself afterwards in talking to her brother of the morning's proceedings in the sick-chamber.

" I admired her at the time for sending away her
fifty pounds so proudly; but I think she has a cold
heart: she hardly thanked me at all for my proposal
of taking her home with us."

" Her thoughts are full of other things just now;
and people have such different ways of showing
feeling: some by silence, some by words. At any
rate, it is unwise to expect gratitude."

"What do you expect—not indifference or ingratitude ? "

" It is better not to expect or calculate consequences.
The longer I live, the more fully I see that. Let us
try simply to do right actions, without thinking of
the feelings they are to call out in others. We know
that no holy or self-denying effort can fall to the
ground vain and useless; but the sweep of eternity
is large, and God alone knows when the effect is to
be produced. We are trying to do right now, and to
feel right; don't let us perplex ourselves with en-
deavouring to map out how she should feel, or how she
should show her feelings."

" That's all very fine, and I dare say very true,"
said Miss Benson, a little chagrined. " But ' a bird
in the hand is worth two in the bush' ; and I would
rather have had one good, hearty ' Thank you,' now,
for all I have been planning to do for her, than the
grand effects you promise me in the ' sweep of eternity.'
Don't be grave and sorrowful, Thurstan, or I'll go out
of the room. I can stand Sally's scoldings, but I
can't bear your look of quiet depression whenever I
am a little hasty or impatient. I had rather you
would give me a good box on the ear."

" And I would often rather you would speak, if
ever so hastily, instead of whistling. So, if I box
your ears when I am vexed with you, will you promise to scold me when you are put out of the way,
instead of whistling ? "

" Very well ! that's a bargain. You box, and I
scold. But, seriously, I began to calculate our
money when she so cavalierly £ent off the fifty-pound

note (I can't help admiring her for it), and I am very much afraid we shall not have enough to pay the doctor's bill, and take her home with us."

" She must go inside the coach whatever we do," said Mr Benson, decidedly. " Who's there? Come in! Oh! Mrs Hughes! Sit down."

" Indeed, sir, and I cannot stay; but the young lady has just made me find up her watch for her, and asked me to get it sold to pay the doctor, and the little things she has had since she came; and please, sir, indeed, I don't know where to sell it nearer than Carnarvon."

" That is good of her," said Miss Benson, her sense of justice satisfied; and, remembering the way in which Ruth had spoken of the watch, she felt what a sacrifice it must have been to resolve to part with it.

" And her goodness just helps us out of our dilemma," said her brother, who was unaware of the feelings with which Ruth regarded her watch, or, perhaps, he might have parted with his Facciolati.

Mrs Hughes patiently awaited their leisure for answering her practical question. Where could the watch be sold? Suddenly her face brightened.

" Mr Jones, the doctor, is going to be married, perhaps he would like nothing better than to give this pretty watch to his bride; indeed, and I think it's very likely; and he'll pay money for it as well as letting alone his bill. I'll ask him, sir, at any rate."

Mr Jones was only too glad to obtain possession of so elegant a present at so cheap a rate. He even, as Mrs Hughes had foretold, " paid money for it "; more than was required to defray the expenses of Ruth's accommodation; as the most of the articles of food she had were paid for at the time by Mr or Miss Benson, but they strictly forbade Mrs Hughes to tell Ruth of this.

" Would you object to my buying you a black gown?" said Miss Benson to her the day after the sale of the watch. She hesitated a little, and then went on:

"My brother and I think it would be better to call you—as if in fact you were—a widow. It will save much awkwardness, and it will spare your child much ——" Mortification she was going to have added, but that word did not exactly do. But, at the mention of her child, Ruth started and turned ruby-red; as she always did when allusion was made to it.

"Oh, yes! certainly. Thank you much for thinking of it. Indeed," said she, very low, as if to herself, "I don't know how to thank you for all you are doing; but I do love you, and will pray for you, if I may."

"If you may, Ruth!" repeated Miss Benson in a tone of surprise.

"Yes, if I may. If you will let me pray for you."

"Certainly, my dear. My dear Ruth, you don't know how often I sin; I do so wrong, with my few temptations. We are both of us great sinners in the eyes of the Most Holy; let us pray for each other. Don't speak so again, my dear; at least, not to me!"

Miss Benson was actually crying. She had always looked upon herself as so inferior to her brother in real goodness; had seen such heights above her, that she was distressed by Ruth's humility. After a short time she resumed the subject.

"Then I may get you a black gown?—and we may call you Mrs Hilton?"

"No; not Mrs Hilton!" said Ruth, hastily.

Miss Benson, who had hitherto kept her eyes averted from Ruth's face from a motive of kindly delicacy, now looked at her with surprise.

"Why not?" asked she.

"It was my mother's name," said Ruth, in a low voice. "I had better not be called by it."

"Then, let us call you by my mother's name," said Miss Benson, tenderly. "She would have—— But I'll talk to you about my mother some other time. Let me call you Mrs Denbigh. It will do

very well, too. People will think you are a distant
relation."

When she told Mr Benson this choice of name, he
was rather sorry ; it was like his sister's impulsive
kindness—impulsive in everything—and he could
imagine how Ruth's humility had touched her. He
was sorry, but he said nothing.

And now the letter was written home, announcing
the probable arrival of the brother and sister on a
certain day, "with a distant relation, early left a
widow," as Miss Benson expressed it. She desired the
spare room might be prepared, and made every provision she could think of for Ruth's comfort ; for Ruth
still remained feeble and weak.

When the black gown, at which she had stitched
away incessantly, was finished—when nothing remained but to rest for the next day's journey—Ruth
could not sit still. She wandered from window to
window, learning off each rock and tree by heart.
Each had its tale, which it was agony to remember ;
but which it would have been worse agony to forget.
The sound of running waters she heard that quiet
evening, was in her ears as she lay on her death-bed ;
so well had she learnt their tune.

And now all was over. She had driven in to Llan-
dhu, sitting by her lover's side, living in the bright
present, and strangely forgetful of the past or the
future ; she had dreamed out her dream, and she had
awakened from the vision of love. She walked slowly
and sadly down the long hill, her tears fast falling,
but as quickly wiped away ; while she strove to make
steady the low quivering voice which was often called
upon to answer some remarks of Miss Benson's.

They had to wait for the coach. Ruth buried her
face in some flowers which Mrs Hughes had given her
on parting ; and was startled when the mail drew up
with a sudden pull, which almost threw the horses on
their haunches. She was placed inside, and the coach
had set off again, before she was fully aware that Mr
and Miss Benson were travelling on the outside ; but

it was a relief to feel she might now cry without
exciting their notice. The shadow of a heavy thunder-
cloud was on the valley, but the little upland village
church (that showed the spot in which so much of her
life had passed) stood out clear in the sunshine. She
grudged the tears that blinded her as she gazed. There
was one passenger, who tried after a while to comfort
her.

"Don't cry, miss," said the kind-hearted woman.
"You're parting from friends, maybe? Well, that's
bad enough, but when you come to my age, you'll
think none of it. Why, I've three sons, and they're
soldiers and sailors, all of them—here, there, and
everywhere. One is in America, beyond seas; another
is in China, making tea; and another is at Gibraltar,
three miles from Spain; and yet, you see, I can laugh
and eat and enjoy myself. I sometimes think I'll try
and fret a bit, just to make myself a better figure; but,
Lord! it's no use, it's against my nature; so I laugh
and grow fat again. I'd be quite thankful for a fit of
anxiety as would make me feel easy in my clothes,
which them manty-makers* will make so tight I'm
fairly throttled."

Ruth durst cry no more; it was no relief, now she
was watched and noticed, and plied with a sandwich
or a gingerbread each time she looked sad. She
lay back with her eyes shut, as if asleep, and went on,
and on, the sun never seeming to move from his high
place in the sky, nor the bright hot day to show the
least sign of waning. Every now and then, Miss
Benson scrambled down, and made kind inquiries of the
pale, weary Ruth; and once they changed coaches.
and the fat old lady left her with a hearty shake of the
hand.

"It is not much further now," said Miss Benson,
apologetically, to Ruth. "See! we are losing sight of
the Welsh mountains. We have about eighteen miles
of plain, and then we come to the moors and the rising
ground, amidst which Eccleston lies. I wish we were
there, for my brother is sadly tired."

The first wonder in Ruth's mind was, why then, if Mr Benson were so tired, did they not stop where they were for the night; for she knew little of the expenses of a night at an inn. The next thought was, to beg that Mr Benson would take her place inside the coach, and allow her to mount up by Miss Benson. She proposed this, and Miss Benson was evidently pleased.

"Well, if you're not tired, it would make a rest and a change for him, to be sure; and if you were by me I could show you the first sight of Eccleston, if we reach there before it is quite dark."

So Mr Benson got down, and changed places with Ruth.

She hardly yet understood the numerous small economies which he and his sister had to practise— the little daily self-denials,—all endured so cheerfully, and simply, that they had almost ceased to require an effort, and it had become natural to them to think of others before themselves. Ruth had not understood that it was for economy that their places had been taken on the outside of the coach, while hers, as an invalid requiring rest, was to be the inside; and that the biscuits which supplied the place of a dinner were, in fact, chosen because the difference in price between the two would go a little way towards fulfilling their plan for receiving her as an inmate. Her thought about money had been hitherto a child's thought; the subject had never touched her; but afterwards, when she had lived a little with the Bensons, her eyes were opened, and she remembered their simple kindness on the journey, and treasured the remembrance of it in her heart.

A low grey cloud was the first sign of Eccleston;*it was the smoke of the town hanging over the plain. Beyond the place where she was expected to believe it existed, arose round, waving uplands; nothing to the fine outlines of the Welsh mountains, but still going up nearer to heaven than the rest of the flat world into which she had now entered. Rumbling stones, lamp-posts, a sudden stop, and they were in the town of

Eccleston; and a strange, uncouth voice, on the dark
side of the coach, was heard to say,

"Be ye there, measter?"

"Yes, yes!" said Miss Benson, quickly. "Did
Sally send you, Ben? Get the ostler's lantern, and
look out the luggage."

CHAPTER XIII

MISS BENSON had resumed every morsel of the brisk-
ness which she had rather lost in the middle of the
day; her foot was on her native stones, and a very
rough set they were, and she was near her home and
among known people. Even Mr Benson spoke very
cheerfully to Ben, and made many inquiries of him
respecting people whose names were strange to Ruth.
She was cold, and utterly weary. She took Miss Benson's offered arm, and could hardly drag herself as far
as the little quiet street in which Mr Benson's house
was situated. The street was so quiet that their footsteps sounded like a loud disturbance, and announced
their approach as effectually as the "trumpet's lordly
blare" did the coming of Abdallah.* A door flew open,
and a lighted passage stood before them. As soon as
they had entered, a stout, elderly servant emerged
from behind the door, her face radiant with welcome.

"Eh, bless ye! are ye back again? I thought I
should ha' been lost without ye."

She gave Mr Benson a hearty shake of the hand,
and kissed Miss Benson warmly; then, turning to
Ruth, she said, in a loud whisper,

"Who's yon?"

Mr Benson was silent, and walked a step onwards.
Miss Benson said boldly out,

"The lady I named in my note, Sally—Mrs Denbigh, a distant relation."

"Aye, but you said hoo was a widow. Is this chit a
widow?"

"Yes, this is Mrs Denbigh," answered Miss Benson.

"If I'd been her mother, I'd ha' given her a lollypop instead of a husband. Hoo looks fitter for it."

"Hush! Sally, Sally! Look, there's your master trying to move that heavy box." Miss Benson calculated well when she called Sally's attention to her master; for it was well believed by every one, and by Sally herself, that his deformity was owing to a fall he had had, when he was scarcely more than a baby, and entrusted to her care—a little nurse-girl, as she then was, not many years older than himself. For years, the poor girl had cried herself to sleep on her pallet-bed, moaning over the blight her carelessness had brought upon her darling; nor was this self-reproach diminished by the forgiveness of the gentle mother, from whom Thurstan Benson derived so much of his character. The way in which comfort stole into Sally's heart was in the gradually-formed resolution that she would never leave him nor forsake him, but serve him faithfully all her life long; and she had kept to her word. She loved Miss Benson, but she almost worshipped the brother. The reverence for him was in her heart, however, and did not always show itself in her manners. But if she scolded him herself, she allowed no one else that privilege. If Miss Benson differed from her brother, and ventured to think his sayings or doings might have been improved, Sally came down upon her like a thunder-clap.

"My goodness gracious, Master Thurstan, when will you learn to leave off meddling with other folk's business! Here, Ben! help me up with these trunks."

The little narrow passage was cleared, and Miss Benson took Ruth into the sitting-room. There were only two sitting-rooms on the ground-floor, one behind the other. Out of the back room the kitchen opened, and for this reason the back parlour was used as the family sitting-room; or else, being, with its garden aspect, so much the pleasanter of the two, both Sally and Miss Benson would have appropriated it for Mr Benson's study. As it was, the front room, which looked to the street, was his room; and many a person

coming for help—help of which giving money was the
lowest kind—was admitted, and let forth by Mr Benson, unknown to any one else in the house. To make
amends for his having the least cheerful room on the
ground-floor, he had the garden bedroom, while his
sister slept over his study. There were two more
rooms again over these, with sloping ceilings, though
otherwise large and airy. The attic looking into the
garden was the spare bedroom; while the front
belonged to Sally. There was no room over the
kitchen, which was, in fact, a supplement to the
house. The sitting-room was called by the pretty,
old-fashioned name of the parlour, while Mr Benson's
room was styled the study.

The curtains were drawn in the parlour; there was
a bright fire and a clean hearth; indeed, exquisite
cleanliness seemed the very spirit of the household, for
the door which was open to the kitchen showed a
delicately-white and spotless floor, and bright glittering
tins, on which the ruddy firelight danced.

From the place in which Ruth sat she could see all
Sally's movements; and though she was not conscious
of close or minute observation at the time (her body
being weary, and her mind full of other thoughts), yet
it was curious how faithfully that scene remained
depicted on her memory in after years. The warm
light filled every corner of the kitchen, in strong distinction to the faint illumination of the one candle in
the parlour, whose radiance was confined, and was lost
in the dead folds of window-curtains, carpet, and
furniture. The square stout, bustling figure, neat and
clean in every respect, but dressed in the peculiar, old-
fashioned costume of the county, namely, a dark-
striped linsey-woolsey* petticoat, made very short,
displaying sturdy legs in woollen stockings beneath;
a loose kind of jacket called there a " bedgown," made
of pink print; a snow-white apron and cap, both of
linen, and the latter made in the shape of a " mutch ";*
—these articles completed Sally's costume, and were
painted on Ruth's memory. Whilst Sally was busied

in preparing tea, Miss Benson took off Ruth's things; and the latter instinctively felt that Sally, in the midst of her movements, was watching their proceedings. Occasionally she also put in a word in the conversation, and these little sentences were uttered quite in the tone of an equal, if not of a superior. She had dropped the more formal "you," with which at first she had addressed Miss Benson, and thou'd her quietly and habitually.

All these particulars sank unconsciously into Ruth's mind; but they did not rise to the surface, and become perceptible, for a length of time. She was weary, and much depressed. Even the very kindness that ministered to her was overpowering. But over the dark, misty moor a little light shone,—a beacon; and on that she fixed her eyes, and struggled out of her present deep dejection—the little child that was coming to her!

Mr Benson was as languid and weary as Ruth, and was silent during all this bustle and preparation. His silence was more grateful to Ruth than Miss Benson's many words, although she felt their kindness. After tea, Miss Benson took her upstairs to her room. The white dimity bed, and the walls, stained green, had something of the colouring and purity of effect of a snowdrop; while the floor, rubbed with a mixture that turned it into a rich dark brown, suggested the idea of the garden-mould out of which the snowdrop grows. As Miss Benson helped the pale Ruth to undress, her voice became less full-toned and hurried; the hush of approaching night subdued her into a softened, solemn kind of tenderness, and the murmured blessing sounded like granted prayer.

When Miss Benson came downstairs, she found her brother reading some letters which had been received during his absence. She went and softly shut the door of communication between the parlour and the kitchen; and then, fetching a grey worsted stocking which she was knitting, sat down near him, her eyes not looking at her work but fixed on the fire; while

the eternal rapid click of the knitting-needles broke
the silence of the room, with a sound as monotonous
and incessant as the noise of a hand-loom. She
expected him to speak, but he did not. She enjoyed
an examination into, and discussion of, her feelings ;
it was an interest and amusement to her, while he
dreaded and avoided all such conversation. There
were times when his feelings, which were always
earnest, and sometimes morbid, burst forth, and defied
control, and overwhelmed him ; when a force was
upon him compelling him to speak. But he, in
general, strove to preserve his composure, from a fear
of the compelling pain of such times, and the consequent
exhaustion. His heart had been very full of Ruth all
day long, and he was afraid of his sister beginning the
subject ; so he read on, or seemed to do so, though he
hardly saw the letter he held before him. It was a
great relief to him when Sally threw open the middle
door with a bang, which did not indicate either calmness of mind or sweetness of temper.

"Is yon young woman going to stay any length o'
time with us ?" asked she of Miss Benson.

Mr Benson put his hand gently on his sister's
arm, to check her from making any reply, while
he said,

"We cannot exactly tell, Sally. She will remain
until after her confinement."

"Lord bless us and save us !—a baby in the house !
Nay, then my time's come, and I'll pack up and
begone. I never could abide them things. I'd sooner
have rats in the house."

Sally really did look alarmed.

"Why, Sally !" said Mr Benson, smiling, "I was
not much more than a baby when you came to take
care of me."

"Yes, you were, Master Thurstan ; you were a fine
bouncing lad of three year old and better."

Then she remembered the change she had wrought
in the "fine bouncing lad," and her eyes filled with
tears, which she was too proud to wipe away with her

apron; for, as she sometimes said to herself, "she could not abide crying before folk."

"Well, it's no use talking, Sally," said Miss Benson, too anxious to speak to be any longer repressed. "We've promised to keep her, and we must do it; you'll have none of the trouble, Sally, so don't be afraid."

"Well, I never! as if I minded trouble! You might ha' known me better nor that. I've scoured master's room twice over, just to make the boards look white, though the carpet is to cover them, and now you go and cast up about me minding my trouble. If them's the fashions you've learnt in Wales, I'm thankful I've never been there."

Sally looked red, indignant, and really hurt. Mr Benson came in with his musical voice and soft words of healing.

"Faith knows you don't care for trouble, Sally; she is only anxious about this poor young woman, who has no friends but ourselves. We know there will be more trouble in consequence of her coming to stay with us; and I think, though we never spoke about it, that in making our plans we reckoned on your kind help, Sally, which has never failed us yet when we needed it."

"You've twice the sense of your sister, Master Thurstan, that you have. Boys always has. It's truth there will be more trouble, and I shall have my share on't, I reckon. I can face it if I'm told out and out, but I cannot abide the way some folk has of denying there's trouble or pain to be met; just as if their saying there was none, would do away with it. Some folk treats one like a babby, and I don't like it. I'm not meaning you, Master Thurstan."

"No, Sally, you need not say that. I know well enough who you mean when you say 'some folk.' However, I admit I was wrong in speaking as if you minded trouble, for there never was a creature minded it less. But I want you to like Mrs Denbigh," said Miss Benson.

" I dare say I should, if you'd let me alone. I did
na like her sitting down in master's chair. Set her up,
indeed, in an arm-chair wi' cushions ! Wenches in my
day were glad enough of stools."

" She was tired to-night," said Mr Benson. " We
are all tired ; so if you have done your work, Sally,
come in to reading."

The three quiet people knelt down side by side, and
two of them prayed earnestly for " them that had gone
astray."* Before ten o'clock, the household were in
bed.

Ruth, sleepless, weary, restless with the oppression
of a sorrow which she dared not face and contemplate
bravely, kept awake all the early part of the night.
Many a time did she rise, and go to the long casement
window, and look abroad over the still and quiet town
—over the grey stone walls, and chimneys, and old
high-pointed roofs—on to the far-away hilly line of the
horizon, lying calm under the bright moonshine.   It
was late in the morning when she woke from her long-
deferred slumbers ; and when she went downstairs,
she found Mr and Miss Benson awaiting her in the
parlour.   That homely, pretty, old-fashioned little
room ! How bright and still and clean it looked !
The window (all the windows at the back of the house
were casements) was open, to let in the sweet morning
air, and streaming eastern sunshine. The long jessamine sprays, with their white-scented stars, forced
themselves almost into the room. The little square
garden beyond, with grey stone walls all round, was
rich and mellow in its autumnal colouring, running
from deep crimson hollyhocks up to amber and gold
nasturtiums, and all toned down by the clear and
delicate air.   It was so still, that the gossamer-webs,
laden with dew, did not tremble or quiver in the least ;
but the sun was drawing to himself the sweet incense
of many flowers, and the parlour was scented with the
odours of mignonette and stocks.   Miss Benson was
arranging a bunch of China and damask roses in an
old-fashioned jar ; they lay, all dewy and fresh, on the

white breakfast-cloth when Ruth entered. Mr Benson
was reading in some large folio.   With gentle morning
speech they greeted her; but the quiet repose of the
scene was instantly broken by Sally popping in from
the kitchen, and glancing at Ruth with sharp reproach.
She said:

"I reckon I may bring in breakfast, now?" with a
strong emphasis on the last word.

"I am afraid I am very late," said Ruth.

"Oh, never mind," said Mr Benson, gently. "It
was our fault for not telling you our breakfast hour.
We always have prayers at half-past seven; and, for
Sally's sake, we never vary from that time; for she
can so arrange her work, if she knows the hour of
prayers, as to have her mind calm and untroubled."

"Ahem!" said Miss Benson, rather inclined to
"testify" against the invariable calmness of Sally's
mind at any hour of the day; but her brother went on
as if he did not hear her.

"But the breakfast does not signify being delayed a
little; and I am sure you were sadly tired with your
long day yesterday."

Sally came slapping in, and put down some withered,
tough, dry toast, with—

"It's not my doing if it is like leather;" but as no
one appeared to hear her, she withdrew to her kitchen,
leaving Ruth's cheeks like crimson at the annoyance
she had caused.

All day long, she had that feeling common to those
who go to stay at a fresh house among comparative
strangers: a feeling of the necessity that she should
become accustomed to the new atmosphere in which
she was placed, before she could move and act freely;
it was, indeed, a purer ether, a diviner air, which she
was breathing in now, than what she had been accustomed to for long months. The gentle, blessed mother,
who had made her childhood's home holy ground, was
in her very nature so far removed from any of earth's
stains and temptations, that she seemed truly one of
those

Who ask not if Thine eye
Be on them ; who, in love and truth,
Where no misgiving is, rely
Upon the genial sense of youth.*

In the Bensons' house there was the same unconsciousness of individual merit, the same absence of in-
trospection and analysis of motive, as there had been
in her mother ; but it seemed that their lives were
pure and good, not merely from a lovely and beautiful
nature, but from some law, the obedience to which was,
of itself, harmonious peace, and which governed them
almost implicitly, and with as little questioning on their
part, as the glorious stars which haste not, rest not, in
their eternal obedience. This household had many
failings : they were but human, and, with all their
loving desire to bring their lives into harmony with
the will of God, they often erred and fell short ; but,
somehow, the very errors and faults of one individual
served to call out higher excellences in another, and
so they re-acted upon each other, and the result of
short discords was exceeding harmony and peace. But
they had themselves no idea of the real state of things ;
they did not trouble themselves with marking their
progress by self-examination ; if Mr Benson did sometimes, in hours of sick incapacity for exertion, turn
inwards, it was to cry aloud with almost morbid despair,
" God be merciful to me a sinner !"* But he strove
to leave his life in the hands of God, and to forget
himself.

Ruth sat still and quiet through the long first day.
She was languid and weary from her journey ; she was
uncertain what help she might offer to give in the
household duties, and what she might not. And, in
her languor and in her uncertainty, it was pleasant to
watch the new ways of the people among whom she
was placed. After breakfast, Mr Benson withdrew to
his study, Miss Benson took away the cups and saucers,
and, leaving the kitchen door open, talked sometimes
to Ruth, sometimes to Sally, while she washed them
up. Sally had upstairs duties to perform, for which

Ruth was thankful, as she kept receiving rather angry glances for her unpunctuality as long as Sally remained downstairs. Miss Benson assisted in the preparation for the early dinner, and brought some kidney-beans to shred into a basin of bright, pure spring-water, which caught and danced in the sunbeams as she sat near the open casement of the parlour, talking to Ruth of things and people which as yet the latter did not understand, and could not arrange and comprehend. She was like a child who gets a few pieces of a dissected map, and is confused until a glimpse of the whole unity is shown him. Mr and Mrs Bradshaw were the centre pieces in Ruth's map; their children, their servants, were the accessories; and one or two other names were occasionally mentioned. Ruth wondered and almost wearied at Miss Benson's perseverance in talking to her about people whom she did not know; but, in truth, Miss Benson heard the long-drawn, quivering sighs which came from the poor heavy heart, when it was left to silence, and had leisure to review the past; and her quick accustomed ear caught also the low mutterings of the thunder in the distance, in the shape of Sally's soliloquies, which, like the asides at a theatre, were intended to be heard. Suddenly, Miss Benson called Ruth out of the room, upstairs into her own bed-chamber, and then began rummaging in little old-fashioned boxes, drawn out of an equally old-fashioned bureau, half desk, half table, and wholly drawers.

"My dear, I've been very stupid and thoughtless. Oh! I'm so glad I thought of it before Mrs Bradshaw came to call. Here it is!" and she pulled out an old wedding-ring, and hurried it on Ruth's finger. Ruth hung down her head, and reddened deep with shame; her eyes smarted with the hot tears that filled them. Miss Benson talked on, in a nervous hurried way:

"It was my grandmother's; it's very broad; they made them so then, to hold a posy inside: there's one in that;

> Thine own sweetheart
> Till death doth part,

I think it is. There, there! Run away, and look as if you'd always worn it."

Ruth went up to her room, and threw herself down on her knees by the bedside, and cried as if her heart would break; and then, as if a light had come down into her soul, she calmed herself and prayed—no words can tell how humbly, and with what earnest feeling. When she came down, she was tear-stained and wretchedly pale; but even Sally looked at her with new eyes, because of the dignity with which she was invested by an earnestness of purpose which had her child for its object. She sat and thought, but she no longer heaved those bitter sighs which had wrung Miss Benson's heart in the morning. In this way the day wore on; early dinner, early tea, seemed to make it preternaturally long to Ruth; the only event was some unexplained absence of Sally's, who had disappeared out of the house in the evening, much to Miss Benson's surprise, and somewhat to her indignation.

At night, after Ruth had gone up to her room, this absence was explained to her at least. She had let down her long waving glossy hair, and was standing absorbed in thought in the middle of the room, when she heard a round clumping knock at her door, different from that given by the small knuckles of delicate fingers, and in walked Sally, with a judge-like severity of demeanour, holding in her hand two widow's caps of commonest make and coarsest texture. Queen Eleanor herself, when she presented the bowl to Fair Rosamond,* had not a more relentless purpose stamped on her demeanour than had Sally at this moment. She walked up to the beautiful, astonished Ruth, where she stood in her long, soft, white dressing-gown, with all her luxuriant brown hair hanging dishevelled down her figure, and thus Sally spoke:

"Missus—or miss, as the case may be—I've my doubts as to you. I'm not going to have my master and Miss Faith put upon, or shame come near them. Widows wears these sort o' caps, and has their hair cut off; and whether widows wears wedding-rings or

not, they shall have their hair cut off—they shall.
I'll have no half work in this house. I've lived with
the family forty-nine year come Michaelmas, and I'll
not see it disgraced by anyone's fine long curls. Sit
down and let me snip off your hair, and let me see you
sham decently in a widow's cap to-morrow, or I'll
leave the house. Whatten's come over Miss Faith, as
used to be as mim a lady as ever was, to be taken by
such as you, I dunnot know. Here! sit down with
ye, and let me crop you.''

She laid no light hand on Ruth's shoulder; and the
latter, partly intimidated by the old servant, who had
hitherto only turned her vixen lining to observation,
and partly because she was broken-spirited enough to
be indifferent to the measure proposed, quietly sat
down. Sally produced the formidable pair of scissors
that always hung at her side, and began to cut in a
merciless manner. She expected some remonstrance
or some opposition, and had a torrent of words ready
to flow forth at the least sign of rebellion; but Ruth
was still and silent, with meekly-bowed head, under
the strange hands that were shearing her beautiful
hair into the clipped shortness of a boy's. Long before
she had finished, Sally had some slight misgivings as
to the fancied necessity of her task; but it was too
late, for half the curls were gone, and the rest must
now come off. When she had done, she lifted up
Ruth's face by placing her hand under the round
white chin. She gazed into the countenance, expecting to read some anger there, though it had not come
out in words; but she only met the large, quiet eyes,
that looked at her with sad gentleness out of their
finely-hollowed orbits. Ruth's soft, yet dignified submission, touched Sally with compunction, though she
did not choose to show the change in her feelings.
She tried to hide it, indeed, by stooping to pick up
the long bright tresses; and, holding them up admiringly, and letting them drop down and float on the
air (like the pendant branches of the weeping birch),
she said: '' I thought we should ha' had some crying

—I did. They're pretty curls enough; you've not
been so bad to let them be cut off neither. You see,
Master Thurstan is no wiser than a babby in some
things; and Miss Faith just lets him have his own
way; so it's all left to me to keep him out of scrapes.
I'll wish you a very good night. I've heard many a
one say as long hair was not wholesome. Good
night."

But in a minute she popped her head into Ruth's
room once more:

" You'll put on them caps to-morrow morning. I'll
make you a present on them."

Sally had carried away the beautiful curls, and she
could not find it in her heart to throw such lovely
chestnut tresses away, so she folded them up carefully in paper, and placed them in a safe corner of her
drawer.

CHAPTER XIV

RUTH felt very shy when she came down (at half-past
seven) the next morning, in her widow's cap. Her
smooth, pale face, with its oval untouched by time,
looked more young and childlike than ever, when
contrasted with the head-gear usually associated with
ideas of age. She blushed very deeply as Mr and
Miss Benson showed the astonishment, which they
could not conceal, in their looks. She said in a low
voice to Miss Benson,

" Sally thought I had better wear it."

Miss Benson made no reply; but was startled at the
intelligence, which she thought was conveyed in this
speech, of Sally's acquaintance with Ruth's real
situation. She noticed Sally's looks particularly this
morning. The manner in which the old servant
treated Ruth, had in it far more of respect than there
had been the day before; but there was a kind of
satisfied way of braving out Miss Benson's glances
which made the latter uncertain and uncomfortable.

She followed her brother into his study.

"Do you know, Thurstan, I am almost certain Sally suspects."

Mr Benson sighed. The deception grieved him, and yet he thought he saw its necessity.

"What makes you think so?" asked he.

"Oh! many little things. It was her odd way of ducking her head about, as if to catch a good view of Ruth's left hand, that made me think of the wedding-ring; and once, yesterday, when I thought I had made up quite a natural speech, and was saying how sad it was for so young a creature to be left a widow, she broke in with 'widow be farred!'*in a very strange, contemptuous kind of manner."

"If she suspects, we had far better tell her the truth, at once. She will never rest till she finds it out, so we must make a virtue of necessity."

"Well, brother, you shall tell her then, for I am sure I daren't. I don't mind doing the thing, since you talked to me that day, and since I've got to know Ruth; but I do mind all the clatter people will make about it."

"But Sally is not 'people.'"

"Oh, I see it must be done; she'll talk as much as all the other persons put together, so that's the reason I call her 'people.' Shall I call her?" (For the house was too homely and primitive to have bells.)

Sally came, fully aware of what was now going to be told her, and determined not to help them out in telling their awkward secret, by understanding the nature of it before it was put into the plainest language. In every pause, when they hoped she had caught the meaning they were hinting at, she persisted in looking stupid and perplexed, and in saying "Well," as if quite unenlightened as to the end of the story. When it was all complete and plain before her, she said, honestly enough,

"It's just as I thought it was; and I think you may thank me for having had the sense to put her into widow's caps, and clip off that bonny brown hair that

was fitter for a bride in lawful matrimony than for
such as her. She took it very well, though. She was
as quiet as a lamb, and I clipped her pretty roughly at
first. I must say, though, if I'd ha' known who your
visitor was, I'd ha' packed up my things and cleared
myself out of the house before such as her came into
it. As it's done, I suppose I must stand by you, and
help you through with it ; I only hope I shan't lose
my character,—and me a parish clerk's daughter."

"Oh, Sally ! people know you too well to think any
ill of you," said Miss Benson, who was pleased to find
the difficulty so easily got over ; for, in truth, Sally
had been much softened by the unresisting gentleness
with which Ruth had submitted to the "clipping" of
the night before.

"If I'd been with you, Master Thurstan, I'd ha'
seen sharp after you, for you're always picking up some
one or another as nobody else would touch with a pair
of tongs. Why, there was that Nelly Brandon's child
as was left at our door, if I hadn't gone to th' overseer *
we should have had that Irish tramp's babby saddled
on us for life ; but I went off and told th' overseer, and
th' mother was caught."

"Yes !" said Mr Benson, sadly, "and I often lie
awake and wonder what is the fate of that poor little
thing, forced back on the mother who tried to get quit
of it. I often doubt whether I did right ; but it's no
use thinking about it now."

"I'm thankful it isn't," said Sally ; "and now, if
we've talked doctrine long enough, I'll go make th'
beds. Yon girl's secret is safe enough for me."

Saying this she left the room, and Miss Benson
followed. She found Ruth busy washing the breakfast
things ; and they were done in so quiet and orderly a
manner, that neither Miss Benson nor Sally, both
particular enough, had any of their little fancies or
prejudices annoyed. She seemed to have an instinctive
knowledge of the exact period when her help was likely
to become a hindrance, and withdrew from the busy
kitchen just at the right time.

That afternoon, as Miss Benson and Ruth sat at their work, Mrs and Miss Bradshaw called. Miss Benson was so nervous as to surprise Ruth, who did not understand the probable and possible questions which might be asked respecting any visitor at the minister's house. Ruth went on sewing, absorbed in her own thoughts, and glad that the conversation between the two elder ladies and the silence of the younger one, who sat at some distance from her, gave her an opportunity of retreating into the haunts of memory; and soon the work fell from her hands, and her eyes were fixed on the little garden beyond, but she did not see its flowers or its walls; she saw the mountains which girdled Llan-dhu, and saw the sun rise from behind their iron outline, just as it had done—how long ago? was it months or was it years?—since she had watched the night through, crouched up at *his* door. Which was the dream and which the reality? that distant life, or this? His moans rang more clearly in her ears than the buzzing of the conversation between Mrs Bradshaw and Miss Benson.

At length the subdued, scared-looking little lady and her bright-eyed silent daughter rose to take leave; Ruth started into the present, and stood up and curtseyed, and turned sick at heart with sudden recollection.

Miss Benson accompanied Mrs Bradshaw to the door; and in the passage gave her a long explanation of Ruth's (fictitious) history. Mrs Bradshaw looked so much interested and pleased, that Miss Benson enlarged a little more than was necessary, and rounded off her invention with one or two imaginary details, which, she was quite unconscious, were overheard by her brother through the half-open study door.

She was rather dismayed when he called her into his room after Mrs Bradshaw's departure, and asked her what she had been saying about Ruth?

"Oh! I thought it was better to explain it thoroughly—I mean, to tell the story we wished to have believed once for all—you know we agreed about that, Thurstan?" deprecatingly.

"Yes; but I heard you saying you believed her husband had been a young surgeon, did I not?"

"Well, Thurstan, you know he must have been something; and young surgeons are so in the way of dying, it seemed very natural. Besides," said she, with sudden boldness, "I do think I've a talent for fiction, it is so pleasant to invent, and make the incidents dovetail together; and after all, if we are to tell a lie, we may as well do it thoroughly, or else it's of no use. A bungling lie would be worse than useless. And, Thurstan—it may be very wrong—but I believe—I am afraid I enjoy not being fettered by truth. Don't look so grave. You know it is necessary, if ever it was, to tell falsehoods now; and don't be angry with me because I do it well."

He was shading his eyes with his hand, and did not speak for some time. At last he said:

"If it were not for the child, I would tell all; but the world is so cruel. You don't know how this apparent necessity for falsehood pains me, Faith, or you would not invent all these details, which are so many additional lies."

"Well, well! I will restrain myself if I have to talk about Ruth again. But Mrs Bradshaw will tell every one who need to know. You don't wish me to contradict it, Thurstan, surely—it was such a pretty, probable story."

"Faith! I hope God will forgive us if we are doing wrong; and pray, dear, don't add one unnecessary word that is not true."

Another day elapsed, and then it was Sunday; and the house seemed filled with a deep peace. Even Sally's movements were less hasty and abrupt. Mr Benson seemed invested with a new dignity, which made his bodily deformity be forgotten in his calm, grave composure of spirit. Every trace of week-day occupation was put away; the night before, a bright new handsome tablecloth had been smoothed down over the table, and the jars had been freshly filled with flowers. Sunday was a festival and a holyday in the house.

After the very early breakfast, little feet pattered into Mr Benson's study, for he had a class for boys—a sort of domestic Sunday school, only that there was more talking between teacher and pupils, than dry, absolute lessons goings on. Miss Benson, too, had her little, neat-tippeted maidens sitting with her in the parlour; and she was far more particular in keeping them to their reading and spelling, than her brother was with his boys. Sally, too, put in her word of instruction from the kitchen, helping, as she fancied, though her assistance was often rather *malapropos*; for instance, she called out, to a little fat, stupid, roly-poly girl, to whom Miss Benson was busy explaining the meaning of the word quadruped,

"Quadruped, a thing wi' four legs, Jenny; a chair is a quadruped, child!"

But Miss Benson had a deaf manner sometimes when her patience was not too severely tried, and she put it on now. Ruth sat on a low hassock, and coaxed the least of the little creatures to her, and showed it pictures till it fell asleep in her arms, and sent a thrill through her, at the thought of the tiny darling who would lie on her breast before long, and whom she would have to cherish and to shelter from the storms of the world.

And then she remembered, that she was once white and sinless as the wee lassie who lay in her arms; and she knew that she had gone astray. By and by the children trooped away, and Miss Benson summoned her to put on her things for chapel.

The chapel was up a narrow street, or rather *cul-de-sac*, close by.* It stood on the outskirts of the town, almost in fields. It was built about the time of Matthew and Philip Henry,* when the Dissenters were afraid of attracting attention or observation, and hid their places of worship in obscure and out-of-the-way parts of the towns in which they were built. Accordingly, it often happened, as in the present case, that the buildings immediately surrounding, as well as the chapels themselves, looked as if they carried you

back to a period a hundred and fifty years ago. The
chapel had a picturesque and old-world look, for luckily
the congregation had been too poor to rebuild it, or
new face it in George the Third's time. The staircases which led to the galleries were outside, at each
end of the building, and the irregular roof and worn
stone steps looked grey and stained by time and
weather. The grassy hillocks, each with a little upright headstone, were shaded by a grand old wych-
elm. A lilac-bush or two, a white rose-tree, and a
few laburnums, all old and gnarled enough, were
planted round the chapel yard; and the casement
windows of the chapel were made of heavy-leaded,
diamond-shaped panes, almost covered with ivy, producing a green gloom, not without its solemnity,
within. This ivy was the home of an infinite number
of little birds, which twittered and warbled, till it
might have been thought that they were emulous of
the power of praise possessed by the human creatures
within, with such earnest, long-drawn strains did this
crowd of winged songsters rejoice and be glad in their
beautiful gift of life. The interior of the building was
plain and simple as plain and simple could be. When
it was fitted up, oak-timber was much cheaper than it
is now, so the wood-work was all of that description;
but roughly hewed, for the early builders had not
much wealth to spare. The walls were whitewashed,
and were recipients of the shadows of the beauty without; on their "white plains" the tracery of the ivy
might be seen, now still, now stirred by the sudden
flight of some little bird. The congregation consisted
of here and there a farmer with his labourers, who
came down from the uplands beyond the town to
worship where their fathers worshipped, and who
loved the place because they knew how much those
fathers had suffered for it, although they never
troubled themselves with the reason why they left
the parish church; of a few shopkeepers, far more
thoughtful and reasoning, who were Dissenters from
conviction, unmixed with old ancestral association; and

of one or two families of still higher worldly station.
With many poor, who were drawn there by love for
Mr Benson's character, and by a feeling that the faith
which made him what he was could not be far wrong,
for the base of the pyramid, and with Mr Bradshaw for
its apex, the congregation stood complete.

The country people came in sleeking down their
hair, and treading with earnest attempts at noiseless
lightness of step over the floor of the aisle ; and by
and by, when all were assembled, Mr Benson followed,
unmarshalled and unattended. When he had closed
the pulpit-door, and knelt in prayer for an instant or
two, he gave out a psalm from the dear old Scottish
paraphrase,*with its primitive inversion of the simple
perfect Bible words ; and a kind of precentor stood up,
and, having sounded the note on a pitch-pipe, sang a
couple of lines by way of indicating the tune ; then
all the congregation stood up, and sang aloud, Mr
Bradshaw's great bass voice being half a note in
advance of the others, in accordance with his place of
precedence as principal member of the congregation.
His powerful voice was like an organ very badly
played, and very much out of tune ; but as he had
no ear, and no diffidence, it pleased him very much
to hear the fine loud sound.   He was a tall, large-
boned, iron man ; stern, powerful, and authoritative
in appearance ; dressed in clothes of the finest broad-
cloth, and scrupulously ill-made, as if to show that he
was indifferent to all outward things. His wife was
sweet and gentle-looking, but as if she was thoroughly
broken into submission.

Ruth did not see this, or hear aught but the words
which were reverently—oh, how reverently !—spoken
by Mr Benson. He had had Ruth present in his
thoughts all the time he had been preparing for his
Sunday duty ; and he had tried carefully to eschew
everything which she might feel as an allusion to her
own case. He remembered how the Good Shepherd,
in Poussin's beautiful picture,* tenderly carried the
lambs which had wearied themselves by going astray,

and felt how like tenderness was required towards
poor Ruth. But where is the chapter which does not
contain something which a broken and contrite spirit
may not apply to itself? And so it fell out that, as he
read, Ruth's heart was smitten, and she sank down;
and down, till she was kneeling on the floor of the
pew, and speaking to God in the spirit, if not in the
words of the Prodigal Son: "Father! I have sinned
against Heaven and before Thee,* and am no more
worthy to be called Thy child!" Miss Benson was
thankful (although she loved Ruth the better for this
self-abandonment) that the minister's seat was far in
the shade of the gallery. She tried to look most
attentive to her brother, in order that Mr Bradshaw
might not suspect anything unusual, while she stealthily
took hold of Ruth's passive hand, as it lay helpless on
the cushion, and pressed it softly and tenderly. But
Ruth sat on the ground, bowed down and crushed in
her sorrow, till all was ended.

Miss Benson loitered in her seat, divided between
the consciousness that she, as *locum tenens* for the
minister's wife, was expected to be at the door to
receive the kind greetings of many after her absence
from home, and her unwillingness to disturb Ruth,
who was evidently praying, and, by her quiet breathing, receiving grave and solemn influences into her
soul. At length she rose up, calm and composed even
to dignity. The chapel was still and empty; but Miss
Benson heard the buzz of voices in the chapel-yard
without. They were probably those of people waiting for her; and she summoned courage, and taking
Ruth's arm in hers, and holding her hand affectionately, they went out into the broad daylight. As
they issued forth, Miss Benson heard Mr Bradshaw's
strong bass voice speaking to her brother, and winced,
as she knew he would be wincing, under the broad
praise, which is impertinence, however little it may be
intended or esteemed as such.

"Oh, yes!—my wife told me yesterday about her—
her husband was a surgeon; my father was a surgeon

too, as I think you have heard. Very much to your
credit, I must say, Mr Benson, with your limited
means, to burden yourself with a poor relation. Very
creditable indeed."

Miss Benson glanced at Ruth ; she either did not
hear or did not understand, but passed on into the
awful sphere of Mr Bradshaw's observation unmoved.
He was in a bland and condescending humour of
universal approval, and when he saw Ruth, he
nodded his head in token of satisfaction. That
ordeal was over, Miss Benson thought, and in the
thought rejoiced.

"After dinner, you must go and lie down, my
dear," said she, untying Ruth's bonnet-strings, and
kissing her. "Sally goes to church again, but you
won't mind staying alone in the house. I am sorry we
have so many people to dinner, but my brother will
always have enough on Sundays for any old or weak
people, who may have come from a distance, to stay and
dine with us ; and to-day they all seem to have come,
because it is his first Sabbath at home."

In this way Ruth's first Sabbath passed over.

CHAPTER XV

"HERE is a parcel for you, Ruth !" said Miss Benson
on the Tuesday morning.

"For me !" said Ruth, all sorts of rushing thoughts
and hopes filling her mind, and turning her dizzy with
expectation. If it had been from "him," the new-
born resolutions would have had a hard struggle for
existence.

"It is directed ' Mrs Denbigh,'" said Miss Benson,
before giving it up. "It is in Mrs Bradshaw's handwriting"; and, far more curious than Ruth, she
awaited the untying of the close-knotted string.
When the paper was opened, it displayed a whole
piece of delicate cambric-muslin; and there was a
short note from Mrs Bradshaw to Ruth, saying her

husband had wished her to send this muslin in aid
of any preparations Mrs Denbigh might have to make.
Ruth said nothing, but coloured up, and sat down
again to her employment.

"Very fine muslin indeed," said Miss Benson,
feeling it, and holding it up against the light, with
the air of a connoisseur; yet all the time she was
glancing at Ruth's grave face. The latter kept silence,
and showed no wish to inspect her present further.
At last she said, in a low voice,

"I suppose I may send it back again?"

"My dear child! send it back to Mr Bradshaw!
You'd offend him for life. You may depend upon it,
he means it as a mark of high favour!"

"What right had he to send it to me?" asked Ruth,
still in her quiet voice.

"What right? Mr Bradshaw thinks —— I don't
know exactly what you mean by 'right.'"

Ruth was silent for a moment, and then said:

"There are people to whom I love to feel that I owe
gratitude—gratitude which I cannot express, and had
better not talk about—but I cannot see why a person
whom I do not know should lay me under an obligation. Oh! don't say I must take this muslin, please,
Miss Benson!"

What Miss Benson might have said if her brother
had not just then entered the room, neither he nor
any other person could tell; but she felt his presence
was most opportune, and called him in as umpire. He
had come hastily, for he had much to do; but he no
sooner heard the case than he sat down, and tried to
draw some more explicit declaration of her feeling
from Ruth, who had remained silent during Miss
Benson's explanation.

"You would rather send this present back?"
said he.

"Yes," she answered, softly. "Is it wrong?"

"Why do you want to return it?"

"Because I feel as if Mr Bradshaw had no right to
offer it me."

Mr Benson was silent.

"It's beautifully fine," said Miss Benson still examining the piece.

"You think that it is a right which must be earned?"

"Yes," said she, after a minute's pause. "Don't you?"

"I understand what you mean. It is a delight to have gifts made to you by those whom you esteem and love, because then such gifts are merely to be considered as fringes to the garment—as inconsiderable additions to the mighty treasure of their affection, adding a grace, but no additional value, to what before was precious, and proceeding as naturally out of that as leaves burgeon out upon the trees; but you feel it to be different when there is no regard for the giver to idealise the gift—when it simply takes its stand among your property as so much money's value. Is this it, Ruth?"

"I think it is. I never reasoned why I felt as I did; I only knew that Mr Bradshaw's giving me a present hurt me, instead of making me glad."

"Well, but there is another side of the case we have not looked at yet—we must think of that, too. You know who said 'Do unto others as ye would that they should do unto you?'* Mr Bradshaw may not have had that in his mind when he desired his wife to send you this; he may have been self-seeking, and only anxious to gratify his love of patronizing—that is the worst motive we can give him; and that would be no excuse for your thinking only of yourself, and returning his present."

"But you would not have me pretend to be obliged?" asked Ruth.

"No, I would not. I have often been similarly situated to you, Ruth; Mr Bradshaw has frequently opposed me on the points on which I feel the warmest—am the most earnestly convinced. He, no doubt, thinks me Quixotic, and often speaks of me, and to me, with great contempt when he is angry. I suppose he has

a little fit of penitence afterwards, or perhaps he
thinks he can pay for ungracious speeches by a present ; so, formerly, he invariably sent me something
after these occasions. It was a time, of all others, to
feel as you are doing now ; but I became convinced
it would be right to accept them, giving only the very
cool thanks which I felt. This omission of all show
of much gratitude had the best effect—the presents
have much diminished ; but if the gifts have lessened,
the unjustifiable speeches have decreased in still greater
proportion, and I am sure we respect each other more.
Take this muslin, Ruth, for the reason I named ; and
thank him as your feelings prompt you. Overstrained
expressions of gratitude always seem like an endeavour
to place the receiver of these expressions in the position
of debtor for future favours. But you won't fall into
this error."

Ruth listened to Mr Benson ; but she had not yet
fallen sufficiently into the tone of his mind to understand him fully. She only felt that he comprehended
her better than Miss Benson, who once more tried to
reconcile her to her present, by calling her attention
to the length and breadth thereof.

"I will do what you wish me," she said, after a
little pause of thoughtfulness. "May we talk of
something else?"

Mr Benson saw that his sister's frame of mind was
not particularly congenial with Ruth's, any more than
Ruth's was with Miss Benson's ; and, putting aside all
thought of returning to the business which had
appeared to him so important when he came into the
room (but which principally related to himself), he
remained above an hour in the parlour, interesting
them on subjects far removed from the present, and
left them at the end of that time soothed and calm.

But the present gave a new current to Ruth's ideas.
Her heart was as yet too sore to speak, but her mind
was crowded with plans. She asked Sally to buy her
(with the money produced by the sale of a ring or two)
the coarsest linen, the homeliest dark blue print, and

similar materials ; on which she set busily to work to make clothes for herself ; and as they were made, she put them on ; and as she put them on, she gave a grace to each, which such homely material and simple shaping had never had before. Then the fine linen and delicate soft white muslin, which she had chosen in preference to more expensive articles of dress when Mr Bellingham had given her *carte blanche* in London, were cut into small garments, most daintily stitched and made ready for the little creature, for whom in its white purity of soul nothing could be too precious.

The love which dictated this extreme simplicity and coarseness of attire, was taken for stiff, hard economy by Mr Bradshaw, when he deigned to observe it. And economy by itself, without any soul or spirit in it to make it living and holy, was a great merit in his eyes. Indeed, Ruth altogether found favour with him. Her quiet manner, subdued by an internal consciousness of a deeper cause for sorrow than he was aware of, he interpreted into a very proper and becoming awe of him. He looked off from his own prayers to observe how well she attended to hers at chapel ; when he came to any verse in the hymn relating to immortality or a future life, he sang it unusually loud, thinking he should thus comfort her in her sorrow for her deceased husband. He desired Mrs Bradshaw to pay her every attention she could ; and even once remarked, that he thought her so respectable a young person that he should not object to her being asked to tea the next time Mr and Miss Benson came. He added, that he thought, indeed, Benson had looked last Sunday as if he rather hoped to get an invitation ; and it was right to encourage the ministers, and to show them respect, even though their salaries were small. The only thing against this Mrs Denbigh was the circumstance of her having married too early, and without any provision for a family. Though Ruth pleaded delicacy of health, and declined accompanying Mr and Miss Benson on their visit to Mr Bradshaw, she still preserved her place in his esteem ; and Miss Benson had to call a

little upon her "talent for fiction" to spare Ruth from
the infliction of further presents, in making which his
love of patronizing delighted.

The yellow and crimson leaves came floating down
on the still October air; November followed, bleak
and dreary; it was more cheerful when the earth put
on her beautiful robe of white, which covered up all
the grey naked stems, and loaded the leaves of the
hollies and evergreens each with its burden of feathery
snow. When Ruth sank down to languor and sadness,
Miss Benson trotted upstairs, and rummaged up every
article of spare or worn-out clothing, and bringing
down a variety of strange materials, she tried to
interest Ruth in making them up into garments for
the poor. But though Ruth's fingers flew through the
work, she still sighed with thought and remembrance.
Miss Benson was at first disappointed, and then she
was angry. When she heard the low, long sigh, and
saw the dreamy eyes filling with glittering tears, she
would say, "What is the matter, Ruth?" in a half-
reproachful tone, for the sight of suffering was painful
to her; she had done all in her power to remedy it;
and, though she acknowledged a cause beyond her
reach for Ruth's deep sorrow, and, in fact, loved and
respected her all the more for these manifestations of
grief, yet at the time they irritated her. Then Ruth
would snatch up the dropped work, and stitch away
with drooping eyes, from which the hot tears fell fast;
and Miss Benson was then angry with herself, yet not
at all inclined to agree with Sally when she asked her
mistress "why she kept 'mithering' the poor lass
with asking her for ever what was the matter, as if she
did not know well enough." Some element of harmony
was wanting—some little angel of peace, in loving
whom all hearts and natures should be drawn together,
and their discords hushed.

The earth was still "hiding her guilty front with
innocent snow,"*when a little baby was laid by the side
of the pale white mother. It was a boy; beforehand
she had wished for a girl, as being less likely to feel

the want of a father—as being what a mother, worse
than widowed, could most effectually shelter. But
now she did not think or remember this. What it
was, she would not have exchanged for a wilderness
of girls. It was her own, her darling, her individual
baby, already, though not an hour old, separate and
sole in her heart, strangely filling up its measure with
love and peace, and even hope. For here was a
new, pure, beautiful, innocent life, which she fondly
imagined, in that early passion of maternal love, she
could guard from every touch of corrupting sin by
ever watchful and most tender care. And *her* mother
had thought the same, most probably; and thousands
of others think the same, and pray to God to purify
and cleanse their souls, that they may be fit guardians
for their little children. Oh, how Ruth prayed, even
while she was yet too weak to speak; and how she felt
the beauty and significance of the words, "Our
Father!"

She was roused from this holy abstraction by the
sound of Miss Benson's voice. It was very much as if
she had been crying.

"Look, Ruth!" it said, softly, "my brother sends
you these. They are the first snowdrops in the
garden." And she put them on the pillow by Ruth;
the baby lay on the opposite side.

"Won't you look at him?" said Ruth; "he is so
pretty!"

Miss Benson had a strange reluctance to see him.
To Ruth, in spite of all that had come and gone, she
was reconciled—nay, more, she was deeply attached;
but over the baby there hung a cloud of shame and
disgrace. Poor little creature, her heart was closed
against it—firmly, as she thought. But she could not
resist Ruth's low faint voice, nor her pleading eyes,
and she went round to peep at him as he lay in his
mother's arm, as yet his shield and guard.

"Sally says he will have black hair, she thinks,"
said Ruth. "His little hand is quite a man's, already.
Just feel how firmly he closes it"; and with her

own weak fingers she opened his little red fist, and
taking Miss Benson's reluctant hand, placed one of her
fingers in his grasp. That baby-touch called out her
love ; the doors of her heart were thrown open wide
for the little infant to go in and take possession.

"Ah, my darling !" said Ruth, falling back weak
and weary. "If God will but spare you to me, never
mother did more than I will. I have done you a
grievous wrong—but, if I may but live, I will spend
my life in serving you !"

"And in serving God !" said Miss Benson, with
tears in her eyes. "You must not make him into an
idol, or God will, perhaps, punish you through him."

A pang of affright shot through Ruth's heart at
these words ; had she already sinned and made her
child into an idol, and was there punishment already
in store for her through him ? But then the internal
voice whispered that God was "Our Father," and that
He knew our frame, and knew how natural was the
first outburst of a mother's love ; so, although she
treasured up the warning, she ceased to affright herself
for what had already gushed forth.

"Now go to sleep, Ruth," said Miss Benson, kissing
her, and darkening the room. But Ruth could not
sleep ; if her heavy eyes closed, she opened them again
with a start, for sleep seemed to be an enemy stealing
from her the consciousness of being a mother. That
one thought excluded all remembrance and all anticipation, in those first hours of delight.

But soon remembrance and anticipation came. Then
was the natural want of the person, who alone could
take an interest similar in kind, though not in amount,
to the mother's. And sadness grew like a giant in the
still watches of the night, when she remembered that
there would be no father to guide and strengthen the
child, and place him in a favourable position for fighting the hard "Battle of Life." She hoped and believed
that no one would know the sin of his parents, and
that that struggle might be spared to him. But a
father's powerful care and mighty guidance would

never be his; and then, in those hours of spiritual
purification, came the wonder and the doubt of how far
the real father would be the one to whom, with her
desire of heaven for her child, whatever might become
of herself, she would wish to entrust him. Slight
speeches, telling of a selfish, worldly nature, unnoticed at
the time, came back upon her ear, having a new significance. They told of a low standard, of impatient self-
indulgence, of no acknowledgment of things spiritual
and heavenly. Even while this examination was forced
upon her, by the new spirit of maternity that had
entered into her, and made her child's welfare supreme,
she hated and reproached herself for the necessity
there seemed upon her of examining and judging the
absent father of her child. And so the compelling
presence that had taken possession of her wearied her
into a kind of feverish slumber; in which she dreamt
that the innocent babe that lay by her side in soft
ruddy slumber had started up into man's growth, and,
instead of the pure and noble being whom she had
prayed to present as her child to "Our Father in
heaven," he was a repetition of his father; and, like
him, lured some maiden (who in her dream seemed
strangely like herself, only more utterly sad and
desolate even than she) into sin, and left her there to
even a worse fate than that of suicide. For Ruth
believed there was a worse. She dreamt she saw the
girl, wandering, lost; and that she saw her son in high
places, prosperous—but with more than blood on his
soul. She saw her son dragged down by the clinging
girl into some pit of horrors into which she dared not
look, but from whence his father's voice was heard,
crying aloud, that in his day and generation he had not
remembered the words of God, and that now he was
"tormented in this flame."* Then she started in sick
terror, and saw, by the dim rushlight, Sally, nodding
in an arm-chair by the fire; and felt her little soft
warm babe, nestled up against her breast, rocked by
her heart, which yet beat hard from the effects of the
evil dream. She dared not go to sleep again, but

prayed. And every time she prayed, she asked with a more complete wisdom, and a more utter and self-forgetting faith. Little child! thy angel was with God, and drew her nearer and nearer to Him, whose face is continually beheld by the angels of little children.

CHAPTER XVI

SALLY and Miss Benson took it in turns to sit up, or rather, they took it in turns to nod by the fire; for if Ruth was awake she lay very still in the moonlight calm of her sick bed. That time resembled a beautiful August evening, such as I have seen. The white snowy rolling mist covers up under its great sheet all trees and meadows, and tokens of earth; but it cannot rise high enough to shut out the heavens, which on such nights seem bending very near, and to be the only real and present objects; and so near, so real and present, did heaven, and eternity, and God seem to Ruth, as she lay encircling her mysterious holy child.

One night Sally found out she was not asleep.

"I'm a rare hand at talking folks to sleep," said she. "I'll try on thee, for thou must get strength by sleeping and eating. What must I talk to thee about, I wonder. Shall I tell thee a love story or a fairy story, such as I've telled Master Thurstan many a time and many a time, for all his father set his face again fairies, and called it vain talking; or shall I tell you the dinner I once cooked, when Mr Harding, as was Miss Faith's sweetheart, came unlooked for, and we'd nought in the house but a neck of mutton, out of which I made seven dishes, all with a different name?"

"Who was Mr Harding?" asked Ruth.

"Oh, he was a grand gentleman from Lunnon, as had seen Miss Faith, and been struck by her pretty looks when she was out on a visit, and came here to ask her to marry him. She said, 'No, she would never leave Master Thurstan, as could never marry';

but she pined a deal at after he went away. She kept up afore Master Thurstan, but I seed her fretting, though I never let on that I did, for I thought she'd soonest get over it and be thankful at after she'd the strength to do right. However, I've no business to be talking of Miss Benson's concerns. I'll tell you of my own sweethearts and welcome, or I'll tell you of the dinner, which was the grandest thing I ever did in my life, but I thought a Lunnoner should never think country folks knew nothing; and, my word! I puzzled him with his dinner. I'm doubting whether to this day he knows whether what he was eating was fish, flesh, or fowl. Shall I tell you how I managed?"

But Ruth said she would rather hear about Sally's sweethearts, much to the disappointment of the latter, who considered the dinner by far the greatest achievement.

"Well, you see, I don't know as I should call them sweethearts; for excepting John Rawson, who was shut up in the mad-house the next week, I never had what you may call a downright offer of marriage but once. But I had once; and so I may say I had a sweetheart. I was beginning to be afeared though, for one likes to be axed; that's but civility; and I remember, after I had turned forty, and afore Jeremiah Dickson had spoken, I began to think John Rawson had perhaps not been so very mad, and that I'd done ill to lightly his offer, as a madman's, if it was to be the only one I was ever to have; I don't mean as I'd have had him, but I thought, if it was to come o'er again, I'd speak respectful of him to folk, and say it were only his way to go about on all fours, but that he was a sensible man in most things. However, I'd had my laugh, and so had others, at my crazy lover, and it was late now to set him up as a Solomon. However, I thought it would be no bad thing to be tried again; but I little thought the trial would come when it did. You see, Saturday night is a leisure night in counting-houses and such-like places,

while it's the busiest of all for servants. Well! it was
a Saturday night, and I'd my baize apron on, and
the tails of my bed-gown pinned together behind,
down on my knees, pipeclaying the kitchen, when
a knock comes to the back door. 'Come in!' says
I; but it knocked again, as if it were too stately to
open the door for itself; so I got up, rather cross,
and opened the door; and there stood Jerry Dixon,
Mr Holt's head clerk; only he was not head clerk
then. So I stood, stopping up the door, fancying he
wanted to speak to master; but he kind of pushed
past me, and telling me summut about the weather (as
if I could not see it for myself), he took a chair, and
sat down by the oven. 'Cool and easy!' thought I;
meaning hisself, not his place, which I knew must be
pretty hot. Well! it seemed no use standing waiting
for my gentleman to go; not that he had much to say
either; but he kept twirling his hat round and round,
and smoothing the nap on't with the back of his hand.
So at last I squatted down to my work, and thinks I, I
shall be on my knees all ready if he puts up a prayer,
for I knew he was a Methodee by bringing-up, and had
only lately turned to master's way of thinking; and
them Methodees are terrible hands at unexpected
prayers when one least looks for 'em. I can't say I
like their way of taking one by surprise, as it were;
but then I'm a parish clerk's daughter, and could
never demean myself to dissenting fashions, always
save and except Master Thurstan's, bless him. However, I'd been caught once or twice unawares, so this
time I thought I'd be up to it, and I moved a dry
duster wherever I went, to kneel upon in case he
began when I were in a wet place. By and by I
thought, if the man would pray it would be a blessing,
for it would prevent his sending his eyes after me
wherever I went; for when they takes to praying they
shuts their eyes, and quivers th' lids in a queer kind o'
way—them Dissenters does. I can speak pretty plain
to you, for you're bred in the Church like mysel', and
must find it as out o' the way as I do to be among

dissenting folk.   God forbid I should speak disrespect-
ful of Master Thurstan and Miss Faith, though ; I
never think on them as Church or Dissenters, but just
as Christians.   But to come back to Jerry.   First, I
tried always to be cleaning at his back ; but when he
wheeled round, so as always to face me, I thought I'd
try a different game.   So, says I, ' Master Dixon, I ax
your pardon, but I must pipeclay under your chair.
Will you please to move ? '   Well, he moved ; and
by and by I was at him again with the same words ;
and at after that, again and again, till he were always
moving about wi' his chair behind him, like a snail as
carries its house on its back.   And the great gaupus
never seed that I were pipeclaying the same places
twice over.   At last I got desperate cross, he were so in
my way ; so I made two big crosses on the tails of his
brown coat ; for you see, whenever he went, up or
down, he drew out the tails of his coat from under
him, and stuck them through the bars of the chair ;
and flesh and blood could not resist pipeclaying them
for him ; and a pretty brushing he'd have, I reckon, to
get it off again.   Well ! at length he clears his throat
uncommon loud ; so I spreads my duster, and shuts
my eyes all ready ; but when nought comed of it, I
opened my eyes a little bit to see what he were about.
My word! if there he wasn't down on his knees right facing me, staring as hard as he could.   Well ! I thought it
would be hard work to stand that, if he made a long
ado ; so I shut my eyes again, and tried to think
serious, as became what I fancied were coming ; but,
forgive me ! but I thought why couldn't the fellow
go in and pray wi' Master Thurstan, as had always a
calm spirit ready for prayer, instead o' me, who had
my dresser to scour, let alone an apron to iron.   At
last he says, says he, ' Sally ! will you oblige me with
your hand ? '   So I thought it were, maybe, Methodee
fashion to pray hand in hand ; and I'll not deny but I
wished I'd washed it better after black-leading the
kitchen fire.   I thought I'd better tell him it were not
so clean as I could wish, so says I, ' Master Dixon, you

shall have it, and welcome, if I may just go and wash
'em first.'   But, says he, 'My dear Sally, dirty or
clean it's all the same to me, seeing I'm only speaking
in a figuring way.   What I'm asking on my bended
knees is, that you'd please to be so kind as to be my
wedded wife ; week after next will suit me, if it's
agreeable to you !'   My word ! I were up on my feet
in an instant !   It were odd now, weren't it?   I never
thought of taking the fellow, and getting married ; for
all, I'll not deny, I had been thinking it would be
agreeable to be axed.   But all at once, I couldn't
abide the chap.   'Sir,' says I, trying to look shame-
faced as became the occasion, but for all that, feeling
a twittering round my mouth that I were afeard might
end in a laugh—'Master Dixon, I'm obleeged to you
for the compliment, and thank ye all the same, but I
think I'd prefer a single life.'   He looked mighty taken
aback ; but in a minute he cleared up, and was as sweet
as ever.   He still kept on his knees, and I wished he'd
take himself up; but, I reckon, he thought it would give
force to his words; says he, 'Think again, my dear Sally.
I've a four-roomed house, and furniture conformable ;
and eighty pound a year.   You may never have such a
chance again.'   There were truth enough in that, but it
was not pretty in the man to say it ; and it put me up
a bit.   'As for that, neither you nor I can tell, Master
Dixon.   You're not the first chap as I've had down on
his knees afore me, axing me to marry him (you see I
were thinking of John Rawson, only I thought there
were no need to say he were on all fours—it were
truth he were on his knees, you know), and maybe you'll not be the last.   Anyhow, I've no wish
to change my condition just now.'   'I'll wait till
Christmas,' says he.   'I've a pig as will be ready for
killing then, so I must get married before that.'   Well
now ! would you believe it ? the pig were a temptation.
I'd a receipt for curing hams, as Miss Faith would
never let me try, saying the old way were good enough.
However, I resisted.   Says I, very stern, because I felt
I'd been wavering, 'Master Dixon, once for all, pig or

no pig, I'll not marry you. And if you'll take my
advice, you'll get up off your knees. The flags is but
damp yet, and it would be an awkward thing to have
rheumatiz just before winter.' With that he got up,
stiff enough. He looked as sulky a chap as ever I
clapped eyes on. And as he were so black and cross,
I thought I'd done well (whatever came of the pig) to
say 'No' to him. 'You may live to repent this,' says
he, very red. 'But I'll not be too hard upon ye, I'll
give you another chance. I'll let you have the night to
think about it, and I'll just call in to hear your second
thoughts, after chapel to-morrow.' Well now! did
ever you hear the like? But that is the way with all
of them men, thinking so much of theirselves, and that
it's but ask and have. They've never had me, though;
and I shall be sixty-one next Martinmas, so there's not
much time left for them to try me, I reckon. Well!
when Jeremiah said that, he put me up more than ever,
and I says, 'My first thoughts, second thoughts, and
third thoughts is all one and the same; you've but
tempted me once, and that was when you spoke of your
pig. But of yoursel' you're nothing to boast on, and
so I'll bid you good night, and I'll keep my manners,
or else, if I told the truth, I should say it had been a
great loss of time listening to you. But I'll be civil—
so good-night.' He never said a word, but went off as
black as thunder, slamming the door after him. The
master called me in to prayers, but I can't say I could
put my mind to them, for my heart was beating so.
However, it was a comfort to have had an offer of holy
matrimony; and though it flustered me, it made me
think more of myself. In the night, I began to wonder
if I'd not been cruel and hard to him. You see, I were
feverish-like; and the old song of Barbary Allen*would
keep running in my head, and I thought I were
Barbary, and he were young Jemmy Gray, and that
maybe he'd die for love of me; and I pictured him to
mysel', lying on his death-bed, with his face turned to
the wall, 'wi' deadly sorrow sighing,' and I could ha'
pinched mysel' for having been so like cruel Barbary

Allen. And when I got up next day, I found it hard to think on the real Jerry Dixon I had seen the night before, apart from the sad and sorrowful Jerry I thought on a-dying, when I were between sleeping and waking. And for many a day I turned sick, when I heard the passing bell, for I thought it were the bell loud-knelling which were to break my heart wi' a sense of what I'd missed in saying 'No' to Jerry, and so killing him with cruelty. But in less than a three week, I heard parish bells a-ringing merrily for a wedding; and in the course of a morning, some one says to me, 'Hark! how the bells is ringing for Jerry Dixon's wedding!' And, all on a sudden, he changed back again from a heart-broken young fellow, like Jemmy Gray, into a stout, middle-aged man, ruddy complexioned, with a wart on his left cheek like life!"

She waited for some exclamation at the conclusion of her tale; but receiving none, she stepped softly to the bedside, and there lay Ruth, peaceful as death, with her baby on her breast.

"I thought I'd lost some of my gifts if I could not talk a body to sleep," said Sally, in a satisfied and self-complacent tone.

Youth is strong and powerful, and makes a hard battle against sorrow. So Ruth strove and strengthened, and her baby flourished accordingly; and before the little celandines were out on the hedge-banks, or the white violets had sent forth their fragrance from the border under the south wall of Miss Benson's small garden, Ruth was able to carry her baby into that sheltered place on sunny days.

She often wished to thank Mr Benson and his sister, but she did not know how to tell the deep gratitude she felt, and therefore she was silent. But they understood her silence well. One day, as she watched her sleeping child, she spoke to Miss Benson, with whom she happened to be alone.

"Do you know of any cottage where the people are clean, and where they would not mind taking me in?" asked she.

"Taking you in! What do you mean?" said Miss Benson, dropping her knitting, in order to observe Ruth more closely.

"I mean," said Ruth, "where I might lodge with my baby—any very poor place would do, only it must be clean, or he might be ill."

"And what in the world do you want to go and lodge in a cottage for?" said Miss Benson, indignantly.

Ruth did not lift up her eyes, but she spoke with a firmness which showed that she had considered the subject.

"I think I could make dresses. I know I did not learn as much as I might, but perhaps I might do for servants, and people who are not particular."

"Servants are as particular as any one," said Miss Benson, glad to lay hold of the first objection that she could.

"Well! somebody who would be patient with me," said Ruth.

"Nobody is patient over an ill-fitting gown," put in Miss Benson. "There's the stuff spoilt, and what not?"

"Perhaps I could find plain work to do," said Ruth, very meekly. "That I can do very well; mamma taught me, and I liked to learn from her. If you would be so good, Miss Benson, you might tell people I could do plain work very neatly, and punctually, and cheaply."

"You'd get sixpence a day, perhaps," said Miss Benson, "and who would take care of baby, I should like to know? Prettily he'd be neglected, would not he? Why, he'd have the croup and the typhus fever in no time, and be burnt to ashes after."

"I have thought of all. Look how he sleeps! Hush, darling," for just at this point he began to cry, and to show his determination to be awake, as if in contradiction to his mother's words. Ruth took him up, and carried him about the room while she went on speaking.

"Yes, just now I know he will not sleep; but very often he will, and in the night he always does."

"And so you'd work in the night and kill yourself, and leave your poor baby an orphan. Ruth! I'm ashamed of you. Now brother " (Mr Benson had just come in), "is not this too bad of Ruth; here she is planning to go away and leave us, just as we—as I, at least, have grown so fond of baby, and he's beginning to know me."

"Where were you thinking of going to, Ruth?" interrupted Mr Benson, with mild surprise.

"Anywhere to be near you and Miss Benson; in any poor cottage where I might lodge very cheaply, and earn my livelihood by taking in plain sewing, and perhaps a little dressmaking; and where I could come and see you and dear Miss Benson sometimes and bring baby."

"If he was not dead before then of some fever, or burn, or scald, poor neglected child; or you had not worked yourself to death with never sleeping," said Miss Benson.

Mr Benson thought a minute or two, and then he spoke to Ruth.

"Whatever you may do when this little fellow is a year old, and able to dispense with some of a mother's care, let me beg you, Ruth, as a favour to me—as a still greater favour to my sister, is it not, Faith?"

"Yes; you may put it so if you like."

"To stay with us," continued he, "till then. When baby is twelve months old, we'll talk about it again, and very likely before then some opening may be shown us. Never fear leading an idle life, Ruth. We'll treat you as a daughter, and set you all the household tasks; and it is not for your sake that we ask you to stay, but for this little dumb helpless child's; and it is not for our sake that you must stay, but for his."

Ruth was sobbing.

"I do not deserve your kindness," said she, in a broken voice; "I do not deserve it."

Her tears fell fast and soft like summer rain, but no further word was spoken. Mr Benson quietly passed on to make the inquiry for which he had entered the room.

But when there was nothing to decide upon, and no necessity for entering upon any new course of action, Ruth's mind relaxed from its strung-up state. She fell into trains of reverie, and mournful regretful recollections which rendered her languid and tearful. This was noticed both by Miss Benson and Sally, and as each had keen sympathies, and felt depressed when they saw anyone near them depressed, and as each, without much reasoning on the cause or reason for such depression, felt irritated at the uncomfortable state into which they themselves were thrown, they both resolved to speak to Ruth on the next fitting occasion.

Accordingly, one afternoon—the morning of that day had been spent by Ruth in housework, for she had insisted on Mr Benson's words, and had taken Miss Benson's share of the more active and fatiguing household duties, but she went through them heavily, and as if her heart was far away—in the afternoon when she was nursing her child, Sally, on coming into the back parlour, found her there alone, and easily detected the fact that she had been crying.

"Where's Miss Benson?" said Sally, gruffly.

"Gone out with Mr Benson," answered Ruth, with an absent sadness in her voice and manner. Her tears, scarce checked while she spoke, began to fall afresh; and as Sally stood and gazed she saw the babe look back in his mother's face, and his little lip begin to quiver, and his open blue eye to grow over-clouded, as with some mysterious sympathy with the sorrowful face bent over him. Sally took him briskly from his mother's arms; Ruth looked up in grave surprise, for in truth she had forgotten Sally's presence, and the suddenness of the motion startled her.

"My bonny boy! are they letting the salt tears drop on thy sweet face before thou'rt weaned! Little somebody knows how to be a mother—I could make a better myself. 'Dance, thumbkin, dance—dance, ye merry men every one.' Aye, that's it! smile, my pretty. Any one but a child like thee," continued

she, turning to Ruth, " would have known better than
to bring ill-luck on thy babby by letting tears fall on
its face before it was weaned.   But thou'rt not fit to
have a babby, and so I've said many a time. I've a great
mind to buy thee a doll, and take thy babby mysel'."

Sally did not look at Ruth, for she was too much
engaged in amusing the baby with the tassel of the
string to the window-blind, or else she would have
seen the dignity which the mother's soul put into
Ruth at that moment.   Sally was quelled into silence
by the gentle composure, the self-command over her
passionate sorrow, which gave to Ruth an unconscious
grandeur of demeanour as she came up to the old
servant.

"Give him back to me, please. I did not know it
brought ill-luck, or if my heart broke I would not
have let a tear drop on his face—I never will again.
Thank you, Sally," as the servant relinquished him to
her who came in the name of a mother. Sally watched
Ruth's grave, sweet smile, as she followed up Sally's
play with the tassel, and imitated, with all the docility
inspired by love, every movement and sound which
had amused her babe.

" Thou'lt be a mother, after all," said Sally, with a
kind of admiration of the control which Ruth was exercising over herself. " But why talk of thy heart
breaking?   I don't question thee about what's past
and gone ; but now thou'rt wanting for nothing, nor
thy child either ; the time to come is the Lord's, and
in His hands ; and yet thou goest about a-sighing and
a-moaning in a way that I can't stand or thole."*

" What do I do wrong?" said Ruth ; " I try to do
all I can."

" Yes, in a way," said Sally, puzzled to know how
to describe her meaning.   " Thou dost it—but there's
a right and a wrong way of setting about everything—
and to my thinking, the right way is to take a thing up
heartily, if it is only making a bed. Why ! dear ah
me, making a bed may be done after a Christian fashion,
I take it, or else what's to come of such as me in heaven,

who've had little enough time on earth for clapping
ourselves down on our knees for set prayers? When
I was a girl, and wretched enough about Master Thurstan, and the crook on his back which came of the fall
I gave him, I took to praying and sighing, and giving
up the world; and I thought it were wicked to care
for the flesh, so I made heavy puddings, and was careless about dinner and the rooms, and thought I was
doing my duty, though I did call myself a miserable
sinner. But one night, the old missus (Master Thurstan's mother) came in, and sat down by me, as I was
a-scolding myself, without thinking of what I was saying; and, says she, 'Sally! what are you blaming
yourself about, and groaning over? We hear you in
the parlour every night, and it makes my heart ache.'
'Oh, ma'am,' says I, 'I'm a miserable sinner, and I'm
travailing in the new birth.' 'Was that the reason,'
says she, 'why the pudding was so heavy to-day?'
'Oh, ma'am, ma'am,' said I, 'if you would not think
of the things of the flesh, but trouble yourself about
your immortal soul.' And I sat a-shaking my head to
think about her soul. 'But,' says she, in her sweet-
dropping voice, 'I do try to think of my soul every
hour of the day, if by that you mean trying to do the
will of God, but we'll talk now about the pudding;
Master Thurstan could not eat it, and I know you'll
be sorry for that.' Well! I was sorry, but I didn't
choose to say so, as she seemed to expect me; so says
I, 'It's a pity to see children brought up to care for
things of the flesh'; and then I could have bitten my
tongue out, for the missus looked so grave, and I
thought of my darling little lad pining for want of his
food. At last, says she, 'Sally, do you think God has
put us into the world just to be selfish, and do nothing
but see after our own souls? or to help one another
with heart and hand, as Christ did to all who wanted
help?' I was silent, for, you see, she puzzled me. So
she went on, 'What is that beautiful answer in your
Church catechism, Sally?' I were pleased to hear a
Dissenter, as I did not think would have done it, speak

so knowledgably about the catechism, and she went
on : 'to do my duty in that station of life unto which
it shall please God to call me' ;*well, your station is a
servant, and it is as honourable as a king's, if you look
at it right ; you are to help and serve others in one way,
just as a king is to help others in another. Now what
way are you to help and serve, or to do your duty, in
that station of life unto which it has pleased God to
call you? Did it answer God's purpose, and serve Him,
when the food was unfit for a child to eat, and un-
wholesome for any one?' Well! I would not give it
up, I was so pig-headed about my soul; so says I, 'I
wish folks would be content with locusts and wild
honey, and leave other folks in peace to work out their
salvation'; and I groaned out pretty loud to think of
missus's soul. I often think since she smiled a bit at
me ; but she said, 'Well, Sally, to-morrow, you shall
have time to work out your salvation ; but as we have
no locusts in England, and I don't think they'd agree
with Master Thurstan if we had, I will come and make
the pudding ; but I shall try and do it well, not only
for him to like it, but because everything may be done
in a right way or a wrong ; the right way is to do it as
well as we can, as in God's sight ; the wrong is to do it
in a self-seeking spirit, which either leads us to neglect
it to follow out some device of our own for our own
ends, or to give up too much time and thought to it
both before and after the doing.' Well! I thought of
all old missus's words this morning, when I saw you
making the beds. You sighed so, you could not half
shake the pillows ; your heart was not in your work ;
and yet it was the duty God had set you, I reckon ;
I know it's not the work parsons preach about ; though
I don't think they go so far off the mark when they
read, 'whatsoever thy hand findeth to do, that do with
all thy might.' Just try for a day to think of all the
odd jobs as has to be done well and truly as in God's
sight, not just slurred over anyhow, and you'll go
through them twice as cheerfully, and have no thought
to spare for sighing or crying."

Sally bustled off to set on the kettle for tea, and felt half ashamed, in the quiet of the kitchen, to think of the oration she had made in the parlour. But she saw with much satisfaction, that henceforward Ruth nursed her boy with a vigour and cheerfulness that were reflected back from him; and the household work was no longer performed with a languid indifference, as if life and duty were distasteful. Miss Benson had her share in this improvement, though Sally placidly took all the credit to herself. One day as she and Ruth sat together, Miss Benson spoke of the child, and thence went on to talk about her own childhood. By degrees they spoke of education, and the book-learning that forms one part of it; and the result was that Ruth determined to get up early all through the bright summer mornings, to acquire the knowledge hereafter to be given to her child. Her mind was uncultivated, her reading scant; beyond the mere mechanical arts of education she knew nothing; but she had a refined taste, and excellent sense and judgement to separate the true from the false. With these qualities, she set to work under Mr Benson's directions. She read in the early morning the books that he marked out; she trained herself with strict perseverance to do all thoroughly; she did not attempt to acquire any foreign language, although her ambition was to learn Latin, in order to teach it to her boy. Those summer mornings were happy, for she was learning neither to look backwards nor forwards, but to live faithfully and earnestly in the present. She rose while the hedge-sparrow was yet singing his *réveillé* to his mate; she dressed and opened her window, shading the soft-blowing air and the sunny eastern light from her baby. If she grew tired, she went and looked at him, and all her thoughts were holy prayers for him. Then she would gaze a while out of the high upper window on to the moorlands, that swelled in waves one behind the other, in the grey, cool morning light. These were her occasional relaxations, and after them she returned with strength to her work.

CHAPTER XVII

IN that body of Dissenters to which Mr Benson belonged,* it is not considered necessary to baptize
infants as early as the ceremony can be performed ;
and many circumstances concurred to cause the solemn
thanksgiving and dedication of the child (for so these
Dissenters look upon christenings) to be deferred until
it was probably somewhere about six months old.
There had been many conversations in the little sitting-
room between the brother and sister and their *protegée*,
which had consisted more of questions betraying a
thoughtful wondering kind of ignorance on the part
of Ruth, and answers more suggestive than explanatory from Mr Benson ; while Miss Benson kept up a
kind of running commentary, always simple and often
quaint, but with that intuition into the very heart of
all things truly religious which is often the gift of those
who seem, at first sight, to be only affectionate and
sensible. When Mr Benson had explained his own
views of what a christening ought to be considered,
and, by calling out Ruth's latent feelings into pious
earnestness, brought her into a right frame of mind,
he felt that he had done what he could to make the
ceremony more than a mere form, and to invest it,
quiet, humble, and obscure as it must necessarily be in
outward shape—mournful and anxious as much of its
antecedents had rendered it—with the severe grandeur
of an act done in faith and truth.

It was not far to carry the little one, for, as I said,
the chapel almost adjoined the minister's house. The
whole procession was to have consisted of Mr and Miss
Benson, Ruth carrying her baby, and Sally, who felt
herself, as a Church-of-England woman, to be condescending and kind in requesting leave to attend a
baptism among "them Dissenters" ; but unless she
had asked permission, she would not have been
desired to attend, so careful was the habit of her
master and mistress that she should be allowed that

freedom which they claimed for themselves. But they
were glad she wished to go; they liked the feeling
that all were of one household, and that the interests
of one were the interests of all. It produced a consequence, however, which they did not anticipate. Sally
was full of the event which her presence was to
sanction, and, as it were, to redeem from the character
of being utterly schismatic; she spoke about it with an
air of patronage to three or four, and among them to
some of the servants at Mr Bradshaw's.

Miss Benson was rather surprised to receive a call
from Jemima Bradshaw, on the very morning of the
day on which little Leonard was to be baptized; Miss
Bradshaw was rosy and breathless with eagerness.
Although the second in the family, she had been at
school when her younger sisters had been christened,
and she was now come, in the full warmth of a girl's
fancy to ask if she might be present at the afternoon's
service. She had been struck with Mrs Denbigh's
grace and beauty at the very first sight, when she had
accompanied her mother to call upon the Bensons on
their return from Wales; and had kept up an enthusiastic interest in the widow only a little older than
herself, whose very reserve and retirement but added
to her unconscious power of enchantment.

"Oh, Miss Benson! I never saw a christening; papa
says I may go, if you think Mr Benson and Mrs
Denbigh would not dislike it; and I will be quite
quiet, and sit up behind the door, or anywhere; and
that sweet little baby! I should so like to see him
christened; is he to be called Leonard, did you say?
After Mr Denbigh, is it?"

"No—not exactly," said Miss Benson, rather discomfited.

"Was not Mr Denbigh's name Leonard, then?
Mamma thought it would be sure to be called after
him, and so did I. But I may come to the christening, may I not, dear Miss Benson?"

Miss Benson gave her consent with a little inward
reluctance. Both her brother and Ruth shared in this

feeling, although no one expressed it ; and it was
presently forgotten.

Jemima stood grave and quiet in the old-fashioned
vestry adjoining the chapel, as they entered with steps
subdued to slowness. She thought Ruth looked so
pale and awed because she was left a solitary parent ;
but Ruth came to the presence of God, as one who had
gone astray, and doubted her own worthiness to be
called His child ; she came as a mother who had
incurred a heavy responsibility, and who entreated
His almighty aid to enable her to discharge it ;
full of passionate, yearning love which craved for
more faith in God, to still her distrust and fear of
the future that might hang over her darling. When
she thought of her boy, she sickened and trembled ;
but when she heard of God's loving kindness, far
beyond all tender mother's love, she was hushed into
peace and prayer.   There she stood, her fair pale
cheek resting on her baby's head, as he slumbered
on her bosom ; her eyes went slanting down under
their half-closed white lids ; but their gaze was not on
the primitive cottage-like room, it was earnestly fixed
on a dim mist, through which she fain would have seen
the life that lay before her child ; but the mist was
still and dense, too thick a veil for anxious human
love to penetrate.   The future was hid with God.

Mr Benson stood right under the casement window
that was placed high up in the room ; he was almost in
shade, except for one or two marked lights which fell on
hair already silvery white ; his voice was always low
and musical when he spoke to few ; it was too weak to
speak so as to be heard by many without becoming
harsh and strange ; but now it filled the little room
with a loving sound, like the stock-dove's brooding
murmur over her young. He and Ruth forgot all in
their earnestness of thought ; and when he said " Let
us pray," and the little congregation knelt down, you
might have heard the baby's faint breathing, scarcely
sighing out upon the stillness, so absorbed were all in
the solemnity.   But the prayer was long ; thought

followed thought, and fear crowded upon fear, and
all were to be laid bare before God, and His aid and
counsel asked.   Before the end Sally had shuffled
quietly out of the vestry into the green chapel-yard,
upon which the door opened. Miss Benson was alive
to this movement, and so full of curiosity as to what it
might mean that she could no longer attend to her
brother, and felt inclined to rush off and question
Sally the moment all was ended.   Miss Bradshaw
hung about the babe and Ruth, and begged to be
allowed to carry the child home, but Ruth pressed him
to her, as if there was no safe harbour for him but in
his mother's breast. Mr Benson saw her feeling, and
caught Miss Bradshaw's look of disappointment.

"Come home with us," said he, "and stay to tea.
You have never drank tea with us since you went to
school."

"I wish I might," said Miss Bradshaw, colouring
with pleasure. "But I must ask papa. May I run
home, and ask?"

"To be sure, my dear!"

Jemima flew off; and fortunately her father was at
home; for her mother's permission would have been
deemed insufficient. She received many directions
about her behaviour.

"Take no sugar in your tea, Jemima. I am sure
the Bensons ought not to be able to afford sugar, with
their means. And do not eat much; you can have
plenty at home on your return; remember Mrs Denbigh's keep must cost them a great deal."

So Jemima returned considerably sobered, and very
much afraid of her hunger leading her to forget Mr
Benson's poverty. Meanwhile Miss Benson and Sally,
acquainted with Mr Benson's invitation to Jemima,
set about making some capital tea-cakes on which they
piqued themselves. They both enjoyed the offices of
hospitality; and were glad to place some home-made
tempting dainty before their guests.

"What made ye leave the chapel-vestry before my
brother had ended?" inquired Miss Benson.

"Indeed, ma'am, I thought master had prayed so long he'd be drouthy. So I just slipped out to put on the kettle for tea."

Miss Benson was on the point of reprimanding her for thinking of anything besides the object of the prayer, when she remembered how she herself had been unable to attend after Sally's departure for wondering what had become of her; so she was silent.

It was a disappointment to Miss Benson's kind and hospitable expectation when Jemima, as hungry as a hound, confined herself to one piece of the cake which her hostess had had such pleasure in making. And Jemima wished she had not a prophetic feeling all tea-time of the manner in which her father would inquire into the particulars of the meal, elevating his eyebrows at every viand named beyond plain bread-and-butter, and winding up with some such sentence as this: "Well, I marvel how, with Benson's salary, he can afford to keep such a table." Sally could have told of self-denial when no one was by, when the left hand did not know what the right hand did, on the part of both her master and mistress, practised without thinking even to themselves that it was either a sacrifice or a virtue, in order to enable them to help those who were in need, or even to gratify Miss Benson's kind, old-fashioned feelings on such occasions as the present, when a stranger came to the house. Her homely, affectionate pleasure in making others comfortable, might have shown that such little occasional extrava-gances were not waste, but a good work; and were not to be gauged by the standard of money spending. This evening her spirits were damped by Jemima's refusal to eat. Poor Jemima! the cakes were so good, and she was so hungry; but still she refused.

While Sally was clearing away the tea-things, Miss Benson and Jemima accompanied Ruth upstairs, when she went to put little Leonard to bed.

"A christening is a very solemn service," said Miss Bradshaw; "I had no idea it was so solemn. Mr

Benson seemed to speak as if he had a weight of care on his heart that God alone could relieve or lighten."

"My brother feels these things very much," said Miss Benson, rather wishing to cut short the conversation, for she had been aware of several parts in the prayer which she knew were suggested by the peculiarity and sadness of the case before him.

"I could not quite follow him all through," continued Jemima; "what did he mean by saying, 'This child, rebuked by the world and bidden to stand apart, thou wilt not rebuke, but wilt suffer it to come to thee and be blessed with thine almighty blessing?' Why is this little darling to be rebuked? I do not think I remember the exact words, but he said something like that."

"My dear! your gown is dripping wet! it must have dipped into the tub; let me wring it out."

"Oh, thank you! Never mind my gown!" said Jemima, hastily, and wanting to return to her question; but just then she caught the sight of tears falling fast down the cheeks of the silent Ruth as she bent over her child, crowing and splashing away in his tub. With a sudden consciousness that unwittingly she had touched on some painful chord, Jemima rushed into another subject, and was eagerly seconded by Miss Benson. The circumstance seemed to die away, and leave no trace; but in after-years it rose, vivid and significant, before Jemima's memory. At present it was enough for her, if Mrs Denbigh would let her serve her in every possible way. Her admiration for beauty was keen, and little indulged at home; and Ruth was very beautiful in her quiet mournfulness; her mean and homely dress left her herself only the more open to admiration, for she gave it a charm by her unconscious wearing of it that made it seem like the drapery of an old Greek statue—subordinate to the figure it covered, yet imbued by it with an unspeakable grace. Then the pretended circumstances of her life were such as to catch the imagination of a young romantic girl. Altogether, Jemima could have kissed her hand and professed herself Ruth's slave. She moved away all the articles used at this little *coucher*;* she folded up Leonard's day-clothes; she felt only too much honoured when Ruth trusted him to her for a few minutes—only too amply rewarded when Ruth thanked her with a grave, sweet smile, and a grateful look of her loving eyes.

When Jemima had gone away with the servant who was sent to fetch her, there was a little chorus of praise.

"She's a warm-hearted girl," said Miss Benson. "She remembers all the old days before she went to school. She is worth two of Mr Richard. They're each of them just the same as they were when they were children, when they broke that window in the chapel, and he ran away home, and she came knocking at our door, with a single knock, just like a beggar's, and I went to see who it was, and was quite startled to see her round, brown, honest face looking up at me, half-frightened, and telling me what she had done, and offering me the money in her savings bank to pay for it. We never should have heard of Master Richard's share in the business if it had not been for Sally."

"But remember," said Mr Benson, "how strict Mr Bradshaw has always been with his children. It is no wonder if poor Richard was a coward in those days."

"He is now, or I'm much mistaken," answered Miss Benson. "And Mr Bradshaw was just as strict with Jemima, and she's no coward. But I've no faith in Richard. He has a look about him that I don't like. And when Mr Bradshaw was away on business in Holland last year, for those months my young gentleman did not come half as regularly to chapel, and I always believe that story of his being seen out with the hounds at Smithiles."

"Those are neither of them great offences in a young man of twenty," said Mr Benson, smiling.

"No! I don't mind them in themselves; but when he could change back so easily to being regular and mim when his father came home, I don't like that."

"Leonard shall never be afraid of me," said Ruth,

following her own train of thought. " I will be his
friend from the very first; and I will try and learn
how to be a wise friend, and you will teach me,
won't you, sir?"

" What made you wish to call him Leonard, Ruth?"
asked Miss Benson.

" It was my mother's father's name ; and she used
to tell me about him and his goodness, and I thought
if Leonard could be like him——"

" Do you remember the discussion there was about
Miss Bradshaw's name, Thurstan? Her father wanting her to be called Hepzibah, but insisting that she
was to have a Scripture name at any rate ; and Mrs
Bradshaw wanting her to be Juliana, after some novel
she had read not long before ; and at last Jemima
was fixed upon, because it would do either for a
Scripture name or a name for a heroine out of a
book."

" I did not know Jemima was a Scripture name,"
said Ruth.

" Oh yes, it is. One of Job's daughters ; Jemima,
Kezia, and Keren-Happuch.* There are a good many
Jemimas in the world, and some Kezias, but I never
heard of a Keren-Happuch ; and yet we know just
as much of one as of another. People really like
a pretty name, whether in Scripture or out of it."

" When there is no particular association with the
name," said Mr Benson.

" Now, I was called Faith after the cardinal virtue ;
and I like my name, though many people would think
it too Puritan ; that was according to our gentle
mother's pious desire. And Thurstan was called by
his name because my father wished it ; for, although
he was what people called a radical and a democrat
in his ways of talking and thinking, he was very
proud in his heart of being descended from some
old Sir Thurstan, who figured away in the French
wars."

" The difference between theory and practice, thinking and being," put in Mr Benson, who was in a

mood for allowing himself a little social enjoyment.
He leant back in his chair, with his eyes looking at,
but not seeing the ceiling. Miss Benson was clicking
away with her eternal knitting-needles, looking at
her brother, and seeing him, too. Ruth was arranging her child's clothes against the morrow. It was
but their usual way of spending an evening; the
variety was given by the different tone which the
conversation assumed on the different nights. Yet,
somehow, the peacefulness of the time, the window
open into the little garden, the scents that came
stealing in, and the clear summer heaven above, made
the time be remembered as a happy festival by Ruth.
Even Sally seemed more placid than usual when she
came in to prayers; and she and Miss Benson followed
Ruth to her bedroom, to look at the beautiful sleeping
Leonard.

"God bless him!" said Miss Benson, stooping down
to kiss his little dimpled hand, which lay outside
the coverlet, tossed abroad in the heat of the evening.

"Now, don't get up too early, Ruth! Injuring
your health will be short-sighted wisdom, and poor
economy. Good night!"

"Good night, dear Miss Benson. Good night,
Sally." When Ruth had shut her door, she went
again to the bed, and looked at her boy till her eyes
filled with tears.

"God bless thee, darling! I only ask to be one
of His instruments, and not thrown aside as useless—
or worse than useless."

So ended the day of Leonard's christening.

Mr Benson had sometimes taught the children of
different people as an especial favour, when requested
by them. But then his pupils were only children,
and by their progress he was little prepared for Ruth's.
She had had early teaching, of that kind which need
never be unlearnt, from her mother; enough to un-
fold many of her powers; they had remained inactive
now for several years, but had grown strong in the
dark and quiet time. Her tutor was surprised at the

bounds by which she surmounted obstacles, the quick
perception and ready adaptation of truths and first
principles, and her immediate sense of the fitness of
things. Her delight in what was strong and beautiful called out her master's sympathy; but, most of
all, he admired the complete unconsciousness of uncommon power, or unusual progress. It was less of
a wonder than he considered it to be, it is true, for
she never thought of comparing what she was now
with her former self, much less with another. Indeed, she did not think of herself at all, but of her
boy, and what she must learn in order to teach him
to be and to do as suited her hope and her prayer.
If anyone's devotion could have flattered her into
self-consciousness, it was Jemima's. Mr Bradshaw
never dreamed that his daughter could feel herself
inferior to the minister's *protegée*, but so it was; and
no knight-errant of old could consider himself more
honoured by his ladye's commands than did Jemima,
if Ruth allowed her to do anything for her or for her
boy. Ruth loved her heartily, even while she was
rather annoyed at the open expressions Jemima used
of admiration.

"Please, I really would rather not be told if people
do think me pretty."

"But it was not merely beautiful; it was sweet-
looking and good, Mrs Postlethwaite called you,"
replied Jemima.

"All the more I would rather not hear it. I may
be pretty, but I know I am not good. Besides, I
don't think we ought to hear what is said of us behind
our backs."

Ruth spoke so gravely, that Jemima feared lest she
was displeased.

"Dear Mrs Denbigh, I never will admire or praise
you again. Only let me love you."

"And let me love you!" said Ruth, with a tender
kiss.

Jemima would not have been allowed to come so
frequently if Mr Bradshaw had not been possessed with

the idea of patronizing Ruth. If the latter had
chosen, she might have gone dressed from head to
foot in the presents which he wished to make her, but
she refused them constantly; occasionally to Miss
Benson's great annoyance. But if he could not load
her with gifts, he could show his approbation by asking
her to his house; and after some deliberation, she
consented to accompany Mr and Miss Benson there.
The house was square and massy-looking, with a great
deal of drab-colour about the furniture. Mrs Bradshaw,
in her lackadaisical, sweet-tempered way, seconded
her husband in his desire of being kind to Ruth; and
as she cherished privately a great taste for what was
beautiful or interesting, as opposed to her husband's
love of the purely useful, this taste of hers had rarely
had so healthy and true a mode of gratification as
when she watched Ruth's movements about the room,
which seemed in its unobtrusiveness and poverty of
colour to receive the requisite ornament of light and
splendour from Ruth's presence. Mrs Bradshaw
sighed, and wished she had a daughter as lovely, about
whom to weave a romance; for castle-building, after
the manner of the Minerva press,* was the outlet by
which she escaped from the pressure of her prosaic
life, as Mr Bradshaw's wife. Her perception was only
of external beauty, and she was not always alive to
that, or she might have seen how a warm, affectionate,
ardent nature, free from all envy or carking care of
self, gave an unspeakable charm to her plain, bright-
faced daughter Jemima, whose dark eyes kept challenging admiration for her friend. The first evening
spent at Mr Bradshaw's passed like many succeeding
visits there. There was tea, the equipage for which
was as handsome and as ugly as money could purchase.
Then the ladies produced their sewing, while Mr
Bradshaw stood before the fire, and gave the assembled
party the benefit of his opinions on many subjects.
The opinions were as good and excellent as the
opinions of any man can be who sees one side of a case
very strongly, and almost ignores the other. They

coincided in many points with those held by Mr
Benson, but he once or twice interposed with a plea
for those who might differ ; and then he was heard by
Mr Bradshaw with a kind of evident and indulgent
pity, such as one feels for a child who unwittingly
talks nonsense. By and by, Mrs Bradshaw and Miss
Benson fell into one *téte à téte*, and Ruth and Jemima
into another. Two well-behaved but unnaturally
quiet children were sent to bed early in the evening,
in an authoritative voice, by their father, because one
of them had spoken too loud while he was enlarging on
an alteration in the tariff. Just before the supper-
tray was brought in, a gentleman was announced whom
Ruth had never previously seen, but who appeared
well known to the rest of the party. It was Mr
Farquhar, Mr Bradshaw's partner ; he had been on the
Continent for the last year, and had only recently
returned. He seemed perfectly at home, but spoke
little. He leaned back in his chair, screwed up his
eyes, and watched everybody ; yet there was nothing
unpleasant or impertinent in his keenness of observation. Ruth wondered to hear him contradict Mr
Bradshaw, and almost expected some rebuff, but Mr
Bradshaw, if he did not yield the point, admitted, for
the first time that evening, that it was possible something might be said on the other side. Mr Farquhar
differed also from Mr Benson, but it was in a more
respectful manner than Mr Bradshaw had done.
For these reasons, although Mr Farquhar had never
spoken to Ruth, she came away with the impression
that he was a man to be respected, and perhaps
liked.

Sally would have thought herself mightily aggrieved
if, on their return, she had not heard some account of
the evening. As soon as Miss Benson came in, the
old servant began :

" Well, and who was there ? and what did they give
you for supper ? "

"Only Mr Farquhar besides ourselves ; and sand-
wiches, sponge-cake, and wine ; there was no occasion

for anything more," replied Miss Benson, who was tired and preparing to go upstairs.

"Mr Farquhar! Why they do say he's thinking of Miss Jemima!"

"Nonsense, Sally! why he's old enough to be her father!" said Miss Benson, half way up the first flight.

"There's no need for it to be called nonsense, though he may be ten year older," muttered Sally, retreating towards the kitchen. "Bradshaw's Betsy knows what she's about, and wouldn't have said it for nothing."

Ruth wondered a little about it. She loved Jemima well enough to be interested in what related to her; but, after thinking for a few minutes, she decided that such a marriage was, and would ever be, very unlikely.

CHAPTER XVIII

ONE afternoon, not long after this, Mr and Miss Benson set off to call upon a farmer, who attended the chapel, but lived at some distance from the town. They intended to stay to tea if they were invited, and Ruth and Sally were left to spend a long afternoon together. At first, Sally was busy in her kitchen, and Ruth employed herself in carrying her baby out into the garden. It was now nearly a year since she came to the Benson's; it seemed like yesterday, and yet as if a lifetime had gone between. The flowers were budding now, that were all in bloom when she came down, on the first autumnal morning, into the sunny parlour. The yellow jessamine, that was then a tender plant, had now taken firm root in the soil, and was sending out strong shoots; the wallflowers, which Miss Benson had sown on the wall a day or two after her arrival, were scenting the air with their fragrant flowers. Ruth knew every plant now; it seemed as though she had always lived here, and always known the inhabi-

tants of the house. She heard Sally singing her
accustomed song in the kitchen, a song she never
varied over her afternoon's work. It began,

> As I was going to Derby, sir,
> Upon a market-day.*

And if music is a necessary element in a song, perhaps
I had better call it by some other name.

But the strange change was in Ruth herself. She
was conscious of it though she could not define it, and
did not dwell upon it. Life had become significant
and full of duty to her. She delighted in the exercise
of her intellectual powers, and liked the idea of the
infinite amount of which she was ignorant; for it was
a grand pleasure to learn—to crave, and be satisfied.
She strove to forget what had gone before this last
twelve months. She shuddered up from contemplating
it; it was like a bad, unholy dream. And yet, there
was a strange yearning kind of love for the father of
the child whom she pressed to her heart, which came,
and she could not bid it begone as sinful, it was so pure
and natural, even when thinking of it, as in the sight
of God. Little Leonard cooed to the flowers, and
stretched after their bright colours; and Ruth laid him
on the dry turf, and pelted him with the gay petals.
He chinked and crowed with laughing delight, and
clutched at her cap, and pulled it off. Her short rich
curls were golden-brown in the slanting sunlight, and
by their very shortness made her look more child like.
She hardly seemed as if she could be the mother of the
noble babe over whom she knelt, now snatching kisses,
now matching his cheek with rose leaves. All at once,
the bells of the old church struck the hour; and far
away, high up in the air, began slowly to play the old
tune of "Life let us cherish";*they had played it for
years—for the life of man—and it always sounded fresh
and strange and aërial. Ruth was still in a moment,
she knew not why; and the tears came into her eyes
as she listened. When it was ended, she kissed her
baby, and bade God bless him.

Just then Sally came out, dressed for the evening,
with a leisurely look about her. She had done her
work, and she and Ruth were to drink tea together in
the exquisitely clean kitchen ; but while the kettle was
boiling, she came out to enjoy the flowers. She gathered
a piece of southern-wood, and stuffed it up her nose,
by way of smelling it.

"Whatten you call this in your country?" asked
she.

"Old-man," replied Ruth.

"We call it here lad's-love.* It and peppermint-
drops always remind me of going to church in the
country. Here! I'll get you a black currant-leaf to
put in the teapot. It gives it a flavour. We had bees
once against this wall ; but when missus died, we forgot
to tell 'em,* and put 'em in mourning, and, in course,
they swarmed away without our knowing, and the next
winter came a hard frost, and they died. Now, I dare
say, the water will be boiling ; and it's time for little
master there to come in, for the dew is falling. See,
all the daisies is shutting themselves up."

Sally was most gracious as a hostess. She quite put
on her company manners to receive Ruth in the kitchen.
They laid Leonard to sleep on the sofa in the parlour,
that they might hear him the more easily, and then
they sat quietly down to their sewing by the bright
kitchen fire. Sally was, as usual, the talker ; and, as
usual, the subject was the family of whom for so many
years she had formed a part.

"Aye! things was different when I was a girl," quoth
she. "Eggs was thirty for a shilling, and butter only
sixpence a pound. My wage when I came here was
but three pound, and I did on it, and was always clean
and tidy, which is more than many a lass can say now
who gets her seven and eight pound a year ; and tea
was kept for an afternoon drink, and pudding was eaten
afore meat in them days, and the upshot was, people
paid their debts better ; aye, aye ! we'n gone backwards,
and we thinken we'n gone forrards."

After shaking her head a little over the degeneracy

of the times, Sally returned to a part of the subject on
which she thought she had given Ruth a wrong idea.

"You'll not go for to think now that I've not more
than three pound a year. I've a deal above that now.
First of all, old missus gave me four pound, for she
said I were worth it, and I thought in my heart that I
were; so I took it without more ado; but after her
death, Master Thurstan and Miss Faith took a fit of
spending, and says they to me, one day as I carried tea
in, 'Sally, we think your wages ought to be raised.'
'What matter what you think!' said I, pretty sharp,
for I thought they'd ha' shown more respect to missus
if they'd let things stand as they were in her time;
and they'd gone and moved the sofa away from the wall
to where it stands now, already that very day. So I
speaks up sharp, and, says I, 'As long as I'm content,
I think it's no business of yours to be meddling wi' me
and my money matters.' 'But,' says Miss Faith (she's
always the one to speak first if you'll notice, though it's
master that comes in and clinches the matter with some
reason she'd never ha' thought of—he were always a
sensible lad), 'Sally, all the servants in the town have
six pound and better, and you have as hard a place as
any of 'em.' 'Did you ever hear me grumble about
my work that you talk about it in that way? wait till I
grumble,' says I, 'but don't meddle wi' me till then.'
So I flung off in a huff; but in the course of the evening,
Master Thurstan came in and sat down in the kitchen,
and he's such winning ways he wiles one over to anything; and besides, a notion had come into my head—
now, you'll not tell," said she, glancing round the
room, and hitching her chair nearer to Ruth in a
confidential manner; Ruth promised, and Sally
went on:

"I thought I should like to be an heiress wi' money,
and leave it all to Master and Miss Faith; and I
thought if I'd six pound a year I could, maybe, get to
be an heiress; all I was feared on was that some chap
or other might marry me for my money, but I've
managed to keep the fellows off; so I looks mim*and

grateful, and I thanks Master Thurstan for his offer, and I takes the wages; and what do you think I've done?" asked Sall, with an exultant air.

"What have you done?" asked Ruth.

"Why," replied Sally, slowly and emphatically, "I've saved thirty pound! but that's not it. I've getten a lawyer to make me a will; that's it, wench!" said she, slapping Ruth on the back.

"How did you manage it?" asked Ruth.

"Aye, that was it," said Sally; "I thowt about it many a night before I hit on the right way. I was afeard the money might be thrown into Chancery, if I didn't make it all safe, and yet I could na' ask Master Thurstan. At last and at length, John Jackson, the grocer, had a nephew come to stay a week with him, as was 'prentice to a lawyer in Liverpool; so now was my time, and here was my lawyer. Wait a minute! I could tell you my story better if I had my will in my hand; and I'll scomfish* you if ever you go for to tell."

She held up her hand, and threatened Ruth as she left the kitchen to fetch the will.

When she came back, she brought a parcel tied up in a blue pocket-handkerchief; she sat down, squared her knees, untied the handkerchief, and displayed a small piece of parchment.

"Now, do you know what this is?" said she, holding it up. "It's parchment, and it's the right stuff to make wills on. People gets into Chancery if they don't make them o' this stuff, and I reckon Tom Jackson thowt he'd have a fresh job on it if he could get it into Chancery; for the rascal went and wrote it on a piece of paper at first, and came and read it me out loud off a piece of paper no better than what one writes letters upon. I were up to him; and, thinks I, come, come, my lad, I'm not a fool, though you may think so; I know a paper will won't stand, but I'll let you run your rig. So I sits and I listens. And would you belie' me, he read it out as if it were as clear a business as your giving me that thimble—no more ado,

though it were thirty pound !   I could understand it
mysel'—that were no law for me.   I wanted summat
to consider about, and for th' meaning to be wrapped
up as I wrap up my best gown.   So says I, 'Tom !
it's not on parchment.   I mun have it on parchment.'
'This 'ill do as well,' says he.   'We'll get it witnessed, and it will stand good.'   Well ! I liked the
notion of having it witnessed, and for a while that
soothed me ; but after a bit, I felt I should like it
done according to law, and not plain out as anybody
might ha' done it ; I mysel', if I could have written.
So says I, 'Tom ! I mun have it on parchment.'
'Parchment costs money,' says he, very grave.   'Oh,
oh, my lad ! are ye there?' thinks I.   'That's the
reason I'm clipped*of law.'   So says I, 'Tom ! I mun
have it on parchment.   I'll pay the money and welcome.   It's thirty pound, and what I can lay to it.
I'll make it safe.   It shall be on parchment, and I'll
tell thee what, lad ! I'll gie ye sixpence for every good
law-word you put in it, sounding like, and not to be
caught up as a person runs.   Your master had need
to be ashamed of you as a 'prentice if you can't do a
thing more tradesman-like than this !'   Well ! he
laughed above a bit, but I were firm, and stood to it.
So he made it out on parchment.   Now, woman, try
and read it ! " said she, giving it to Ruth.

Ruth smiled, and began to read ; Sally listening with
rapt attention.   When Ruth came to the word, " testatrix," Sally stopped her.

"That was the first sixpence," said she.   "I thowt
he was going to fob me off again wi' plain language ;
but when that word came, I out wi' my sixpence, and
gave it to him on the spot.   Now go on."

Presently Ruth read, " accruing."

"That was the second sixpence.   Four sixpences it
were in all, besides six-and-eightpence as we bargained
at first, and three-and-fourpence parchment.   There !
that's what I call a will ; witnessed according to law,
and all.   Master Thurstan will be prettily taken in
when I die, and he finds all his extra wage left back to

him.   But it will teach him it's not so easy as he
thinks for, to make a woman give up her way."

The time was now drawing near when little Leonard
might be weaned—the time appointed by all three for
Ruth to endeavour to support herself in some way
more or less independent of Mr and Miss Benson.
This prospect dwelt much in all of their minds, and
was in each shaded with some degree of perplexity;
but they none of them spoke of it for fear of acceler-
ating the event.   If they had felt clear and determined as to the best course to be pursued, they were
none of them deficient in courage to commence upon
that course at once.   Miss Benson would, perhaps,
have objected the most to any alteration in their
present daily mode of life; but that was because she
had the habit of speaking out her thoughts as they
arose, and she particularly disliked and dreaded
change.   Besides this, she had felt her heart open
out, and warm towards the little helpless child, in a
strong and powerful manner.   Nature had intended
her warm instincts to find vent in a mother's duties;
her heart had yearned after children, and made her
restless in her childless state, without her well knowing why; but now, the delight she experienced in
tending, nursing, and contriving for the little boy—
even contriving to the point of sacrificing many of her
cherished whims—made her happy and satisfied and
peaceful.   It was more difficult to sacrifice her whims
than her comforts; but all had been given up when
and where required by the sweet lordly baby, who
reigned paramount in his very helplessness.

From some cause or other, an exchange of ministers
for one Sunday was to be effected with a neighbouring
congregation, and Mr Benson went on a short absence
from home.   When he returned on Monday, he was
met at the house-door by his sister, who had evidently
been looking out for him some time.   She stepped out
to greet him.

"Don't hurry yourself, Thurstan! all's well; only
I wanted to tell you something.   Don't fidget yourself

—baby is quite well, bless him! It's only good news. Come into your room, and let me talk a little quietly with you."

She drew him into his study, which was near the outer door, and then she took off his coat, and put his carpet-bag in a corner, and wheeled a chair to the fire, before she would begin.

"Well, now! to think how often things fall out just as we want them, Thurstan! Have not you often wondered what was to be done with Ruth when the time came at which we promised her she should earn her living? I am sure you have, because I have so often thought about it myself. And yet I never dared to speak out my fear, because that seemed giving it a shape. And now Mr Bradshaw has put all to rights. He invited Mr Jackson to dinner yesterday, just as we were going into chapel; and then he turned to me and asked me if I would come to tea—straight from afternoon chapel, because Mrs Bradshaw wanted to speak to me. He made it very clear I was not to bring Ruth; and, indeed, she was only too happy to stay at home with baby. And so I went; and Mrs Bradshaw took me into her bedroom, and shut the doors, and said Mr Bradshaw had told her, that he did not like Jemima being so much confined with the younger ones while they were at their lessons, and that he wanted some one above a nursemaid to sit with them while their masters were there—some one who would see about their learning their lessons, and who would walk out with them; a sort of nursery governess, I think she meant, though she did not say so; and Mr Bradshaw (for, of course, I saw his thoughts and words constantly peeping out, though he had told her to speak to me) believed that our Ruth would be the very person. Now, Thurstan, don't look so surprised, as if she had never come into your head! I am sure I saw what Mrs Bradshaw was driving at, long before she came to the point; and I could scarcely keep from smiling, and saying, 'We'd jump at the proposal'—long before I ought to have known anything about it."

"Oh, I wonder what we ought to do!" said Mr Benson. "Or rather, I believe I see what we ought to do, if I durst but do it."

"Why, what ought we to do?" asked his sister, in surprise.

"I ought to go and tell Mr Bradshaw the whole story——"

"And get Ruth turned out of our house," said Miss Benson, indignantly.

"They can't make us do that," said her brother. "I do not think they would try."

"Yes, Mr Bradshaw would try; and he would blazon out poor Ruth's sin, and there would not be a chance for her left. I know him well, Thurstan; and why should he be told now, more than a year ago?"

"A year ago, he did not want to put her in a situation of trust about his children."

"And you think she'll abuse that trust, do you? You've lived a twelvemonth in the house with Ruth, and the end of it is, you think she will do his children harm! Besides, who encouraged Jemima to come to the house so much to see Ruth? Did you not say it would do them both good to see something of each other?"

Mr Benson sat thinking.

"If you had not known Ruth as well as you do—if during her stay with us you had marked anything wrong, or forward, or deceitful, or immodest, I would say at once, don't allow Mr Bradshaw to take her into his house; but still I would say, don't tell of her sin and her sorrow to so severe a man—so unpitiful a judge. But here I ask you, Thurstan, can you, or I, or Sally (quick-eyed as she is), say, that in any one thing we have had true, just occasion to find fault with Ruth? I don't mean that she is perfect—she acts without thinking, her temper is sometimes warm and hasty; but have we any right to go and injure her prospects for life, by telling Mr Bradshaw all we know of her errors—only sixteen when she did so wrong, and never to escape from it all her many years to come—to have

the despair which would arise rrom its being known,
clutching her back into worse sin? What harm do
you think she can do? What is the risk to which you
think you are exposing Mr Bradshaw's children?"
She paused, out of breath, her eyes glittering with
tears of indignation, and impatient for an answer, that
she might knock it to pieces.

"I do not see any danger that can arise," said he at
length, and with slow difficulty, as if not fully convinced. "I have watched Ruth, and I believe she is
pure and truthful; and the very sorrow and penitence
she has felt—the very suffering she has gone through—
has given her a thoughtful conscientiousness beyond
her age."

"That and the care of her baby," said Miss Benson,
secretly delighted at the tone of her brother's thoughts.

"Ah, Faith! that baby you so much dreaded once,
is turning out a blessing, you see," said Thurstan, with
a faint, quiet smile.

"Yes! anyone might be thankful, and better too,
for Leonard; but how could I tell that it would be like
him?"

"But to return to Ruth and Mr Bradshaw. What
did you say?"

"Oh! with my feelings, of course, I was only too
glad to accept the proposal, and so I told Mrs Bradshaw then; and I afterwards repeated it to Mr Bradshaw, when he asked me if his wife had mentioned
their plans. They would understand that I must
consult you and Ruth, before it could be considered
as finally settled."

"And have you named it to her?"

"Yes," answered Miss Benson, half afraid lest he
should think she had been too precipitate.

"And what did she say?" asked he, after a little
pause of grave silence.

"At first she seemed very glad, and fell into my
mood of planning how it should all be managed; how
Sally and I should take care of the baby the hours that
she was away at Mr Bradshaw's; but by and by she

became silent and thoughtful, and knelt down by me and hid her face in my lap, and shook a little as if she was crying ; and then I heard her speak in a very low smothered voice, for her head was still bent down— quite hanging down, indeed, so that I could not see her face, so I stooped to listen, and I heard her say, ' Do you think I should be good enough to teach little girls, Miss Benson?' She said it so humbly and fearfully that all I thought of was how to cheer her, and I answered and asked her if she did not hope to be good enough to bring up her own darling to be a brave Christian man? And she lifted up her head, and I saw her eyes looking wild and wet and earnest, and she said, ' With God's help, that will I try to make my child.' And I said then, ' Ruth, as you strive and as you pray for your own child, so you must strive and pray to make Mary and Elizabeth good, if you are trusted with them.' And she said out quite clear, though her face was hiding from me once more, ' I will strive, and I will pray.' You would not have had any fears, Thurstan, if you could have heard and seen her last night."

"I have no fear," said he, decidedly. "Let the plan go on." After a minute, he added, "But I am glad it was so far arranged before I heard of it. My indecision about right and wrong—my perplexity as to how far we are to calculate consequences—grows upon me, I fear."

"You look tired and weary, dear. You should blame your body rather than your conscience at these times."

"A very dangerous doctrine."

The scroll of Fate was closed, and they could not foresee the Future ; and yet, if they could have seen it, though they might have shrunk fearfully at first, they would have smiled and thanked God when all was done and said.

CHAPTER XIX

The quiet days grew into weeks and months, and even years, without any event to startle the little circle into the consciousness of the lapse of time. One who had known them at the date of Ruth's becoming a governess in Mr Bradshaw's family, and had been absent until the time of which I am now going to tell you, would have noted some changes which had imperceptibly come over all; but he, too, would have thought, that the life which had brought so little of turmoil and vicissitude must have been calm and tranquil, and in accordance with the bygone activity of the town in which their existence passed away.

The alterations that he would have perceived were those caused by the natural progress of time. The Benson home was brightened into vividness by the presence of the little Leonard, now a noble boy of six, large and grand in limb and stature, and with a face of marked beauty and intelligence. Indeed, he might have been considered by many as too intelligent for his years; and often the living with old and thoughtful people gave him, beyond most children, the appearance of pondering over the mysteries which meet the young on the threshold of life, but which fade away as advancing years bring us more into contact with the practical and tangible—fade away and vanish, until it seems to require the agitation of some great storm of the soul before we can again realize spiritual things.

But, at times, Leonard seemed oppressed and bewildered, after listening intent, with grave and wondering eyes, to the conversation around him; at others, the bright animal life shone forth radiant, and no three-months' kitten—no foal, suddenly tossing up its heels by the side of its sedate dam, and careering around the pasture in pure mad enjoyment—no young creature of any kind, could show more merriment and gladness of heart.

" For ever in mischief," was Sally's account of him

at such times; but it was not intentional mischief;
and Sally herself would have been the first to scold anyone else who had used the same words in reference to
her darling.   Indeed, she was once nearly giving
warning, because she thought the boy was being
ill-used.   The occasion was this: Leonard had for
some time shown a strange odd disregard of truth; he
invented stories, and told them with so grave a face,
that unless there was some internal evidence of their
incorrectness (such as describing a cow with a bonnet
on), he was generally believed, and his statements,
which were given with the full appearance of relating
a real occurrence, had once or twice led to awkward
results.   All the three, whose hearts were pained by
this apparent unconsciousness of the difference between
truth and falsehood, were unaccustomed to children, or
they would have recognized this as a stage through
which most infants, who have lively imaginations,
pass; and, accordingly, there was a consultation in Mr
Benson's study one morning.   Ruth was there, quiet,
very pale, and with compressed lips, sick at heart as
she heard Miss Benson's arguments for the necessity
of whipping, in order to cure Leonard of his story-
telling.   Mr Benson looked unhappy and uncomfortable.   Education was but a series of experiments to
them all, and they all had a secret dread of spoiling the
noble boy, who was the darling of their hearts.   And,
perhaps, this very intensity of love begot an impatient,
unnecessary anxiety, and made them resolve on sterner
measures than the parent of a large family (where love
was more spread abroad) would have dared to use.   At
any rate, the vote for whipping carried the day; and
even Ruth, trembling and cold, agreed that it must be
done; only she asked, in a meek, sad voice, if she need
be present (Mr Benson was to be the executioner—the
scene, the study); and being instantly told that she
had better not, she went slowly and languidly up to
her room, and kneeling down, she closed her ears, and
prayed.
    Miss Benson, having carried her point, was very

sorry for the child, and would have begged him off; but Mr Benson had listened more to her arguments than now to her pleadings, and only answered, "If it is right, it shall be done!" He went into the garden, and deliberately, almost as if he wished to gain time, chose and cut off a little switch from the laburnum-tree. Then he returned through the kitchen, and gravely taking the awed and wondering little fellow by the hand, he led him silently into the study, and placing him before him, began an admonition on the importance of truthfulness, meaning to conclude with what he believed to be the moral of all punishment: "As you cannot remember this of yourself, I must give you a little pain to make you remember it. I am very sorry it is necessary, and that you cannot recollect without my doing so."

But before he had reached this very proper and desirable conclusion, and while he was yet working his way, his heart aching with the terrified look of the child at the solemnly sad face and words of upbraiding, Sally burst in :

"And what may ye be going to do with that fine switch I saw ye gathering, Master Thurstan?" asked she, her eyes gleaming with anger at the answer she knew must come, if answer she had at all.

"Go away, Sally," said Mr Benson, annoyed at the fresh difficulty in his path.

"I'll not stir never a step till you give me that switch, as you've got for some mischief, I'll be bound."

"Sally! remember where it is said, 'He that spareth the rod, spoileth the child,'"*said Mr Benson austerely.

"Aye, I remember ; and I remember a bit more than you want me to remember, I reckon. It were King Solomon as spoke them words, and it were King Solomon's son that were King Rehoboam, and no great shakes either. I can remember what is said on him, 2 Chronicles, xii. chapter, 14th verse : 'And he,' that's King Rehoboam, the lad that tasted the rod, 'did evil, because he prepared not his heart to seek the Lord.'

I've not been reading my chapters every night for fifty
year to be caught napping by a Dissenter, neither!"
said she, triumphantly. "Come along, Leonard."
She stretched out her hand to the child, thinking that
she had conquered.

But Leonard did not stir. He looked wistfully at
Mr Benson. "Come!" said she, impatiently. The
boy's mouth quivered.

"If you want to whip me, uncle, you may do it. I
don't much mind."

Put in this form, it was impossible to carry out his
intentions; and so Mr Benson told the lad he might
go—that he would speak to him another time. Leonard
went away, more subdued in spirit than if he had been
whipped. Sally lingered a moment. She stopped to
add: "I think it's for them without sin to throw
stones at a poor child, and cut up good laburnum
branches to whip him. I only do as my betters do,
when I call Leonard's mother Mrs ——." The moment
she had said this she was sorry; it was an ungenerous
advantage after the enemy had acknowledged himself
defeated. Mr Benson dropped his head upon his hands,
and hid his face, and sighed deeply.

Leonard flew in search of his mother, as in search of
a refuge. If he had found her calm, he would have
burst into a passion of crying after his agitation; as it
was, he came upon her kneeling and sobbing, and he
stood quite still. Then he threw his arms round her
neck, and said: "Mamma! mamma! I will be good—
I make a promise; I will speak true—I make a
promise." And he kept his word.

Miss Benson piqued herself upon being less carried
away by her love for this child than anyone else in the
house; she talked severely, and had capital theories;
but her severity ended in talk, and her theories would
not work. However, she read several books on education, knitting socks for Leonard all the while; and,
upon the whole, I think, the hands were more usefully
employed than the head, and the good honest heart
better than either. She looked older than when we

first knew her, but it was a ripe, kindly age that was coming over her. Her excellent practical sense, perhaps, made her a more masculine character than her brother. He was often so much perplexed by the problems of life, that he let the time for action go by ; but she kept him in check by her clear, pithy talk, which brought back his wandering thoughts to the duty that lay straight before him, waiting for action ; and then he remembered that it was the faithful part to "wait patiently upon God,"*and leave the ends in His hands, who alone knows why Evil exists in this world, and why it ever hovers on either side of Good. In this respect, Miss Benson had more faith than her brother—or so it seemed ; for quick, resolute action in the next step of Life was all she required, while he deliberated and trembled, and often did wrong from his very deliberation, when his first instinct would have led him right.

But although decided and prompt as ever, Miss Benson was grown older since the summer afternoon when she dismounted from the coach at the foot of the long Welsh hill that led to Llan-dhu, where her brother awaited her to consult her about Ruth. Though her eye was as bright and straight-looking as ever, quick and brave in its glances, her hair had become almost snowy white ; and it was on this point she consulted Sally, soon after the date of Leonard's last untruth. The two were arranging Miss Benson's room one morning, when, after dusting the looking-glass, she suddenly stopped in her operation, and after a close inspection of herself, startled Sally by this speech :

"Sally ! I'm looking a great deal older than I used to do !"

Sally, who was busy dilating on the increased price of flour, considered this remark of Miss Benson's as strangely irrelevant to the matter in hand, and only noticed it by a

"To be sure ! I suppose we all on us do. But two and fourpence a dozen is too much to make us pay for it."

Miss Benson went on with her inspection of herself, and Sally with her economical projects.

"Sally!" said Miss Benson, "my hair is nearly white. The last time I looked it was only pepper-and-salt. What must I do?"

"Do—why, what would the wench do?" asked Sally, contemptuously. "Ye're never going to be taken in, at your time of life, by hair dyes and such gimcracks, as can only take in young girls whose wisdom teeth are not cut."

"And who are not very likely to want them," said Miss Benson, quietly. "No! but you see, Sally, it's very awkward having such grey hair, and feeling so young. Do you know, Sally, I've as great a mind for dancing, when I hear a lively tune on the street organs, as ever; and as great a mind to sing when I'm happy—to sing in my old way, Sally, you know."

"Aye, you had it from a girl," said Sally; "and many a time, when the door's been shut, I did not know if it was you in the parlour, or a big bumble-bee in the kitchen, as was making that drumbling noise. I heard you at it yesterday."

"But an old woman with grey hair ought not to have a fancy for dancing or singing," continued Miss Benson.

"Whatten nonsense are ye talking?" said Sally, roused to indignation. "Calling yoursel' an old woman when you're better than ten years younger than me! and many a girl has grey hair at five-and-twenty."

"But I'm more than five-and-twenty, Sally. I'm fifty-seven next May!"

"More shame for ye, then, not to know better than to talk of dyeing your hair. I cannot abide such vanities!"

"Oh, dear! Sally, when will you understand what I mean? I want to know how I am to keep remembering how old I am, so as to prevent myself from feeling so young? I was quite startled just now to see my hair in the glass, for I can generally tell if my cap is straight by feeling. I'll tell you what I'll do—I'll cut off a piece of my grey hair, and plait it together for a marker in my Bible!" Miss Benson expected applause for this bright idea, but Sally only made answer :

"You'll be taking to painting your cheeks next, now you've once thought of dyeing your hair." So Miss Benson plaited her grey hair in silence and quietness, Leonard holding one end of it while she wove it, and admiring the colour and texture all the time, with a sort of implied dissatisfaction at the auburn colour of his own curls, which was only half-comforted away by Miss Benson's information, that, if he lived long enough, his hair would be like hers.

Mr Benson, who had looked old and frail while he was yet but young, was now stationary as to the date of his appearance. But there was something more of nervous restlessness in his voice and ways than formerly ; that was the only change six years had brought to him. And as for Sally, she chose to forget age and the passage of years altogether, and had as much work in her, to use her own expression, as she had at sixteen ; nor was her appearance very explicit as to the flight of time. Fifty, sixty, or seventy, she might be—not more than the last, not less than the first—though her usual answer to any circuitous inquiry as to her age was now (what it had been for many years past), "I'm feared I shall never see thirty again."

Then as to the house. It was not one where the sitting-rooms are refurnished every two or three years ; not now, even (since Ruth came to share their living) a place where, as an article grew shabby or worn, a new one was purchased. The furniture looked poor, and the carpets almost threadbare ; but there was such a dainty spirit of cleanliness abroad, such ex-quisite neatness of repair, and altogether so bright and cheerful a look about the rooms—everything so above-board—no shifts to conceal poverty under flimsy

ornament—that many a splendid drawing-room would
give less pleasure to those who could see evidences of
character in inanimate things. But whatever poverty
there might be in the house, there was full luxuriance
in the little square wall-encircled garden, on two sides
of which the parlour and kitchen looked. The laburnum-tree, which when Ruth came was like a twig
stuck into the ground, was now a golden glory in
spring, and a pleasant shade in summer. The wild
hop, that Mr Benson had brought home from one of
his country rambles, and planted by the parlour-
window, while Leonard was yet a baby in his mother's
arms, was now a garland over the casement, hanging
down long tendrils, that waved in the breezes, and
threw pleasant shadows and traceries, like some
Bacchanalian carving, on the parlour walls, at "morn
or dusky eve." The yellow rose had clambered up to
the window of Mr Benson's bedroom, and its blossom-
laden branches were supported by a jargonelle pear
tree rich in autumnal fruit.*

But, perhaps, in Ruth herself there was the greatest
external change; for of the change which had gone on in
her heart, and mind, and soul, or if there had been
any, neither she nor anyone around her was conscious;
but sometimes Miss Benson did say to Sally, "How
very handsome Ruth is grown!" To which Sally
made ungracious answer, "Yes! she's well enough.
Beauty is deceitful, and favour a snare, and I'm thankful the Lord has spared me from such man-traps and
spring-guns." But even Sally could not help secretly
admiring Ruth. If her early brilliancy of colour was
gone, a clear ivory skin, as smooth as satin, told of
complete and perfect health, and was as lovely, if not
so striking in effect, as the banished lilies and roses.
Her hair had grown darker and deeper, in the shadow
that lingered in its masses; her eyes, even if you could
have guessed that they had shed bitter tears in their day,
had a thoughtful spiritual look about them, that made
you wonder at their depth, and look—and look again.
The increase of dignity in her face had been imparted

to her form. I do not know if she had grown taller
since the birth of her child, but she looked as if she
had. And although she had lived in a very humble
home, yet there was something about either it or her,
or the people amongst whom she had been thrown
during the last few years, which had so changed her,
that whereas, six or seven years ago, you would have
perceived that she was not altogether a lady by birth
and education, yet now she might have been placed
among the highest in the land, and would have been
taken by the most critical judge for their equal,
although ignorant of their conventional etiquette—
an ignorance which she would have acknowledged in a
simple childlike way, being unconscious of any false
shame.

Her whole heart was in her boy. She often feared
that she loved him too much—more than God Himself—yet she could not bear to pray to have her
love for her child lessened. But she would kneel
down by his little bed at night—at the deep, still mid-
night—with the stars that kept watch over Rizpah*
shining down upon her, and tell God what I have now
told you, that she feared she loved her child too much,
yet could not, would not, love him less; and speak to
Him of her one treasure as she could speak to no
earthly friend. And so, unconsciously, her love for
her child led her up to love to God, to the All-
knowing, who read her heart.

It might be superstition—I dare say it was—but,
somehow, she never lay down to rest without saying,
as she looked her last on her boy, "Thy will, not
mine, be done;"* and even while she trembled and
shrank with infinite dread from sounding the depths
of what that will might be, she felt as if her treasure
were more secure to waken up rosy and bright in the
morning, as one over whose slumbers God's holy
angels had watched, for the very words which she had
turned away in sick terror from realizing the night
before.

Her daily absence at her duties to the Bradshaw

children only ministered to her love for Leonard.
Everything does minister to love when its foundation
lies deep in a true heart, and it was with an exquisite
pang of delight that, after a moment of vague fear,

> (Oh, mercy ! to myself I said,
> If Lucy should be dead !),*

she saw her child's bright face of welcome as he threw
open the door every afternoon on her return home.
For it was his silently-appointed work to listen for her
knock, and rush breathless to let her in. If he were
in the garden, or upstairs among the treasures of the
lumber room, either Miss Benson, or her brother, or
Sally, would fetch him to his happy little task ; no one
so sacred as he to the allotted duty. And the joyous
meeting was not deadened by custom, to either mother
or child.

Ruth gave the Bradshaws the highest satisfaction, as
Mr Bradshaw often said both to her and to the Bensons ;
indeed, she rather winced under his pompous approbation. But his favourite recreation was patronizing ;
and when Ruth saw how quietly and meekly Mr Benson
submitted to gifts and praise, when an honest word of
affection, or a tacit, implied acknowledgment of
equality, would have been worth everything said and
done, she tried to be more meek in spirit, and to
recognize the good that undoubtedly existed in Mr
Bradshaw. He was richer and more prosperous than
ever ;—a keen, far-seeing man of business, with an
undisguised contempt for all who failed in the success
which he had achieved. But it was not alone those
who were less fortunate in obtaining wealth than himself that he visited with severity of judgement ; every
moral error or delinquency came under his unsparing
comment. Stained by no vice himself, either in his
own eyes or in that of any human being who cared to
judge him, having nicely and wisely proportioned and
adapted his means to his ends, he could afford to speak
and act with a severity which was almost sanctimonious
in its ostentation of thankfulness as to himself. Not a

misfortune or a sin was brought to light but Mr Bradshaw could trace it to its cause in some former mode of
action, which he had long ago foretold would lead to
shame. If another's son turned out wild or bad, Mr
Bradshaw had little sympathy; it might have been
prevented by a stricter rule, or more religious life at
home; young Richard Bradshaw was quiet and steady,
and other fathers might have had sons like him if they
had taken the same pains to enforce obedience.
Richard was an only son, and yet Mr Bradshaw might
venture to say, he had never had his own way in his
life. Mrs Bradshaw was, he confessed (Mr Bradshaw
did not dislike confessing his wife's errors), rather less
firm than he should have liked with the girls; and
with some people, he believed, Jemima was rather
headstrong; but to his wishes she had always shown
herself obedient. All children were obedient, if their
parents were decided and authoritative; and everyone
would turn out well, if properly managed. If they
did not prove good, they must take the consequences
of their errors.

Mrs Bradshaw murmured faintly at her husband
when his back was turned; but if his voice was heard,
or his footsteps sounded in the distance, she was mute,
and hurried her children into the attitude or action
most pleasing to their father. Jemima, it is true,
rebelled against this manner of proceeding, which
savoured to her a little of deceit; but even she had
not, as yet, overcome her awe of her father sufficiently
to act independently of him, and according to her own
sense of right—or rather, I should say, according to
her own warm, passionate impulses. Before him, the
wilfulness which made her dark eyes blaze out at
times was hushed and still; he had no idea of her self-
tormenting, no notion of the almost southern jealousy
which seemed to belong to her brunette complexion.
Jemima was not pretty, the flatness and shortness of
her face made her almost plain; yet most people looked
twice at her expressive countenance, at the eyes which
flamed or melted at every trifle, at the rich colour

which came at every expressed emotion into her usually sallow face, at the faultless teeth which made her smile like a sunbeam. But then, again, when she thought she was not kindly treated, when a suspicion crossed her mind, or when she was angry with herself, her lips were tight-pressed together, her colour was wan and almost livid, and a stormy gloom clouded her eyes as with a film. But before her father her words were few, and he did not notice looks or tones.

Her brother Richard had been equally silent before his father, in boyhood and early youth; but since he had gone to be clerk in a London house, preparatory to assuming his place as junior partner in Mr Bradshaw's business, he spoke more on his occasional visits at home. And very proper and highly moral was his conversation; set sentences of goodness, which were like the flowers that children stick in the ground, and that have not sprung upwards from roots—deep down in the hidden life and experience of the heart. He was as severe a judge as his father of other people's conduct, but you felt that Mr Bradshaw was sincere in his condemnation of all outward error and vice, and that he would try himself by the same laws as he tried others; somehow, Richard's words were frequently heard with a lurking distrust, and many shook their heads over the pattern son; but then it was those whose sons had gone astray, and been condemned, in no private or tender manner, by Mr Bradshaw, so it might be revenge in them. Still, Jemima felt that all was not right; her heart sympathized in the rebellion against his father's commands, which her brother had confessed to her in an unusual moment of confidence, but her uneasy conscience condemned the deceit which he had practised.

The brother and sister were sitting alone over a blazing Christmas fire, and Jemima held an old newspaper in her hand to shield her face from the hot light. They were talking of family events, when, during a pause, Jemima's eye caught the name of a great actor, who had lately given prominence and

life to a character in one of Shakspeare's plays.   The
criticism in the paper was fine, and warmed Jemima's
heart.

"How I should like to see a play!" exclaimed she.

"Should you?" said her brother, listlessly.

"Yes, to be sure!   Just hear this!" and she began
to read a fine passage of criticism.

"Those newspaper people can make an article out of
anything," said he, yawning.   "I've seen the man
myself, and it was all very well, but nothing to make
such a fuss about."

"You! you seen——!   Have you seen a play,
Richard?   Oh, why did you never tell me before?
Tell me all about it!   Why did you never name
seeing —— in your letters?"

He half smiled, contemptuously enough.   "Oh! at
first it strikes one rather, but after a while one cares no
more for the theatre than one does for mince-pies."

"Oh, I wish I might go to London!" said Jemima,
impatiently.   "I've a great mind to ask papa to let me
go to the George Smiths', and then I could see——.
I would not think him like mince-pies."

"You must not do any such thing!" said Richard,
now neither yawning nor contemptuous.   "My father
would never allow you to go to the theatre; and the
George Smiths are such old fogeys—they would be sure
to tell."

"How do you go, then?   Does my father give you
leave?"

"Oh! many things are right for men which are not
for girls."

Jemima sat and pondered.   Richard wished he had
not been so confidential.

"You need not name it," said he, rather anxiously.

"Name what?" said she, startled, for her thoughts
had gone far a-field.

"Oh, name my going once or twice to the theatre!"

"No, I shan't name it!" said she.   "No one here
would care to hear it."

But it was with some little surprise, and almost with

a feeling of disgust, that she heard Richard join with her father in condemning some one, and add to Mr Bradshaw's list of offences, by alleging that the young man was a playgoer. He did not think his sister heard his words.

Mary and Elizabeth were the two girls whom Ruth had in charge; they resembled Jemima more than their brother in character. The household rules were occasionally a little relaxed in their favour, for Mary, the elder, was nearly eight years younger than Jemima, and three intermediate children had died. They loved Ruth dearly, made a great pet of Leonard, and had many profound secrets together, most of which related to their wonders if Jemima and Mr Farquhar would ever be married. They watched their sister closely; and every day had some fresh confidence to make to each other, confirming or discouraging to their hopes.

Ruth rose early, and shared the household work with Sally and Miss Benson, till seven; and then she helped Leonard to dress, and had a quiet time alone with him till prayers and breakfast. At nine she was to be at Mr Bradshaw's house. She sat in the room with Mary and Elizabeth during the Latin, the writing, and arithmetic lessons, which they received from masters; then she read, and walked with them, they clinging to her as to an elder sister; she dined with her pupils at the family lunch, and reached home by four. That happy home—those quiet days!

And so the peaceful days passed on into weeks, and months, and years, and Ruth and Leonard grew and strengthened into the riper beauty of their respective ages; while as yet no touch of decay had come on the quaint, primitive elders of the household.

CHAPTER XX

IT was no wonder that the lookers-on were perplexed as to the state of affairs between Jemima and Mr Farquhar, for they too were sorely puzzled themselves at the sort of relationship between them. Was it love, or was it not? that was the question in Mr Farquhar's mind. He hoped it was not; he believed it was not; and yet he felt as if it were. There was something preposterous, he thought, in a man, nearly forty years of age, being in love with a girl of twenty. He had gone on reasoning through all the days of his manhood on the idea of a staid, noble-minded wife, grave and sedate, the fit companion in experience of her husband. He had spoken with admiration of reticent characters, full of self-control and dignity; and he hoped—he trusted, that all this time he had not been allowing himself unconsciously to fall in love with a wild-hearted, impetuous girl, who knew nothing of life beyond her father's house, and who chafed under the strict discipline enforced there. For it was rather a suspicious symptom of the state of Mr Farquhar's affections, that he had discovered the silent rebellion which continued in Jemima's heart, unperceived by any of her own family, against the severe laws and opinions of her father. Mr Farquhar shared in these opinions; but in him they were modified, and took a milder form. Still he approved of much that Mr Brad-shaw did and said; and this made it all the more strange that he should wince so for Jemima, whenever anything took place which he instinctively knew that she would dislike. After an evening at Mr Brad-shaw's, when Jemima had gone to the very verge of questioning or disputing some of her father's severe judgements, Mr Farquhar went home in a dissatisfied, restless state of mind, which he was almost afraid to analyse. He admired the inflexible integrity—and almost the pomp of principle—evinced by Mr Bradshaw on every occasion; he wondered how it was that Jemima could not see how grand a life might be, whose every action was shaped in obedience to some eternal law; instead of which, he was afraid she rebelled against every law, and was only guided by impulse. Mr Farquhar had been taught to dread impulses as promptings of the devil. Sometimes, if

he tried to present her father's opinions before her in
another form, so as to bring himself and her rather
more into that state of agreement he longed for, she
flashed out upon him with the indignation of difference
that she dared not show to, or before, her father, as if
she had some diviner instinct which taught her more
truly than they knew, with all their experience; at
least, in her first expressions there seemed something
good and fine; but opposition made her angry and
irritable, and the arguments which he was constantly
provoking (whenever he was with her in her father's
absence) frequently ended in some vehemence of
expression on her part that offended Mr Farquhar,
who did not see how she expiated her anger in tears
and self-reproaches when alone in her chamber. Then
he would lecture himself severely on the interest he
could not help feeling in a wilful girl; he would determine not to interfere with her opinions in future, and
yet, the very next time they differed, he strove to
argue her into harmony with himself, in spite of all
resolutions to the contrary.

Mr Bradshaw saw just enough of this interest which
Jemima had excited in his partner's mind, to determine him in considering their future marriage as a
settled affair. The fitness of the thing had long ago
struck him; her father's partner—so the fortune he
meant to give her might continue in the business; a
man of such steadiness of character, and such a
capital eye for a desirable speculation as Mr Farquhar
—just the right age to unite the paternal with the
conjugal affection, and consequently the very man for
Jemima, who had something unruly in her, which
might break out under a *régime* less wisely adjusted to
the circumstances than was Mr Bradshaw's (in his own
opinion)—a house ready-furnished, at a convenient
distance from her home—no near relations on Mr
Farquhar's side, who might be inclined to consider his
residence as their own for an indefinite time, and so
add to the household expenses—in short, what could
be more suitable in every way? Mr Bradshaw re-

spected the very self-restraint he thought he saw in
Mr Farquhar's demeanour, attributing it to a wise
desire to wait until trade should be rather more slack,
and the man of business more at leisure to become the
lover.

As for Jemima, at times she thought she almost
hated Mr Farquhar.

"What business has he," she would think, "to
lecture me? Often I can hardly bear it from papa,
and I will not bear it from him. He treats me just
like a child, and as if I should lose all my present
opinions when I know more of the world. I am sure
I should like never to know the world, if it was to
make me think as he does, hard man that he is! I
wonder what made him take Jem Brown on as
gardener again, if he does not believe that above one
criminal in a thousand is restored to goodness. I'll
ask him, some day, if that was not acting on impulse
rather than principle. Poor impulse! how you do get
abused. But I will tell Mr Farquhar, I will not let
him interfere with me. If I do what papa bids me,
no one has a right to notice whether I do it willingly
or not."

So then she tried to defy Mr Farquhar, by doing
and saying things that she knew he would disapprove.
She went so far that he was seriously grieved, and did
not even remonstrate and "lecture," and then she
was disappointed and irritated; for, somehow, with all
her indignation at interference, she liked to be lectured by him; not that she was aware of this liking of
hers, but still it would have been more pleasant to be
scolded than so quietly passed over. Her two little
sisters, with their wide-awake eyes, had long ago put
things together, and conjectured. Every day they had
some fresh mystery together, to be imparted in garden
walks and whispered talks.

"Lizzie, did you see how the tears came into Mimie's
eyes when Mr Farquhar looked so displeased when
she said good people were always dull? I think
she's in love." Mary said the last words with grave

emphasis, and felt like an oracle of twelve years of age.

"I don't," said Lizzie. "I know I cry often enough when papa is cross, and I'm not in love with him."

"Yes! but you don't look as Mimie did."

"Don't call her Mimie—you know papa does not like it."

"Yes; but there are so many things papa does not like I can never remember them all. Never mind about that; but listen to something I've got to tell you, if you'll never, never tell."

"No, indeed I won't, Mary. What is it?"

"Not to Mrs Denbigh?"

"No, not even to Mrs Denbigh."

"Well, then, the other day—last Friday, Mimie ——"

"Jemima!" interrupted the more conscientious Elizabeth.

"Jemima, if it must be so," jerked out Mary, "sent me to her desk for an envelope, and what do you think I saw?"

"What?" asked Elizabeth, expecting nothing less than a red-hot Valentine, signed Walter Farquhar, *pro* Bradshaw, Farquhar, and Co., in full.

"Why a piece of paper, with dull-looking lines upon it, just like the scientific dialogues; and I remembered all about it. It was once when Mr Farquhar had been telling us that a bullet does not go in a straight line, but in a something curve, and he drew some lines on a piece of paper; and Mimie——"

"Jemima," put in Elizabeth.

"Well, well! she had treasured it up, and written in a corner, 'W. F., April 3rd.' Now, that's rather like love, is not it? For Jemima hates useful information just as much as I do, and that's saying a great deal; and yet she had kept this paper, and dated it."

"If that's all, I know Dick keeps a paper with Miss Benson's name written on it, and yet he's not in love with her; and perhaps Jemima may like Mr Farquhar,

and he may not like her.   It seems such a little while
since her hair was turned up, and he has always been
a grave middle-aged man ever since I can recollect ;
and then, have you never noticed how often he finds
fault with her—almost lectures her ? ”

"To be sure," said Mary ; " but he may be in love,
for all that.   Just think how often papa lectures
mamma ; and yet, of course, they're in love with each
other.”

" Well ! we shall see," said Elizabeth.

Poor Jemima little thought of the four sharp eyes
that watched her daily course while she sat alone, as
she fancied, with her secret in her own room.   For, in
a passionate fit of grieving, at the impatient hasty
temper which had made her so seriously displease Mr
Farquhar that he had gone away without remonstrance, without more leave-taking than a distant bow,
she had begun to suspect that rather than not be
noticed at all by him, rather than be an object of
indifference to him—oh ! far rather would she be an
object of anger and upbraiding ; and the thoughts
that followed this confession to herself, stunned and
bewildered her ; and for once that they made her
dizzy with hope, ten times they made her sick with
fear.   For an instant she planned to become and to be
all he could wish her ; to change her very nature for
him.   And then a great gush of pride came over her,
and she set her teeth tight together, and determined
that he should either love her as she was, or not at all.
Unless he could take her with all her faults, she would
not care for his regard ; " love " was too noble a word
to call such cold calculating feeling as his must be,
who went about with a pattern idea in his mind, trying
to find a wife to match.   Besides, there was something
degrading, Jemima thought, in trying to alter herself
to gain the love of any human creature.   And yet, if
he did not care for her, if this late indifference were
to last, what a great shroud was drawn over life !
Could she bear it ?

From the agony she dared not look at, but which

she was going to risk encountering, she was aroused
by the presence of her mother.

"Jemima! your father wants to speak to you in the
dining-room."

"What for?" asked the girl.

"Oh! he is fidgeted by something Mr Farquhar
said to me, and which I repeated. I am sure I
thought there was no harm in it, and your father
always likes me to tell him what everybody says in
his absence."

Jemima went with a heavy heart into her father's
presence.

He was walking up and down the room, and did not
see her at first.

"Oh, Jemima! is that you? Has your mother told
you what I want to speak to you about?"

"No!" said Jemima. "Not exactly."

"She has been telling me, what proves to me how
very seriously you must have displeased and offended
Mr Farquhar, before he could have expressed himself
to her as he did, when he left the house; you know
what he said?"

"No!" said Jemima, her heart swelling within her.
"He has no right to say anything about me." She
was desperate, or she durst not have said this before
her father.

"No right!—what do you mean, Jemima?" said
Mr Bradshaw, turning sharp round. "Surely you
must know that I hope he may one day be your
husband; that is to say, if you prove yourself worthy
of the excellent training I have given you. I cannot
suppose Mr Farquhar would take any undisciplined
girl as a wife."

Jemima held tight by a chair near which she was
standing. She did not speak; her father was pleased
by her silence—it was the way in which he liked his
projects to be received.

"But you cannot suppose," he continued, "that Mr
Farquhar will consent to marry you—"

"Consent to marry me!" repeated Jemima, in a low

tone of brooding indignation; were those the terms upon which her rich, woman's heart was to be given, with a calm consent of acquiescent acceptance, but a little above resignation on the part of the receiver?

—" if you give way to a temper which, although you have never dared to show it to me, I am well aware exists, although I hoped the habits of self-examination I had instilled had done much to cure you of manifesting it. At one time, Richard promised to be the more headstrong of the two; now, I must desire you to take pattern by him. Yes," he continued, falling into his old train of thought, "it would be a most fortunate connexion for you in every way. I should have you under my own eye, and could still assist you in the formation of your character, and I should be at hand to strengthen and confirm your principles. Mr Farquhar's connexion with the firm would be convenient and agreeable to me in a pecuniary point of view. He ——" Mr Bradshaw was going on in his enumeration of the advantages which he in particular, and Jemima in the second place, would derive from this marriage, when his daughter spoke, at first so low that he could not hear her, as he walked up and down the room with his creaking boots, and he had to stop to listen.

"Has Mr Farquhar ever spoken to you about it?" Jemima's cheek was flushed as she asked the question; she wished that she might have been the person to whom he had first addressed himself.

Mr Bradshaw answered,

"No! not spoken. It has been implied between us for some time. At least, I have been so aware of his intentions that I have made several allusions, in the course of business, to it, as a thing that might take place. He can hardly have misunderstood; he must have seen that I perceived his design, and approved of it," said Mr Bradshaw, rather doubtfully; as he remembered how very little, in fact, passed between him and his partner which could have reference to the subject, to any but a mind prepared to receive it. Perhaps Mr Farquhar had not really thought of it;

but then again, that would imply that his own penetration had been mistaken, a thing not impossible certainly, but quite beyond the range of probability.   So
he reassured himself, and (as he thought) his daughter,
by saying,

"The whole thing is so suitable—the advantages
arising from the connexion are so obvious; besides
which, I am quite aware, from many little speeches
of Mr Farquhar's, that he contemplates marriage at no
very distant time; and he seldom leaves Eccleston,
and visits few families besides our own—certainly, none
that can compare with ours in the advantages you have
all received in moral and religious training." But then
Mr Bradshaw was checked in his implied praises of
himself (and only himself could be his martingale when
he once set out on such a career), by a recollection that
Jemima must not feel too secure, as she might become
if he dwelt too much on the advantages of her being her
father's daughter.   Accordingly, he said : "But you
must be aware, Jemima, that you do very little credit
to the education I have given you, when you make such
an impression as you must have done to-day, before
Mr Farquhar could have said what he did of you !"

"What did he say?" asked Jemima, still in the low,
husky tone of suppressed anger.

"Your mother says he remarked to her, 'What a
pity it is, that Jemima cannot maintain her opinions
without going into a passion; and what a pity it is,
that her opinions are such as to sanction, rather than
curb, these fits of rudeness and anger !'"

"Did he say that?" said Jemima, in a still lower
tone, not questioning her father, but speaking rather
to herself.

"I have no doubt he did," replied her father, gravely.
"Your mother is in the habit of repeating accurately
to me what takes place in my absence; besides which,
the whole speech is not one of hers; she has not
altered a word in the repetition, I am convinced.   I
have trained her to habits of accuracy very unusual in
a woman."

At another time, Jemima might have been inclined
to rebel against this system of carrying constant intelligence to headquarters, which she had long ago felt
as an insurmountable obstacle to any free communication with her mother; but now, her father's means of
acquiring knowledge faded into insignificance before the
nature of the information he imparted. She stood
quite still, grasping the chair-back, longing to be
dismissed.

"I have said enough now, I hope, to make you behave in a becoming manner to Mr Farquhar; if your
temper is too unruly to be always under your own
control, at least have respect to my injunctions, and
take some pains to curb it before him."

"May I go?" asked Jemima, chafing more and more.

"You may," said her father. When she left the
room he gently rubbed his hands together, satisfied
with the effect he had produced, and wondering how it
was, that one so well brought up as his daughter, could
ever say or do anything to provoke such a remark from
Mr Farquhar as that which he had heard repeated.

"Nothing can be more gentle and docile than she is
when spoken to in the proper manner. I must give
Farquhar a hint," said Mr Bradshaw to himself.

Jemima rushed upstairs, and locked herself into
her room. She began pacing up and down at first,
without shedding a tear; but then she suddenly
stopped, and burst out crying with passionate indignation.

"So! I am to behave well, not because it is right—
not because it is right—but to show off before Mr
Farquhar. Oh, Mr Farquhar!" said she, suddenly
changing to a sort of upbraiding tone of voice, "I did
not think so of you an hour ago. I did not think you
could choose a wife in that cold-hearted way, though
you did profess to act by rule and line; but you think
to have me, do you? because it is fitting and suitable, and
you want to be married, and can't spare time for wooing"
(she was lashing herself up by an exaggeration of all
her father had said). "And how often I have thought

you were too grand for me! but now I know better.
Now I can believe that all you do is done from cal-
culation; you are good because it adds to your business
credit—you talk in that high strain about principle
because it sounds well, and is respectable—and even
these things are better than your cold way of looking
out for a wife, just as you would do for a carpet, to add
to your comforts, and settle you respectably. But I
won't be that wife. You shall see something of me
which shall make you not acquiesce so quietly in the
arrangements of the firm." She cried too vehemently
to go on thinking or speaking. Then she stopped, and
said:

"Only an hour ago I was hoping—I don't know
what I was hoping—but I thought—oh! how I was
deceived!—I thought he had a true, deep, loving,
manly heart, which God might let me win; but now I
know he has only a calm, calculating head——"

If Jemima had been vehement and passionate before
this conversation with her father, it was better than
the sullen reserve she assumed now whenever Mr
Farquhar came to the house. He felt it deeply; no
reasoning with himself took off the pain he experienced. He tried to speak on the subjects she liked, in
the manner she liked, until he despised himself for the
unsuccessful efforts.

He stood between her and her father once or twice,
in obvious inconsistency with his own previously expressed opinions; and Mr Bradshaw piqued himself
upon his admirable management, in making Jemima
feel that she owed his indulgence or forbearance to
Mr Farquhar's interference; but Jemima—perverse,
miserable Jemima—thought that she hated Mr Farquhar
all the more. She respected her father inflexible,
much more than her father pompously giving up to
Mr Farquhar's subdued remonstrances on her behalf.
Even Mr Bradshaw was perplexed, and shut himself
up to consider how Jemima was to be made more fully
to understand his wishes and her own interests. But
there was nothing to take hold of as a ground for any

further conversation with her. Her actions were so submissive that they were spiritless ; she did all her father desired ; she did it with a nervous quickness and haste, if she thought that otherwise Mr Farquhar would interfere in any way. She wished evidently to owe nothing to him. She had begun by leaving the room when he came in, after the conversation she had had with her father ; but at Mr Bradshaw's first expression of his wish that she should remain, she remained— silent, indifferent, inattentive to all that was going on ; at least there was this appearance of inattention. She would work away at her sewing as if she were to earn her livelihood by it ; the light was gone out of her eyes as she lifted them up heavily before replying to any question, and the eyelids were often swollen with crying.

But in all this there was no positive fault. Mr Bradshaw could not have told her not to do this, or to do that, without her doing it ; for she had become much more docile of late.

It was a wonderful proof of the influence Ruth had gained in the family, that Mr Bradshaw, after much deliberation, congratulated himself on the wise deter- mination he had made of requesting her to speak to Jemima, and find out what feeling was at the bottom of all this change in her ways of going on.

He rang the bell.

"Is Mrs Denbigh here?" he inquired of the servant who answered it.

"Yes, sir ; she is just come."

"Beg her to come to me in this room as soon as she can leave the young ladies."

Ruth came.

"Sit down, Mrs Denbigh, sit down. I want to have a little conversation with you ; not about your pupils, they are going on well under your care, I am sure ; and I often congratulate myself on the choice I made— I assure you I do. But now I want to speak to you about Jemima. She is very fond of you, and perhaps you could take some opportunity of observing to her—

in short, of saying to her, that she is behaving very
foolishly—in fact, disgusting Mr Farquhar (who was, I
know, inclined to like her) by the sullen, sulky way
she behaves in, when he is by."

He paused for the ready acquiescence he expected.
But Ruth did not quite comprehend what was required
of her, and disliked the glimpse she had gained of the
task very much.

"I hardly understand, sir. You are displeased with
Miss Bradshaw's manners to Mr Farquhar."

"Well, well! not quite that; I am displeased with
her manners—they are sulky and abrupt, particularly
when he is by—and I want you (of whom she is so
fond) to speak to her about it."

"But I have never had the opportunity of noticing
them. Whenever I have seen her, she has been most
gentle and affectionate."

"But I think you do not hesitate to believe me,
when I say that I have noticed the reverse," said Mr
Bradshaw, drawing himself up.

"No, sir. I beg your pardon if I have expressed
myself so badly as to seem to doubt. But am I to tell
Miss Bradshaw that you have spoken of her faults to
me?" asked Ruth, a little astonished, and shrinking
more than ever from the proposed task.

"If you would allow me to finish what I have got to
say, without interruption, I could then tell you what I
do wish."

"I beg your pardon, sir," said Ruth, gently.

"I wish you to join our circle occasionally in an
evening; Mrs Bradshaw shall send you an invitation
when Mr Farquhar is likely to be here. Warned
by me, and, consequently, with your observation
quickened, you can hardly fail to notice instances of
what I have pointed out; and then I will trust to your
own good sense" (Mr Bradshaw bowed to her at this
part of his sentence) "to find an opportunity to remonstrate with her."

Ruth was beginning to speak, but he waved his hand
for another minute of silence.

"Only a minute, Mrs Denbigh; I am quite aware that, in requesting your presence occasionally in the evening, I shall be trespassing upon the time which is, in fact, your money; you may be assured that I shall not forget this little circumstance, and you can explain what I have said on this head to Benson and his sister."

"I am afraid I cannot do it," Ruth began; but while she was choosing words delicate enough to express her reluctance to act as he wished, he had almost bowed her out of the room; and thinking that she was modest in her estimate of her qualifications for remonstrating with his daughter, he added, blandly,

"No one so able, Mrs Denbigh. I have observed many qualities in you—observed when, perhaps, you have little thought it."

If he had observed Ruth that morning, he would have seen an absence of mind, and depression of spirits, not much to her credit as a teacher; for she could not bring herself to feel that she had any right to go into the family purposely to watch over and find fault with any one member of it. If she had seen anything wrong in Jemima, Ruth loved her so much that she would have told her of it in private; and with many doubts, how far she was the one to pull out the mote from any-one's eye, even in the most tender manner;—she would have had to conquer reluctance before she could have done even this; but there was something undefinably repugnant to her in the manner of acting which Mr Bradshaw had proposed, and she determined not to accept the invitations which were to place her in so false a position.

But as she was leaving the house, after the end of the lessons, while she stood in the hall tying on her bonnet, and listening to the last small confidences of her two pupils, she saw Jemima coming in through the garden-door, and was struck by the change in her looks. The large eyes, so brilliant once, were dim and clouded; the complexion sallow and colourless; a lowering expression was on the dark brow, and the corners of her mouth drooped as with sorrowful thoughts. She looked up, and her eyes met Ruth's.

"Oh! you beautiful creature!" thought Jemima, "with your still, calm, heavenly face, what are you to know of earth's trials! You have lost your beloved by death—but that is a blessed sorrow; the sorrow I have pulls me down and down, and makes me despise and hate every one—not you, though." And her face changing to a soft, tender look, she went up to Ruth, and kissed her fondly; as if it were a relief to be near some one on whose true pure heart she relied. Ruth returned the caress; and even while she did so, she suddenly rescinded her resolution to keep clear of what Mr Bradshaw had desired her to do. On her way home she resolved, if she could, to find out what were Jemima's secret feelings; and if (as from some previous knowledge she suspected) they were morbid and exaggerated in any way, to try and help her right with all the wisdom which true love gives. It was time that some one should come to still the storm in Jemima's turbulent heart, which was daily and hourly knowing less and less of peace. The irritating difficulty was to separate the two characters, which at two different times she had attributed to Mr Farquhar— the old one, which she had formerly believed to be true, that he was a man acting up to a high standard of lofty principle, and acting up without a struggle (and this last had been the circumstance which had made her rebellious and irritable once); the new one, which her father had excited in her suspicious mind, that Mr Farquhar was cold and calculating in all he did, and that she was to be transferred by the former, and accepted by the latter, as a sort of stock in trade —these were the two Mr Farquhars who clashed together in her mind. And in this state of irritation and prejudice, she could not bear the way in which he gave up his opinions to please her; that was not the way to win her; she liked him far better when he inflexibly and rigidly adhered to his idea of right and wrong, not even allowing any force

to temptation, and hardly any grace to repentance,
compared with that beauty of holiness which had
never yielded to sin. He had been her idol in those
days, as she found out now, however much at the time
she had opposed him with violence.

As for Mr Farquhar, he was almost weary of himself;
no reasoning, even no principle, seemed to have influence over him, for he saw that Jemima was not
at all what he approved of in woman. He saw her
uncurbed and passionate, affecting to despise the rules
of life he held most sacred, and indifferent to, if not
positively disliking him ; and yet he loved her dearly.
But he resolved to make a great effort of will, and
break loose from these trammels of sense. And
while he resolved, some old recollection would bring
her up, hanging on his arm, in all the confidence of
early girlhood, looking up in his face with her soft
dark eyes, and questioning him upon the mysterious
subjects which had so much interest for both of them
at that time, although they had become only matter
for dissension in these later days.

It was also true, as Mr Bradshaw had said, Mr
Farquhar wished to marry, and had not much choice
in the small town of Eccleston. He never put this
so plainly before himself, as a reason for choosing
Jemima, as her father had done to her ; but it was
an unconscious motive all the same. However, now
he had lectured himself into the resolution to make
a pretty long absence from Eccleston, and see if,
amongst his distant friends, there was no woman more
in accordance with his ideal, who could put the naughty,
wilful, plaguing Jemima Bradshaw out of his head, if
he did not soon perceive some change in her for the
better.

A few days after Ruth's conversation with Mr Bradshaw, the invitation she had been expecting, yet
dreading, came. It was to her alone. Mr and Miss
Benson were pleased at the compliment to her, and
urged her acceptance of it. She wished that they
had been included ; she had not thought it right, or

kind to Jemima, to tell them why she was going, and she feared now lest they should feel a little hurt that they were not asked too. But she need not have been afraid. They were glad and proud of the attention to her, and never thought of themselves.

"Ruthie, what gown shall you wear to-night? your dark grey one, I suppose?" asked Miss Benson.

"Yes, I suppose so. I never thought of it; but that is my best."

"Well, then, I shall quill up a ruff for you. You know I am a famous quiller of net."

Ruth came downstairs with a little flush on her cheeks when she was ready to go. She held her bonnet and shawl in her hand, for she knew Miss Benson and Sally would want to see her dressed.

"Is not mamma pretty?" asked Leonard, with a child's pride.

"She looks very nice and tidy," said Miss Benson, who had an idea that children should not talk or think about beauty.

"I think my ruff looks so nice," said Ruth, with gentle pleasure. And indeed it did look nice, and set off the pretty round throat most becomingly. Her hair, now grown long and thick, was smoothed as close to her head as its waving nature would allow, and plaited up in a great rich knot low down behind. The grey gown was as plain as plain could be.

"You should have light gloves, Ruth," said Miss Benson. She went upstairs, and brought down a delicate pair of Limerick ones, which had been long treasured up in a walnut-shell.*

"They say them gloves is made of chicken's-skins," said Sally, examining them curiously. "I wonder how they set about skinning 'em."

"Here, Ruth," said Mr Benson, coming in from the garden, "here's a rose or two for you. I am sorry there are no more; I hoped I should have had my yellow rose out by this time, but the damask and the white are in a warmer corner, and have got the start."

Miss Benson and Leonard stood at the door, and watched her down the little passage-street till she was out of sight.

She had hardly touched the bell at Mr Bradshaw's door, when Mary and Elizabeth opened it with boisterous glee.

"We saw you coming—we've been watching for you —we want you to come round the garden before tea ; papa is not come in yet. Do come."

She went round the garden with a little girl clinging to each arm. It was full of sunshine and flowers, and this made the contrast between it and the usual large family room (which fronted the north-east, and therefore had no evening sun to light up its cold drab furniture) more striking than usual. It looked very gloomy. There was the great dining-table, heavy and square ; the range of chairs, straight and square ; the work-boxes, useful and square ; the colouring of walls, and carpet, and curtains, all of the coldest description ; everything was handsome, and everything was ugly. Mrs Bradshaw was asleep in her easy chair when they came in. Jemima had just put down her work, and, lost in thought, she leant her cheek on her hand. When she saw Ruth she brightened a little, and went to her and kissed her. Mrs Bradshaw jumped up at the sound of their entrance, and was wide awake in a moment.

"Oh ! I thought your father was here," said she, evidently relieved to find that he had not come in and caught her sleeping.

"Thank you, Mrs Denbigh, for coming to us to-night," said she, in the quiet tone in which she generally spoke in her husband's absence. When he was there, a sort of constant terror of displeasing him made her voice sharp and nervous ; the children knew that many a thing passed over by their mother when their father was away, was sure to be noticed by her when he was present ; and noticed, too, in a cross and querulous manner, for she was so much afraid of the blame which on any occasion of their misbehaviour fell

upon her.   And yet she looked up to her husband with
a reverence, and regard, and a faithfulness of love,
which his decision of character was likely to produce
on a weak and anxious mind.   He was a rest and a
support to her, on whom she cast all her respon-
sibilities ; she was an obedient, unremonstrating wife
to him ; no stronger affection had ever brought her
duty to him into conflict with any desire of her heart.
She loved her children dearly, though they all perplexed her very frequently.   Her son was her especial
darling, because he very seldom brought her into any
scrapes with his father ; he was so cautious and prudent,
and had the art of " keeping a calm sough "*about any
difficulty he might be in.   With all her dutiful sense
of the obligation, which her husband enforced upon
her, to notice and tell him everything that was going
wrong in the household, and especially among his
children, Mrs Bradshaw, somehow, contrived to be
honestly blind to a good deal that was not praiseworthy
in Master Richard.

Mr Bradshaw came in before long, bringing with
him Mr Farquhar. Jemima had been talking to Ruth
with some interest before then ; but, on seeing Mr
Farquhar, she bent her head down over her work, went
a little paler, and turned obstinately silent.   Mr
Bradshaw longed to command her to speak ; but even
he had a suspicion that what she might say, when so
commanded, might be rather worse in its effect than
her gloomy silence ; so he held his peace, and a dis-
contented, angry kind of peace it was.   Mrs Bradshaw
saw that something was wrong, but could not tell what ;
only she became every moment more trembling, and
nervous, and irritable, and sent Mary and Elizabeth
off on all sorts of contradictory errands to the servants,
and made the tea twice as strong, and sweetened it
twice as much as usual, in hopes of pacifying her
husband with good things.

Mr Farquhar had gone for the last time, or so he
thought.   He had resolved (for the fifth time) that he
would go and watch Jemima once more, and if her

temper got the better of her, and she showed the old sullenness again, and gave the old proofs of indifference to his good opinion, he would give her up altogether, and seek a wife elsewhere. He sat watching her with folded arms, and in silence. Altogether they were a pleasant family party!

Jemima wanted to wind a skein of wool. Mr Farquhar saw it, and came to her, anxious to do her this little service. She turned away pettishly, and asked Ruth to hold it for her.

Ruth was hurt for Mr Farquhar, and looked sorrowfully at Jemima; but Jemima would not see her glance of upbraiding, as Ruth, hoping that she would relent, delayed a little to comply with her request. Mr Farquhar did; and went back to his seat to watch them both. He saw Jemima turbulent and stormy in look; he saw Ruth, to all appearance, heavenly calm as the angels, or with only that little tinge of sorrow which her friend's behaviour had called forth. He saw the unusual beauty of her face and form, which he had never noticed before; and he saw Jemima, with all the brilliancy she once possessed in eyes and complexion, dimmed and faded. He watched Ruth, speaking low and soft to the little girls, who seemed to come to her in every difficulty; and he remarked her gentle firmness when their bedtime came, and they pleaded to stay up longer (their father was absent in his counting-house, or they would not have dared to do so). He liked Ruth's soft, distinct, unwavering "No! you must go. You must keep to what is right," far better than the good-natured yielding to entreaty he had formerly admired in Jemima. He was wandering off into this comparison, while Ruth, with delicate and unconscious tact, was trying to lead Jemima into some subject which should take her away from the thoughts, whatever they were, that made her so ungracious and rude.

Jemima was ashamed of herself before Ruth, in a way which she had never been before anyone else. She valued Ruth's good opinion so highly, that she

dreaded lest her friend should perceive her faults.
She put a check upon herself—a check at first; but
after a little time she had forgotten something of her
trouble, and listened to Ruth, and questioned her
about Leonard, and smiled at his little witticisms; and
only the sighs, that would come up from the very force
of habit, brought back the consciousness of her unhappiness. Before the end of the evening, Jemima
had allowed herself to speak to Mr Farquhar in the
old way—questioning, differing, disputing. She was
recalled to the remembrance of that miserable conversation by the entrance of her father. After that she
was silent. But he had seen her face more animated,
and bright with a smile, as she spoke to Mr Farquhar;
and although he regretted the loss of her complexion
(for she was still very pale), he was highly pleased
with the success of his project. He never doubted but
that Ruth had given her some sort of private exhortation to behave better. He could not have understood
the pretty art with which, by simply banishing unpleasant subjects, and throwing a wholesome natural
sunlit tone over others, Ruth had insensibly drawn
Jemima out of her gloom. He resolved to buy Mrs
Denbigh a handsome silk gown the very next day.
He did not believe she had a silk gown, poor creature!
He had noticed that dark grey stuff, this long long
time, as her Sunday dress. He liked the colour; the
silk one should be just the same tinge. Then he
thought that it would, perhaps, be better to choose a
lighter shade, one which might be noticed as different
to the old gown. For he had no doubt she would like
to have it remarked, and, perhaps, would not object to
tell people that it was a present from Mr Bradshaw—
a token of his approbation. He smiled a little to
himself as he thought of this additional source of
pleasure to Ruth. She, in the meantime, was getting
up to go home. While Jemima was lighting the bed-
candle at the lamp, Ruth came round to bid good
night. Mr Bradshaw could not allow her to remain till
the morrow, uncertain whether he was satisfied or not.

"Good night, Mrs Denbigh," said he.   "Good
night. Thank you. I am obliged to you—I am
exceedingly obliged to you."

He laid emphasis on these words, for he was pleased
to see Mr Farquhar step forward to help Jemima in
her little office.

Mr Farquhar offered to accompany Ruth home ; but
the streets that intervened between Mr Bradshaw's
and the Chapel-house were so quiet that he desisted,
when he learnt from Ruth's manner how much she
disliked his proposal. Mr Bradshaw, too, instantly
observed :

"Oh ! Mrs Denbigh need not trouble you, Farquhar.
I have servants at liberty at any moment to attend on
her, if she wishes it."

In fact, he wanted to make hay while the sun shone,
and to detain Mr Farquhar a little longer, now that
Jemima was so gracious. She went upstairs with Ruth
to help her to put on her things.

"Dear Jemima !" said Ruth, "I am so glad to see
you looking better to-night ! You quite frightened
me this morning, you looked so ill."

"Did I ?" replied Jemima. "Oh, Ruth ! I have
been so unhappy lately. I want you to come and put
me to rights," she continued, half smiling. "You
know I'm a sort of out-pupil of yours, though we are
so nearly of an age. You ought to lecture me, and
make me good."

"Should I, dear ?" said Ruth. "I don't think I'm
the one to do it."

"Oh, yes ! you are — you've done me good to-
night."

"Well, if I can do anything for you, tell me what
it is ?" asked Ruth, tenderly.

"Oh, not now—not now," replied Jemima. "I
could not tell you here. It's a long story, and I don't
know that I can tell you at all. Mamma might come
up at any moment, and papa would be sure to ask
what we had been talking about so long."

"Take your own time, love," said Ruth ; "only

remember, as far as I can, how glad I am to help you."

"You're too good, my darling!" said Jemima, fondly.

"Don't say so," replied Ruth, earnestly, almost as if she were afraid. "God knows I am not."

"Well! we're none of us too good," answered Jemima; "I know that. But you *are* very good. Nay, I won't call you so, if it makes you look sb miserable. But come away downstairs."

With the fragrance of Ruth's sweetness lingering about her, Jemima was her best self during the next half hour. Mr Bradshaw was more and more pleased, and raised the price of the silk, which he was going to give Ruth, sixpence a yard during the time. Mr Farquhar went home through the garden-way, happier than he had been this long time. He even caught himself humming the old refrain:

> On revient, on revient toujours,
> A ses premiers amours.*

But as soon as he was aware of what he was doing, he cleared away the remnants of the song into a cough, which was sonorous, if not perfectly real.

CHAPTER XXI

THE next morning, as Jemima and her mother sat at their work, it came into the head of the former to remember her father's very marked way of thanking Ruth the evening before.

"What a favourite Mrs Denbigh is with papa," said she. "I am sure I don't wonder at it. Did you notice, mamma, how he thanked her for coming here last night?"

"Yes, dear; but I don't think it was all——" Mrs Bradshaw stopped short. She was never certain if it was right or wrong to say anything.

"Not all what?" asked Jemima, when she saw her mother was not going to finish the sentence.

"Not all because Mrs Denbigh came to tea here," replied Mrs Bradshaw.

"Why, what else could he be thanking her for? What has she done?" asked Jemima, stimulated to curiosity by her mother's hesitating manner.

"I don't know if I ought to tell you," said Mrs Bradshaw.

"Oh, very well!" said Jemima, rather annoyed.

"Nay, dear! your papa never said I was not to tell; perhaps I may."

"Never mind! I don't want to hear," in a piqued tone.

There was silence for a little while. Jemima was trying to think of something else, but her thoughts would revert to the wonder what Mrs Denbigh could have done for her father.

"I think I may tell you, though," said Mrs Bradshaw, half questioning.

Jemima had the honour not to urge any confidence, but she was too curious to take any active step towards repressing it.

Mrs Bradshaw went on. "I think you deserve to know. It is partly your doing that papa is so pleased with Mrs Denbigh. He is going to buy her a silk gown this morning, and I think you ought to know why."

"Why?" asked Jemima.

"Because papa is so pleased to find that you mind what she says."

"I mind what she says! to be sure I do, and always did. But why should papa give her a gown for that? I think he ought to give it me rather," said Jemima, half laughing.

"I am sure he would, dear; he will give you one, I am certain, if you want one. He was so pleased to see you like your old self to Mr Farquhar last night. We neither of us could think what had come over you this last month; but now all seems right."

A dark cloud came over Jemima's face. She did
not like this close observation and constant comment
upon her manners ; and what had Ruth to do with it ?

" I am glad you were pleased," said she, very coldly.
Then, after a pause, she added, " But you have not
told me what Mrs Denbigh had to do with my good
behaviour."

" Did not she speak to you about it ? " asked Mrs
Bradshaw, looking up.

" No ; why should she.   She has no right to criti-
cise what I do.   She would not be so impertinent,"
said Jemima, feeling very uncomfortable and suspicious.

" Yes, love ! she would have had a right, for papa
had desired her to do it."

" Papa desired her ! What do you mean, mamma ? "

" Oh, dear ! I dare say I should not have told
you," said Mrs Bradshaw, perceiving, from Jemima's
tone of voice, that something had gone wrong.   " Only
you spoke as if it would be impertinent in Mrs
Denbigh, and I am sure she would not do anything
that was impertinent.   You know, it would be but
right for her to do what papa told her ; and he said a
great deal to her, the other day, about finding out
why you were so cross, and bringing you right.   And
you are right now, dear ! " said Mrs Bradshaw, soothingly, thinking that Jemima was annoyed (like a
good child) at the recollection of how naughty she had
been.

" Then papa is going to give Mrs Denbigh a gown
because I was civil to Mr Farquhar last night ? "

" Yes, dear ! " said Mrs Bradshaw, more and more
frightened at Jemima's angry manner of speaking—
low-toned, but very indignant.

Jemima remembered, with smouldered anger, Ruth's
pleading way of wiling her from her sullenness the
night before.   Management everywhere ! but in this
case it was peculiarly revolting ; so much so, that she
could hardly bear to believe that the seemingly-trans-
parent Ruth had lent herself to it.

"Are you sure, mamma, that papa asked Mrs Denbigh to make me behave differently? It seems so strange."

"I am quite sure. He spoke to her last Friday morning in the study. I remember it was Friday, because Mrs Dean was working here."

Jemima remembered now that she had gone into the school-room on the Friday, and found her sisters lounging about, and wondering what papa could possibly want with Mrs Denbigh.

After this conversation, Jemima repulsed all Ruth's timid efforts to ascertain the cause of her disturbance, and to help her if she could. Ruth's tender, sympathizing manner, as she saw Jemima daily looking more wretched, was distasteful to the latter in the highest degree. She could not say that Mrs Denbigh's conduct was positively wrong—it might even be quite right; but it was inexpressibly repugnant to her to think of her father consulting with a stranger (a week ago she almost considered Ruth as a sister) how to manage his daughter, so as to obtain the end he wished for; yes, even if that end was for her own good.

She was thankful and glad to see a brown paper parcel lying on the hall table, with a note in Ruth's handwriting, addressed to her father. She *knew* what it was, the grey silk dress. That she was sure Ruth would never accept.

No one henceforward could induce Jemima to enter into conversation with Mr Farquhar. She suspected manoeuvring in the simplest actions, and was miserable in this constant state of suspicion. She would not allow herself to like Mr Farquhar, even when he said things the most after her own heart. She heard him, one evening, talking with her father about the principles of trade. Her father stood out for the keenest, sharpest work, consistent with honesty; if he had not been her father she would, perhaps, have thought some of his sayings inconsistent with true Christian honesty. He was for driving hard bargains, exacting interest and payment of just bills to a day. That was (he said) the only way in which trade could be conducted. Once allow a margin of uncertainty, or where feelings, instead of maxims, were to be the guide, and all hope of there ever being any good men of business was ended.

"Suppose a delay of a month in requiring payment might save a man's credit—prevent his becoming a bankrupt?" put in Mr Farquhar.

"I would not give it him. I would let him have money to set up again as soon as he had passed the Bankruptcy Court; if he never passed, I might, in some cases, make him an allowance, but I would always keep my justice and my charity separate."

"And yet charity (in your sense of the word) degrades; justice, tempered with mercy and consideration, elevates."

"That is not justice—justice is certain and inflexible. No! Mr Farquhar, you must not allow any Quixotic notions to mingle with your conduct as a tradesman."

And so they went on; Jemima's face glowing with sympathy in all Mr Farquhar said; till once, on looking up suddenly with sparkling eyes, she saw a glance of her father's which told her, as plain as words could say, that he was watching the effect of Mr Farquhar's speeches upon his daughter. She was chilled thenceforward; she thought her father prolonged the argument, in order to call out those sentiments which he knew would most recommend his partner to his daughter. She would so fain have let herself love Mr Farquhar; but this constant manœuvring, in which she did not feel clear that he did not take a passive part, made her sick at heart. She even wished that they might not go through the form of pretending to try to gain her consent to the marriage, if it involved all this premeditated action and speech-making—such moving about of every one into their right places, like pieces at chess. She felt as if she would rather be bought openly, like an Oriental daughter, where no one is degraded in their own eyes by being parties to such a contract. The consequences of all this "admirable management" of Mr Bradshaw's would have been very unfortunate to Mr Farquhar (who was innocent of all connivance in any of the plots—indeed, would have been as much annoyed at them as Jemima, had he been aware of them), but that the impression made upon him by Ruth on the evening I have so lately described, was deepened by the contrast which her behaviour made to Miss Bradshaw's on one or two more recent occasions.

There was no use, he thought, in continuing attentions so evidently distasteful to Jemima. To her, a young girl hardly out of the schoolroom, he probably appeared like an old man; and he might even lose the friendship with which she used to regard him, and which was, and ever would be, very dear to him, if he persevered in trying to be considered as a lover. He should always feel affectionately towards her; her very faults gave her an interest in his eyes, for which he had blamed himself most conscientiously and most uselessly when he was looking upon her as his future wife, but which the said conscience would learn to approve of when she sank down to the place of a young friend, over whom he might exercise a good and salutary interest. Mrs Denbigh, if not many months older in years, had known sorrow and cares so early that she was much older in character. Besides, her shy reserve, and her quiet daily walk within the lines of duty, were much in accordance with Mr Farquhar's notion of what a wife should be. Still, it was a wrench to take his affections away from Jemima. If she had not helped him to do so by every means in her power, he could never have accomplished it.

Yes! by every means in her power had Jemima alienated her lover, her beloved—for so he was in fact. And now her quick-sighted eyes saw he was gone for ever—past recall; for did not her jealous, sore heart feel, even before he himself was conscious of the fact, that he was drawn towards sweet, lovely, composed, and dignified Ruth—one who always thought before she spoke (as Mr Farquhar used to bid Jemima do)—who never was tempted by sudden impulse, but walked the world calm and self-governed. What now availed Jemima's reproaches, as she remembered the days when he had watched her with earnest, attentive eyes, as he now watched Ruth; and the times since, when, led astray by her morbid fancy, she had turned away from all his advances!

"It was only in March—last March, he called me 'dear Jemima.' Ah, don't I remember it well? The pretty nosegay of green-house flowers that he gave me in exchange for the wild daffodils—and how he seemed to care for the flowers I gave him—and how he looked at me, and thanked me—that is all gone and over now."

Her sisters came in bright and glowing.

"Oh, Jemima, how nice and cool you are, sitting in this shady room!" (She had felt it even chilly.) "We have been such a long walk! We are so tired. It is so hot."

"Why did you go, then?" said she.

"Oh! we wanted to go. We would not have stayed at home on any account. It has been so pleasant," said Mary.

"We've been to Scaurside Wood, to gather wild strawberries," said Elizabeth. "Such a quantity! We've left a whole basketful in the dairy. Mr Farquhar says he'll teach us how to dress them in the way he learnt in Germany, if we can get him some hock. Do you think papa will let us have some?"

"Was Mr Farquhar with you?" asked Jemima, a dull light coming into her eyes.

"Yes, we told him this morning that mamma wanted us to take some old linen to the lame man at Scaurside Farm, and that we meant to coax Mrs Denbigh to let us go into the wood and gather strawberries," said Elizabeth.

"I thought he would make some excuse and come," said the quick-witted Mary, as eager and thoughtless an observer of one love affair as of another, and quite forgetting that, not many weeks ago, she had fancied an attachment between him and Jemima.

"Did you? I did not," replied Elizabeth. "At least I never thought about it. I was quite startled when I heard his horse's feet behind us on the road."

"He said he was going to the farm, and could take our basket. Was not it kind of him?" Jemima did not answer, so Mary continued:

"You know it's a great pull up to the farm, and we were so hot already. The road was quite white and baked; it hurt my eyes terribly. I was so glad when Mrs Denbigh said we might turn into the wood. The light was quite green there, the branches are so thick overhead."

"And there are whole beds of wild strawberries," said Elizabeth, taking up the tale now Mary was out of breath. Mary fanned herself with her bonnet, while Elizabeth went on:

"You know where the grey rock crops out, don't you, Jemima? Well, there was a complete carpet of strawberry runners. So pretty! And we could hardly step without treading the little bright scarlet berries under foot."

"We did so wish for Leonard," put in Mary.

"Yes! but Mrs Denbigh gathered a great many for him. And Mr Farquhar gave her all his."

"I thought you said he had gone on to Dawson's farm," said Jemima.

"Oh, yes! he just went up there; and then he left his horse there, like a wise man, and came to us in the pretty, cool, green wood. Oh, Jemima, it was so pretty—little flecks of light coming down here and there through the leaves, and quivering on the ground. You must go with us to-morrow."

"Yes," said Mary, "we're going again to-morrow. We could not gather nearly all the strawberries."

"And Leonard is to go too, to-morrow."

"Yes! we thought of such a capital plan. That's to say, Mr Farquhar thought of it—we wanted to carry

Leonard up the hill in a king's cushion, but Mrs Denbigh would not hear of it."

"She said it would tire us so; and yet she wanted him to gather strawberries!"

"And so," interrupted Mary, for by this time the two girls were almost speaking together, "Mr Farquhar is to bring him up before him on his horse."

"You'll go with us, won't you, dear Jemima?" asked Elizabeth; "it will be at——"

"No! I can't go!" said Jemima, abruptly. "Don't ask me—I can't."

The little girls were hushed into silence by her manner; for whatever she might be to those above her in age and position, to those below her Jemima was almost invariably gentle. She felt that they were wondering at her.

"Go upstairs and take off your things. You know papa does not like you to come into this room in the shoes in which you have been out."

She was glad to cut her sisters short in the details which they were so mercilessly inflicting—details which she must harden herself to, before she could hear them quietly and unmoved. She saw that she had lost her place as the first object in Mr Farquhar's eyes—a position she had hardly cared for while she was secure in the enjoyment of it; but the charm of it now was redoubled, in her acute sense of how she had forfeited it by her own doing, and her own fault. For if he were the cold, calculating man her father had believed him to be, and had represented him as being to her, would he care for a portionless widow in humble circumstances like Mrs Denbigh; no money, no connexion, encumbered with her boy? The very action which proved Mr Farquhar to be lost to Jemima, reinstated him on his throne in her fancy. And she must go on in hushed quietness, quivering with every fresh token of his preference for another! That other, too, one so infinitely more worthy of him than herself; so that she could not have even the poor comfort of thinking, that he had no discrimination, and was throwing himself away on a common or worthless person. Ruth was beautiful, gentle, good, and conscientious. The hot colour flushed up into Jemima's sallow face as she became aware that, even while she acknowledged these excellences on Mrs Denbigh's part, she hated her. The recollection of her marble face wearied her even to sickness; the tones of her low voice were irritating from their very softness. Her goodness, undoubted as it was, was more distasteful than many faults which had more savour of human struggle in them.

"What was this terrible demon in her heart?" asked Jemima's better angel. "Was she, indeed, given up to possession? Was not this the old stinging hatred which had prompted so many crimes? The hatred of all sweet virtues which might win the love denied to us? The old anger that wrought in the elder brother's heart, till it ended in the murder of the gentle Abel, while yet the world was young?"

"Oh, God! help me! I did not know I was so wicked," cried Jemima aloud in her agony. It had been a terrible glimpse into the dark lurid gulf—the capability for evil, in her heart. She wrestled with the demon, but he would not depart; it was to be a struggle whether or not she was to be given up to him, in this her time of sore temptation.

All the next day long, she sat and pictured the happy strawberry gathering going on, even then, in pleasant Scaurside Wood. Every touch of fancy which could heighten her idea of their enjoyment, and of Mr Farquhar's attention to the blushing, conscious Ruth—every such touch which would add a pang to her self-reproach and keen jealousy, was added by her imagination. She got up and walked about, to try and stop her over-busy fancy by bodily exercise. But she had eaten little all day, and was weak and faint in the intense heat of the sunny garden. Even the long grass walk under the filbert hedge, was parched and dry in the glowing August sun. Yet her sisters found her there when they re-

turned, walking quickly up and down, as if to warm
herself on some winter's day. They were very weary;
and not half so communicative as on the day before,
now that Jemima was craving for every detail to add
to her agony.

"Yes! Leonard came up before Mr Farquhar. Oh!
how hot it is, Jemima; do sit down, and I'll tell you
about it, but I can't if you keep walking so!"

"I can't sit still to-day," said Jemima, springing up
from the turf as soon as she had sat down. "Tell me!
I can hear you while I walk about."

"Oh! but I can't shout; I can hardly speak I am
so tired. Mr Farquhar brought Leonard——"

"You've told me that before," said Jemima, sharply.

"Well! I don't know what else to tell. Somebody
had been since yesterday, and gathered nearly all the
strawberries off the grey rock. Jemima! Jemima!"
said Elizabeth, faintly, "I am so dizzy—I think I am
ill."

The next minute the tired girl lay swooning on the
grass. It was an outlet for Jemima's fierce energy.
With a strength she had never again, and never had
known before, she lifted up her fainting sister, and
bidding Mary run and clear the way, she carried her
in through the open garden-door, up the wide old-
fashioned stairs, and laid her on the bed in her own
room, where the breeze from the window came softly
and pleasantly through the green shade of the vine-
leaves and jessamine.

"Give me the water. Run for mamma, Mary,"
said Jemima, as she saw that the fainting-fit did not
yield to the usual remedy of a horizontal position, and
the water sprinkling.

"Dear! dear Lizzie!" said Jemima, kissing the
pale, unconscious face. "I think you loved me,
darling."

The long walk on the hot day had been too much
for the delicate Elizabeth, who was fast outgrowing
her strength. It was many days before she regained
any portion of her spirit and vigour. After that faint-

ing-fit, she lay listless and weary, without appetite or
interest, through the long sunny autumn weather, on
the bed or on the couch in Jemima's room, whither she
had been carried at first. It was a comfort to Mrs
Bradshaw to be able at once to discover what it was
that had knocked up Elizabeth; she did not rest easily
until she had settled upon a cause for every ailment or
illness in the family. It was a stern consolation to Mr
Bradshaw, during his time of anxiety respecting his
daughter, to be able to blame somebody. He could
not, like his wife, have taken comfort from an inanimate fact; he wanted the satisfaction of feeling that
some one had been in fault, or else this never could
have happened. Poor Ruth did not need his implied
reproaches. When she saw her gentle Elizabeth lying
feeble and languid, her heart blamed her for thought-
lessness, so severely as to make her take all Mr Bradshaw's words and hints as too light censure for the
careless way in which, to please her own child, she had
allowed her two pupils to fatigue themselves with such
long walks. She begged hard to take her share of
nursing. Every spare moment she went to Mr Bradshaw's, and asked, with earnest humility, to be allowed
to pass them with Elizabeth; and, as it was often a
relief to have her assistance, Mrs Bradshaw received
these entreaties very kindly, and desired her to go upstairs, where Elizabeth's pale countenance brightened
when she saw her, but where Jemima sat in silent
annoyance that her own room was now become open
ground for one, whom her heart rose up against, to
enter in and be welcomed. Whether it was that Ruth,
who was not an inmate of the house, brought with her
a fresher air, more change of thought to the invalid, I
do not know, but Elizabeth always gave her a peculiarly
tender greeting; and if she had sunk down into languid
fatigue, in spite of all Jemima's endeavours to interest
her, she roused up into animation when Ruth came in
with a flower, a book, or a brown and ruddy pear,
sending out the warm fragrance it retained from the
sunny garden wall at Chapel-house.

The jealous dislike which Jemima was allowing to
grow up in her heart against Ruth was, as she thought,
never shown in word or deed. She was cold in manner,
because she could not be hypocritical ; but her words
were polite and kind in purport ; and she took pains
to make her actions the same as formerly. But rule
and line may measure out the figure of a man ; it is
the soul that gives it life ; and there was no soul, no
inner meaning, breathing out in Jemima's actions.
Ruth felt the change acutely. She suffered from it
some time before she ventured to ask what had occasioned it. But, one day, she took Miss Bradshaw by
surprise, when they were alone together for a few
minutes, by asking her if she had vexed her in any
way, she was so changed? It is sad when friendship
has cooled so far as to render such a question necessary.
Jemima went rather paler than usual, and then made
answer :
"Changed ! How do you mean? How am I
changed? What do I say or do different from what I
used to do?"
But the tone was so constrained and cold, that
Ruth's heart sank within her. She knew now, as well
as words could have told her, that not only had the
old feeling of love passed away from Jemima, but that
it had gone unregretted, and no attempt had been
made to recall it. Love was very precious to Ruth
now, as of old time. It was one of the faults of her
nature to be ready to make any sacrifices for those
who loved her, and to value affection almost above its
price. She had yet to learn the lesson, that it is more
blessed to love than to be beloved ; and lonely as the
impressible years of her youth had been—without
parents, without brother or sister—it was, perhaps, no
wonder that she clung tenaciously to every symptom
of regard, and could not relinquish the love of anyone
without a pang.
The doctor who was called in to Elizabeth prescribed
sea-air as the best means of recruiting her strength.
Mr Bradshaw, who liked to spend money ostentatiously,

went down straight to Abermouth,*and engaged a house
for the remainder of the autumn ; for, as he told the
medical man, money was no object to him in comparison with his children's health ; and the doctor
cared too little about the mode in which his remedy
was administered, to tell Mr Bradshaw that lodgings
would have done as well, or better, than the complete
house he had seen fit to take.   For it was now necessary
to engage servants, and take much trouble, which
might have been obviated, and Elizabeth's removal
effected more quietly and speedily, if she had gone
into lodgings.   As it was, she was weary of hearing
all the planning and talking, and deciding and un-
deciding, and re-deciding, before it was possible for
her to go.   Her only comfort was in the thought, that
dear Mrs Denbigh was to go with her.

It had not been entirely by way of pompously spending his money that Mr Bradshaw had engaged this seaside house.   He was glad to get his little girls and
their governess out of the way ; for a busy time was
impending, when he should want his head clear for
electioneering purposes, and his house clear for electioneering hospitality.   He was the mover of a project
for bringing forward a man, on the Liberal and Dissenting interest, to contest the election*with the old
Tory member, who had on several successive occasions
walked over the course, as he and his family owned
half the town, and votes and rent were paid alike to
the landlord.

Kings of Eccleston had Mr Cranworth and his ancestors been this many a long year ; their right was so
little disputed that they never thought of acknowledging the allegiance so readily paid to them.   The old
feudal feeling between landowner and tenant did not
quake prophetically at the introduction of manufac-
tures ; the Cranworth family ignored the growing
power of the manufacturers, more especially as the
principal person engaged in the trade was a Dissenter.
But notwithstanding this lack of patronage from the
one great family in the neighbourhood, the business

flourished, increased, and spread wide ; and the Dissenting head thereof looked around, about the time of which I speak, and felt himself powerful enough to defy the great Cranworth interest even in their hereditary stronghold, and, by so doing, avenge the slights of many years—slights which rankled in Mr Bradshaw's mind as much as if he did not go to chapel twice every Sunday, and pay the largest pew-rent of any member of Mr Benson's congregation.

Accordingly, Mr Bradshaw had applied to one Coppoc, one of the Liberal parliamentary agents in London—a man whose only principle was to do wrong on the Liberal side ; he would not act, right or wrong, for a Tory, but for a Whig the latitude of his conscience had never yet been discovered. It was possible Mr Bradshaw was not aware of the character of this agent ; at any rate, he knew he was the man for his purpose, which was to hear of some one who would come forward as a candidate for the representation of Eccleston on the Dissenting interest.

"There are in round numbers about six hundred voters," said he ; "two hundred are decidedly in the Cranworth interest—dare not offend Mr Cranworth, poor souls ! Two hundred more we may calculate upon as pretty certain—factory hands, or people connected with our trade in some way or another—who are indignant at the stubborn way in which Cranworth has contested the right of water ; two hundred are doubtful."

"Don't much care either way," said the parliamentary agent. "Of course, we must make them care."

Mr Bradshaw rather shrunk from the knowing look with which this was said. He hoped that Mr Pilson did not mean to allude to bribery ; but he did not express this hope, because he thought it would deter the agent from using this means, and it was possible it might prove to be the only way. And if he (Mr Bradshaw) once embarked on such on enterprise, there must be no failure. By some expedient or another, success must be certain, or he could have nothing to do with it.

The parliamentary agent was well accustomed to deal with all kinds and shades of scruples. He was most at home with men who had none; but still he could allow for human weakness; and he perfectly understood Mr Bradshaw.

"I have a notion I know of a man who will just suit your purpose. Plenty of money—does not know what to do with it, in fact—tired of yachting, travelling, wants something new. I heard, through some of the means of intelligence I employ, that not very long ago he was wishing for a seat in Parliament."

"A Liberal?" said Mr Bradshaw.

"Decidedly. Belongs to a family who were in the Long Parliament in their day."

Mr Bradshaw rubbed his hands.

"Dissenter?" asked he.

"No, no! Not so far as that. But very lax Church."

"What is his name?" asked Mr Bradshaw, eagerly.

"Excuse me. Until I am certain that he would like to come forward for Eccleston, I think I had better not mention his name."

The anonymous gentleman did like to come forward, and his name proved to be Donne. He and Mr Bradshaw had been in correspondence during all the time of Mr Ralph Cranworth's illness, and when he died, everything was arranged ready for a start, even before the Cranworths had determined who should keep the seat warm till the eldest son came of age, for the father was already member for the county. Mr Donne was to come down to canvass in person, and was to take up his abode at Mr Bradshaw's; and therefore it was that the seaside house, within twenty miles' distance of Eccleston was found to be so convenient as an infirmary and nursery for those members of his family who were likely to be useless, if not positive encumbrances, during the forthcoming election.

CHAPTER XXII

JEMIMA did not know whether she wished to go to
Abermouth or not. She longed for change. She
wearied of the sights and sounds of home. But yet
she could not bear to leave the neighbourhood of Mr
Farquhar; especially as, if she went to Abermouth,
Ruth would in all probability be left to take her
holiday at home.

When Mr Bradshaw decided that she was to go,
Ruth tried to feel glad that he gave her the means of
repairing her fault towards Elizabeth; and she resolved
to watch over the two girls most faithfully and carefully, and to do all in her power to restore the invalid
to health. But a tremor came over her whenever
she thought of leaving Leonard; she had never
quitted him for a day, and it seemed to her as if
her brooding, constant care, was his natural and
necessary shelter from all evils—from very death
itself. She would not go to sleep at nights, in order
to enjoy the blessed consciousness of having him near
her; when she was away from him teaching her pupils,
she kept trying to remember his face, and print it
deep on her heart, against the time when days and
days would elapse without her seeing that little darling
countenance. Miss Benson would wonder to her
brother that Mr Bradshaw did not propose that
Leonard should accompany his mother; he only
begged her not to put such an idea into Ruth's
head, as he was sure Mr Bradshaw had no thoughts
of doing any such thing, yet to Ruth it might be a
hope, and then a disappointment. His sister scolded
him for being so cold-hearted; but he was full of
sympathy, although he did not express it, and made
some quiet little sacrifices in order to set himself at
liberty to take Leonard a long walking expedition on
the day when his mother left Eccleston.

Ruth cried until she could cry no longer, and felt
very much ashamed of herself as she saw the grave

and wondering looks of her pupils, whose only feeling
on leaving home was delight at the idea of Abermouth,
and into whose mind the possibility of death to any of
their beloved ones never entered.   Ruth dried her
eyes, and spoke cheerfully as soon as she caught the
perplexed expression of their faces ; and by the time
they arrived at Abermouth, she was as much delighted
with all the new scenery as they were, and found it hard
work to resist their entreaties to go rambling out on
the seashore at once ; but Elizabeth had undergone
more fatigue that day, than she had had before for
many weeks, and Ruth was determined to be prudent.

Meanwhile, the Bradshaw's house at Eccleston was
being rapidly adapted for electioneering hospitality.
The partition wall between the unused drawing-room
and the school-room was broken down, in order to
admit of folding doors ; the "ingenious" upholsterer
of the town (and what town does not boast of the
upholsterer full of contrivances and resources, in
opposition to the upholsterer of steady capital and
no imagination, who looks down with uneasy contempt on ingenuity ?) had come in to give his
opinion that "nothing could be easier than to
convert a bathroom into a bedroom, by the assistance of a little drapery to conceal the shower-bath,"
the string of which was to be carefully concealed, for
fear that the unconscious occupier of the bath-bed
might innocently take it for a bell-rope.   The professional cook of the town had been already engaged
to take up her abode for a month at Mr Bradshaw's,
much to the indignation of Betsy, who became a
vehement partisan of Mr Cranworth, as soon as ever
she heard of the plan of her deposition from sovereign
authority in the kitchen, in which she had reigned
supreme for fourteen years.   Mrs Bradshaw sighed
and bemoaned herself in all her leisure moments,
which were not many, and wondered why their house
was to be turned into an inn for this Mr Donne, when
everybody knew that the George was good enough
for the Cranworths, who never thought of asking

the electors to the Hall ;—and they had lived at Cranworth ever since Julius Cæsar's time, and if that was
not being an old family, she did not know what was.
The excitement soothed Jemima.   There was something to do.   It was she who planned with the
upholsterer ; it was she who soothed Betsy into
angry silence ; it was she who persuaded her mother
to lie down and rest, while she herself went out to buy
the heterogeneous things required to make the family
and house presentable to Mr Donne, and his precursor
—the friend of the parliamentary agent.   This latter
gentleman never appeared himself on the scene of
action, but pulled all the strings notwithstanding.
The friend was a Mr Hickson, a lawyer—a briefless
barrister, some people called him ; but he himself
professed a great disgust to the law, as a " great sham,"
which involved an immensity of underhand action,
and truckling and time-serving, and was perfectly
encumbered by useless forms and ceremonies, and dead
obsolete words.   So, instead of putting his shoulder to
the wheel to reform the law, he talked eloquently
against it, in such a high-priest style, that it was
occasionally a matter of surprise how he could ever
have made a friend of the parliamentary agent before
mentioned.   But, as Mr Hickson himself said, it was
the very corruptness of the law which he was fighting
against, in doing all he could to effect the return of
certain members to Parliament ; these certain members
being pledged to effect a reform in the law, according
to Mr Hickson.   And, as he once observed confidentially, " If you had to destroy a hydra-headed monster, would you measure swords with the demon as
if he were a gentleman?   Would you not rather seize
the first weapon that came to hand?   And so do I.
My great object in life, sir, is to reform the law of
England, sir.   Once get a majority of Liberal members
into the House, and the thing is done.   And I consider
myself justified, for so high—for, I may say, so holy—
an end, in using men's weaknesses to work out my
purpose.   Of course, if men were angels, or even

immaculate—men invulnerable to bribes, we would not bribe."*

"Could you?" asked Jemima, for the conversation took place at Mr Bradshaw's dinner-table, where a few friends were gathered together to meet Mr Hickson; and among them was Mr Benson.

"We neither would nor could," said the ardent barrister, disregarding in his vehemence the point of the question, and floating on over the bar of argument into the wide ocean of his own eloquence : "As it is— as the world stands, they who would succeed even in good deeds, must come down to the level of expediency ; and therefore, I say once more, if Mr Donne is the man for your purpose, and your purpose is a good one, a lofty one, a holy one" (for Mr Hickson remembered the Dissenting character of his little audience, and privately considered the introduction of the word 'holy' a most happy hit), "then, I say, we must put all the squeamish scruples which might befit Utopia, or some such place, on one side, and treat men as they are. If they are avaricious, it is not we who have made them so ; but as we have to do with them, we must consider their failings in dealing with them ; if they have been careless or extravagant, or have had their little peccadillos, we must administer the screw. The glorious reform of the law will justify, in my idea, all means to obtain the end—that law, from the profession of which I have withdrawn myself from perhaps a too scrupulous conscience !" He concluded softly to himself.

"We are not to do evil that good may come,"*said Mr Benson. He was startled at the deep sound of his own voice as he uttered these words ; but he had not been speaking for some time, and his voice came forth strong and unmodulated.

"True, sir ; most true," said Mr Hickson, bowing. "I honour you for the observation." And he profited by it, insomuch that he confined his further remarks on elections to the end of the table, where he sat near Mr Bradshaw, and one or two equally eager, though

not equally influential partisans of Mr Donne's.
Meanwhile, Mr Farquhar took up Mr Benson's quota-
tion, at the end where he and Jemima sat near to Mrs
Bradshaw and him.

"But in the present state of the world, as Mr
Hickson says, it is rather difficult to act upon that
precept."

"Oh, Mr Farquhar!" said Jemima, indignantly,
the tears springing to her eyes with a feeling of disappointment. For she had been chafing under all that
Mr Hickson had been saying, perhaps the more for one
or two attempts on his part at a flirtation with the
daughter of his wealthy host, which she resented with
all the loathing of a pre-occupied heart; and she had
longed to be a man, to speak out her wrath at this
paltering with right and wrong. She had felt grateful
to Mr Benson for his one, clear, short precept, coming
down with a divine force against which there was no
appeal; and now to have Mr Farquhar taking the side
of expediency! It was too bad.

"Nay, Jemima!" said Mr Farquhar, touched, and
secretly flattered by the visible pain his speech had
given. "Don't be indignant with me till I have
explained myself a little more. I don't understand
myself yet; and it is a very intricate question, or so it
appears to me, which I was going to put, really,
earnestly, and humbly, for Mr Benson's opinion.
Now, Mr Benson, may I ask, if you always find it
practicable to act strictly in accordance with that
principle? For if you do not, I am sure no man living
can! Are there not occasions when it is absolutely
necessary to wade through evil to good? I am not
speaking in the careless, presumptuous way of that
man yonder," said he, lowering his voice, and addressing himself to Jemima more exclusively, "I am really
anxious to hear what Mr Benson will say on the
subject, for I know no one to whose candid opinion I
should attach more weight."

But Mr Benson was silent. He did not see Mrs
Bradshaw and Jemima leave the room. He was really,

as Mr Farquhar supposed him, completely absent, questioning himself as to how far his practice tallied with his principle. By degrees he came to himself; he found the conversation still turned on the election; and Mr Hickson, who felt that he had jarred against the little minister's principles, and yet knew, from the *carte du pays* which the scouts of the parliamentary agent had given him, that Mr Benson was a person to be conciliated, on account of his influence over many of the working people, began to ask him questions with an air of deferring to superior knowledge, that almost surprised Mr Bradshaw, who had been accustomed to treat "Benson" in a very different fashion, of civil condescending indulgence, just as one listens to a child who can have had no opportunities of knowing better.

At the end of a conversation that Mr Hickson held with Mr Benson, on a subject in which the latter was really interested, and on which he had expressed himself at some length, the young barrister turned to Mr Bradshaw, and said very audibly,

"I wish Donne had been here. This conversation during the last half hour would have interested him almost as much as it has done me."

Mr Bradshaw little guessed the truth, that Mr Donne was, at that very moment, coaching up the various subjects of public interest in Eccleston, and privately cursing the particular subject on which Mr Benson had been holding forth, as being an unintelligible piece of Quixotism; or the leading Dissenter of the town need not have experienced a pang of jealousy, at the possible future admiration his minister might excite in the possible future member for Eccleston. And if Mr Benson had been clairvoyant, he need not have made an especial subject of gratitude out of the likelihood that he might have an opportunity of so far interesting Mr Donne in the condition of the people of Eccleston as to induce him to set his face against any attempts at bribery.

Mr Benson thought of this, half the night through;

and ended by determining to write a sermon on the Christian view of political duties, which might be good for all, both electors and member, to hear on the eve of an election. For Mr Donne was expected at Mr Bradshaw's before the next Sunday ; and, of course, as Mr and Miss Benson had settled it, he would appear at the chapel with them on that day. But the stinging conscience refused to be quieted. No present plan of usefulness allayed the aching remembrance of the evil he had done that good might come. Not even the look of Leonard, as the early dawn fell on him, and Mr Benson's sleepless eyes saw the rosy glow on his firm round cheeks ; his open mouth, through which the soft, long-drawn breath came gently quivering ; and his eyes not fully shut, but closed to outward sight—not even the aspect of the quiet innocent child could soothe the troubled spirit.

Leonard and his mother dreamt of each other that night. Her dream of him was one of undefined terror —terror so great that it wakened her up, and she strove not to sleep again, for fear that ominous ghastly dream should return. He, on the contrary, dreamt of her sitting watching and smiling by his bedside, as her gentle self had been many a morning ; and when she saw him awake (so it fell out in the dream), she smiled still more sweetly, and bending down she kissed him, and then spread out large, soft, white-feathered wings (which in no way surprised her child—he seemed to have known they were there all along), and sailed away through the open window far into the blue sky of a summer's day. Leonard wakened up then, and re- membered how far away she really was—far more distant and inaccessible than the beautiful blue sky to which she had betaken herself in his dream—and cried himself to sleep again.

In spite of her absence from her child, which made one great and abiding sorrow, Ruth enjoyed her sea- side visit exceedingly. In the first place, there was the delight of seeing Elizabeth's daily and almost hourly improvement. Then, at the doctor's express orders,

there were so few lessons to be done, that there was
time for the long-exploring rambles, which all three
delighted in. And when the rain came and the storms
blew, the house with its wild sea views was equally
delightful.

It was a large house, built on the summit of a rock,
which nearly overhung the shore below; there were,
to be sure, a series of zigzag tacking paths down the
face of this rock, but from the house they could not be
seen. Old or delicate people would have considered
the situation bleak and exposed; indeed, the present
proprietor wanted to dispose of it on this very account;
but by its present inhabitants, this exposure and
bleakness were called by other names, and considered
as charms. From every part of the rooms, they saw
the grey storms gather on the sea horizon, and put
themselves in marching array; and soon the march
became a sweep, and the great dome of the heavens
was covered with the lurid clouds, between which and
the vivid green earth below there seemed to come a
purple atmosphere, making the very threatening
beautiful; and by and by the house was wrapped in
sheets of rains shutting out sky and sea, and inland
view; till, of a sudden, the storm was gone by, and the
heavy rain-drops glistened in the sun as they hung on
leaf and grass, and the " little birds sang east, and the
little birds sang west,"*and there was a pleasant sound
of running waters all abroad.

" Oh! if papa would but buy this house!" exclaimed
Elizabeth, after one such storm, which she had watched
silently from the very beginning of the " little cloud
no bigger than a man's hand."*

" Mamma would never like it, I am afraid," said
Mary. " She would call our delicious gushes of air,
draughts, and think we should catch cold."

" Jemima would be on our side. But how long Mrs
Denbigh is! I hope she was near enough the post
office when the rain come on!"

Ruth had gone to " the shop" in the little village,
about half a mile distant, where all letters were left

till fetched. She only expected one, but that one was
to tell her of Leonard. She, however, received two ; the
unexpected one was from Mr Bradshaw, and the news it
contained was, if possible, a greater surprise than the
letter itself. Mr Bradshaw informed her, that he
planned arriving by dinner-time the following Saturday,
at Eagle's Crag ; and more, that he intended bringing
Mr Donne and one or two other gentlemen with him,
to spend the Sunday there ! The letter went on to give
every possible direction regarding the household preparations. The dinner-hour was fixed to be at six ;
but, of course, Ruth and the girls would have dined
long before. The (professional) cook would arrive the
day before, laden with all the provisions that could not
be obtained on the spot. Ruth was to engage a waiter
from the inn, and this it was that detained her so long.
While she sat in the little parlour, awaiting the coming
of the landlady, she could not help wondering why Mr
Bradshaw was bringing this strange gentleman to spend
two days at Abermouth, and thus giving himself so
much trouble and fuss of preparation.

There were so many small reasons that went to make
up the large one which had convinced Mr Bradshaw of
the desirableness of this step, that it was not likely that
Ruth should guess at one half of them. In the first
place, Miss Benson, in the pride and fulness of her
heart, had told Mrs Bradshaw what her brother had
told her ; how he meant to preach upon the Christian
view of the duties involved in political rights ; and as,
of course, Mrs Bradshaw had told Mr Bradshaw, he
began to dislike the idea of attending chapel on that
Sunday at all ; for he had an uncomfortable idea that
by the Christian standard—that divine test of the true
and pure—bribery would not be altogether approved
of ; and yet he was tacitly coming round to the understanding that " packets " would be required, for what
purpose both he and Mr Donne were to be supposed to
remain ignorant. But it would be very awkward, so
near to the time, if he were to be clearly convinced
that bribery, however disguised by names and words,

was in plain terms a sin. And yet he knew Mr Benson had once or twice convinced him against his will of certain things, which he had thenceforward found it impossible to do, without such great uneasiness of mind, that he had left off doing them, which was sadly against his interest. And if Mr Donne (who he had intended to take with him to chapel, as fair Dissenting prey) should also become convinced, why the Cranworths would win the day, and he should be the laughing-stock of Eccleston. No! in this one case bribery must be allowed—was allowable ; but it was a great pity human nature was so corrupt, and if his member succeeded, he would double his subscription to the schools, in order that the next generation might be taught better. There were various other reasons, which strengthened Mr Bradshaw in the bright idea of going down to Abermouth for the Sunday ; some connected with the out-of-door politics, and some with the domestic. For instance, it had been the plan of the house to have a cold dinner on the Sundays—Mr Bradshaw had piqued himself on this strictness—and yet he had an instinctive feeling that Mr Donne was not quite the man to partake of cold meat for conscience' sake with cheerful indifference to his fare.

Mr Donne had, in fact, taken the Bradshaw household a little by surprise. Before he came, Mr Bradshaw had pleased himself with thinking, that more unlikely things had happened than the espousal of his daughter with the member of a small borough. But this pretty airy bubble burst as soon as he saw Mr Donne ; and its very existence was forgotten in less than half an hour, when he felt the quiet, but incontestible difference of rank and standard that there was, in every respect, between his guest and his own family. It was not through any circumstance so palpable, and possibly accidental, as the bringing down a servant, whom Mr Donne seemed to consider as much a matter of course as a carpet-bag (though the smart gentleman's arrival "fluttered the Volscians in Corioli"*considerably more

than his gentle-spoken master's).   It was nothing like
this ; it was something indescribable—a quiet being at
ease, and expecting every one else to be so—an attention to women, which was so habitual as to be unconsciously exercised to those subordinate persons in Mr
Bradshaw's family—a happy choice of simple and expressive words, some of which it must be confessed
were slang, but fashionable slang, and that makes all
the difference—a measured, graceful way of utterance,
with a style of pronunciation quite different to that of
Eccleston.   All these put together make but a part of
the indescribable whole which unconsciously affected
Mr Bradshaw, and established Mr Donne in his estimation as a creature quite different to any he had seen
before, and as most unfit to mate with Jemima.   Mr
Hickson, who had appeared as a model of gentlemanly
ease before Mr Donne's arrival, now became vulgar
and coarse in Mr Bradshaw's eyes.   And yet, such was
the charm of that languid, high-bred manner, that Mr
Bradshaw "cottoned" (as he expressed it to Mr Farquhar) to his new candidate at once.   He was only
afraid lest Mr Donne was too indifferent to all things
under the sun, to care whether he gained or lost the
election ; but he was reassured, after the first conversation they had together on the subject.   Mr
Donne's eye lightened with an eagerness that was
almost fierce, though his tones were as musical, and
nearly as slow as ever ; and when Mr Bradshaw alluded
distantly to "probable expenses" and "packets," Mr
Donne replied,

   "Oh, of course ! disagreeable necessity !   Better
speak as little about such things as possible ; other
people can be found to arrange all the dirty work.
Neither you nor I would like to soil our fingers by it,
I am sure.   Four thousand pounds are in Mr Pilson's
hands, and I shall never inquire what becomes of
them ; they may, very probably, be absorbed in the
law expenses, you know.   I shall let it be clearly
understood from the hustings, that I most decidedly
disapprove of bribery, and leave the rest to Hickson's

management. He is accustomed to these sort of things. I am not."

Mr Bradshaw was rather perplexed by this want of bustling energy on the part of the new candidate; and if it had not been for the four thousand pounds aforesaid, would have doubted whether Mr Donne cared sufficiently for the result of the election. Jemima thought differently. She watched her father's visitor attentively, with something like the curious observation which a naturalist bestows on a new species of animal.

"Do you know what Mr Donne reminds me of, mamma?" said she, one day, as the two sat at work, while the gentlemen were absent canvassing.

"No! he is not like anybody I ever saw. He quite frightens me, by being so ready to open the door for me if I am going out of the room, and by giving me a chair when I come in. I never saw anyone like him. Who is it, Jemima?"

"Not any person—not any human being, mamma," said Jemima, half smiling. "Do you remember our stopping at Wakefield once, on our way to Scarborough, and there were horse-races going on somewhere, and some of the racers were in the stables at the inn where we dined?"

"Yes! I remember it; but what about that?"

"Why Richard, somehow, knew one of the jockeys, and, as we were coming in from our ramble through the town, this man, or boy, asked us to look at one of the racers he had the charge of."

"Well, my dear!"

"Well, mamma! Mr Donne is like that horse!"

"Nonsense, Jemima; you must not say so. I don't know what your father would say, if he heard you likening Mr Donne to a brute."

"Brutes are sometimes very beautiful, mamma. I am sure I should think it a compliment to be likened to a race-horse, such as the one we saw. But the thing in which they are alike, is the sort of repressed eagerness in both."

"Eager! Why, I should say there never was any
one cooler than Mr Donne. Think of the trouble
your papa has had this month past, and then remember
the slow way in which Mr Donne moves when he is
going out to canvass, and the low drawling voice in
which he questions the people who bring him intelligence. I can see your papa standing by, ready to
shake them to get out their news."

"But Mr Donne's questions are always to the point,
and force out the grain without the chaff. And look
at him, if anyone tells him ill news about the election!
Have you never seen a dull red light come into his
eyes? That is like my race-horse. Her flesh quivered
all over, at certain sounds and noises which had some
meaning to her; but she stood quite still, pretty
creature! Now, Mr Donne is just as eager as she was,
though he may be too proud to show it. Though he
seems so gentle, I almost think he is very headstrong
in following out his own will."

"Well! don't call him like a horse again, for I am
sure papa would not like it. Do you know, I thought
you were going to say he was like little Leonard, when
you asked me who he was like."

"Leonard! Oh, mamma, he is not in the least like
Leonard. He is twenty times more like my race-
horse."

"Now, my dear Jemima, do be quiet. Your father
thinks racing so wrong, that I am sure he would be
very seriously displeased if he were to hear you."

To return to Mr Bradshaw, and to give one more of
his various reasons for wishing to take Mr Donne to
Abermouth. The wealthy Eccleston manufacturer was
uncomfortably impressed with an indefinable sense of
inferiority to his visitor. It was not in education, for
Mr Bradshaw was a well-educated man; it was not in
power, for, if he chose, the present object of Mr
Donne's life might be utterly defeated; it did not arise
from anything overbearing in manner, for Mr Donne
was habitually polite and courteous, and was just now
anxious to propitiate his host, whom he looked upon

as a very useful man. Whatever this sense of inferiority arose from, Mr Bradshaw was anxious to
relieve himself of it, and imagined that if he could
make more display of his wealth his object would be
obtained. Now his house in Eccleston was old-
fashioned, and ill-calculated to exhibit money's worth.
His mode of living, though strained to a high pitch
just at this time, he became aware was no more than
Mr Donne was accustomed to every day of his life.
The first day at dessert, some remark (some opportune
remark, as Mr Bradshaw in his innocence had thought)
was made regarding the price of pine-apples, which
was rather exorbitant that year, and Mr Donne asked
Mrs Bradshaw, with quiet surprise, if they had no
pinery, as if to be without a pinery were indeed a depth
of pitiable destitution. In fact, Mr Donne had been
born and cradled in all that wealth could purchase,
and so had his ancestors before him for so many
generations, that refinement and luxury seemed the
natural condition of man, and they that dwelt without
were in the position of monsters. The absence was
noticed ; but not the presence.

Now Mr Bradshaw knew that the house and grounds
of Eagle's Crag were exorbitantly dear, and yet he
really thought of purchasing them. And as one
means of exhibiting his wealth, and so raising himself
up to the level of Mr Donne, he thought that if he
could take the latter down to Abermouth, and show
him the place for which, " because his little girls had
taken a fancy to it," he was willing to give the fancy-
price of fourteen thousand pounds, he should at last
make those half-shut dreamy eyes open wide, and their
owner confess that, in wealth at least, the Eccleston
manufacturer stood on a par with him.

All these mingled motives caused the determination
which made Ruth sit in the little inn-parlour at Abermouth during the wild storm's passage.

She wondered if she had fulfilled all Mr Bradshaw's
directions. She looked at the letter. Yes ! everything was done. And now home with her news,

through the wet lane, where the little pools by the roadside reflected the deep blue sky and the round white clouds with even deeper blue and clearer white ; and the rain-drops hung so thick on the trees, that even a little bird's flight was enough to shake them down in a bright shower as of rain.   When she told the news, Mary exclaimed,

"Oh, how charming !   Then we shall see this new member after all !" while Elizabeth added,

"Yes ! I shall like to do that.   But where must we be?   Papa will want the dining-room and this room, and where must we sit ?"

"Oh !" said Ruth, "in the dressing-room next to my room.   All that your papa wants always, is that you are quiet and out of the way."

CHAPTER XXIII

SATURDAY came.   Torn, ragged clouds were driven across the sky.   It was not a becoming day for the scenery, and the little girls regretted it much.   First they hoped for a change at twelve o'clock, and then at the afternoon tide-turning.   But at neither time did the sun show his face.

"Papa will never buy this dear place," said Elizabeth, sadly, as she watched the weather.   "The sun is everything to it.   The sea looks quite leaden to-day, and there is no sparkle on it.   And the sands, that were so yellow and sun-speckled on Thursday, are all one dull brown now."

"Never mind ! to-morrow may be better," said Ruth, cheerily.

"I wonder what time they will come at?" inquired Mary.

"Your papa said they would be at the station at five o'clock.   And the landlady at the Swan said it would take them half an hour to get here."

"And they are to dine at six?" asked Elizabeth.

"Yes," answered Ruth.   "And I think if we had

our tea half an hour earlier, at half-past four, and then went out for a walk, we should be nicely out of the way just during the bustle of the arrival and dinner ; and we could be in the drawing-room ready against your papa came in after dinner."

"Oh ! that would be nice," said they ; and tea was ordered accordingly.

The south-westerly wind had dropped, and the clouds were stationary, when they went out on the sands.   They dug little holes near the in-coming tide, and made canals to them from the water, and blew the light sea-foam against each other ; and then stole on tiptoe near to the groups of grey and white sea-gulls, which despised their caution, flying softly and slowly away to a little distance as soon as they drew near. And in all this Ruth was as great a child as any. Only she longed for Leonard with a mother's longing, as indeed she did every day, and all hours of the day. By and by the clouds thickened yet more, and one or two drops of rain were felt.   It was very little, but Ruth feared a shower for her delicate Elizabeth, and besides, the September evening was fast closing in the dark and sunless day.   As they turned homewards in the rapidly increasing dusk, they saw three figures on the sand near the rocks, coming in their direction.

"Papa and Mr Donne !" exclaimed Mary.   "Now we shall see him !"

"Which do you make out is him?" asked Elizabeth.

"Oh ! the tall one, to be sure.   Don't you see how papa always turns to him, as if he was speaking to him and not to the other?"

"Who is the other?" asked Elizabeth.

"Mr Bradshaw said that Mr Farquhar and Mr Hickson would come with him.   But that is not Mr Farquhar, I am sure," said Ruth.

The girls looked at each other, as they always did, when Ruth mentioned Mr Farquhar's name ; but she was perfectly unconscious both of the look and of the conjectures which gave rise to it.

As soon as the two parties drew near, Mr Bradshaw called out in his strong voice,

"Well, my dears! we found there was an hour before dinner, so we came down upon the sands, and here you are."

The tone of his voice assured them that he was in a bland and indulgent mood, and the two little girls ran towards him. He kissed them, and shook hands with Ruth; told his companions that these were the little girls who were tempting him to this extravagance of purchasing Eagle's Crag; and then, rather doubtfully, and because he saw that Mr Donne expected it, he introduced "My daughters' governess, Mrs Denbigh."

It was growing darker every moment, and it was time they should hasten back to the rocks, which were even now indistinct in the grey haze. Mr Bradshaw held a hand of each of his daughters, and Ruth walked alongside, the two strange gentlemen being on the outskirts of the party.

Mr Bradshaw began to give his little girls some home news. He told them that Mr Farquhar was ill, and could not accompany them; but Jemima and their mamma were quite well.

The gentleman nearest to Ruth spoke to her.

"Are you fond of the sea?" asked he. There was no answer, so he repeated his question in a different form.

"Do you enjoy staying by the seaside I should rather ask?"

The reply was "Yes," rather breathed out in a deep inspiration than spoken in a sound. The sands heaved and trembled beneath Ruth. The figures near her vanished into strange nothingness; the sounds of their voices were as distant sounds in a dream, while the echo of one voice thrilled through and through. She could have caught at his arm for support, in the awful dizziness which wrapped her up, body and soul. That voice! No! if name, and face, and figure, were all changed, that voice was the same which had touched

her girlish heart, which had spoken most tender words
of love, which had won, and wrecked her, and which
she had last heard in the low mutterings of fever. She
dared not look round to see the figure of him who
spoke, dark as it was. She knew he was there—she
heard him speak in the manner in which he used to
address strangers years ago ; perhaps she answered
him, perhaps she did not—God knew. It seemed as if
weights were tied to her feet—as if the steadfast rocks
receded—as if time stood still ;—it was so long, so
terrible, that path across the reeling sand.

At the foot of the rocks they separated. Mr Bradshaw, afraid lest dinner should cool, preferred the
shorter way for himself and his friends. On Elizabeth's
account, the girls were to take the longer and easier
path, which wound upwards through a rocky field,
where larks' nests abounded, and where wild thyme
and heather were now throwing out their sweets to the
soft night air.

The little girls spoke in eager discussion of the
strangers. They appealed to Ruth, but Ruth did not
answer, and they were too impatient to convince each
other to repeat the question. The first little ascent
from the sands to the field surmounted, Ruth sat down
suddenly, and covered her face with her hands. This
was so unusual—their wishes, their good, was so invariably the rule of motion or of rest in their walks—
that the girls, suddenly checked, stood silent and
affrighted in surprise. They were still more startled
when Ruth wailed aloud some inarticulate words.

"Are you not well, dear Mrs Denbigh?" asked
Elizabeth, gently, kneeling down on the grass by Ruth.
She sat facing the west. The low watery twilight
was on her face as she took her hands away. So pale,
so haggard, so wild and wandering a look, the girls had
never seen on human countenance before.

"Well! what are you doing here with me? You
should not be with me," said she, shaking her head
slowly.

They looked at each other.

"You are sadly tired," said Elizabeth, soothingly.
"Come home, and let me help you to bed. I will tell
papa you are ill, and ask him to send for a doctor."

Ruth looked at her, as if she did not understand the
meaning of her words. No more she did at first. But
by and by the dulled brain began to think most vividly
and rapidly, and she spoke in a sharp way which
deceived the girls into a belief that nothing had been
the matter.

"Yes! I was tired. I am tired. Those sands—oh!
those sands, those weary, dreadful sands! But that is
all over now. Only my heart aches still. Feel how it
flutters and beats," said she, taking Elizabeth's hand,
and holding it to her side. "I am quite well, though,"
she continued, reading pity in the child's looks, as
she felt the trembling, quivering beat. "We will go
straight to the dressing-room, and read a chapter, that
will still my heart; and then I'll go to bed, and Mr
Bradshaw will excuse me, I know, this one night. I
only ask for one night. Put on your right frocks,
dears, and do all you ought to do. But I know you
will," said she, bending down to kiss Elizabeth, and
then, before she had done so, raising her head abruptly.
"You are good and dear girls—God keep you so!"

By a strong effort at self-command, she went onwards
at an even pace, neither rushing nor pausing to sob
and think. The very regularity of motion calmed her.
The front and back doors of the house were on two
sides, at right angles with each other. They all
shrunk a little from the idea of going in at the front
door, now that the strange gentlemen were about, and,
accordingly, they went through the quiet farm-yard
right into the bright, ruddy kitchen, where the servants
were dashing about with the dinner things. It was a
contrast in more than colour to the lonely dusky field,
which even the little girls perceived; and the noise,
the warmth, the very bustle of the servants, were a
positive relief to Ruth, and for the time lifted off the
heavy press of pent-up passion. A silent house, with
moonlit rooms, or with a faint gloom brooding over the

apartments, would have been more to be dreaded. Then, she must have given way, and cried out. As it was, she went up the old awkward back stairs, and into the room they were to sit in. There was no candle. Mary volunteered to go down for one; and when she returned she was full of the wonders of preparation in the drawing-room, and ready and eager to dress, so as to take her place there before the gentlemen had finished dinner. But she was struck by the strange paleness of Ruth's face, now that the light fell upon it.

" Stay up here, dear Mrs Denbigh ! We'll tell papa you are tired, and are gone to bed."

Another time Ruth would have dreaded Mr Bradshaw's displeasure ; for it was an understood thing that no one was to be ill or tired in his household without leave asked, and cause given and assigned. But she never thought of that now. Her great desire was to hold quiet till she was alone. Quietness it was not— it was rigidity ; but she succeeded in being rigid in look and movement, and went through her duties to Elizabeth (who preferred remaining with her upstairs) with wooden precision. But her heart felt at times like ice, at times like burning fire ; always a heavy, heavy weight within her. At last Elizabeth went to bed. Still Ruth dared not think. Mary would come upstairs soon ; and with a strange, sick, shrinking yearning, Ruth awaited her—and the crumbs of intelligence she might drop out about *him*. Ruth's sense of hearing was quickened to miserable intensity as she stood before the chimney-piece, grasping it tight with both hands—gazing into the dying fire, but seeing— not the dead grey embers, or the little sparks of vivid light that ran hither and thither among the wood-ashes —but an old farm-house, and climbing winding road, and a little golden breezy common, with a rural inn on the hill-top, far, far away. And through the thoughts of the past came the sharp sounds of the present—of three voices, one of which was almost silence, it was so hushed. Indifferent people would only have guessed that Mr Donne was speaking by the quietness in which the others listened; but Ruth heard the voice and many of the words, though they conveyed no idea to her mind. She was too much stunned even to feel curious to know to what they related. *He* spoke. That was her one fact.

Presently up came Mary, bounding, exultant. Papa had let her stay up one quarter of an hour longer, because Mr Hickson had asked. Mr Hickson was so clever! She did not know what to make of Mr Donne, he seemed such a dawdle. But he was very handsome. Had Ruth seen him? Oh, no! She could not, it was so dark on those stupid sands. Well, never mind, she would see him to-morrow. She *must* be well to-morrow. Papa seemed a good deal put out that neither she nor Elizabeth were in the drawing-room to-night; and his last words were, "Tell Mrs Denbigh I hope" (and papa's "hopes" always meant "expect") "she will be able to make breakfast at nine o'clock;" and then she would see Mr Donne.

That was all Ruth heard about him. She went with Mary into her bedroom, helped her to undress, and put the candle out. At length she was alone in her own room! At length!

But the tension did not give way immediately. She fastened her door, and threw open the window, cold and threatening as was the night. She tore off her gown; she put her hair back from her heated face. It seemed now as if she could not think—as if thought and emotion had been repressed so sternly that they would not come to relieve her stupified brain. Till all at once, like a flash of lightning, her life, past and present, was revealed to her in its minutest detail. And when she saw her very present "Now," the strange confusion of agony was too great to be borne, and she cried aloud. Then she was quite dead, and listened to the sound of galloping armies.

"If I might see him! If I might see him! If I might just ask him why he left me; if I had vexed him in any way; it was so strange—so cruel! It was not him, it was his mother," said she, almost fiercely, as if answering herself. "Oh, God! but he might have found me out before this," she continued, sadly. "He did not care for me, as I did for him. He did not care for me at all," she went on wildly and sharply. "He did me cruel harm. I can never again lift up my face in innocence. They think I have forgotten all, because I do not speak. Oh, darling love! am I talking against you?" asked she, tenderly. "I am so torn and perplexed! You, who are the father of my child!"

But that very circumstance, full of such tender meaning in many cases, threw a new light into her mind. It changed her from the woman into the mother—the stern guardian of her child. She was still for a time, thinking. Then she began again, but in a low, deep voice,

"He left me. He might have been hurried off, but he might have inquired—he might have learnt, and explained. He left me to bear the burden and the shame; and never cared to learn, as he might have done, of Leonard's birth. He has no love for his child, and I will have no love for him."

She raised her voice while uttering this determination, and then, feeling her own weakness, she moaned out, "Alas! alas!"

And then she started up, for all this time she had been rocking herself backwards and forwards as she sat on the ground, and began to pace the room with hurried steps.

"What am I thinking of? Where am I? I who have been praying these years and years to be worthy to be Leonard's mother. My God! what a depth of sin is in my heart! Why, the old time would be as white as snow to what it would be now, if I sought him out, and prayed for the explanation, which should re-establish him in my heart. I who have striven (or made a mock of trying) to learn God's holy will, in order to bring up Leonard into the full strength of a Christian—I who have taught his sweet innocent lips to pray 'Lead us not into temptation, but deliver us

from evil'; and yet, somehow, I've been longing to
give him to his father, who is—who is——" she almost
choked, till at last she cried sharp out, " Oh, my God !
I do believe Leonard's father is a bad man, and yet, oh !
pitiful God, I love him ; I cannot forget—I cannot ! "

She threw her body half out of the window into the
cold night air. The wind was rising, and came in
great gusts. The rain beat down on her. It did her
good. A still, calm night would not have soothed her
as this did. The wild tattered clouds, hurrying past
the moon, gave her a foolish kind of pleasure that
almost made her smile a vacant smile. The blast-
driven rain came on her again, and drenched her hair
through and through. The words " stormy wind
fulfilling his word "*came into her mind.

She sat down on the floor. This time her hands
were clasped round her knees. The uneasy rocking
motion was stilled.

" I wonder if my darling is frightened with this
blustering, noisy wind. I wonder if he is awake."

And then her thoughts went back to the various
times of old, when, affrighted by the weather—sounds
so mysterious in the night—he had crept into her bed
and clung to her, and she had soothed him, and
sweetly awed him into stillness and childlike faith, by
telling him of the goodness and power of God.

Of a sudden, she crept to a chair, and there knelt
as in the very presence of God, hiding her face, at first
not speaking a word (for did He not know her heart),
but by and by moaning out, amid her sobs and tears
(and now for the first time she wept),

" Oh, my God, help me, for I am very weak. My
God ! I pray thee be my rock and my strong fortress,
for I of myself am nothing. If I ask in His name,
thou wilt give it me. In the name of Jesus Christ I
pray for strength to do Thy will ! "

She could not think, or, indeed, remember anything
but that she was weak, and God was strong, and " a
very present help in time of trouble " ;*and the wind
rose yet higher, and the house shook and vibrated as,

in measured time, the great and terrible gusts came from the four quarters of the heavens and blew around it, dying away in the distance with loud and unearthly wails, which were not utterly still before the sound of the coming blast was heard like the trumpets of the vanguard of the Prince of Air.

There was a knock at the bedroom door—a little gentle knock, and a soft, child's voice.

"Mrs Denbigh, may I come in, please? I am so frightened!"

It was Elizabeth. Ruth calmed her passionate breathing by one hasty draught of water, and opened the door to the timid girl.

"Oh, Mrs Denbigh! did you ever hear such a night? I am so frightened! and Mary sleeps so sound."

Ruth was too much shaken to be able to speak all at once; but she took Elizabeth in her arms to reassure her. Elizabeth stood back.

"Why, how wet you are, Mrs Denbigh! and there's the window open, I do believe! Oh, how cold it is!" said she, shivering.

"Get into my bed, dear!" said Ruth.

"But do come too! The candle gives such a strange light with that long wick, and, somehow, your face does not look like you. Please, put the candle out, and come to bed. I am so frightened, and it seems as if I should be safer if you were by me."

Ruth shut the window, and went to bed. Elizabeth was all shivering and quaking. To soothe her, Ruth made a great effort; and spoke of Leonard and his fears, and, in a low hesitating voice, she spoke of God's tender mercy, but very humbly, for she feared lest Elizabeth should think her better and holier than she was. The little girl was soon asleep, her fears forgotten; and Ruth, worn out by passionate emotion, and obliged to be still for fear of awaking her bedfellow, went off into a short slumber, through the depths of which the echoes of her waking sobs quivered up.

When she awoke, the grey light of autumnal dawn
was in the room. Elizabeth slept on ; but Ruth heard
the servants about, and the early farmyard sounds.
After she had recovered from the shock of consciousness and recollection, she collected her thoughts with
a stern calmness. He was here. In a few hours she
must meet him. There was no escape, except through
subterfuges and contrivances that were both false and
cowardly. How it would all turn out she could not
say, or even guess. But of one thing she was clear,
and to one thing she would hold fast ; that was, that,
come what might, she would obey God's law, and, be
the end of all what it might, she would say " Thy will
be done ! "* She only asked for strength enough to do
this when the time came. How the time would come
—what speech or action would be requisite on her part,
she did not know—she did not even try to conjecture.
She left that in His hands.

She was icy cold, but very calm when the breakfast-
bell rang. She went down immediately ; because she
felt that there was less chance of a recognition, if she
were already at her place beside the tea-urn, and busied
with the cups, than if she came in after all were
settled. Her heart seemed to stand still, but she felt
almost a strange exultant sense of power over herself.
She felt, rather than saw, that he was not there. Mr
Bradshaw and Mr Hickson were, and so busy talking
election-politics that they did not interrupt their conversation even when they bowed to her. Her pupils
sat one on each side of her. Before they were quite
settled, and while the other two gentlemen yet hung
over the fire, Mr Donne came in. Ruth felt as if that
moment was like death. She had a kind of desire to
make some sharp sound, to relieve a choking sensation,
but it was over in an instant, and she sat on very composed and silent—to all outward appearance, the very
model of a governess who knew her place. And by and
by she felt strangely at ease in her sense of power.
She could even listen to what was being said. She
had never dared as yet to look at Mr Donne, though

her heart burnt to see him once again. He sounded
changed. The voice had lost its fresh and youthful
eagerness of tone, though in peculiarity of modulation
it was the same. It could never be mistaken for the
voice of another person.   There was a good deal said
at that breakfast, for none seemed inclined to hurry,
although it was Sunday morning. Ruth was compelled
to sit there, and it was good for her that she did. That
half-hour seemed to separate the present Mr Donne
very effectively, from her imagination of what Mr
Bellingham had been.   She was no analyser; she
hardly even had learnt to notice character; but she
felt there was some strange difference between the
people she had lived with lately and the man who now
leant back in his chair, listening in a careless manner
to the conversation, but never joining in, or expressing
any interest in it, unless it somewhere, or somehow,
touched him himself.   Now, Mr Bradshaw always
threw himself into a subject; it might be in a pompous,
dogmatic sort of way, but he did do it, whether it
related to himself or not; and it was part of Mr
Hickson's trade to assume an interest if he felt it not.
But Mr Donne did neither the one nor the other.
When the other two were talking of many of the topics
of the day, he put his glass in his eye, the better to
examine into the exact nature of a cold game-pie at the
other side of the table.   Suddenly Ruth felt that his
attention was caught by her. Until now, seeing his
short-sightedness, she had believed herself safe; now
her face flushed with a painful, miserable blush. But,
in an instant, she was strong and quiet. She looked
up straight at his face; and, as if this action took him
aback, he dropped his glass, and began eating away
with great diligence. She had seen him. He was
changed, she knew not how. In fact, the expression,
which had been only occasional formerly, when his
worse self predominated, had become permanent. He
looked restless and dissatisfied.   But he was very
handsome still; and her quick eye had recognized,
with a sort of strange pride, that the eyes and mouth

were like Leonard's. Although perplexed by the straightforward brave look she had sent right at him, he was not entirely baffled. He thought this Mrs Denbigh was certainly like poor Ruth ; but this woman was far handsomer. Her face was positively Greek ; and then such a proud, superb turn of her head ; quite queenly ! A governess in Mr Bradshaw's family ! Why, she might be a Percy or a Howard for the grandeur of her grace ! Poor Ruth ! This woman's hair was darker, though ; and she had less colour ; altogether a more refined-looking person. Poor Ruth ! and, for the first time for several years, he wondered what had become of her ; though, of course, there was but one thing that could have happened, and perhaps it was as well he did not know her end, for most likely it would have made him very uncomfortable. He leant back in his chair, and, unobserved (for he would not have thought it gentlemanly to look so fixedly at her, if she or any one noticed him), he put up his glass again. She was speaking to one of her pupils, and did not see him.

By Jove ! it must be she, though ! There were little dimples came out about the mouth as she spoke, just like those he used to admire so much in Ruth, and which he had never seen in anyone else—the sunshine without the positive movement of a smile. The longer he looked the more he was convinced ; and it was with a jerk that he recovered himself enough to answer Mr Bradshaw's question, whether he wished to go to church or not.

"Church? how far—a mile? No, I think I shall perform my devotions at home to-day."

He absolutely felt jealous when Mr Hickson sprang up to open the door, as Ruth and her pupils left the room. He was pleased to feel jealous again. He had been really afraid he was too much "used-up" for such sensations. But Hickson must keep his place. What he was paid for, was doing the talking to the electors, not paying attention to the ladies in their families. Mr Donne had noticed

that Mr Hickson had tried to be gallant to Miss
Bradshaw ; let him, if he liked ; but let him beware
how he behaved to this fair creature, Ruth or no
Ruth. It certainly was Ruth ; only how the devil had
she played her cards so well as to be the governess
—the respected governess, in such a family as Mr
Bradshaw's?

Mr Donne's movements were evidently to be the
guide of Mr Hickson's. Mr Bradshaw always disliked
going to church,*partly from principle, partly because
he never could find the places in the Prayer-book. Mr
Donne was in the drawing-room as Mary came down
ready equipped ; he was turning over the leaves of the
large and handsome Bible. Seeing Mary, he was
struck with a new idea.

"How singular it is," said he, "that the name of
Ruth is so seldom chosen by those good people who go
to the Bible before they christen their children. It is
a pretty name, I think."

Mr Bradshaw looked up. "Why, Mary !" said he,
"Is not that Mrs Denbigh's name?"

"Yes, papa," replied Mary, eagerly ; "and I know
two other Ruths ; there's Ruth Brown here, and Ruth
Macartney at Eccleston."

"And I have an aunt called Ruth, Mr Donne ! I
don't think your observation holds good.   Besides
my daughter's governess, I know three other Ruths."

"Oh ! I have no doubt I was wrong. It was just a
speech of which one perceives the folly the moment it
is made."

But, secretly, he rejoiced with a fierce joy over
the success of his device.

Elizabeth came to summon Mary.

Ruth was glad when she got into the open air, and
away from the house. Two hours were gone and over.
Two out of a day, a day and a half—for it might be
late on Monday morning before the Eccleston party
returned.

She felt weak and trembling in body, but strong in
power over herself. They had left the house in good

time for church, so they needed not to hurry; and
they went leisurely along the road, now and then
passing some country person whom they knew, and
with whom they exchanged a kindly placid greeting.
But presently, to Ruth's dismay, she heard a step
behind, coming at a rapid pace, a peculiar clank of
rather high-heeled boots, which gave a springy sound
to the walk, that she had known well long ago. It
was like a nightmare, where the Evil dreaded is never
avoided, never completely shunned, but is by one's
side at the very moment of triumph in escape.
There he was by her side; and there was a quarter
of a mile intervening between her and the church;
but even yet she trusted that he had not recognized
her.

"I have changed my mind, you see," said he,
quietly. "I have some curiosity to see the archi-
tecture of the church; some of these old country
churches have singular bits about them.   Mr Bradshaw kindly directed me part of the way, but I was
so much puzzled by 'turns to the right,' and 'turns
to the left,' that I was quite glad to espy your
party."

That speech required no positive answer of any
kind; and no answer did it receive. He had not
expected a reply. He knew, if she were Ruth, she
could not answer any indifferent words of his; and
her silence made him more certain of her identity with
the lady by his side.

"The scenery here is of a kind new to me; neither
grand, wild, nor yet marked by high cultivation; and
yet it has great charms. It reminds me of some parts
of Wales."   He breathed deeply, and then added,
"You have been in Wales, I believe?"

He spoke low; almost in a whisper. The little
church-bell began to call the lagging people with its
quick sharp summons. Ruth writhed in body and
spirit, but struggled on. The church-door would be
gained at last; and in that holy place she would
find peace.

He repeated in a louder tone, so as to compel an answer in order to conceal her agitation from the girls.

"Have you never been in Wales?" He used " never," instead of " ever," and laid the emphasis on that word, in order to mark his meaning to Ruth, and Ruth only. But he drove her to bay.

"I have been in Wales, sir," she replied, in a calm, grave tone. "I was there many years ago. Events took place there, which contribute to make the recollection of that time most miserable to me. I shall be obliged to you, sir, if you will make no further reference to it."

The little girls wondered how Mrs Denbigh could speak in such a tone of quiet authority to Mr Donne, who was almost a member of Parliament. But they settled that her husband must have died in Wales, and, of course, that would make the recollection of the country " most miserable," as she said.

Mr Donne did not dislike the answer, and he posisively admired the dignity with which she spoke. His leaving her as he did, must have made her very miserable ; and he liked the pride that made her retain her indignation, until he could speak to her in private, and explain away a good deal of what she might complain of with some justice.

The church was reached. They all went up the middle aisle into the Eagle's Crag pew. He followed them in, entered himself, and shut the door. Ruth's heart sank as she saw him there ; just opposite to her ; coming between her and the clergyman who was to read out the Word of God. It was merciless—it was cruel to haunt her there. She durst not lift her eyes to the bright eastern light—she could not see how peacefully the marble images of the dead lay on their tomb, for he was between her and all Light and Peace. She knew that his look was on her ; that he never turned his glance away. She could not join in the prayer for the remission of sins while he was there, for his very presence seemed as a sign that their stain would

never be washed out of her life.   But, although goaded
and chafed by her thoughts and recollections, she kept
very still.   No sign of emotion, no flush of colour was
on her face, as he looked at her.   Elizabeth could not
find her place, and then Ruth breathed once, long and
deeply, as she moved up the pew, and out of the
straight burning glance of those eyes of evil meaning.
When they sat down for the reading of the first lesson,
Ruth turned the corner of the seat so as no longer to
be opposite to him.   She could not listen.   The words
seemed to be uttered in some world far away, from
which she was exiled and cast out;   their sound, and
yet more their meaning, was dim and distant.   But in
this extreme tension of mind to hold in her bewildered
agony, it so happened that one of her senses was preternaturally acute.   While all the church and the
people swam in misty haze, one point in a dark corner
grew clearer and clearer till she saw (what, at another
time she could not have discerned at all) a face—a
gargoyle I think they call it—at the end of the arch
next to the narrowing of the nave into the chancel,
and in the shadow of that contraction.   The face was
beautiful in feature (the next to it was a grinning
monkey), but it was not the features that were the
most striking part.   There was a half-open mouth,
not in any way distorted out of its exquisite beauty
by the intense expression of suffering it conveyed.
Any distortion of the face by mental agony, implies
that a struggle with circumstance is going on.   But in
this face, if such struggle had been, it was over now.
Circumstance had conquered ; and there was no hope
from mortal endeavour, or help from mortal creature
to be had.   But the eyes looked onward and upward
to the "Hills from whence cometh our help."* And
though the parted lips seemed ready to quiver with
agony, yet the expression of the whole face, owing
to these strange, stony, and yet spiritual eyes, was
high and consoling.   If mortal gaze had never sought
its meaning before, in the deep shadow where it had
been placed long centuries ago, yet Ruth's did now.

Who could have imagined such a look? Who could have
witnessed—perhaps felt—such infinite sorrow, and yet
dared to lift it up by Faith into a peace so pure? Or
was it a mere conception? If so, what a soul the
unknown carver must have had! for creator and
handicraftsman must have been one; no two minds
could have been in such perfect harmony. Whatever it
was—however it came there—imaginer, carver, sufferer,
all were long passed away. Human art was ended—
human life done—human suffering over; but this
remained; it stilled Ruth's beating heart to look on
it. She grew still enough to hear words, which have
come to many in their time of need, and awed them in
the presence of the extremest suffering that the hushed
world has ever heard of.

The second lesson for the morning of the 25th of
September, is the 26th chapter of St Matthew's Gospel.*

And when they prayed again, Ruth's tongue was
unloosed, and she also could pray, in His name, who
underwent the agony in the garden.

As they came out of church, there was a little pause
and gathering at the door. It had begun to rain; those
who had umbrellas were putting them up; those who
had not were regretting, and wondering how long it
would last. Standing for a moment, impeded by the
people who were thus collected under the porch, Ruth
heard a voice close to her say, very low but very
distinctly,

"I have much to say to you—much to explain. I
entreat you to give me the opportunity."

Ruth did not reply. She would not acknowledge
that she heard; but she trembled nevertheless, for the
well-remembered voice was low and soft, and had yet
its power to thrill. She earnestly desired to know why
and how he had left her. It appeared to her as if that
knowledge could alone give her a relief from the restless wondering that distracted her mind, and that one
explanation could do no harm.

"*No!*" the higher spirit made answer; "*it must
not be.*"

Ruth and the girls had each an umbrella. She turned to Mary, and said,

"Mary, give your umbrella to Mr Donne, and come under mine." Her way of speaking was short and decided; she was compressing her meaning into as few words as possible. The little girls obeyed in silence. As they went first through the churchyard stile, Mr Donne spoke again.

"You are unforgiving," said he. "I only ask you to hear me. I have a right to be heard, Ruth! I won't believe you are so much changed, as not to listen to me when I entreat."

He spoke in a tone of soft complaint. But he himself had done much to destroy the illusion which had hung about his memory for years, whenever Ruth had allowed herself to think of it. Besides which, during the time of her residence in the Benson family, her feeling of what people ought to be had been unconsciously raised and refined; and Mr Donne, even while she had to struggle against the force of past recollections, repelled her so much by what he was at present, that every speech of his, every minute they were together, served to make her path more and more easy to follow. His voice retained something of its former influence. When he spoke, without her seeing him, she could not help remembering former days.

She did not answer this last speech any more than the first. She saw clearly, that, putting aside all thought as to the character of their former relationship, it had been dissolved by his will—his act and deed; and that, therefore, the power to refuse any further intercourse whatsoever remained with her.

It sometimes seems a little strange how, after having earnestly prayed to be delivered from temptation, and having given ourselves with shut eyes into God's hand, from that time every thought, every outward influence, every acknowledged law of life, seems to lead us on from strength to strength. It seems strange sometimes, because we notice the coincidence; but it is the natural, unavoidable consequence of all.

truth and goodness being one and the same, and therefore carried out in every circumstance, external and
internal, of God's creation.

When Mr Donne saw that Ruth would not answer
him, he became only the more determined that she
should hear what he had to say. What that was he
did not exactly know. The whole affair was most
mysterious and piquant.

The umbrella protected Ruth from more than the
rain on that walk homewards, for under its shelter she
could not be spoken to unheard. She had not rightly
understood at what time she and the girls were to dine.
From the gathering at meal-times she must not shrink.
She must show no sign of weakness. But, oh! the
relief, after that walk, to sit in her own room, locked
up, so that neither Mary nor Elizabeth could come by
surprise, and to let her weary frame (weary with being
so long braced up to rigidity and stiff quiet) fall into a
chair anyhow—all helpless, nerveless, motionless, as
if the very bones had melted out of her!

The peaceful rest which her mind took was in thinking of Leonard. She dared not look before or behind,
but she could see him well at present. She brooded
over the thought of him, till she dreaded his father
more and more. By the light of her child's purity
and innocence, she saw evil clearly, and yet more
clearly. She thought that, if Leonard ever came to
know the nature of his birth, she had nothing for it
but to die out of his sight. He could never know—
human heart could never know, her ignorant innocence, and all the small circumstances which had impelled her onwards. But God knew. And if Leonard
heard of his mother's error, why nothing remained
but death; for she felt, then, as if she had it in her
power to die innocently out of such future agony; but
that escape is not so easy. Suddenly a fresh thought
came, and she prayed that, through whatever suffering, she might be purified. Whatever trials, woes,
measureless pangs, God might see fit to chastise her
with, she would not shrink, if only at last she might

come into His presence in Heaven. Alas ! the shrinking from suffering we cannot help. That part of her
prayer was vain. And as for the rest, was not the
sure justice of His law finding her out even now ? His
laws once broken, His justice and the very nature of
those laws bring the immutable retribution ; but if we
turn penitently to Him, He enables us to bear our
punishment with a meek and docile heart, " for His
mercy endureth for ever."*

Mr Bradshaw had felt himself rather wanting in
proper attention to his guest, inasmuch as he had been
unable, all in a minute, to comprehend Mr Donne's
rapid change of purpose ; and, before it had entered
into his mind that, notwithstanding the distance of the
church, Mr Donne was going thither, that gentleman
was out of the sight, and far out of the reach, of his
burly host. But though the latter had so far neglected
the duties of hospitality as to allow his visitor to sit in
the Eagle's Crag pew with no other guard of honour
than the children and the governess, Mr Bradshaw
determined to make up for it by extra attention during
the remainder of the day. Accordingly he never left
Mr Donne. Whatever wish that gentleman expressed,
it was the study of his host to gratify. Did he hint at
the pleasure which a walk in such beautiful scenery
would give him, Mr Bradshaw was willing to accompany him, although at Eccleston it was a principle
with him not to take any walks for pleasure on a Sunday. When Mr Donne turned round, and recollected
letters which must be written, and which would compel
him to stay at home, Mr Bradshaw instantly gave up
the walk, and remained at hand, ready to furnish him
with any writing materials which could be wanted,
and which were not laid out in the half-furnished
house. Nobody knew where Mr Hickson was all this
time. He had sauntered out after Mr Donne, when
the latter set off for church, and he had never returned. Mr Donne kept wondering if he could have
met Ruth—if, in fact, she had gone out with her
pupils, now that the afternoon had cleared up. This

uneasy wonder, and a few mental imprecations on his host's polite attention, together with the letter-writing pretence, passed away the afternoon — the longest afternoon he had ever spent; and of weariness he had had his share. Lunch was lingering in the dining-room, left there for the truant Mr Hickson; but of the children or Ruth there was no sign. He ventured on a distant inquiry as to their whereabouts.

"They dine early; they are gone to church again. Mrs Denbigh was a member of the Establishment once; and, though she attends chapel at home, she seems glad to have an opportunity of going to church."

Mr Donne was on the point of asking some further questions about "Mrs Denbigh," when Mr Hickson came in, loud-spoken, cheerful, hungry, and as ready to talk about his ramble, and the way in which he had lost and found himself, as he was about everything else. He knew how to dress up the commonest occurrence with a little exaggeration, a few puns, and a happy quotation or two, so as to make it sound very agreeable. He could read faces, and saw that he had been missed; both host and visitor looked moped to death. He determined to devote himself to their amusement during the remainder of the day, for he had really lost himself, and felt that he had been away too long on a dull Sunday, when people were apt to get hypped if not well amused.

"It is really a shame to be indoors in such a place. Rain? yes, it rained some hours ago, but now it is splendid weather. I feel myself quite qualified for guide, I assure you. I can show you all the beauties of the neighbourhood, and throw in a bog and a nest of vipers to boot."

Mr Donne languidly assented to this proposal of going out, and then he became restless until Mr Hickson had eaten a hasty lunch, for he hoped to meet Ruth on the way from church, to be near her, and watch her, though he might not be able to speak to her. To have the slow hours roll away—to know

he must leave the next day—and yet, so close to her,
not to be seeing her—was more than he could bear.
In an impetuous kind of way, he disregarded all Mr
Hickson's offers of guidance to lovely views, and
turned a deaf ear to Mr Bradshaw's expressed wish of
showing him the land belonging to the house ("very
little for fourteen thousand pounds"), and set off wil-
fully on the road leading to the church, from which,
he averred, he had seen a view which nothing else
about the place could equal.

They met the country people dropping homewards.
No Ruth was there. She and her pupils had returned
by the field-way, as Mr Bradshaw informed his guests
at dinner-time. Mr Donne was very captious all
through dinner. He thought it would never be over,
and cursed Hickson's interminable stories, which were
told on purpose to amuse him. His heart gave a
fierce bound when he saw her in the drawing-room
with the little girls.

She was reading to them — with how sick and
trembling a heart, no words can tell. But she could
master and keep down outward signs of her emotion.
An hour more to-night (part of which was to be spent
in family prayer, and all in the safety of company),
another hour in the morning (when all would be engaged in the bustle of departure)—if, during this short
space of time, she could not avoid speaking to him,
she could at least keep him at such a distance as to
make him feel that henceforward her world and his
belonged to separate systems, wide as the heavens
apart.

By degrees she felt that he was drawing near to
where she stood. He was by the table examining the
books that lay upon it. Mary and Elizabeth drew off
a little space, awe-stricken by the future member for
Eccleston. As he bent his head over a book, he said,
"I implore you ; five minutes alone."

The little girls could not hear ; but Ruth, hemmed
in so that no escape was possible, did hear.

She took sudden courage, and said, in a clear voice,

" Will you read the whole passage aloud ? I do not remember it."

Mr Hickson, hovering at no great distance, heard these words, and drew near to second Mrs Denbigh's request. Mr Bradshaw, who was very sleepy after his unusually late dinner, and longing for bedtime, joined in the request, for it would save the necessity for making talk, and he might, perhaps, get in a nap, undisturbed and unnoticed, before the servants came in to prayers.

Mr Donne was caught; he was obliged to read aloud, although he did not know what he was reading. In the middle of some sentence, the door opened, a rush of servants came in, and Mr Bradshaw became particularly wide awake in an instant, and read them a long sermon with great emphasis and unction, winding up with a prayer almost as long.

Ruth sat with her head drooping, more from exhaustion after a season of effort than because she shunned Mr Donne's looks. He had so lost his power over her—his power, which had stirred her so deeply the night before—that, except as one knowing her error and her shame, and making a cruel use of such knowledge, she had quite separated him from the idol of her youth. And yet, for the sake of that first and only love, she would gladly have known what explanation he could offer to account for leaving her. It would have been something gained to her own self-respect, if she had learnt that he was not then, as she felt him to be now, cold and egotistical, caring for no one and nothing but what related to himself.

Home, and Leonard—how strangely peaceful the two seemed ! Oh, for the rest that a dream about Leonard would bring !

Mary and Elizabeth went to bed immediately after prayers, and Ruth accompanied them. It was planned that the gentlemen should leave early the next morning. They were to breakfast half an hour sooner, to catch the railway train ; and this by Mr Donne's own arrangement, who had been as eager about his canvassing, the week before, as it was possible for him to be, but who now wished Eccleston and the Dissenting interest therein very fervently at the devil.

Just as the carriage came round, Mr Bradshaw turned to Ruth : " Any message for Leonard beyond love, which is a matter of course?"

Ruth gasped—for she saw Mr Donne catch at the name ; she did not guess the sudden sharp jealousy called out by the idea that Leonard was a grown-up man.

" Who is Leonard?" said he, to the little girl standing by him ; he did not know which she was.

" Mrs Denbigh's little boy," answered Mary.

Under some pretence or other, he drew near to Ruth ; and in that low voice, which she had learnt to loathe, he said,

" Our child !"

By the white misery that turned her face to stone— by the wild terror in her imploring eyes—by the gasping breath, which came out as the carriage drove away —he knew that he had seized the spell to make her listen at last.

CHAPTER XXIV

" HE will take him away from me. He will take the child from me."

These words rang like a tolling bell through Ruth's head. It seemed to her that her doom was certain. Leonard would be taken from her ! She had a firm conviction—not the less firm because she knew not on what it was based—that a child, whether legitimate or not, belonged of legal right to the father. And Leonard, of all children was the prince and monarch. Every man's heart would long to call Leonard " Child !" She had been too strongly taxed to have much power left her to reason coolly and dispassionately, just then, even if she had been with anyone who could furnish her with information from which to draw correct conclusions. The one thought haunted her night and day. "He will take my child away from me!" In her dreams she saw Leonard borne away into some dim land, to which she could not follow. Sometimes he sat in a swiftly-moving carriage, at his father's side, and smiled on her as he passed by, as if going to promised pleasure. At another time, he was struggling to return to her; stretching out his little arms, and crying to her for the help she could not give. How she got through the days, she did not know; her body moved about and habitually acted, but her spirit was with her child. She thought often of writing and warning Mr Benson of Leonard's danger: but then she shrank from recurring to circumstances, all mention of which had ceased years ago; the very recollection of which seemed buried deep for ever. Besides, she feared occasioning discord or commotion in the quiet circle in which she lived. Mr Benson's deep anger against her betrayer had been shown too clearly in the old time to allow her to think that he would keep it down without expression now. He would cease to do anything to forward his election; he would oppose him as much as he could; and Mr Bradshaw would be angry, and a storm would arise, from the bare thought of which Ruth shrank with the cowardliness of a person thoroughly worn out with late contest. She was bodily wearied with her spiritual buffeting.

One morning, three or four days after their departure, she received a letter from Miss Benson. She could not open it at first, and put it on one side, clenching her hand over it all the time. At last she tore it open. Leonard was safe as yet. There were a few lines in his great round hand, speaking of events no larger than the loss of a beautiful "alley."* There was a sheet from Miss Benson. She always wrote letters in the manner of a diary. "Monday we did so-and-so; Tuesday, so-and-so, etc." Ruth glanced rapidly down the page. Yes, here it was! Sick, fluttering heart, be still!

"In the middle of the damsons, when they were just on the fire, there was a knock at the door. My brother was out, and Sally was washing up, and I was stirring the preserve with my great apron and bib on; so I bade Leonard come in from the garden, and open the door. But I would have washed his face first, if I had known who it was! It was Mr Bradshaw, and the Mr Donne that they hope to send up to the House of Commons, as member of Parliament for Eccleston, and another gentleman, whose name I never heard. They had come canvassing; and when they found my brother was out, they asked Leonard if they could see me. The child said 'Yes! if I could leave the damsons;' and straightway came to call me, leaving them standing in the passage. I whipped off my apron, and took Leonard by the hand, for I fancied I should feel less awkward if he was with me, and then I went and asked them all into the study, for I thought I should like them to see how many books Thurstan had got. Then they began talking politics at me in a very polite manner, only I could not make head or tail of what they meant; and Mr Donne took a deal of notice of Leonard, and called him to him; and I am sure he noticed what a noble, handsome boy he was, though his face was very brown and red, and hot with digging, and his curls all tangled. Leonard talked back as if he had known him all his life, till, I think, Mr Bradshaw thought he was making too much noise, and bid him remember he ought to be seen, not heard. So he stood as still and stiff as a soldier, close to Mr Donne; and as I could not help looking at the two, and thinking how handsome they both were in their different ways, I could not tell Thurstan half the messages the gentlemen left for him. But there was one thing more I must tell you, though I said I would not. When Mr Donne was talking to Leonard, he took off his watch and chain and put it round the boy's neck, who was pleased enough, you may be sure. I bade him give it back to the gentleman, when they were all going away; and I was quite surprised, and very uncomfortable, when Mr Donne said he had given it to Leonard, and that he was to keep it for his own. I could see Mr Bradshaw was annoyed, and he and the other gentleman spoke to Mr Donne, and I heard them say, 'too barefaced'; and I shall never forget Mr Donne's proud, stubborn look back at them, nor his way of saying, 'I allow no one to interfere with what I choose to do with my own.' And he looked so haughty and displeased, I durst say nothing at the time. But when I told Thurstan, he was very grieved and angry; and said he had heard that our party were bribing, but that he never could have thought they would have tried to do it at his house. Thurstan is very much out of spirits about this election altogether; and, indeed, it does make sad work up and down the town. However, he sent back the watch with a letter to Mr Bradshaw; and Leonard was very good about it, so I gave him a taste of the new damson preserve on his bread for supper."

Although a stranger might have considered this letter wearisome from the multiplicity of the details, Ruth craved greedily after more. What had Mr Donne said to Leonard? Had Leonard liked his new acquaintance? Were they likely to meet again? After wondering and wondering over these points, Ruth composed herself by the hope that in a day or two she should hear again; and to secure this end, she answered the letters by return of post. That was on Thursday. On Friday she had another letter, in a strange hand. It was from Mr Donne. No name, no initials were given. If it had fallen into another person's hands, they could not have recognized the writer, nor guessed to whom it was sent. It contained simply these words:

"For our child's sake, and in his name, I summon you to appoint a place where I can speak, and you can listen, undisturbed. The time must be on Sunday; the limit of distance may be the circumference of your power of walking. My words may be commands, but my fond heart entreats. More I shall not say now, but, remember! your boy's welfare depends on your

acceding to this request. Address B. D., Post Office,
Eccleston."

Ruth did not attempt to answer this letter till the
last five minutes before the post went out. She could
not decide until forced to it. Either way she dreaded.
She was very nearly leaving the letter altogether un-
answered. But suddenly she resolved she would know
all, the best, the worst. No cowardly dread of herself, or of others, should make her neglect aught that
came to her in her child's name. She took up a pen
and wrote :

"The sands below the rocks, where we met you the
other night. Time, afternoon church."

Sunday came.

"I shall not go to church this afternoon. You know
the way, of course ; and I can trust you to go steadily
by yourselves."

When they came to kiss her before leaving her,
according to their fond wont, they were struck by the
coldness of her face and lips.

"Are you not well, dear Mrs Denbigh ? How cold
you are !"

"Yes, darling ! I am well" ; and tears sprang into
her eyes as she looked at their anxious little faces.
"Go now, dears. Five o'clock will soon be here, and
then we will have tea."

"And that will warm you !" said they, leaving the
room.

"And then it will be over," she murmured—
"over."

It never came into her head to watch the girls, as
they disappeared down the lane on their way to
church. She knew them too well to distrust their
doing what they were told. She sat still, her head
bowed on her arms for a few minutes, and then rose
up and went to put on her walking things. Some
thoughts impelled her to sudden haste. She crossed
the field by the side of the house, ran down the steep
and rocky path, and was carried by the impetus of her
descent far out on the level sands—but not far enough

for her intent. Without looking to the right hand or
to the left, where comers might be seen, she went
forwards to the black posts, which, rising above the
heaving waters, marked where the fishermen's nets
were laid. She went straight towards this place, and
hardly stinted her pace even where the wet sands were
glittering with the receding waves. Once there, she
turned round, and in a darting glance, saw that as yet
no one was near. She was perhaps half a mile or more
from the grey silvery rocks, which sloped away into
brown moorland, interspersed with a field here and
there of golden, waving corn. Behind were purple
hills, with sharp, clear outlines, touching the sky. A
little on one side from where she stood, she saw the
white cottages and houses which formed the village of
Abermouth, scattered up and down, and, on a windy
hill, about a mile inland, she saw the little grey
church, where even now many were worshipping in
peace.

"Pray ror me!" she sighed out, as this object caught
her eye.

And now, close under the heathery fields, where
they fell softly down and touched the sands, she saw a
figure moving in the direction of the great shadow
made by the rocks—going towards the very point
where the path from Eagle's Crag came down to the
shore.

"It is he!" said she to herself. And she turned
round and looked seaward. The tide had turned; the
waves were slowly receding, as if loath to lose the hold
they had, so lately, and with such swift bounds, gained
on the yellow sands. The eternal moan they have
made since the world began filled the ear, broken only
by the skirl of the grey sea-birds as they alighted in
groups on the edge of the waters, or as they rose up
with their measured, balancing motion, and the sunlight caught their white breasts. There was no sign
of human life to be seen; no boat, or distant sail, or
near shrimper. The black posts there were all that
spoke of men's work or labour. Beyond a stretch of

the waters, a few pale grey hills showed like films;
their summits clear, though faint, their bases lost in a
vapoury mist.

On the hard, echoing sands, and distinct from the
ceaseless murmur of the salt sea waves, came footsteps
—nearer—nearer. Very near they were when Ruth,
unwilling to show the fear that rioted in her heart,
turned round, and faced Mr Donne.

He came forward, with both hands extended.

"This is kind! my own Ruth," said he. Ruth's
arms hung down motionless at her sides.

"What! Ruth, have you no word for me?"

"I have nothing to say," said Ruth.

"Why, you little revengeful creature! And so I
am to explain all before you will even treat me with
decent civility."

"I do not want explanations," said Ruth, in a
trembling tone. "We must not speak of the past.
You asked me to come in Leonard's—in my child's
name, and to hear what you had to say about him."

"But what I have to say about him relates to you
even more. And how can we talk about him without
recurring to the past? That past, which you try to
ignore—I know you cannot do it in your heart—is full
of happy recollections to me. Were you not happy in
Wales?" he said, in his tenderest tone.

But there was no answer; not even one faint sigh,
though he listened intently.

"You dare not speak; you dare not answer me.
Your heart will not allow you to prevaricate, and you
know you were happy."

Suddenly Ruth's beautiful eyes were raised to him,
full of lucid splendour, but grave and serious in their
expression; and her cheeks, heretofore so faintly
tinged with the tenderest blush, flashed into a ruddy
glow.

"I was happy. I do not deny it. Whatever comes,
I will not blench from the truth. I have answered
you."

"And yet," replied he, secretly exulting in her

admission, and not perceiving the inner strength of which she must have been conscious before she would have dared to make it—" and yet, Ruth, we are not to recur to the past! Why not? If it was happy at the time, is the recollection of it so miserable to you?"

He tried once more to take her hand, but she quietly stepped back.

"I came to hear what you had to say about my child," said she, beginning to feel very weary.

"*Our* child, Ruth."

She drew herself up, and her face went very pale.

"What have you to say about him?" asked she, coldly.

"Much," exclaimed he—"much that may affect his whole life. But it all depends upon whether you will hear me or not."

"I listen."

"Good Heavens! Ruth, you will drive me mad. Oh! what a changed person you are from the sweet, loving creature you were! I wish you were not so beautiful." She did not reply, but he caught a deep, involuntary sigh.

"Will you hear me if I speak, though I may not begin all at once to talk of this boy—a boy of whom any mother—any parent, might be proud? I could see that, Ruth. I have seen him; he looked like a prince in that cramped, miserable house, and with no earthly advantages. It is a shame he should not have every kind of opportunity laid open before him."

There was no sign of maternal ambition on the motionless face, though there might be some little spring in her heart, as it beat quick and strong at the idea of the proposal she imagined he was going to make of taking her boy away to give him the careful education she had often craved for him. She should refuse it, as she would everything else which seemed to imply that she acknowledged a claim over Leonard; but yet sometimes, for her boy's sake, she had longed for a larger opening—a more extended sphere.

"Ruth! you acknowledge we were happy once;—
there were circumstances which, if I could tell you
them all in detail, would show you how in my weak,
convalescent state I was almost passive in the hands
of others. Ah, Ruth! I have not forgotten the tender
nurse who soothed me in my delirium. When I am
feverish, I dream that I am again at Llan-dhu, in the
little old bedchamber, and you, in white—which you
always wore then, you know—flitting about me."

The tears dropped, large and round, from Ruth's
eyes—she could not help it—how could she?

"We were happy then," continued he, gaining confidence from the sight of her melted mood, and recurring once more to the admission which he considered
so much in his favour. "Can such happiness never
return?" Thus he went on, quickly, anxious to lay
before her all he had to offer, before she should fully
understand his meaning.

"If you would consent, Leonard should be always
with you—educated where and how you liked—money
to any amount you might choose to name should be
secured to you and him—if only, Ruth—if only those
happy days might return."

Ruth spoke.

"I said that I was happy, because I had asked God
to protect and help me—and I dared not tell a lie. I
was happy. Oh! what is happiness or misery that we
should talk about them now?"

Mr Donne looked at her, as she uttered these words,
to see if she was wandering in her mind, they seemed
to him so utterly strange and incoherent.

"I dare not think of happiness—I must not look
forward to sorrow. God did not put me here to consider either of these things."

"My dear Ruth, compose yourself! There is no
hurry in answering the question I asked."

"What was it?" said Ruth.

"I love you so, I cannot live without you. I offer
you my heart, my life—I offer to place Leonard wherever
you would have him placed. I have the power and the

means to advance him in any path of life you choose.
All who have shown kindness to you shall be rewarded
by me, with a gratitude even surpassing your own. If
there is anything else I can do that you can suggest, I
will do it."

"Listen to me!" said Ruth, now that the idea of
what he proposed had entered her mind. "When I
said that I was happy with you long ago, I was choked
with shame as I said it. And yet it may be a vain,
false excuse that I make for myself. I was very young;
I did not know how such a life was against God's pure
and holy will—at least, not as I know it now; and I
tell you truth—all the days of my years since I have
gone about with a stain on my hidden soul—a stain
which made me loathe myself, and envy those who
stood spotless and undefiled; which made me shrink
from my child—from Mr Benson, from his sister, from
the innocent girls whom I teach—nay, even I have
cowered away from God Himself; and what I did wrong
then, I did blindly to what I should do now if I listened
to you."

She was so strongly agitated that she put her hands
over her face, and sobbed without restraint. Then,
taking them away, she looked at him with a glowing
face, and beautiful, honest, wet eyes, and tried to speak
calmly, as she asked if she needed to stay longer (she
would have gone away at once but that she thought of
Leonard, and wished to hear all that his father might
have to say). He was so struck anew by her beauty,
and understood her so little, that he believed that she
only required a little more urging to consent to what
he wished; for in all she had said there was no trace
of the anger and resentment for his desertion of her,
which he had expected would be a prominent feature—
the greatest obstacle he had to encounter. The deep
sense of penitence she expressed, he mistook for earthly
shame; which he imagined he could soon soothe away.

"Yes, I have much more to say. I have not said
half. I cannot tell you how fondly I will—how fondly
I do love you—how my life shall be spent in minister-

ing to your wishes. Money, I see—I know, you
despise——"

"Mr Bellingham! I will not stay to hear you speak
to me so again. I have been sinful, but it is not you
who should——" She could not speak, she was so
choking with passionate sorrow.

He wanted to calm her, as he saw her shaken with
repressed sobs. He put his hand on her arm. She
shook it off impatiently, and moved away in an instant.

"Ruth!" said he, nettled by her action of repugnance, "I begin to think you never loved me."

"I!—I never loved you! Do you dare to say so?"
Her eyes flamed on him as she spoke. Her red,
round lip curled into beautiful contempt.

"Why do you shrink so from me?" said he, in his
turn getting impatient.

"I did not come here to be spoken to in this way,"
said she. "I came, if by any chance I could do Leonard
good. I would submit to many humiliations for his
sake—but to no more from you."

"Are not you afraid to brave me so?" said he.
"Don't you know how much you are in my power?"

She was silent. She longed to go away, but dreaded
lest he should follow her, where she might be less
subject to interruption than she was here—near the
fisherman's nets, which the receding tide was leaving
every moment barer and more bare, and the posts they
were fastened to more blackly uprising above the
waters.

Mr Donne put his hands on her arms as they hung
down before her—her hands tightly clasped together.

"Ask me to let you go," said he. "I will, if you
will ask me." He looked very fierce and passionate
and determined. The vehemence of his action took
Ruth by surprise, and the painful tightness of the
grasp almost made her exclaim. But she was quite
still and mute.

"Ask me," said he, giving her a little shake. She
did not speak. Her eyes, fixed on the distant shore,
were slowly filling with tears. Suddenly a light came

through the mist that obscured them, and the shut lips parted. She saw some distant object that gave her hope.

"It is Stephen Bromley," said she. "He is coming to his nets. They say he is a very desperate, violent man, but he will protect me."

"You obstinate, wilful creature!" said Mr Donne, releasing his grasp. "You forget that one word of mine could undeceive all these good people at Eccleston; and that if I spoke out ever so little, they would throw you off in an instant. Now!" he continued, "do you understand how much you are in my power?"

"Mr and Miss Benson know all—they have not thrown me off," Ruth gasped out. "Oh! for Leonard's sake! you would not be so cruel."

"Then do not you be cruel to him—to me. Think once more!"

"I think once more;" she spoke solemnly. "To save Leonard from the shame and agony of knowing my disgrace, I would lie down and die. Oh! perhaps it would be best for him—for me, if I might; my death would be a stingless grief—but to go back into sin would be the real cruelty to him. The errors of my youth may be washed away by my tears—it was so once when the gentle, blessed Christ was upon earth;*but now, if I went into wilful guilt, as you would have me, how could I teach Leonard God's holy will? I should not mind his knowing my past sin, compared to the awful corruption it would be if he knew me living now, as you would have me, lost to all fear of God——" Her speech was broken by sobs. "Whatever may be my doom—God is just—I leave myself in His hands. I will save Leonard from evil. Evil would it be for him if I lived with you. I will let him die first!" She lifted her eyes to heaven, and clasped and wreathed her hands together tight. Then she said: "You have humbled me enough, sir. I shall leave you now."

She turned away resolutely. The dark, grey fisherman was at hand. Mr Donne folded his arms, and set his teeth, and looked after her.

"What a stately step she has! How majestic and
graceful all her attitudes were! She thinks she has
baffled me now. We will try something more, and bid
a higher price." He unfolded his arms, and began to
follow her. He gained upon her, for her beautiful
walk was now wavering and unsteady. The works
which had kept her in motion were running down fast.

"Ruth!" said he, overtaking her. "You shall hear
me once more. Aye, look round! Your fisherman is
near. He may hear me, if he chooses—hear your
triumph. I am come to offer to marry you, Ruth;
come what may, I will have you. Nay—I will make
you hear me. I will hold this hand till you have
heard me. To-morrow I will speak to anyone in
Eccleston you like—to Mr Bradshaw; Mr ——, the
little minister, I mean. We can make it worth while
for him to keep our secret, and no one else need know
but what you are really Mrs Denbigh. Leonard shall
still bear this name, but in all things else he shall be
treated as my son. He and you would grace any
situation. I will take care the highest paths are open
to him!"

He looked to see the lovely face brighten into
sudden joy; on the contrary, the head was still hung
down with a heavy droop.

"I cannot," said she; her voice was very faint and low.

"It is sudden for you, my dearest. But be calm.
It will all be easily managed. Leave it to me."

"I cannot," repeated she, more distinct and clear,
though still very low.

"Why! what on earth makes you say that?"
asked he, in a mood to be irritated by any repetition
of such words.

"I do not love you. I did once. Don't say I did
not love you then; but I do not now. I could never
love you again. All you have said and done since you
came with Mr Bradshaw to Abermouth first, has only
made me wonder how I ever could have loved
you. We are very far apart. The time that has
pressed down my life like brands of hot iron, and

scarred me for ever, has been nothing to you. You
have talked of it with no sound of moaning in your
voice—no shadow over the brightness of your face;
it has left no sense of sin on your conscience, while me
it haunts and haunts; and yet I might plead that I
was an ignorant child—only I will not plead anything,
for God knows all—— But this is only one piece of
our great difference——"

"You mean that I am no saint," he said, impatient
at her speech. "Granted. But people who are no
saints have made very good husbands before now.
Come, don't let any morbid, overstrained conscientiousness interfere with substantial happiness—happiness both to you and to me—for I am sure I can make
you happy—aye! and make you love me, too, in spite of
your pretty defiance. I love you so dearly I must win
love back. And here are advantages for Leonard, to
be gained by you quite in a holy and legitimate way."

She stood very erect.

"If there was one thing needed to confirm me, you
have named it. You shall have nothing to do with
my boy, by my consent, much less by my agency.
I would rather see him working on the roadside than
leading such a life—being such a one as you are.
You have heard my mind now, Mr Bellingham. You
have humbled me—you have baited me; and if at
last I have spoken out too harshly, and too much in
a spirit of judgement, the fault is yours. If there
were no other reason to prevent our marriage but the
one fact that it would bring Leonard into contact with
you, that would be enough."

"It is enough!" said he, making her a low bow.
"Neither you nor your child shall ever more be
annoyed by me. I wish you a good evening."

They walked apart—he back to the inn, to set off
instantly, while the blood was hot in him, from the
place where he had been so mortified—she to steady
herself along till she reached the little path, more
like a rude staircase than anything else, by which she
had to climb to the house.

She did not turn round for some time after she
was fairly lost to the sight of anyone on the shore;
she clambered on, almost stunned by the rapid beating of her heart. Her eyes were hot and dry; and
at last became as if she were suddenly blind. Unable to go on, she tottered into the tangled under-
wood which grew among the stones, filling every niche
and crevice, and little shelving space, with green and
delicate tracery. She sank down behind a great over-
hanging rock, which hid her from anyone coming
up the path. An ash tree was rooted in this rock,
slanting away from the sea-breezes that were prevalent
in most weathers; but this was a still autumnal
Sabbath evening. As Ruth's limbs fell, so they lay.
She had no strength, no power of volition to move a
finger. She could not think or remember. She was
literally stunned. The first sharp sensation which
roused her from her torpor was a quick desire to see
him once more; up she sprang, and climbed to an
out-jutting dizzy point of rock, but a little above her
sheltered nook, yet commanding a wide view over the
bare naked sands;—far away below, touching the
rippling water-line, was Stephen Bromley, busily
gathering in his nets; besides him there was no living
creature visible. Ruth shaded her eyes, as if she
thought they might have deceived her; but no, there
was no one there. She went slowly down to her old
place, crying sadly as she went.

"Oh! if I had not spoken so angrily to him—the
last things I said were so bitter—so reproachful!—and
I shall never, never see him again!"

She could not take in the general view and scope
of their conversation—the event was too near her for
that; but her heart felt sore at the echo of her last
words, just and true as their severity was. Her
struggle, her constant flowing tears, which fell from
very weakness, made her experience a sensation of intense bodily fatigue; and her soul had lost the power
of throwing itself forward, or contemplating anything
beyond the dreary present, when the expanse of grey,

wild, bleak moors, stretching wide away below a sunless sky, seemed only an outward sign of the waste
world within her heart, for which she could claim no
sympathy ;—for she could not even define what its woes
were ; and if she could, no one would understand how
the present time was haunted by the terrible ghost of
the former love.

"I am so weary! I am so weary!" she moaned
aloud at last. "I wonder if I might stop here, and
just die away."

She shut her eyes, until through the closed lids came
a ruddy blaze of light. The clouds had parted away,
and the sun was going down in a crimson glory behind the distant purple hills. The whole western sky
was one flame of fire. Ruth forgot herself in looking
at the gorgeous sight. She sat up gazing, and, as she
gazed, the tears dried on her cheeks ; and, somehow,
all human care and sorrow were swallowed up in the
unconscious sense of God's infinity. The sunset calmed
her more than any words, however wise and tender,
could have done. It even seemed to give her strength
and courage; she did not know how or why, but so
it was.

She rose, and went slowly towards home. Her
limbs were very stiff, and every now and then she
had to choke down an unbidden sob. Her pupils
had been long returned from church, and had busied
themselves in preparing tea—an occupation which had
probably made them feel the time less long.

If they had ever seen a sleep-walker, they might
have likened Ruth to one for the next few days, so
slow and measured did her movements seem—so far
away was her intelligence from all that was passing
around her—so hushed and strange were the tones of
her voice ! They had letters from home announcing
the triumphant return of Mr Donne as M.P. for
Eccleston. Mrs Denbigh heard the news without a
word, and was too languid to join in the search after
purple and yellow flowers with which to deck the
sitting-room at Eagle's Crag.

A letter from Jemima came the next day, summoning them home. Mr Donne and his friends had
left the place, and quiet was restored in the Bradshaw household; so it was time that Mary's and
Elizabeth's holiday should cease. Mrs Denbigh had
also a letter—a letter from Miss Benson, saying that
Leonard was not quite well. There was so much pains
taken to disguise anxiety, that it was very evident
much anxiety was felt; and the girls were almost
alarmed by Ruth's sudden change from taciturn lan-
gour to eager, vehement energy. Body and mind
seemed strained to exertion. Every plan that could
facilitate packing and winding-up affairs at Abermouth,
every errand and arrangement that could expedite
their departure by one minute, was done by Ruth
with stern promptitude. She spared herself in nothing.
She made them rest, made them lie down, while she
herself lifted weights and transacted business with
feverish power, never resting, and trying never to
have time to think.

For in remembrance of the Past there was Remorse,—how had she forgotten Leonard these last few
days!—how had she repined and been dull of heart
to her blessing! And in anticipation of the Future
there was one sharp point of red light in the darkness
which pierced her brain with agony, and which she
would not see or recognize—and saw and recognized
all the more for such mad determination—which is not
the true shield against the bitterness of the arrows
of Death.

When the seaside party arrived in Eccleston, they
were met by Mrs and Miss Bradshaw and Mr Benson.
By a firm resolution, Ruth kept from shaping the
question, "Is he alive?" as if by giving shape to
her fears she made their realization more imminent.
She said merely, "How is he?" but she said it with
drawn, tight, bloodless lips, and in her eyes Mr
Benson read her anguish of anxiety.

"He is very ill, but we hope he will soon be better.
It is what every child has to go through."

CHAPTER XXV

Mr Bradshaw had been successful in carrying his
point. His member had been returned; his proud
opponents mortified. So the public thought he ought
to be well pleased; but the public were disappointed
to see that he did not show any of the gratification they
supposed him to feel.

The truth was, that he had met with so many small
mortifications during the progress of the election, that
the pleasure which he would otherwise have felt in the
final success of his scheme was much diminished.

He had more than tacitly sanctioned bribery; and
now that the excitement was over, he regretted it; not
entirely from conscientious motives, though he was
uneasy from a slight sense of wrong-doing; but he
was more pained, after all, to think that, in the eyes
of some of his townsmen, his hitherto spotless character
had received a blemish. He, who had been so stern
and severe a censor on the undue influence exercised
by the opposite party in all preceding elections, could
not expect to be spared by their adherents now, when
there were rumours that the hands of the scrupulous
Dissenters were not clean. Before, it had been his
boast that neither friend nor enemy could say one
word against him; now, he was constantly afraid of
an indictment for bribery, and of being compelled to
appear before a Committee to swear to his own share
in the business.

His uneasy, fearful consciousness made him stricter
and sterner than ever; as if he would quench all wondering, slanderous talk about him in the town by a
renewed austerity of uprightness; that the slack-
principled Mr Bradshaw of one month of ferment
and excitement, might not be confounded with the
highly-conscientious and deeply-religious Mr Bradshaw, who went to chapel twice a day, and gave a
hundred pounds a-piece to every charity in the town,
as a sort of thank-offering that his end was gained.

But he was secretly dissatisfied with Mr Donne.   In
general, that gentleman had been rather too willing
to act in accordance with anyone's advice, no matter
whose; as if he had thought it too much trouble to weigh
the wisdom of his friends, in which case Mr Bradshaw's
would have, doubtless, proved the most valuable.   But
now and then he unexpectedly, and utterly without
reason, took the conduct of affairs into his own hands,
as when he had been absent without leave only just
before the day of nomination.   No one guessed whither
he had gone; but the fact of his being gone was enough
to chagrin Mr Bradshaw, who was quite ready to pick
a quarrel on this very head, if the election had not
terminated favourably.   As it was, he had a feeling
of proprietorship in Mr Donne which was not disagreeable.   He had given the new M.P. his seat;
his resolution, his promptitude, his energy, had made
Mr Donne "our member"; and Mr Bradshaw began
to feel proud of him accordingly.   But there had
been no one circumstance during this period to bind
Jemima and Mr Farquhar together.   They were still
misunderstanding each other with all their power.
The difference in the result was this.   Jemima loved
him all the more, in spite of quarrels and coolness.
He was growing utterly weary of the petulant temper
of which he was never certain; of the reception which
varied day after day, according to the mood she was in
and the thoughts that were uppermost; and he was
almost startled to find how very glad he was that the little
girls and Mrs Denbigh were coming home.   His was
a character to bask in peace; and lovely, quiet Ruth,
with her low tones and quiet replies, her delicate
waving movements, appeared to him the very type
of what a woman should be—a calm, serene soul,
fashioning the body to angelic grace.

It was, therefore, with no slight interest that Mr
Farquhar inquired daily after the health of little
Leonard.   He asked at the Bensons' house; and
Sally answered him, with swollen and tearful eyes,
that the child was very bad—very bad indeed.   He

asked at the doctor's ; and the doctor told him, in a few short words, that "it was only a bad kind of measles, and that the lad might have a struggle for it, but he thought he would get through. Vigorous children carried their force into everything ; never did things by halves ; if they were ill, they were sure to be in a high fever directly ; if they were well, there was no peace in the house for their rioting. For his part," continued the doctor, "he thought he was glad he had had no children ; as far as he could judge, they were pretty much all plague and no profit." But as he ended his speech he sighed ; and Mr Farquhar was none the less convinced that common report was true, which represented the clever, prosperous surgeon of Eccleston as bitterly disappointed at his failure of offspring.

While these various interests and feelings had their course outside the Chapel-house, within there was but one thought which possessed all the inmates. When Sally was not cooking for the little invalid, she was crying ; for she had a dream about green rushes, not three months ago, which, by some queer process of oneiromancy,* she interpreted to mean the death of a child ; and all Miss Benson's endeavours were directed to making her keep silence to Ruth about this dream. Sally thought that the mother ought to be told ; what were dreams sent for but for warnings ; but it was just like a pack of Dissenters, who would not believe anything like other folks. Miss Benson was too much accustomed to Sally's contempt for Dissenters, as viewed from the pinnacle of the Establishment, to pay much attention to all this grumbling ; especially as Sally was willing to take as much trouble about Leonard as if she believed he was going to live, and that his recovery depended upon her care. Miss Benson's great object was to keep her from having any confidential talks with Ruth ; as if any repetition of the dream could have deepened the conviction in Ruth's mind that the child would die.

It seemed to her that his death would only be the

fitting punishment for the state of indifference towards
him—towards life and death—towards all things earthly
or divine, into which she had suffered herself to fall
since her last interview with Mr Donne. She did not
understand that such exhaustion is but the natural consequence of violent agitation and severe tension of
feeling. The only relief she experienced was in constantly serving Leonard; she had almost an animal's
jealousy lest anyone should come between her and her
young. Mr Benson saw this jealous suspicion, although he could hardly understand it; but he calmed
his sister's wonder and officious kindness, so that the
two patiently and quietly provided all that Ruth might
want, but did not interfere with her right to nurse
Leonard. But when he was recovering, Mr Benson,
with the slight tone of authority he knew how to assume when need was, bade Ruth lie down and take some
rest, while his sister watched. Ruth did not answer,
but obeyed in a dull, weary kind of surprise at being so
commanded. She lay down by her child, gazing her
fill at his calm slumber, and as she gazed, her large
white eyelids were softly pressed down as with a
gentle irresistible weight, and she fell asleep.

She dreamed that she was once more on the lonely
shore, striving to carry Leonard away from some
pursuer—some human pursuer—she knew he was
human, and she knew who he was, although she
dared not say his name even to herself, he seemed so
close and present, gaining on her flying footsteps,
rushing after her as with the sound of the roaring
tide. Her feet seemed heavy weights fixed to the
ground; they would not move. All at once, just
near the shore, a great black whirlwind of waves
clutched her back to her pursuer; she threw Leonard
on to land, which was safety; but whether he reached
it or no, or was swept back like her into a mysterious
something too dreadful to be borne, she did not know,
for the terror awakened her. At first the dream
seemed yet a reality, and she thought that the pursuer
was couched even there, in that very room, and the

great boom of the sea was still in her ears. But as full consciousness returned, she saw herself safe in the dear old room—the haven of rest—the shelter from storms. A bright fire was glowing in the little old-fashioned, cup-shaped grate, niched into a corner of the wall, and guarded on either side by whitewashed bricks, which rested on hobs. On one of these the kettle hummed and buzzed, within two points of boiling whenever she or Leonard required tea. In her dream that home-like sound had been the roaring of the relentless sea, creeping swiftly on to seize its prey. Miss Benson sat by the fire, motionless and still; it was too dark to read any longer without a candle; but yet on the ceiling and upper part of the walls the golden light of the setting sun was slowly moving—so slow, and yet a motion gives the feeling of rest to the weary yet more than perfect stillness. The old clock on the staircase told its monotonous click-clack, in that soothing way which more marked the quiet of the house than disturbed with any sense of sound. Leonard still slept that renovating slumber, almost in her arms, far from that fatal pursuing sea, with its human form of cruelty. The dream was a vision; the reality which prompted the dream was over and past—Leonard was safe—she was safe; all this loosened the frozen springs, and they gushed forth in her heart, and her lips moved in accordance with her thoughts.

"What were you saying, my darling?" said Miss Benson, who caught sight of the motion, and fancied she was asking for something. Miss Benson bent over the side of the bed on which Ruth lay, to catch the low tones of her voice.

"I only said," replied Ruth, timidly, "thank God! I have so much to thank Him for, you don't know."

"My dear, I am sure we have all of us cause to be thankful that our boy is spared. See! he is wakening up; and we will have a cup of tea together."

Leonard strode on to perfect health; but he was made older in character and looks by his severe illness.

He grew tall and thin, and the lovely child was lost in
the handsome boy. He began to wonder, and to question. Ruth mourned a little over the vanished baby-
hood, when she was all in all, and over the childhood,
whose petals had fallen away; it seemed as though
two of her children were gone—the one an infant, the
other a bright thoughtless darling; and she wished
that they could have remained quick in her memory
for ever, instead of being absorbed in loving pride for
the present boy. But these were only fanciful regrets,
flitting like shadows across a mirror. Peace and thankfulness were once more the atmosphere of her mind;
nor was her unconsciousness disturbed by any suspicion
of Mr Farquhar's increasing approbation and admiration, which he was diligently nursing up into love for
her. She knew that he had sent—she did not know
how often he had brought—fruit for the convalescent
Leonard. She heard, on her return from her daily
employment, that Mr Farquhar had brought a little
gentle pony, on which Leonard, weak as he was,
might ride. To confess the truth, her maternal pride
was such that she thought that all kindness shown to
such a boy as Leonard was but natural; she believed
him to be

A child whom all that looked on, loved.*

As in truth he was; and the proof of this was daily
shown in many kind inquiries, and many thoughtful
little offerings, besides Mr Farquhar's. The poor
(warm and kind of heart to all sorrow common to
humanity) were touched with pity for the young
widow, whose only child lay ill, and nigh unto death.
They brought what they could—a fresh egg, when
eggs were scarce—a few ripe pears that grew on the
sunniest side of the humble cottage, where the fruit
was regarded as a source of income—a call of inquiry,
and a prayer that God would spare the child, from an
old crippled woman, who could scarcely drag herself
so far as the Chapel-house, yet felt her worn and
weary heart stirred with a sharp pang of sympathy,

and a very present remembrance of the time when she too was young, and saw the life-breath quiver out of her child, now an angel in that heaven, which felt more like home to the desolate old creature than this empty earth. To all such, when Leonard was better, Ruth went, and thanked them from her heart. She and the old cripple sat hand in hand over the scanty fire on the hearth of the latter, while she told in solemn, broken, homely words, how her child sickened and died. Tears fell like rain down Ruth's cheeks; but those of the old woman were dry. All tears had been wept out of her long ago, and now she sat patient and quiet, waiting for death. But after this, Ruth "clave unto her," and the two were henceforward a pair of friends. Mr Farquhar was only included in the general gratitude which she felt towards all who had been kind to her boy.

The winter passed away in deep peace after the storms of the autumn, yet every now and then a feeling of insecurity made Ruth shake for an instant. Those wild autumnal storms had torn aside the quiet flowers and herbage that had gathered over the wreck of her early life, and shown her that all deeds, however hidden, and long passed by, have their eternal consequences. She turned sick and faint whenever Mr Donne's name was casually mentioned. No one saw it; but she felt the miserable stop in her heart's beating, and wished that she could prevent it by any exercise of self-command. She had never named his identity with Mr Bellingham, nor had she spoken about the seaside interview. Deep shame made her silent and reserved on all her life before Leonard's birth; from that time she rose again in her self-respect, and spoke as openly as a child (when need was) of all occurrences which had taken place since then; except that she could not, and would not, tell of this mocking echo, this haunting phantom, this past, that would not rest in its grave. The very circumstance that it was stalking abroad in the world, and might reappear at any moment, made her a

coward : she trembled away from contemplating what
the reality had been ; only she clung more faithfully
than before to the thought of the great God, who was
a rock in the dreary land, where no shadow was.

Autumn and winter, with their lowering skies, were
less dreary than the woeful, desolate feelings that shed
a gloom on Jemima.   She found too late that she had
considered Mr Farquhar so securely her own for so
long a time, that her heart refused to recognize him as
lost to her, unless her reason went through the same
weary, convincing, miserable evidence day after day,
and hour after hour.   He never spoke to her now,
except from common civility.   He never cared for her
contradictions ;   he never tried, with patient perseverance, to bring her over to his opinions ;   he never
used the wonted wiles (so tenderly remembered now
they had no existence but in memory) to bring her
round out of some wilful mood—and such moods were
common enough now !   Frequently she was sullenly
indifferent to the feelings of others—not from any unkindness, but because her heart seemed numb and
stony, and incapable of sympathy.   Then afterwards
her self-reproach was terrible—in the dead of night,
when no one saw it.   With a strange perversity, the
only intelligence she cared to hear, the only sights she
cared to see, were the circumstances which gave con-
firmation to the idea that Mr Farquhar was thinking of
Ruth for a wife.   She craved with stinging curiosity to
hear something of their affairs every day ; partly because the torture which such intelligence gave was
almost a relief from the deadness of her heart to all
other interests.

And so spring (*gioventu dell'anno*)*came back to her,
bringing all the contrasts which spring alone can bring
to add to the heaviness of the soul.   The little winged
creatures filled the air with bursts of joy ; the vegetation came bright and hopefully onwards, without any
check of nipping frost.   The ash trees in the Bradshaws'
garden were out in leaf by the middle of May, which
that year wore more the aspect of summer than most

Junes do. The sunny weather mocked Jemima, and the unusual warmth oppressed her physical powers. She felt very weak and languid: she was acutely sensible that no one else noticed her want of strength; father, mother, all seemed too full of other things to care if, as she believed, her life was waning. She herself felt glad that it was so. But her delicacy was not unnoticed by all. Her mother often anxiously asked her husband if he did not think Jemima was looking ill; nor did his affirmation to the contrary satisfy her, as most of his affirmations did. She thought every morning, before she got up, how she could tempt Jemima to eat, by ordering some favourite dainty for dinner; in many other little ways she tried to minister to her child; but the poor girl's own abrupt irritability of temper had made her mother afraid of openly speaking to her about her health.

Ruth, too, saw that Jemima was not looking well. How she had become an object of dislike to her former friend she did not know; but she was sensible that Miss Bradshaw disliked her now. She was not aware that this feeling was growing and strengthening almost into repugnance, for she seldom saw Jemima out of school-hours, and then only for a minute or two. But the evil element of a fellow-creature's dislike oppressed the atmosphere of her life. That fellow-creature was one who had once loved her so fondly, and whom she still loved, although she had learnt to fear her, as we fear those whose faces cloud over when we come in sight—who cast unloving glances at us, of which we, though not seeing, are conscious, as of some occult influence; and the cause of whose dislike is unknown to us, though every word and action seems to increase it. I believe that this sort of dislike is only shown by the jealous, and that it renders the disliker even more miserable, because more continually conscious than the object; but the growing evidence of Jemima's feeling made Ruth very unhappy at times. This very May, too, an idea had come into her mind, which she had tried to repress—namely, that Mr Farquhar was in love with her. It annoyed her extremely; it made her reproach herself that she ever should think such a thing possible. She tried to strangle the notion, to drown it, to starve it out by neglect—its existence caused her such pain and distress.

The worst was, he had won Leonard's heart, who was constantly seeking him out; or, when absent, talking about him. The best was some journey connected with business, which would take him to the continent for several weeks; and, during that time, surely this disagreeable fancy of his would die away, if untrue; and if true, some way would be opened by which she might put a stop to all increase of predilection on his part, and yet retain him as a friend for Leonard—that darling for whom she was far-seeing and covetous, and miserly of every scrap of love and kindly regard.

Mr Farquhar would not have been flattered if he had known how much his departure contributed to Ruth's rest of mind on the Saturday afternoon on which he set out on his journey. It was a beautiful day; the sky of that intense quivering blue which seemed as though you could look through it for ever, yet not reach the black, infinite space which is suggested as lying beyond. Now and then a thin, torn, vaporous cloud floated slowly within the vaulted depth; but the soft air that gently wafted it was not perceptible among the leaves on the trees, which did not even tremble. Ruth sat at her work in the shadow formed by the old grey garden wall; Miss Benson and Sally—the one in the parlour window-seat mending stockings, the other hard at work in her kitchen—were both within talking distance, for it was weather for open doors and windows; but none of the three kept up any continued conversation; and in the intervals Ruth sang low a brooding song, such as she remembered her mother singing long ago. Now and then she stopped to look at Leonard, who was labouring away with vehement energy at digging over a small plot of ground, where he meant to prick out some celery plants that had been given to him. Ruth's heart warmed at the earnest,

spirited way in which he thrust his large spade deep
down into the brown soil, his ruddy face glowing, his
curly hair wet with the exertion ; and yet she sighed to
think that the days were over when her deeds of skill
could give him pleasure.   Now, his delight was in
acting himself ; last year, not fourteen months ago, he
had watched her making a daisy-chain for him, as if he
could not admire her cleverness enough ; this year—
this week, when she had been devoting every spare
hour to the simple tailoring which she performed for
her boy (she had always made every article he wore,
and felt almost jealous of the employment), he had
come to her with a wistful look, and asked when he
might begin to have clothes made by a man?

Ever since the Wednesday when she had accompanied Mary and Elizabeth, at Mrs Bradshaw's desire,
to be measured for spring clothes by the new Eccleston
dressmaker, she had been looking forward to this
Saturday afternoon's pleasure of making summer
trousers for Leonard ; but the satisfaction of the employment was a little taken away by Leonard's speech.
It was a sign, however, that her life was very quiet and
peaceful that she had leisure to think upon the thing at
all ; and often she forgot it entirely in her low,
chanting song, or in listening to the thrush warbling
out his afternoon ditty to his patient mate in the
holly-bush below.

The distant rumble of carts through the busy streets
(it was market-day) not only formed a low rolling bass
to the nearer and pleasanter sounds, but enhanced the
sense of peace by the suggestion of the contrast afforded
to the repose of the garden by the bustle not far off.

But besides physical din and bustle there is mental
strife and turmoil.

That afternoon, as Jemima was restlessly wandering
about the house, her mother desired her to go on an
errand to Mrs Pearson's, the new dressmaker, in order
to give some directions about her sisters' new frocks.
Jemima went, rather than have the trouble of resisting ;
or else she would have preferred staying at home,

moving or being outwardly quiet according to her own
fitful will. Mrs Bradshaw, who, as I have said, had
been aware for some time that something was wrong
with her daughter, and was very anxious to set it to
rights if she only knew how, had rather planned this
errand with a view to dispel Jemima's melancholy.

"And Mimie, dear," said her mother, "when you
are there, look out for a new bonnet for yourself; she
has got some very pretty ones, and your old one is so
shabby."

"It does for me, mother," said Jemima, heavily.
"I don't want a new bonnet."

"But I want you to have one, my lassie. I want
my girl to look well and nice."

There was something of homely tenderness in Mrs
Bradshaw's tone that touched Jemima's heart. She
went to her mother, and kissed her with more of affection than she had shown to anyone for weeks before;
and the kiss was returned with warm fondness.

"I think you love me, mother," said Jemima.

"We all love you, dear, if you would but think so.
And if you want anything, or wish for anything, only
tell me, and with a little patience I can get your father
to give it you, I know. Only be happy, there's a good
girl."

"Be happy! as if one could by an effort of will!"
thought Jemima, as she went along the street, too
absorbed in herself to notice the bows of acquaintances
and friends, but instinctively guiding herself right
among the throng and press of carts, and gigs, and
market people in High Street.

But her mother's tones and looks, with their comforting power, remained longer in her recollection than
the inconsistency of any words spoken. When she had
completed her errand about the frocks, she asked to
look at some bonnets, in order to show her recognition
of her mother's kind thought.

Mrs Pearson was a smart, clever-looking woman of
five or six and thirty. She had all the variety of small-
talk at her finger ends that was formerly needed by

barbers to amuse the people who came to be shaved.
She had admired the town till Jemima was weary of its
praises, sick and oppressed by its sameness, as she had
been these many weeks.

"Here are some bonnets, ma'am, that will be just
the thing for you—elegant and tasty, yet quite of the
simple style, suitable to young ladies. Oblige me by
trying on this white silk !"

Jemima looked at herself in the glass ; she was
obliged to own it was very becoming, and perhaps not
the less so for the flush of modest shame which came
into her cheeks as she heard Mrs Pearson's open praises
of the "rich, beautiful hair," and the "Oriental eyes"
of the wearer.

"I induced the young lady who accompanied your
sisters the other day—the governess, is she, ma'am ?"

"Yes—Mrs Denbigh is her name," said Jemima,
clouding over.

"Thank you, ma'am. Well, I persuaded Mrs Denbigh to try on that bonnet, and you can't think how
charming she looked in it ; and yet I don't think it
became her as much as it does you."

"Mrs Denbigh is very beautiful," said Jemima,
taking off the bonnet, and not much inclined to try
on any other.

"Very, ma'am. Quite a peculiar style of beauty.
If I might be allowed, I should say that hers was a
Grecian style of loveliness, while yours was Oriental.
She reminded me of a young person I once knew in
Fordham."   Mrs Pearson sighed an audible sigh.

"In Fordham !" said Jemima, remembering that
Ruth had once spoken of the place as one in which she
had spent some time, while the county in which it was
situated was the same in which Ruth was born. "In
Fordham ! Why, I think Mrs Denbigh comes from
that neighbourhood."

"Oh, ma'am ! she cannot be the young person I
mean—I am sure, ma'am—holding the position she
does in your establishment. I should hardly say I
knew her myself ; for I only saw her two or three times

at my sister's house; but she was so remarked for her
beauty, that I remember her face quite well—the
more so, on account of her vicious conduct afterwards."

"Her vicious conduct!" repeated Jemima, convinced by these words that there could be no identity
between Ruth and the "young person" alluded to.
"Then it could not have been our Mrs Denbigh."

"Oh, no, ma'am! I am sure I should be sorry to be
understood to have suggested anything of the kind.
I beg your pardon if I did so. All I meant to say—
and perhaps that was a liberty I ought not to have
taken, considering what Ruth Hilton was——"

"Ruth Hilton!" said Jemima, turning suddenly
round, and facing Mrs Pearson.

"Yes, ma'am, that was the name of the young person
I allude to."

"Tell me about her—what did she do?" asked
Jemima, subduing her eagerness of tone and look as
best she might, but trembling as on the verge of some
strange discovery.

"I don't know whether I ought to tell you, ma'am—
it is hardly a fit story for a young lady; but this Ruth
Hilton was an apprentice to my sister-in-law, who had
a first-rate business in Fordham, which brought her a
good deal of patronage from the county families; and
this young creature was very artful and bold, and
thought sadly too much of her beauty; and, somehow,
she beguiled a young gentleman, who took her into
keeping (I am sure, ma'am, I ought to apologize for
polluting your ears——)"

"Go on," said Jemima, breathlessly.

"I don't know much more. His mother followed
him into Wales. She was a lady of a great deal of
religion, and of a very old family, and was much
shocked at her son's misfortune in being captivated by
such a person; but she led him to repentance, and
took him to Paris, where, I think, she died; but I am
not sure, for, owing to family differences, I have not
been on terms for some years with my sister-in-law,
who was my informant."

"Who died?" interrupted Jemima—"the young man's mother, or—or Ruth Hilton?"

"Oh dear, ma'am! pray don't confuse the two. It was the mother, Mrs —— I forget the name—something like Billington. It was the lady who died."

"And what became of the other?" asked Jemima, unable, as her dark suspicion seemed thickening, to speak the name.

"The girl? Why, ma'am, what could become of her? Not that I know exactly—only one knows they can but go from bad to worse, poor creatures! God forgive me, if I am speaking too transiently of such degraded women, who, after all, are a disgrace to our sex."

"Then you know nothing more about her?" asked Jemima.

"I did hear that she had gone off with another gentleman that she met with in Wales, but I'm sure I can't tell who told me."

There was a little pause. Jemima was pondering on all she had heard. Suddenly she felt that Mrs Pearson's eyes were upon her, watching her; not with curiosity, but with a newly-awakened intelligence;—and yet she must ask one more question; but she tried to ask it in an indifferent, careless tone, handling the bonnet while she spoke.

"How long is it since all this—all you have been telling me about—happened?" (Leonard was eight years old.)

"Why—let me see. It was before I was married, and I was married three years, and poor dear Pearson has been deceased five—I should say, going on for nine years this summer. Blush roses would become your complexion, perhaps, better than these lilacs," said she, as with superficial observation she watched Jemima, turning the bonnet round and round on her hand—the bonnet that her dizzy eyes did not see.

"Thank you. It is very pretty. But I don't want a bonnet. I beg your pardon for taking up your time."

And with an abrupt bow to the discomfited Mrs
Pearson, she was out and away in the open air, thread-
ing her way with instinctive energy along the crowded
street. Suddenly she turned round, and went back to
Mrs Pearson's, with even more rapidity than she had
been walking away from the house.

"I have changed my mind," said she, as she came,
breathless, up into the show-room. "I will take the
bonnet. How much is it?"

"Allow me to change the flowers; it can be done in
an instant, and then you can see if you would not
prefer the roses; but with either foliage it is a lovely
little bonnet," said Mrs Pearson, holding it up admiringly on her hand.

"Oh! never mind the flowers—yes! change them
to roses." And she stood by, agitated (Mrs Pearson
thought with impatience) all the time the milliner was
making the alteration with skilful, busy haste.

"By the way," said Jemima, when she saw the last
touches were being given, and that she must not delay
executing the purpose which was the real cause of her
return—"Papa, I am sure, would not like your con-
necting Mrs Denbigh's name with such a—story as
you have been telling me."

"Oh dear! ma'am, I have too much respect for you
all to think of doing such a thing! Of course I know,
ma'am, that it is not to be cast up to any lady that
she is like anybody disreputable."

"But I would rather you did not name the likeness
to anyone," said Jemima; "not to anyone. Don't
tell anyone the story you have told me this morning."

"Indeed, ma'am, I should never think of such a
thing! My poor husband could have borne witness
that I am as close as the grave where there is anything
to conceal."

"Oh dear!" said Jemima, "Mrs Pearson, there is
nothing to conceal; only you must not speak about
it."

"I certainly shall not do it, ma'am; you may rest
assured of me."

This time Jemima did not go towards home, but in the direction of the outskirts of the town, on the hilly side. She had some dim recollection of hearing her sisters ask if they might not go and invite Leonard and his mother to tea; and how could she face Ruth, after the conviction had taken possession of her heart that she, and the sinful creature she had just heard of, were one and the same?

It was yet only the middle of the afternoon; the hours were early in the old-fashioned town of Eccleston. Soft white clouds had come slowly sailing up out of the west; the plain was flecked with thin floating shadows, gently borne along by the westerly wind that was waving the long grass in the hay fields into alternate light and shade. Jemima went into one of these fields, lying by the side of the upland road. She was stunned by the shock she had received. The diver, leaving the green sward, smooth and known, where his friends stand with their familiar smiling faces, admiring his glad bravery—the diver, down in an instant in the horrid depths of the sea, close to some strange, ghastly, lidless-eyed monster, can hardly more feel his blood curdle at the near terror than did Jemima now. Two hours ago—but a point of time on her mind's dial—she had never imagined that she should ever come in contact with anyone who had committed open sin; she had never shaped her conviction into words and sentences, but still it was *there*, that all the respectable, all the family and religious circumstances of her life, would hedge her in, and guard her from ever encountering the great shock of coming face to face with vice. Without being pharisaical in her estimation of herself, she had all a Pharisee's dread of publicans and sinners, and all a child's cowardliness—that cowardliness which prompts it to shut its eyes against the object of terror, rather than acknowledge its existence with brave faith. Her father's often reiterated speeches had not been without their effect. He drew a clear line of partition, which separated mankind into two great groups, to one of

which, by the grace of God, he and his belonged;
while the other was composed of those whom it was
his duty to try and reform, and bring the whole force
of his morality to bear upon, with lectures, admoni-
tions, and exhortations—a duty to be performed,
because it was a duty—but with very little of that Hope
and Faith which is the Spirit that maketh alive.
Jemima had rebelled against these hard doctrines of
her father's, but their frequent repetition had had its
effect, and led her to look upon those who had gone
astray with shrinking, shuddering recoil, instead of
with a pity, so Christ-like as to have both wisdom and
tenderness in it.

And now she saw among her own familiar associates
one, almost her housefellow, who had been stained
with that evil most repugnant to her womanly modesty,
that would fain have ignored its existence altogether.
She loathed the thought of meeting Ruth again. She
wished that she could take her up, and put her down
at a distance somewhere—anywhere—where she might
never see or hear of her more; never be reminded, as
she must be whenever she saw her, that such things
were, in this sunny, bright, lark-singing earth, over
which the blue dome of heaven bent softly down as
Jemima sat down in the hayfield that June afternoon;
her cheeks flushed and red, but her lips pale and compressed, and her eyes full of a heavy, angry sorrow.
It was Saturday, and the people in that part of the
country left their work an hour earlier on that day.
By this, Jemima knew it must be growing time for
her to be at home. She had had so much of
conflict in her own mind of late, that she had grown to
dislike struggle, or speech, or explanation; and so
strove to conform to times and hours much more than
she had done in happier days. But oh! how full of
hate her heart was growing against the world! And
oh! how she sickened at the thought of seeing Ruth!
Who was to be trusted more, if Ruth—calm, modest,
delicate, dignified Ruth—had a memory blackened by
sin?

As she went heavily along, the thought of Mr
Farquhar came into her mind. It showed how terrible
had been the stun, that he had been forgotten until
now. With the thought of him came in her first
merciful feeling towards Ruth. This would never
have been, had there been the least latent suspicion in
Jemima's jealous mind that Ruth had purposely done
aught—looked a look—uttered a word—modulated a
tone — for the sake of attracting. As Jemima recalled all the passages of their intercourse, she
slowly confessed to herself how pure and simple had
been all Ruth's ways in relation to Mr Farquhar. It
was not merely that there had been no coquetting,
but there had been simple unconsciousness on Ruth's
part, for so long a time after Jemima had discovered
Mr Farquhar's inclination for her; and when at length
she had slowly awakened to some perception of the
state of his feelings, there had been a modest, shrinking dignity of manner, not startled, or emotional, or
even timid, but pure, grave, and quiet; and this conduct of Ruth's, Jemima instinctively acknowledged to
be of necessity transparent and sincere. Now, and
here, there was no hypocrisy; but some time, somewhere, on the part of somebody, what hypocrisy, what
lies must have been acted, if not absolutely spoken,
before Ruth could have been received by them all as
the sweet, gentle, girlish widow, which she remembered they had all believed Mrs Denbigh to be when
first she came among them. Could Mr and Miss
Benson know? Could they be a party to the deceit?
Not sufficiently acquainted with the world to understand how strong had been the temptation to play the
part they did, if they wished to give Ruth a chance,
Jemima could not believe them guilty of such deceit
as the knowledge of Mrs Denbigh's previous conduct
would imply; and yet how it darkened the latter into
a treacherous hypocrite, with a black secret shut up in
her soul for years—living in apparent confidence, and
daily household familiarity with the Bensons for years,
yet never telling the remorse that ought to be corrod-

ing her heart! Who was true? Who was not?
Who was good and pure? Who was not? The very
foundations of Jemima's belief in her mind were
shaken.

Could it be false? Could there be two Ruth Hil-
tons. She went over every morsel of evidence. It
could not be. She knew that Mrs Denbigh's former
name had been Hilton. She had heard her speak
casually, but charily, of having lived in Fordham.
She knew she had been in Wales but a short time
before she made her appearance in Eccleston. There
was no doubt of the identity. Into the middle of
Jemima's pain and horror at the afternoon's discovery,
there came a sense of the power which the knowledge
of this secret gave her over Ruth; but this was no
relief, only an aggravation of the regret with which
Jemima looked back on her state of ignorance. It was
no wonder that when she arrived at home, she was
so oppressed with headache that she had to go to bed
directly.

"Quiet, mother! quiet, dear, dear mother" (for
she clung to the known and tried goodness of her
mother more than ever now), "that is all I want."
And she was left to the stillness of her darkened room,
the blinds idly flapping to and fro in the soft evening
breeze, and letting in the rustling sound of the
branches which waved close to her window, and the
thrush's gurgling warble, and the distant hum of the
busy town.

Her jealousy was gone—she knew not how or where.
She might shun and recoil from Ruth, but she now
thought that she could never more be jealous of her.
In her pride of innocence, she felt almost ashamed
that such a feeling could have had existence. Could
Mr Farquhar hesitate between her own self and one
who—— No! she could not name what Ruth had
been, even in thought. And yet he might never
know, so fair a seeming did her rival wear. Oh! for
one ray of God's holy light to know what was seeming,
and what was truth in this traitorous hollow earth!

It might be—she used to think such things possible,
before sorrow had embittered her — that Ruth had
worked her way through the deep purgatory of repentance up to something like purity again ; God only
knew! If her present goodness was real—if, after
having striven back thus far on the heights, a fellow-
woman was to throw her down into some terrible depth
with her unkind, incontinent tongue, that would be
too cruel! And yet, if—there was such woeful uncertainty and deceit somewhere—if Ruth—— No!
that Jemima, with noble candour, admitted was impossible. Whatever Ruth had been, she was good,
and to be respected as such, now. It did not follow
that Jemima was to preserve the secret always ; she
doubted her own power to do so, if Mr Farquhar came
home again, and were still constant in his admiration
of Mrs Denbigh, and if Mrs Denbigh gave him any—
the least encouragement. But this last she thought,
from what she knew of Ruth's character, was impossible. Only, what was impossible after this afternoon's
discovery? At any rate, she would watch, and wait.
Come what might, Ruth was in her power. And,
strange to say, this last certainty gave Jemima a kind
of protecting, almost pitying, feeling for Ruth. Her
horror at the wrong was not diminished ; but the more
she thought of the struggles that the wrong-doer must
have made to extricate herself, the more she felt how
cruel it would be to baffle all by revealing what had
been. But for her sisters' sake she had a duty to
perform ; she must watch Ruth. For her love's sake
she could not have helped watching ; but she was too
much stunned to recognize the force of her love, while
duty seemed the only stable thing to cling to. For
the present she would neither meddle nor mar in
Ruth's course of life.

CHAPTER XXVI

So it was that Jemima no longer avoided Ruth, nor
manifested by word or look the dislike which for a
long time she had been scarce concealing. Ruth could
not help noticing that Jemima always sought to be in
her presence while she was at Mr Bradshaw's house ;
either when daily teaching Mary and Elizabeth, or
when she came as an occasional visitor with Mr and
Miss Benson, or by herself.   Up to this time, Jemima
had used no gentle skill to conceal the abruptness
with which she would leave the room rather than that
Ruth and she should be brought into contact—rather
than that it should fall to her lot to entertain Ruth
during any part of the evening.   It was months since
Jemima had left off sitting in the schoolroom, as had
been her wont during the first few years of Ruth's
governess-ship.   Now, each morning, Miss Bradshaw
seated herself at a little round table in the window, at
her work, or at her writing ; but whether she sewed,
or wrote, or read, Ruth felt that she was always watching—watching.   At first, Ruth had welcomed all these
changes in habit and behaviour, as giving her a chance,
she thought, by some patient waiting or some opportune show of enduring constant love, to regain her
lost friend's regard ; but, by and by, the icy chillness,
immovable and grey, struck more to her heart than
many sudden words of unkindness could have done.
They might be attributed to the hot impulses of a
hasty temper—to the vehement anger of an accuser ;
but this measured manner was the conscious result of
some deep-seated feeling ; this cold sternness befitted
the calm implacability of some severe judge.   The
watching, which Ruth felt was ever upon her, made
her unconsciously shiver, as you would if you saw that
the passionless eyes of the dead were visibly gazing
upon you.   Her very being shrivelled and parched up
in Jemima's presence, as if blown upon by a bitter,
keen, east wind.

Jemima bent every power she possessed upon the one object of ascertaining what Ruth really was. Sometimes the strain was very painful; the constant tension made her soul weary; and she moaned aloud, and upbraided circumstance (she dared not go higher —to the maker of circumstance) for having deprived her of her unsuspicious happy ignorance.

Things were in this state when Mr Richard Bradshaw came on his annual home visit. He was to remain another year in London, and then to return and be admitted into the firm. After he had been a week at home, he grew tired of the monotonous regularity of his father's household, and began to complain of it to Jemima.

"I wish Farquhar were at home. Though he is such a stiff, quiet old fellow, his coming in in the evenings makes a change. What has become of the Millses? They used to drink tea with us sometimes, formerly."

"Oh! papa and Mr Mills took opposite sides at the election, and we have never visited since. I don't think they are any great loss."

"Anybody is a loss—the stupidest bore that ever was would be a blessing, if he only would come in sometimes."

"Mr and Miss Benson have drank tea here twice since you came."

"Come, that's capital! Apropos of stupid bores, you talk of the Bensons. I did not think you had so much discrimination, my little sister."

Jemima looked up in surprise; and then reddened angrily.

"I never meant to say a word against Mr or Miss Benson, and that you know quite well, Dick."

"Never mind! I won't tell tales. They are stupid old fogeys, but they are better than nobody, especially as that handsome governess of the girls always comes with them to be looked at."

There was a little pause; Richard broke it by saying:

"Do you know, Minnie, I've a notion, it she plays her cards well, she may hook Farquhar!"

"Who?" asked Jemima, shortly, though she knew quite well.

"Mrs Denbigh, to be sure. We were talking ot her, you know. Farquhar asked me to dine with him at his hotel as he passed through town, and—I'd my own reasons for going and trying to creep up his sleeve —I wanted him to tip me, as he used to do."

"For shame! Dick," burst in Jemima.

"Well! well! not tip me exactly, but lend me some money. The governor keeps me so deucedly short."

"Why! it was only yesterday, when my father was speaking about your expenses, and your allowance, I heard you say that you'd more than you knew how to spend."

"Don't you see that was the perfection of art. If my father had thought me extravagant, he would have kept me in with a tight rein; as it is, I'm in great hopes of a handsome addition, and I can tell you it's needed. If my father had given me what I ought to have had at first, I should not have been driven to the speculations and messes I've got into."

"What speculations? What messes?" asked Jemima, with anxious eagerness.

"Oh! messes was not the right word. Speculations hardly was; for they are sure to turn out well, and then I shall surprise my father with my riches." He saw that he had gone a little too far in his confidence, and was trying to draw in.

"But, what do you mean? Do explain it to me."

"Never you trouble your head about my business, my dear. Women can't understand the share-market, and such things. Don't think I've forgotten the awful blunders you made when you tried to read the state of the money-market aloud to my father, that night when he had lost his spectacles. What were we talking of? Oh! of Farquhar and pretty Mrs Denbigh. Yes! I soon found out that was the subject my gentleman liked me to dwell on. He did not talk about her much himself, but his eyes sparkled when I told him what enthusiastic letters Polly and Elizabeth wrote about her. How old d'ye think she is?"

" I know!" said Jemima. " At least, I heard her age spoken about, amongst other things, when first she came. She will be five-and-twenty this autumn."

"And Farquhar is forty, if he is a day. She's young, too, to have such a boy as Leonard; younger-looking, or full as young-looking as she is! I tell you what, Minnie, she looks younger than you. How old are you? Three-and-twenty, ain't it?"

"Last March," replied Jemima.

" You'll have to make haste and pick up somebody, if you're losing your good looks at this rate. Why, Jemima, I thought you had a good chance of Farquhar a year or two ago. How come you to have lost him? I'd far rather you'd had him than that proud, haughty Mrs Denbigh, who flashes her great grey eyes upon me if ever I dare to pay her a compliment. She ought to think it an honour that I take that much notice of her. Besides, Farquhar is rich, and it's keeping the business of the firm in one's own family ; and if he marries Mrs Denbigh she will be sure to be wanting Leonard in when he's of age, and I won't have that. Have a try for Farquhar, Minnie! Ten to one it's not too late. I wish I'd brought you a pink bonnet down. You go about so dowdy—so careless of how you look."

" If Mr Farquhar has not liked me as I am," said Jemima, choking, " I don't want to owe him to a pink bonnet."

"Nonsense! I don't like to have my sisters' gover-ness stealing a march on my sister. I tell you Farquhar is worth trying for. If you'll wear the pink bonnet I'll give it you, and I'll back you against Mrs Denbigh. I think you might have done something with 'our member,' as my father calls him, when you had him so long in the house. But, altogether, I should like Farquhar best for a brother-in-law. By the way, have you heard down here that Donne is

going to be married? I heard of it in town, just
before I left, from a man that was good authority.
Some Sir Thomas Campbell's seventh daughter: a girl
without a penny; father ruined himself by gambling,
and obliged to live abroad. But Donne is not a man
to care for any obstacle, from all accounts, when once
he has taken a fancy. It was love at first sight, they
say. I believe he did not know of her existence a
month ago."

"No! we have not heard of it," replied Jemima.
"My father will like to know; tell it him;" continued she, as she was leaving the room, to be alone,
in order to still her habitual agitation whenever she
heard Mr Farquhar and Ruth coupled together.

Mr Farquhar came home the day before Richard
Bradshaw left for town. He dropped in after tea at
the Bradshaws'; he was evidently disappointed to see
none but the family there, and looked round whenever
the door opened.

"Look! look!" said Dick to his sister. "I wanted
to make sure of his coming in to-night, to save me my
father's parting exhortations against the temptations
of the world (as if I did not know much more of the
world than he does!), so I used a spell I thought
would prove efficacious; I told him that we should be
by ourselves, with the exception of Mrs Denbigh, and
look how he is expecting her to come in!"

Jemima did see; did understand. She understood,
too, why certain packets were put carefully on one
side, apart from the rest of the purchases of Swiss toys
and jewellery, by which Mr Farquhar proved that none
of Mr Bradshaw's family had been forgotten by him
during his absence. Before the end of the evening,
she was very conscious that her sore heart had not
forgotten how to be jealous. Her brother did not
allow a word, a look, or an incident, which might be
supposed on Mr Farquhar's side to refer to Ruth, to
pass unnoticed; he pointed out all to his sister, never
dreaming of the torture he was inflicting, only anxious
to prove his own extreme penetration. At length

Jemima could stand it no longer, and left the room. She went into the schoolroom, where the shutters were not closed, as it only looked into the garden. She opened the window, to let the cool night air blow in on her hot cheeks. The clouds were hurrying over the moon's face in a tempestuous and unstable manner, making all things seem unreal; now clear out in its bright light, now trembling and quivering in shadow. The pain at her heart seemed to make Jemima's brain grow dull; she laid her head on her arms, which rested on the window-sill, and grew dizzy with the sick weary notion that the earth was wandering lawless and aimless through the heavens, where all seemed one tossed and whirling wrack of clouds. It was a waking night mare, from the uneasy heaviness of which she was thankful to be roused by Dick's entrance.

"What, you are here, are you? I have been looking everywhere for you. I wanted to ask you if you have any spare money you could lend me for a few weeks?"

"How much do you want?" asked Jemima, in a dull, hopeless voice.

"Oh! the more the better. But I should be glad of any trifle, I am kept so confoundedly short."

When Jemima returned with her little store, even her careless, selfish brother was struck by the wanness of her face, lighted by the bed-candle she carried.

"Come, Minnie, don't give it up. If I were you, I would have a good try against Mrs Denbigh. I'll send you the bonnet as soon as ever I get back to town, and you pluck up a spirit, and I'll back you against her even yet."

It seemed to Jemima strange—and yet only a fitting part of this strange, chaotic world—to find that her brother, who was the last person to whom she could have given her confidence in her own family, and almost the last person of her acquaintance to whom she could look for real help and sympathy, should have been the only one to hit upon the secret of her love. And the idea passed away from his mind as quickly as all ideas not bearing upon his own self-interests did.

The night, the sleepless night, was so crowded and haunted by miserable images, that she longed for day ; and when day came, with its stinging realities, she wearied and grew sick for the solitude of night. For the next week, she seemed to see and hear nothing but what confirmed the idea of Mr Farquhar's decided attachment to Ruth. Even her mother spoke of it as a thing which was impending, and which she wondered how Mr Bradshaw would like ; for his approval or dis- approval was the standard by which she measured all things.

"Oh! merciful God," prayed Jemima, in the dead silence of the night, "the strain is too great—I cannot bear it longer—my life—my love—the very essence of me, which is myself through time and eternity ; and on the other side there is all-pitying Charity. If she had not been what she is—if she had shown any sign of triumph—any knowledge of her prize—if she had made any effort to gain his dear heart, I must have given way long ago, and taunted her, even if I did not tell others—taunted her, even though I sank down to the pit the next moment."

"The temptation is too strong for me. Oh Lord! where is Thy peace that I believed in, in my child- hood?—that I hear people speaking of now, as if it hushed up the troubles of life, and had not to be sought for—sought for, as with tears of blood!"

There was no sound nor sight in answer to this wild imploring cry, which Jemima half thought must force out a sign from Heaven. But there was a dawn steal- ing on through the darkness of her night.

It was glorious weather for the end of August. The nights were as full of light as the days—everywhere, save in the low dusky meadows by the river-side, where the mists rose and blended the pale sky with the lands below. Unknowing of the care and trouble around them, Mary and Elizabeth exulted in the weather, and saw some new glory in every touch of the year's decay. They were clamorous for an expedition to the hills, before the calm stillness of the autumn should be dis-

turbed by storms. They gained permission to go on
the next Wednesday—the next half-holiday. They
had won their mother over to consent to a full holiday,
but their father would not hear of it. Mrs Bradshaw
had proposed an early dinner, but the idea was scouted
at by the girls. What would the expedition be worth
if they did not carry their dinners with them in baskets?
Anything out of a basket, and eaten in the open air,
was worth twenty times as much as the most sumptuous
meal in the house. So the baskets were packed up,
while Mrs Bradshaw wailed over probable colds to be
caught from sitting on the damp ground. Ruth and
Leonard were to go; they four. Jemima had refused
all invitations to make one of the party; and yet she
had a half sympathy with her sisters' joy—a sort of
longing, lingering look back to the time when she too
would have revelled in the prospect that lay before
them. They too would grow up, and suffer; though
now they played, regardless of their doom.

The morning was bright and glorious; just cloud
enough, as some one said, to make the distant plain
look beautiful from the hills, with its floating shadows
passing over the golden cornfields. Leonard was to
join them at twelve, when his lessons with Mr Benson,
and the girls' with their masters, should be over. Ruth
took off her bonnet, and folded her shawl with her
usual dainty, careful neatness, and laid them aside in a
corner of the room to be in readiness. She tried to
forget the pleasure she always anticipated from a long
walk towards the hills, while the morning's work went
on; but she showed enough of sympathy to make the
girls cling round her with many a caress of joyous love.
Everything was beautiful in their eyes; from the
shadows of the quivering leaves on the wall to the
glittering beads of dew, not yet absorbed by the sun,
which decked the gossamer web in the vine outside the
window. Eleven o'clock struck. The Latin master
went away, wondering much at the radiant faces of his
pupils, and thinking that it was only very young people
who could take such pleasure in the "Delectus."*

Ruth said, "Now, do let us try to be very steady this next hour," and Mary pulled back Ruth's head, and gave the pretty budding mouth a kiss. They sat down to work, while Mrs Denbigh read aloud. A fresh sun-gleam burst into the room, and they looked at each other with glad, anticipating eyes.

Jemima came in, ostensibly to seek for a book, but really from that sort of restless weariness of any one place or employment, which had taken possession of her since Mr Farquhar's return. She stood before the bookcase in the recess, languidly passing over the titles in search of the one she wanted. Ruth's voice lost a tone or two of its peacefulness, and her eyes looked more dim and anxious at Jemima's presence. She wondered in her heart if she dared to ask Miss Brad-shaw to accompany them in their expedition. Eighteen months ago she would have urged it on her friend with soft, loving entreaty ; now she was afraid even to pro-pose it as a hard possibility, everything she did or said was taken so wrongly—seemed to add to the old dis-like, or the later stony contempt with which Miss Bradshaw had regarded her. While they were in this way Mr Bradshaw came into the room. His entrance —his being at home at all at this time—was so unusual a thing, that the reading was instantly stopped ; and all four involuntarily looked at him, as if expecting some explanation of his unusual proceeding.

His face was almost purple with suppressed agitation. "Mary and Elizabeth, leave the room. Don't stay to pack up your books. Leave the room, I say !" He spoke with trembling anger, and the frightened girls obeyed without a word. A cloud passing over the sun, cast a cold gloom into the room which was late so bright and beaming ; but, by equalizing the light, it took away the dark shadow from the place where Jemima had been standing, and her figure caught her father's eye.

"Leave the room, Jemima," said he.

"Why, father?" replied she, in an opposition that was strange even to herself, but which was prompted

by the sullen passion which seethed below the stagnant
surface of her life, and which sought a vent in defiance.
She maintained her ground, facing round upon her
father, and Ruth—Ruth, who had risen, and stood
trembling, shaking, a lightning-fear having shown her
the precipice on which she stood. It was of no use ;
no quiet, innocent life—no profound silence, even to
her own heart as to the Past ; the old offence could
never be drowned in the Deep ; but thus, when all was
calm on the great, broad, sunny sea, it rose to the surface, and faced her with its unclosed eyes, and its
ghastly countenance. The blood bubbled up to her
brain, and made such a sound there, as of boiling
waters, that she did not hear the words which Mr Bradshaw first spoke ; indeed, his speech was broken and
disjointed by intense passion. But she needed not to
hear ; she knew. As she rose up at first, so she stood
now—numb and helpless. When her ears heard again
(as if the sounds were drawing nearer, and becoming
more distinct, from some faint, vague distance of
space), Mr Bradshaw was saying, " If there be one sin
I hate—I utterly loathe—more than all others, it is
wantonness. It includes all other sins. It is but of a
piece that you should have come with your sickly,
hypocritical face, imposing upon us all. I trust Benson
did not know of it—for his own sake, I trust not.
Before God, if he got you into my house on false pre-
tences, he shall find his charity at other men's expense
shall cost him dear—you—the common talk of Eccleston for your profligacy——" He was absolutely
choked by his boiling indignation. Ruth stood speech-
less, motionless. Her head drooped a little forward,
her eyes were more than half veiled by the large
quivering lids, her arms hung down straight and
heavy. At last she heaved the weight off her heart
enough to say, in a faint, moaning voice, speaking with
infinite difficulty :

" I was so young."

"The more depraved, the more disgusting you," Mr
Bradshaw exclaimed, almost glad that the woman, un-

resisting so long, should now begin to resist. But to his surprise (for in his anger he had forgotten her presence) Jemima moved forwards, and said, "Father!"

"You hold your tongue, Jemima. You have grown more and more insolent—more and more disobedient everyday. I now know who to thank for it. When such a woman came into my family there is no wonder at any corruption—any evil—any defilement——"

"Father!"

"Not a word! If, in your disobedience, you choose to stay and hear what no modest young woman would put herself in the way of hearing, you shall be silent when I bid you. The only good you can gain is in the way of warning. Look at that woman" (indicating Ruth, who moved her drooping head a little on one side, as if by such motion she could avert the pitiless pointing—her face growing whiter and whiter still every instant)—"look at that woman, I say—corrupt long before she was your age—hypocrite for years! If ever you, or any child of mine, cared for her, shake her off from you, as St Paul shook off the viper—even into the fire."* He stopped for very want of breath. Jemima, all flushed and panting, went up and stood side by side with wan Ruth. She took the cold, dead hand which hung next to her in her warm convulsive grasp, and holding it so tight, that it was blue and discoloured for days, she spoke out beyond all power of restraint from her father.

"Father, I will speak. I will not keep silence. I will bear witness to Ruth. I have hated her—so keenly, may God forgive me! but you may know, from that, that my witness is true. I have hated her, and my hatred was only quenched into contempt —not contempt now, dear Ruth—dear Ruth"—(this was spoken with infinite softness and tenderness, and in spite of her father's fierce eyes and passionate gesture)—"I heard what you have learnt now, father, weeks and weeks ago—a year it may be, all time of late has been so long; and I shuddered up from her and from her sin; and I might have

spoken of it, and told it there and then, if I had not
been afraid that it was from no good motive I should
act in so doing, but to gain a way to the desire of
my own jealous heart.   Yes, father, to show you what a
witness I am for Ruth, I will own that I was stabbed
to the heart with jealousy ; some one—some one
cared for Ruth that—oh, father ! spare me saying
all."   Her face was double-dyed with crimson blushes,
and she paused for one moment—no more.

"I watched her, and I watched her with my wild-beast
eyes.   If I had seen one paltering with duty—if I had
witnessed one flickering shadow of untruth in word or
action—if, more than all things, my woman's instinct
had ever been conscious of the faintest speck of
impurity in thought, or word, or look, my old hate
would have flamed out with the flame of hell! my
contempt would have turned to loathing disgust,
instead of my being full of pity, and the stirrings of
new-awakened love, and most true respect.   Father,
I have borne my witness ! "

"And I will tell you how much your witness is
worth," said her father, beginning low, that his pent-
up wrath might have room to swell out.   "It only
convinces me more and more how deep is the corruption this wanton has spread in my family.   She has
come amongst us with her innocent seeming, and
spread her nets well and skilfully.   She has turned
right into wrong, and wrong into right, and taught
you all to be uncertain whether there be any such
thing as Vice in the world, or whether it ought not
to be looked upon as virtue.   She has led you to the
brink of the deep pit, ready for the first chance circumstance to push you in.   And I trusted her—I trusted
her—I welcomed her."

"I have done very wrong," murmured Ruth, but
so low, that perhaps he did not hear her, for he went
on, lashing himself up.

"I welcomed her.   I was duped into allowing her
bastard—(I sicken at the thought of it)——"

At the mention of Leonard, Ruth lifted up her eyes

for the first time since the conversation began, the
pupils dilating, as if she were just becoming aware
of some new agony in store for her. I have seen
such a look of terror on a poor dumb animal's
countenance, and once or twice on human faces. I
pray I may never see it again on either! Jemima
felt the hand she held in her strong grasp writhe itself
free. Ruth spread her arms before her, clasping and
lacing her fingers together, her head thrown a little
back, as if in intensest suffering.

Mr Bradshaw went on:

"That very child and heir of shame to associate
with my own innocent children! I trust they are not
contaminated."

"I cannot bear it—I cannot bear it," were the words
wrung out of Ruth.

"Cannot bear it! cannot bear it!" he repeated.
"You must bear it, madam. Do you suppose your
child is to be exempt from the penalties of his birth?
Do you suppose that he alone is to be saved from the
upbraiding scoff? Do you suppose that he is ever to
rank with other boys, who are not stained and marked
with sin from their birth? Every creature in Eccleston may know what he is, do you think they will spare
him their scorn? 'Cannot bear it,' indeed! Before
you went into your sin, you should have thought
whether you could bear the consequences or not—
have had some idea how far your offspring would be
degraded and scouted, till the best thing that could
happen to him would be for him to be lost to all sense
of shame, dead to all knowledge of guilt, for his
mother's sake."

Ruth spoke out. She stood like a wild creature at
bay, past fear now. "I appeal to God against such a
doom for my child. I appeal to God to help me. I
am a mother, and as such I cry to God for help—for
help to keep my boy in His pitying sight, and to bring
him up in His holy fear. Let the shame fall on me!
I have deserved it, but he—he is so innocent and
good."

Ruth had caught up her shawl, and was tying on
her bonnet with her trembling hands. What if
Leonard was hearing of her shame from common
report? What would be the mysterious shock of the
intelligence? She must face him, and see the look
in his eyes, before she knew whether he recoiled from
her; he might have his heart turned to hate her, by
their cruel jeers.

Jemima stood by, dumb and pitying. Her sorrow
was past her power. She helped in arranging the
dress, with one or two gentle touches, which were
hardly felt by Ruth, but which called out all Mr
Bradshaw's ire afresh; he absolutely took her by the
shoulders and turned her by force out of the room.
In the hall, and along the stairs, her passionate woeful
crying was heard. The sound only concentrated Mr
Bradshaw's anger on Ruth. He held the street door
open wide; and said, between his teeth, "If ever you,
or your bastard, darken this door again, I will have
you both turned out by the police."

He need not have added this, if he had seen
Ruth's face.

CHAPTER XXVII

As Ruth went along the accustomed streets, every
sight and every sound seemed to bear a new meaning,
and each and all to have some reference to her boy's
disgrace. She held her head down, and scudded along
dizzy with fear, lest some word should have told him
what she had been, and what he was, before she could
reach him. It was a wild unreasoning fear, but it took
hold of her as strongly as if it had been well founded.
And, indeed, the secret whispered by Mrs Pearson,
whose curiosity and suspicion had been excited by
Jemima's manner, and confirmed since by many a little
corroborating circumstance, had spread abroad, and
was known to most of the gossips in Eccleston before
it reached Mr Bradshaw's ears.

As Ruth came up to the door of the Chapel-house, it was opened, and Leonard came out, bright and hopeful as the morning, his face radiant at the prospect of the happy day before him. He was dressed in the clothes it had been such a pleasant pride to her to make for him. He had the dark blue ribbon tied round his neck that she had left out for him that very morning, with a smiling thought of how it would set off his brown handsome face. She caught him by the hand as they met, and turned him, with his face homewards, without a word. Her looks, her rushing movement, her silence, awed him; and although he wondered, he did not stay to ask why she did so. The door was on the latch; she opened it, and only said, "Upstairs," in a hoarse whisper. Up they went into her own room. She drew him in, and bolted the door; and then, sitting down, she placed him (she had never let go of him) before her, holding him with her hands on each of his shoulders, and gazing into his face with a woeful look of the agony that could not find vent in words. At last she tried to speak; she tried with strong bodily effort, almost amounting to convulsion. But the words would not come; it was not till she saw the absolute terror depicted on his face that she found utterance; and then the sight of that terror changed the words from what she meant them to have been. She drew him to her, and laid her head upon his shoulder; hiding her face even there.

"My poor, poor boy! my poor, poor darling! Oh! would that I had died—I had died, in my innocent girlhood!"

"Mother! mother!" sobbed Leonard. "What is the matter? Why do you look so wild and ill? Why do you call me your ' poor boy'? Are we not going to Scaurside-hill? I don't much mind it, mother; only please don't gasp and quiver so. Dearest mother, are you ill? Let me call Aunt Faith!"

Ruth lifted herself up, and put away the hair that had fallen over and was blinding her eyes. She looked at him with intense wistfulness.

"Kiss me, Leonard!" said she—"kiss me, my darling, once more in the old way!" Leonard threw himself into her arms, and hugged her with all his force, and their lips clung together as in the kiss given to the dying.

"Leonard!" said she at length, holding him away from her, and nerving herself up to tell him all by one spasmodic effort—"Listen to me." The boy stood breathless and still, gazing at her. On her impetuous transit from Mr Bradshaw's to the Chapel-house, her wild desperate thought had been that she would call herself by every violent, coarse name which the world might give her—that Leonard should hear those words applied to his mother first from her own lips; but the influence of his presence—for he was a holy and sacred creature in her eyes, and this point remained steadfast, though all the rest were upheaved—subdued her; and now it seemed as if she could not find words fine enough, and pure enough, to convey the truth that he must learn, and should learn from no tongue but hers.

"Leonard—when I was very young I did very wrong. I think God, who knows all, will judge me more tenderly than men—but I did wrong in a way which you cannot understand yet" (she saw the red flush come into his cheek, and it stung her as the first token of that shame which was to be his portion through life)—"in a way people never forget, never forgive. You will hear me called the hardest names that ever can be thrown at women—I have been, to-day; and, my child, you must bear it patiently, because they will be partly true. Never get confused, by your love for me, into thinking that what I did was right.—Where was I?" said she, suddenly faltering, and forgetting all she had said and all she had got to say; and then, seeing Leonard's face of wonder, and burning shame and indignation, she went on more rapidly, as fearing lest her strength should fail before she had ended.

"And Leonard," continued she, in a trembling, sad voice, "this is not all. The punishment of punishments lies awaiting me still. It is to see you suffer

for my wrongdoing.   Yes, darling! they will speak
shameful things of you, poor innocent child, as well
as of me, who am guilty.   They will throw it in
your teeth through life, that your mother was never
married—was not married when you were born——"

"Were not you married?   Are not you a widow?"
asked he abruptly, for the first time getting anything
like a clear idea of the real state of the case.

"No!   May God forgive me, and help me!" exclaimed she, as she saw a strange look of repugnance
cloud over the boy's face, and felt a slight motion on
his part to extricate himself from her hold.   It was as
slight, as transient as it could be—over in an instant.
But she had taken her hands away, and covered up
her face with them as quickly—covered up her face in
shame before her child; and in the bitterness of her
heart she was wailing out, "Oh, would to God I had
died—that I had died as a baby—that I had died as a
little baby hanging at my mother's breast!"

"Mother," said Leonard, timidly putting his hand
on her arm; but she shrunk from him, and continued
her low, passionate wailing.   "Mother," said he, after
a pause, coming nearer, though she saw it not—
"mammy darling," said he, using the caressing name,
which he had been trying to drop as not sufficiently
manly, "mammy, my own, own dear, dear, darling
mother, I don't believe them—I don't, I don't, I don't,
I don't!"   He broke out into a wild burst of crying,
as he said this.   In a moment her arms were round
the poor boy, and she was hushing him up like a baby
on her bosom.   "Hush, Leonard! Leonard, be still,
my child!   I have been too sudden with you!—I have
done you harm—oh! I have done you nothing but
harm," cried she, in a tone of bitter self-reproach.

"No, mother," said he, stopping his tears, and his
eyes blazing out with earnestness, "there never was
such a mother as you have been to me, and I won't
believe anyone who says it.   I won't; and I'll knock
them down if they say it again, I will!"   He clenched
his fist, with a fierce defiant look on his face.

"You forget, my child," said Ruth, in the sweetest, saddest tone that ever was heard, "I said it of myself; I said it because it was true." Leonard threw his arms tight round her, and hid his face against her bosom. She felt him pant there like some hunted creature. She had no soothing comfort to give him. "Oh, that she and he lay dead!"

At last, exhausted, he lay so still and motionless, that she feared to look. She wanted him to speak, yet dreaded his first words. She kissed his hair, his head, his very clothes; murmuring low inarticulate moaning sounds.

"Leonard," said she, "Leonard, look up at me! Leonard, look up!" But he only clung the closer, and hid his face the more.

"My boy!" said she, "what can I do or say? If I tell you never to mind it—that it is nothing—I tell you false. It is a bitter shame and a sorrow that I have drawn down upon you. A shame, Leonard, because of me, your mother; but, Leonard, it is no disgrace or lowering of you in the eyes of God." She spoke now as if she had found the clue which might lead him to rest and strength at last. "Remember that, always. Remember that, when the time of trial comes—and it seems a hard and cruel thing that you should be called reproachful names by men, and all for what was no fault of yours—remember God's pity and God's justice; and though my sin shall have made you an outcast in the world—oh, my child, my child!"— (she felt him kiss her, as if mutely trying to comfort her—it gave her strength to go on)—"remember, darling of my heart, it is only your own sin that can make you an outcast from God."

She grew so faint that her hold of him relaxed. He looked up affrighted. He brought her water—he threw it over her; in his terror at the notion that she was going to die and leave him, he called her by every fond name, imploring her to open her eyes.

When she partially recovered, he helped her to the bed, on which she lay still, wan and deathlike. She

almost hoped the swoon that hung around her might
be Death, and in that imagination she opened her eyes
to take a last look at her boy. She saw him pale and
terror-stricken; and pity for his affright roused her,
and made her forget herself in the wish that he should
not see her death, if she were indeed dying.

"Go to Aunt Faith!" whispered she; "I am weary,
and want sleep."

Leonard arose slowly and reluctantly. She tried to
smile upon him, that what she thought would be her
last look might dwell in his remembrance as tender
and strong; she watched him to the door, she saw him
hesitate, and return to her. He came back to her, and
said in a timid, apprehensive tone:

"Mother—will *they* speak to me about——it?"

Ruth closed her eyes, that they might not express
the agony she felt, like a sharp knife, at this question.
Leonard had asked it with a child's desire of avoiding
painful and mysterious topics,—from no personal sense
of shame as she understood it, shame beginning thus
early, thus instantaneously.

"No," she replied. "You may be sure they will
not."

So he went. But now she would have been thankful
for the unconsciousness of fainting; that one little
speech bore so much meaning to her hot irritable
brain. Mr and Miss Benson, all in their house, would
never speak to the boy—but in his home alone would
he be safe from what he had already learnt to dread.
Every form in which shame and opprobrium could
overwhelm her darling, haunted her. She had been
exercising strong self-control for his sake ever since
she had met him at the house-door; there was now a
reaction. His presence had kept her mind on its
perfect balance. When that was withdrawn, the
effect of the strain of power was felt. And athwart
the fever-mists that arose to obscure her judgement, all
sorts of will-o'-the-wisp plans flittered before her;
tempting her to this and that course of action—to
anything rather than patient endurance—to relieve

her present state of misery by some sudden spasmodic
effort, that took the semblance of being wise and right.
Gradually all her desires, all her longing, settled
themselves on one point. What had she done—what
could she do, to Leonard, but evil? If she were away,
and gone no one knew where—lost in mystery, as if
she were dead—perhaps the cruel hearts might reflect,
and show pity on Leonard ; while her perpetual
presence would but call up the remembrance of his
birth. Thus she reasoned in her hot dull brain ; and
shaped her plans in accordance.

Leonard stole downstairs noiselessly. He listened
to find some quiet place where he could hide himself.
The house was very still. Miss Benson thought the
purposed expedition had taken place, and never
dreamed but that Ruth and Leonard were on distant
sunny Scaurside-hill ; and after a very early dinner,
she had set out to drink tea with a farmer's wife who
lived in the country two or three miles off. Mr Benson
meant to have gone with her ; but while they were at
dinner, he had received an unusually authoritative
note from Mr Bradshaw desiring to speak with him, so
he went to that gentleman's house instead. Sally was
busy in her kitchen, making a great noise (not unlike
a groom rubbing down a horse) over her cleaning.
Leonard stole into the sitting-room, and crouched
behind the large old-fashioned sofa to ease his sore,
aching heart, by crying with all the prodigal waste
and abandonment of childhood.

Mr Benson was shown into Mr Bradshaw's own
particular room. The latter gentleman was walking
up and down, and it was easy to perceive that something had occurred to chafe him to great anger.

" Sit down, sir ! " said he to Mr Benson, nodding to
a chair.

Mr Benson sat down. But Mr Bradshaw continued
his walk for a few minutes longer without speaking.
Then he stopped abruptly, right in front of Mr Benson ;
and in a voice which he tried to render calm, but which
trembled with passion—with a face glowing purple as

he thought of his wrongs (and real wrongs they were)
he began :

"Mr Benson, I have sent for you to ask—I am
almost too indignant at the bare suspicion to speak as
becomes me—but did you——I really shall be obliged
to beg your pardon, if you are as much in the dark as
I was yesterday, as to the character of that woman
who lives under your roof?"

There was no answer from Mr Benson. Mr Bradshaw looked at him very earnestly. His eyes were
fixed on the ground—he made no inquiry—he uttered
no expression of wonder or dismay. Mr Bradshaw
ground his foot on the floor with gathering rage ; but,
just as he was about to speak, Mr Benson rose up—a
poor deformed old man—before the stern and portly
figure that was swelling and panting with passion.

"Hear me, sir !" (stretching out his hand as if to
avert the words which were impending). "Nothing
you can say, can upbraid me like my own conscience ;
no degradation you can inflict, by word or deed, can
come up to the degradation I have suffered for years,
at being a party to a deceit, even for a good end——"

"For a good end !—Nay ! what next ?"

The taunting contempt with which Mr Bradshaw
spoke these words, almost surprised himself by what
he imagined must be its successful power of withering ;
but in spite of it, Mr Benson lifted his grave eyes to
Mr Bradshaw's countenance, and repeated :

"For a good end. The end was not, as perhaps you
consider it to have been, to obtain her admission into
your family—nor yet to put her in the way of gaining
her livelihood ; my sister and I would willingly have
shared what we have with her ; it was our intention to
do so at first, if not for any length of time, at least as
long as her health might require it. Why I advised
(perhaps I only yielded to advice) a change of name—
an assumption of a false state of widowhood—was
because I earnestly desired to place her in circumstances in which she might work out her self-
redemption ; and you, sir, know how terribly the

world goes against all such as have sinned as Ruth did. She was so young, too."

"You mistake, sir; my acquaintance has not lain so much among that class of sinners as to give me much experience of the way in which they are treated. But, judging from what I have seen, I should say they meet with full as much leniency as they deserve; and supposing they do not—I know there are plenty of sickly sentimentalists just now who reserve all their interest and regard for criminals—why not pick out one of these to help you in your task of washing the blackamoor white? Why choose me to be imposed upon—my household into which to intrude your protégée? Why were my innocent children to be exposed to corruption? I say," said Mr Bradshaw, stamping his foot, "how dared you come into this house, where you were looked upon as a minister of religion, with a lie in your mouth? How dared you single me out, of all people, to be gulled and deceived, and pointed at through the town as the person who had taken an abandoned woman into his house to teach his daughters?"

"I own my deceit was wrong and faithless."

"Yes! you can own it, now it is found out! There is small merit in that, I think!"

"Sir! I claim no merit. I take shame to myself. I did not single you out. You applied to me with your proposal that Ruth should be your children's governess."

"Pah!"

"And the temptation was too great—No! I will not say that—but the temptation was greater than I could stand—it seemed to open out a path of usefulness."

"Now, don't let me hear you speak so," said Mr Bradshaw, blazing up. "I can't stand it. It is too much to talk in that way when the usefulness was to consist in contaminating my innocent girls."

"God knows that if I had believed there had been any danger of such contamination—God knows how I would have died sooner than have allowed her to enter

your family. Mr Bradshaw, you believe me, don't
you?" asked Mr Benson, earnestly.

"I really must be allowed the privilege of doubting
what you say in future," said Mr Bradshaw, in a cold,
contemptuous manner.

"I have deserved this," Mr Benson replied. "But,"
continued he, after a moment's pause, "I will not speak
of myself, but of Ruth. Surely, sir, the end I aimed
at (the means I took to obtain it were wrong, you cannot feel that more than I do) was a right one; and you
will not—you cannot say, that your children have
suffered from associating with her. I had her in my
family, under the watchful eyes of three anxious persons for a year or more; we saw faults—no human
being is without them—and poor Ruth's were but slight
venial errors; but we saw no sign of a corrupt mind—
no glimpse of boldness or forwardness—no token of
want of conscientiousness; she seemed, and was, a
young and gentle girl, who had been led astray before
she fairly knew what life was."

"I suppose most depraved women have been innocent
in their time," said Mr Bradshaw, with bitter contempt.

"Oh, Mr Bradshaw! Ruth was not depraved, and
you know it. You cannot have seen her—have known
her daily, all these years, without acknowledging
that!" Mr Benson was almost breathless, awaiting
Mr Bradshaw's answer. The quiet self-control which
he had maintained so long, was gone now.

"I saw her daily—I did *not* know her. If I had
known her, I should have known she was fallen and
depraved, and consequently not fit to come into my
house, nor to associate with my pure children."

"Now I wish God would give me power to speak
out convincingly what I believe to be His truth, that
not every woman who has fallen is depraved; that
many—how many the Great Judgment Day will reveal
to those who have shaken off the poor, sore, penitent
hearts on earth—many, many crave and hunger after a
chance for virtue—the help which no man gives to
them—help—that gentle tender help which Jesus gave

once to Mary Magdalen."* Mr Benson was almost
choked by his own feelings.

"Come, come, Mr Benson, let us have no more of
this morbid way of talking. The world has decided
how such women are to be treated; and, you may
depend upon it, there is so much practical wisdom in
the world that its way of acting is right in the long
run, and that no one can fly in its face with impunity,
unless, indeed, they stoop to deceit and imposition."

"I take my stand with Christ against the world,"
said Mr Benson, solemnly, disregarding the covert
allusion to himself. "What have the world's ways
ended in? Can we be much worse than we are?"

"Speak for yourself, if you please."

"Is it not time to change some of our ways of
thinking and acting? I declare before God, that if I
believe in any one human truth, it is this—that to every
woman, who, like Ruth, has sinned, should be given a
chance of self-redemption—and that such a chance
should be given in no supercilious or contemptuous
manner, but in the spirit of the holy Christ."

"Such as getting her into a friend's house under
false colours."

"I do not argue on Ruth's case. In that I have
acknowledged my error. I do not argue on any case.
I state my firm belief, that it is God's will that we
should not dare to trample any of His creatures down
to the hopeless dust; that it is God's will that the
women who have fallen should be numbered among
those who have broken hearts to be bound up, not cast
aside as lost beyond recall. If this be God's will, as a
thing of God it will stand; and He will open a
way."

"I should have attached much more importance to
all your exhortation on this point, if I could have
respected your conduct in other matters. As it is,
when I see a man who has deluded himself into considering falsehood right, I am disinclined to take his
opinion on subjects connected with morality; and I can
no longer regard him as a fitting exponent of the will

of God. You perhaps understand what I mean, Mr
Benson. I can no longer attend your chapel."

If Mr Benson had felt any hope of making Mr
Bradshaw's obstinate mind receive the truth, that he
acknowledged and repented of his connivance at the
falsehood by means of which Ruth had been received
into the Bradshaw family, this last sentence prevented
his making the attempt. He simply bowed and took
his leave—Mr Bradshaw attending him to the door
with formal ceremony.

He felt acutely the severance of the tie which Mr
Bradshaw had just announced to him. He had experienced many mortifications in his intercourse with
that gentleman, but they had fallen off from his meek
spirit like drops of water from a bird's plumage ; and
now he only remembered the acts of substantial kindness rendered (the ostentation all forgotten)—many
happy hours and pleasant evenings—the children whom
he had loved dearer than he thought till now—the
young people about whom he had cared, and whom he
had striven to lead aright. He was but a young man
when Mr Bradshaw first came to his chapel ; they had
grown old together ; he had never recognized Mr
Bradshaw as an old familiar friend so completely, as
now when they were severed.

It was with a heavy heart that he opened his own
door. He went to his study immediately ; he sat down
to steady himself into his position.

How long he was there—silent and alone—reviewing
his life—confessing his sins—he did not know ; but he
heard some unusual sound in the house that disturbed
him—roused him to present life. A slow, languid
step came along the passage to the front door—the
breathing was broken by many sighs.

Ruth's hand was on the latch when Mr Benson came
out. Her face was very white, except two red spots on
each cheek—her eyes were deep sunk and hollow, but
glittered with feverish lustre. "Ruth!" exclaimed
he. She moved her lips, but her throat and mouth
were too dry for her to speak.

"Where are you going?" asked he; for she had all her walking things on, yet trembled so, even as she stood, that it was evident she could not walk far without falling.

She hesitated—she looked up at him, still with the same dry glittering eyes. At last she whispered (for she could only speak in a whisper), "To Helmsby— I am going to Helmsby."

"Helmsby! my poor girl—may God have mercy upon you!" for he saw she hardly knew what she was saying. "Where is Helmsby?"

"I don't know. In Lincolnshire, I think."

"But why are you going there?"

"Hush! he's asleep," said she, as Mr Benson had unconsciously raised his voice.

"Who is asleep?" asked Mr Benson.

"That poor little boy," said she, beginning to quiver and cry.

"Come here!" said he, authoritatively, drawing her into the study.

"Sit down in that chair. I will come back directly."

He went in search of his sister, but she had not returned. Then he had recourse to Sally, who was as busy as ever about her cleaning.

"How long has Ruth been at home?" asked he.

"Ruth! She has never been at home sin' morning. She and Leonard were to be off for the day somewhere or other with them Bradshaw girls."

"Then she has had no dinner?"

"Not here, at any rate. I can't answer for what she may have done at other places."

"And Leonard—where is he?"

"How should I know? With his mother, I suppose. Leastways, that was what was fixed on. I've enough to do of my own, without routing after other folks."

She went on scouring in no very good temper. Mr Benson stood silent for a moment.

"Sally," he said, "I want a cup of tea. Will you

make it as soon as you can ; and some dry toast too.
I'll come for it in ten minutes."

Struck by something in his voice, she looked up at
him for the first time.

"What ha' ye been doing to yourself, to look so
grim and grey. Tiring yourself all to tatters, looking
after some naught, I'll be bound ! Well ! well ! I mun
make ye your tea, I reckon ; but I did hope as you
grew older you'd ha' grown wiser ! "

Mr Benson made no reply, but went to look for
Leonard, hoping that the child's presence might bring
back to his mother the power of self-control. He
opened the parlour-door, and looked in, but saw no
one. Just as he was shutting it, however, he heard a
deep, broken, sobbing sigh ; and, guided by the sound,
he found the boy lying on the floor, fast asleep, but
with his features all swollen and disfigured by passionate crying.

"Poor child ! This was what she meant, then,"
thought Mr Benson. "He has begun his share of the
sorrows too," he continued, pitifully. "No ! I will
not waken him back to consciousness." So he returned alone into the study. Ruth sat where he had
placed her, her head bent back, and her eyes shut.
But when he came in she started up.

"I must be going," she said, in a hurried way.

"Nay, Ruth, you must not go. You must not
leave us. We cannot do without you. We love you
too much."

"Love me ! " said she, looking at him wistfully.
As she looked, her eyes filled slowly with tears. It
was a good sign, and Mr Benson took heart to go
on.

"Yes ! Ruth. You know we do. You may have
other things to fill up your mind just now, but you
know we love you ; and nothing can alter our love for
you. You ought not to have thought of leaving us.
You would not, if you had been quite well."

"Do you know what has happened ? " she asked, in a
low, hoarse voice.

"Yes. I know all," he answered. "It makes no difference to us. Why should it?"

"Oh! Mr Benson, don't you know that my shame is discovered?" she replied, bursting into tears—"and I must leave you, and leave Leonard, that you may not share in my disgrace."

"You must do no such thing. Leave Leonard! You have no right to leave Leonard. Where could you go to?"

"To Helmsby," she said, humbly. "It would break my heart to go, but I think I ought, for Leonard's sake. I know I ought." She was crying sadly by this time, but Mr Benson knew the flow of tears would ease her brain. "It will break my heart to go, but I know I must."

"Sit still here at present," said he, in a decided tone of command. He went for the cup of tea. He brought it to her without Sally's being aware for whom it was intended.

"Drink this!" He spoke as you would do to a child, if desiring it to take medicine. "Eat some toast." She took the tea, and drank it feverishly; but when she tried to eat, the food seemed to choke her. Still she was docile, and she tried.

"I cannot," said she at last, putting down the piece of toast. There was a return to something of her usual tone in the words. She spoke gently and softly; no longer in the shrill, hoarse voice she had used at first. Mr Benson sat down by her.

"Now, Ruth, we must talk a little together. I want to understand what your plan was. Where is Helmsby? Why did you fix to go there?"

"It is where my mother lived," she answered. "Before she was married she lived there; and wherever she lived, the people all loved her dearly; and I thought—I think, that for her sake some one would give me work. I meant to tell them the truth," said she, dropping her eyes; "but still they would, perhaps, give me some employment—I don't care what—for her sake. I could do many things," said

she, suddenly looking up. "I am sure I could weed
—I could in gardens—if they did not like to have me
in their houses. But perhaps some one, for my
mother's sake—oh! my dear, dear mother!—do you
know where and what I am?" she cried out, sobbing
afresh.

Mr Benson's heart was very sore, though he spoke
authoritatively, and almost sternly.

"Ruth! you must be still and quiet. I cannot
have this. I want you to listen to me. Your thought
of Helmsby would be a good one, if it was right for
you to leave Eccleston; but I do not think it is. I
am certain of this, that it would be a great sin in you
to separate yourself from Leonard. You have no
right to sever the tie by which God has bound you
together."

"But if I am here they will all know and remember
the shame of his birth; and if I go away they may
forget——"

"And they may not. And if you go away, he may
be unhappy or ill; and you, who above all others
have—and have from God—remember *that*, Ruth!—
the power to comfort him, the tender patience to nurse
him, have left him to the care of strangers. Yes; I
know! But we ourselves are as strangers, dearly as
we love him, compared to a mother. He may turn to
sin, and want the long forbearance, the serene
authority of a parent; and where are you? No dread
of shame, either for yourself, or even for him, can
ever make it right for you to shake off your responsibility." All this time he was watching her narrowly,
and saw her slowly yield herself up to the force of
what he was saying.

"Besides, Ruth," he continued, "we have gone on
falsely hitherto. It has been my doing, my mistake,
my sin. I ought to have known better. Now, let us
stand firm on the truth. You have no new fault to
repent of. Be brave and faithful. It is to God you
answer, not to men. The shame of having your sin
known to the world, should be as nothing to the

shame you felt at having sinned. We have dreaded men too much, and God too little, in the course we have taken. But now be of good cheer. Perhaps you will have to find your work in the world very low— not quite working in the fields," said he, with a gentle smile, to which she, downcast and miserable, could give no response. "Nay, perhaps, Ruth," he went on, "you may have to stand and wait for some time; no one may be willing to use the services you would gladly render; all may turn aside from you, and may speak very harshly of you. Can you accept all this treatment meekly, as but the reasonable and just penance God has laid upon you — feeling no anger against those who slight you, no impatience for the time to come (and come it surely will—I speak as having the word of God for what I say) when He, having purified you, even as by fire, will make a straight path for your feet? My child, it is Christ the Lord who has told us of this infinite mercy of God. Have you faith enough in it to be brave, and bear on, and do rightly in patience and in tribulation?"

Ruth had been hushed and very still until now, when the pleading earnestness of his question urged her to answer:

"Yes!" said she. "I hope—I believe I can be faithful for myself, for I have sinned and done wrong. But Leonard——" She looked up at him.

"But Leonard," he echoed. "Ah! there it is hard, Ruth. I own the world is hard and persecuting to such as he." He paused to think of the true comfort for this sting. He went on. "The world is not everything, Ruth; nor is the want of men's good opinion and esteem the highest need which man has. Teach Leonard this. You would not wish his life to be one summer's day. You dared not make it so, if you had the power. Teach him to bid a noble, Christian welcome, to the trials which God sends— and this is one of them. Teach him not to look on a life of struggle, and perhaps of disappointment and incompleteness, as a sad and mournful end, but as the

means permitted to the heroes and warriors in the
army of Christ, by which to show their faithful
following.   Tell him of the hard and thorny path
which was trodden once by the bleeding feet of One.
Ruth! think of the Saviour's life and cruel death,
and of His divine faithfulness.   Oh, Ruth!" exclaimed he, "when I look and see what you may
be—what you *must* be to that boy, I cannot think
how you could be coward enough, for a moment,
to shrink from your work!   But we have all been
cowards hitherto," he added, in bitter self-accusation.
"God help us to be so no longer!"

Ruth sat very quiet.   Her eyes were fixed on the
ground, and she seemed lost in thought.   At length
she rose up.

"Mr Benson!" said she, standing before him, and
propping herself by the table, as she was trembling
sadly from weakness, "I mean to try very, very hard,
to do my duty to Leonard—and to God," she added,
reverently.   "I am only afraid my faith may sometimes fail about Leonard——"

"Ask, and it shall be given unto you.* That is no
vain or untried promise, Ruth!"

She sat down again, unable longer to stand.   There
was another long silence.

"I must never go to Mr Bradshaw's again," she
said at last, as if thinking aloud.

"No, Ruth, you shall not," he answered.

"But I shall earn no money!" added she, quickly,
for she thought that he did not perceive the difficulty
that was troubling her.

"You surely know, Ruth, that while Faith and I
have a roof to shelter us, or bread to eat, you and
Leonard share it with us."

"I know—I know your most tender goodness,"
said she, "but it ought not to be."

"It must be at present," he said, in a decided
manner.   "Perhaps before long you may have some
employment; perhaps it may be some time before an
opportunity occurs."

"Hush," said Ruth; "Leonard is moving about in the parlour. I must go to him."

But when she stood up, she turned so dizzy, and tottered so much, that she was glad to sit down again immediately.

"You must rest here. I will go to him," said Mr Benson. He left her; and when he was gone, she leaned her head on the back of the chair, and cried quietly and incessantly; but there was a more patient, hopeful, resolved feeling in her heart, which all along, through all the tears she shed, bore her onwards to higher thoughts, until at last she rose to prayers.

Mr Benson caught the new look of shrinking shame in Leonard's eye, as it first sought, then shunned, meeting his. He was pained, too, by the sight of the little sorrowful, anxious face, on which, until now, hope and joy had been predominant. The constrained voice, the few words the boy spoke, when formerly there would have been a glad and free utterance—all this grieved Mr Benson inexpressibly, as but the beginning of an unwonted mortification, which must last for years, He himself made no allusion to any unusual occurrence; he spoke of Ruth as sitting, overcome by headache, in the study for quietness: he hurried on the preparations for tea, while Leonard sat by in the great arm-chair, and looked on with sad dreamy eyes. He strove to lessen the shock which he knew Leonard had received, by every mixture of tenderness and cheerfulness that Mr Benson's gentle heart prompted; and now and then a languid smile stole over the boy's face. When his bedtime came, Mr Benson told him of the hour, although he feared that Leonard would have but another sorrowful crying of himself to sleep; but he was anxious to accustom the boy to cheerful movement within the limits of domestic law, and by no disobedience to it to weaken the power of glad submission to the Supreme; to begin the new life that lay before him, where strength to look up to God as the Lawgiver and Ruler of events would be pre-eminently required. When Leonard had gone upstairs, Mr Benson went immediately to Ruth, and said,

"Ruth! Leonard is just gone up to bed," secure in the instinct which made her silently rise, and go up to the boy—certain, too, that they would each be the other's best comforter, and that God would strengthen each through the other.

Now, for the first time, he had leisure to think of himself; and to go over all the events of the day. The half hour of solitude in his study, that he had before his sister's return, was of inestimable value; he had leisure to put events in their true places, as to importance and eternal significance.

Miss Faith came in laden with farm produce. Her kind entertainers had brought her in their shandry to the opening of the court in which the Chapel-house stood; but she was so heavily burdened with eggs, mushrooms, and plums, that when her brother opened the door she was almost breathless.

"Oh, Thurstan! take this basket—it is such a weight! Oh, Sally, is that you? Here are some magnum-bonums which we must preserve to-morrow. There are guinea-fowl eggs in that basket."

Mr Benson let her unburden her body, and her mind too, by giving charges to Sally respecting her housekeeping treasures, before he said a word; but when she returned into the study, to tell him the small pieces of intelligence respecting her day at the farm, she stood aghast.

"Why, Thurstan, dear! What's the matter? Is your back hurting you?"

He smiled to reassure her; but it was a sickly and forced smile.

"No, Faith! I am quite well, only rather out of spirits, and wanting to talk to you to cheer me."

Miss Faith sat down, straight, sitting bolt-upright to listen the better.

"I don't know how, but the real story about Ruth is found out."

"Oh, Thurstan!" exclaimed Miss Benson, turning quite white.

For a moment, neither of them said another word. Then she went on.

"Does Mr Bradshaw know?"

"Yes! He sent for me, and told me."

"Does Ruth know that it has all come out?"

"Yes. And Leonard knows."

"How? Who told him?"

"I do not know. I have asked no questions. But of course it was his mother."

"She was very foolish and cruel, then," said Miss Benson, her eyes blazing, and her lips trembling, at the thought of the suffering her darling boy must have gone through.

"I think she was wise. I am sure it was not cruel. He must have soon known that there was some mystery, and it was better that it should be told him openly and quietly by his mother than by a stranger."

"How could she tell him quietly?" asked Miss Benson, still indignant.

"Well! perhaps I used the wrong word—of course no one was by—and I don't suppose even they themselves could now tell how it was told, or in what spirit it was borne."

Miss Benson was silent again.

"Was Mr Bradshaw very angry?"

"Yes, very; and justly so. I did very wrong in making that false statement at first."

"No! I am sure you did not," said Miss Faith. "Ruth has had some years of peace, in which to grow stronger and wiser, so that she can bear her shame now in a way she never could have done at first."

"All the same it was wrong in me to do what I did."

"I did it too, as much or more than you. And I don't think it wrong. I'm certain it was quite right, and I would do just the same again."

"Perhaps it has not done you the harm it has done me."

"Nonsense! Thurstan. Don't be morbid. I'm sure you are as good—and better than ever you were."

"No, I am not. I have got what you call morbid just in consequence of the sophistry by which I persuaded myself that wrong could be right. I torment myself. I have lost my clear instincts of conscience. Formerly, if I believed that such or such an action was according to the will of God, I went and did it, or at least I tried to do it, without thinking of consequences. Now, I reason and weigh what will happen if I do so and so—I grope where formerly I saw. Oh, Faith! it is such a relief to me to have the truth known, that I am afraid I have not been sufficiently sympathizing with Ruth."

"Poor Ruth!" said Miss Benson. "But at any rate our telling a lie has been the saving of her. There is no fear of her going wrong now."

"God's omnipotence did not need our sin."

They did not speak for some time.

"You have not told me what Mr Bradshaw said."

"One can't remember the exact words that are spoken on either side in moments of such strong excitement. He was very angry, and said some things about me that were very just, and some about Ruth that were very hard. His last words were that he should give up coming to chapel."

"Oh, Thurstan! did it come to that?"

"Yes."

"Does Ruth know all he said?"

"No! Why should she? I don't know if she knows he has spoken to me at all. Poor creature! she had enough to craze her almost without that! She was for going away and leaving us that we might not share in her disgrace. I was afraid of her being quite delirious. I did so want you, Faith! However, I did the best I could, I spoke to her very coldly, and almost sternly, all the while my heart was bleeding for her. I dared not give her sympathy; I tried to give her strength. But I did so want you, Faith."

"And I was so full of enjoyment, I am ashamed to

think of it. But the Dawsons are so kind—and the day was so fine——   Where is Ruth now?"

"With Leonard. He is her great earthly motive—I thought that being with him would be best. But he must be in bed and asleep now."

"I will go up to her," said Miss Faith.

She found Ruth keeping watch by Leonard's troubled sleep; but when she saw Miss Faith she rose up, and threw herself on her neck and clung to her, without speaking. After a while Miss Benson said:

"You must go to bed, Ruth!" So, after she had kissed the sleeping boy, Miss Benson led her away, and helped to undress her, and brought her up a cup of soothing violet tea—not so soothing as tender actions, and soft loving tones.

CHAPTER XXVIII

It was well they had so early and so truly strengthened the spirit to bear, for the events which had to be endured soon came thick and threefold.

Every evening Mr and Miss Benson thought the worst must be over; and everyday brought some fresh occurrence to touch upon the raw place. They could not be certain, until they had seen all their acquaintances, what difference it would make in the cordiality of their reception: in some cases it made much; and Miss Benson was proportionably indignant. She felt this change in behaviour more than her brother. His great pain arose from the coolness of the Bradshaws. With all the faults which had at times grated on his sensitive nature (but which he now forgot, and remembered only their kindness), they were his old familiar friends—his kind, if ostentatious, patrons—his great personal interest, out of his own family; and he could not get over the suffering he experienced from seeing their large square pew empty on Sundays—from perceiving how Mr Bradshaw, though he bowed in a distant manner when he and Mr Benson met face to face, shunned him as often as he possibly could. All that happened in the household, which once was as patent to him as his own, was now a sealed book; he heard of its doings by chance, if he heard at all. Just at the time when he was feeling the most depressed from this cause, he met Jemima at a sudden turn of the street. He was uncertain for a moment how to accost her, but she saved him all doubt; in an instant she had his hand in both of hers, her face flushed with honest delight.

"Oh, Mr Benson, I am so glad to see you! I have so wanted to know all about you! How is poor Ruth? dear Ruth! I wonder if she has forgiven me my cruelty to her? And I may not go to her now, when I should be so glad and thankful to make up for it."

"I never heard you had been cruel to her. I am sure she does not think so."

"She ought, she must. What is she doing? Oh! I have so much to ask, I can never hear enough; and papa says"—she hesitated a moment, afraid of giving pain, and then, believing that they would understand the state of affairs, and the reason for her behaviour better if she told the truth, she went on: "Papa says I must not go to your house—I suppose it's right to obey him?"

"Certainly, my dear. It is your clear duty. We know how you feel towards us."

"Oh! but if I could do any good—if I could be of any use or comfort to any of you—especially to Ruth, I should come, duty or not. I believe it would be my duty," said she, hurrying on to try and stop any decided prohibition from Mr Benson. "No! don't be afraid; I won't come till I know I can do some good. I hear bits about you through Sally every now and then, or I could not have waited so long. Mr Benson," continued she, reddening very much, "I think you did quite right about poor Ruth."

"Not in the falsehood, my dear."

"No! not perhaps in that. I was not thinking of that. But I have been thinking a great deal about poor Ruth's——you know I could not help it when everybody was talking about it—and it made me think of myself, and what I am. With a father and mother, and home and careful friends, I am not likely to be tempted like Ruth; but oh! Mr Benson," said she, lifting her eyes, which were full of tears, to his face, for the first time since she began to speak, "if you knew all I have been thinking and feeling this last year, you would see how I have yielded to every temptation that was able to come to me; and, seeing how I have no goodness or strength in me, and how I might just have been like Ruth, or rather, worse than she ever was, because I am more headstrong and passionate by nature, I do so thank you and love you for what you did for her! And will you tell me really and truly now if I can ever do anything for Ruth? If you'll promise me that, I wont rebel unnecessarily against papa; but if you don't, I will, and come and see you all this very afternoon. Remember! I trust you!" said she, breaking away. Then turning back, she came to ask after Leonard.

"He must know something of it," said she. "Does he feel it much?"

"Very much," said Mr Benson. Jemima shook her head sadly.

"It is hard upon him," said she.

"It is," Mr Benson replied.

For in truth, Leonard was their greatest anxiety indoors. His health seemed shaken, he spoke half sentences in his sleep, which showed that in his dreams he was battling on his mother's behalf against an unkind and angry world. And then he would wail to himself, and utter sad words of shame, which they never thought had reached his ears. By day, he was in general grave and quiet; but his appetite varied, and he was evidently afraid of going into the streets, dreading to be pointed at as an object of remark. Each separately in their hearts longed to give him

change of scene, but they were all silent, for where
was the requisite money to come from?

His temper became fitful and variable.   At times he
would be most sullen against his mother ; and then
give way to a passionate remorse.   When Mr Benson
caught Ruth's look of agony at her child's rebuffs, his
patience failed ; or rather, I should say, he believed
that a stronger, severer hand than hers was required
for the management of the lad.   But, when she heard
Mr Benson say so, she pleaded with him.

"Have patience with Leonard," she said.   "I have
deserved the anger that is fretting in his heart.   It is
only I who can reinstate myself in his love and respect.
I have no fear.   When he sees me really striving hard
and long to do what is right, he must love me.   I am
not afraid."

Even while she spoke, her lips quivered, and her
colour went and came with eager anxiety.   So Mr
Benson held his peace, and let her take her course.
It was beautiful to see the intuition by which she
divined what was passing in every fold of her child's
heart, so as to be always ready with the right words to
soothe or to strengthen him.   Her watchfulness was
unwearied, and with no thought of self tainting it, or
else she might have often paused to turn aside and
weep at the clouds of shame which came over Leonard's
love for her, and hid it from all but her faithful heart ;
she believed and knew that he was yet her own affectionate boy, although he might be gloomily silent, or
apparently hard and cold.   And in all this, Mr Benson
could not choose but admire the way in which she was
insensibly teaching Leonard to conform to the law of
right, to recognize Duty in the mode in which every
action was performed.   When Mr Benson saw this, he
knew that all goodness would follow, and that the
claims which his mother's infinite love had on the boy's
heart would be acknowledged at last, and all the more
fully because she herself never urged them, but silently
admitted the force of the reason that caused them to
be for a time forgotten.   By and by Leonard's remorse

at his ungracious and sullen ways to his mother—ways
that alternated with passionate, fitful bursts of clinging
love—assumed more the character of repentance; he
tried to do so no more. But still his health was
delicate; he was averse to going out of doors; he was
much graver and sadder than became his age. It
was what must be; an inevitable consequence of what
had been; and Ruth had to be patient, and pray in
secret, and with many tears, for the strength she
needed.

She knew what it was to dread the going out into
the streets after her story had become known. For
days and days she had silently shrunk from this effort.
But one evening towards dusk, Miss Benson was busy,
and asked her to go an errand for her; and Ruth got
up and silently obeyed her. That silence as to inward
suffering was only one part of her peculiar and exquisite
sweetness of nature; part of the patience with which
she "accepted her penance."* Her true instincts told
her that it was not right to disturb others with many
expressions of her remorse; that the holiest repentance
consisted in a quiet and daily sacrifice. Still there
were times when she wearied pitifully of her inaction.
She was so willing to serve and work, and every one
despised her services. Her mind, as I have said
before, had been well cultivated during these last few
years; so now she used all the knowledge she had
gained in teaching Leonard, which was an employment
that Mr Benson relinquished willingly, because he felt
that it would give her some of the occupation that
she needed. She endeavoured to make herself useful
in the house in every way she could; but the waters of
housekeeping had closed over her place during the
time of her absence at Mr Bradshaw's—and, besides,
now that they were trying to restrict every unnecessary
expense, it was sometimes difficult to find work for
three women. Many and many a time Ruth turned
over in her mind every possible chance of obtaining
employment for her leisure hours, and nowhere could
she find it. Now and then Sally, who was her con-

fidante in this wish, procured her some needlework,
but it was of a coarse and common kind, soon done,
lightly paid for. But whatever it was, Ruth took it,
and was thankful, although it added but a few pence
to the household purse. I do not mean that there was
any great need of money; but a new adjustment of
expenditure was required—a reduction of wants which
had never been very extravagant.

Ruth's salary of forty pounds was gone, while more
of her " keep," as Sally called it, was thrown upon
the Bensons. Mr Benson received about eighty
pounds a year for his salary as minister. Of this, he
knew that twenty pounds came from Mr Bradshaw;
and when the old man appointed to collect the pew-
rents brought him the quarterly amount, and he found
no diminution in them, he inquired how it was, and
learnt that, although Mr Bradshaw had expressed to
the collector his determination never to come to
chapel again, he had added, that of course his pew-
rent should be paid all the same. But this Mr Benson
could not suffer; and the old man was commissioned
to return the money to Mr Bradshaw, as being what
his deserted minister could not receive.

Mr and Miss Benson had about thirty or forty
pounds coming in annually from a sum which, in
happier days, Mr Bradshaw had invested in Canal
shares for them. Altogether their income did not
fall much short of a hundred a year, and they lived in
the Chapel-house free of rent. So Ruth's small earnings were but very little in actual hard commercial
account, though in another sense they were much;
and Miss Benson always received them with quiet
simplicity. By degrees, Mr Benson absorbed some
of Ruth's time in a gracious and natural way. He
employed her mind in all the kind offices he was
accustomed to render to the poor around him. And
as much of the peace and ornament of life as they
gained now, was gained on a firm basis of truth. If
Ruth began low down to find her place in the world,
at any rate there was no flaw in the foundation.

Leonard was still their great anxiety. At times the
question seemed to be, could he live through all this
trial of the elasticity of childhood? And then they
knew how precious a blessing—how true a pillar of
fire, he was to his mother: and how black the night,
and how dreary the wilderness would be, when he was
not. The child and the mother were each messengers
of God—angels to each other.

They had long gaps between the pieces of intelligence respecting the Bradshaws. Mr Bradshaw had
at length purchased the house at Abermouth, and
they were much there. The way in which the Bensons
heard most frequently of the family of their former
friends, was through Mr Farquhar. He called on Mr
Benson about a month after the latter had met Jemima
in the street. Mr Farquhar was not in the habit of
paying calls on anyone; and though he had always
entertained and evinced the most kind and friendly
feeling towards Mr Benson, he had rarely been in the
Chapel-house. Mr Benson received him courteously,
but he rather expected that there would be some
especial reason alleged, before the conclusion of the
visit, for its occurrence; more particularly as Mr
Farquhar sat talking on the topics of the day in a
somewhat absent manner, as if they were not the
subjects most present to his mind. The truth was,
he could not help recurring to the last time when he
was in that room, waiting to take Leonard a ride, and
his heart beating rather more quickly than usual at
the idea that Ruth might bring the boy in when he
was equipped. He was very full now of the remembrance of Ruth; and yet he was also most thankful,
most self-gratulatory, that he had gone no further in
his admiration of her—that he had never expressed
his regard in words—that no one, as he believed, was
cognizant of the incipient love which had grown partly
out of his admiration, and partly out of his reason.
He was thankful to be spared any implication in the
nine-days' wonder which her story had made in Eccleston. And yet his feeling for her had been of so

strong a character, that he winced, as with extreme
pain, at every application of censure to her name.
These censures were often exaggerated, it is true;
but when they were just in their judgement of the outward circumstances of the case, they were not the less
painful and distressing to him. His first rebound to
Jemima was occasioned by Mrs Bradshaw's account
of how severely her husband was displeased at her
daughter's having taken part with Ruth; and he could
have thanked and almost blessed Jemima when she
dropped in (she dared do no more) her pleading
excuses and charitable explanations on Ruth's behalf.
Jemima had learnt some humility from the discovery
which had been to her so great a shock; standing, she
had learnt to take heed lest she fell; and when she
had once been aroused to a perception of the violence
of the hatred which she had indulged against Ruth,
she was more reticent and measured in the expression
of all her opinions. It showed how much her character
had been purified from pride, that now she felt aware
that what in her was again attracting Mr Farquhar
was her faithful advocacy of her rival, wherever such
advocacy was wise or practicable. He was quite unaware that Jemima had been conscious of his great
admiration for Ruth; he did not know that she had
ever cared enough for him to be jealous. But the
unacknowledged bond between them now was their
grief, and sympathy, and pity for Ruth; only in
Jemima these feelings were ardent, and would fain
have become active; while in Mr Farquhar they were
strongly mingled with thankfulness that he had escaped
a disagreeable position, and a painful notoriety. His
natural caution induced him to make a resolution
never to think of any woman as a wife until he had
ascertained all her antecedents, from her birth upwards; and the same spirit of caution, directed in-
wardly, made him afraid of giving too much pity to
Ruth, for fear of the conclusions to which such a
feeling might lead him. But still his old regard for
her, for Leonard, and his esteem and respect for the

Bensons, induced him to lend a willing ear to Jemima's earnest entreaty that he would go and call on Mr Benson, in order that she might learn something about the family in general, and Ruth in particular. It was thus that he came to sit by Mr Benson's study fire, and to talk, in an absent way, to that gentleman. How they got on the subject he did not know, more than one-half of his attention being distracted, but they were speaking about politics, when Mr Farquhar learned that Mr Benson took in no newspaper.

"Will you allow me to send you over my *Times?* I have generally done with it before twelve o'clock, and after that it is really waste-paper in my house. You will oblige me by making use of it."

"I am sure I am very much obliged to you for thinking of it. But do not trouble yourself to send it ; Leonard can fetch it."

"How is Leonard now?" asked Mr Farquhar, and he tried to speak indifferently ; but a grave look of intelligence clouded his eyes as he looked for Mr Benson's answer. "I have not met him lately."

"No !" said Mr Benson, with an expression of pain in his countenance, though he, too, strove to speak in his usual tone.

"Leonard is not strong, and we find it difficult to induce him to go much out of doors."

There was a little silence for a minute or two, during which Mr Farquhar had to check an unbidden sigh. But, suddenly rousing himself into a determination to change the subject, he said :

"You will find rather a lengthened account of the exposure of Sir Thomas Campbell's conduct at Baden. He seems to be a complete blackleg, in spite of his baronetcy. I fancy the papers are glad to get hold of anything just now."

"Who is Sir Thomas Campbell?" asked Mr Benson.

"Oh, I thought you might have heard the report— a true one, I believe—of Mr Donne's engagement to his daughter. He must be glad she jilted him now, I fancy, after this public exposure of her father's conduct." (That was an awkward speech, as Mr Farquhar felt ; and he hastened to cover it, by going on without much connexion :)

"Dick Bradshaw is my informant about all these projected marriages in high life—they are not much in my way ; but since he has come down from London to take his share in the business, I think I have heard more of the news and the scandal of what, I suppose, would be considered high life, than ever I did before ; and Mr Donne's proceedings seem to be an especial object of interest to him."

"And Mr Donne is engaged to a Miss Campbell, is he ?"

"Was engaged ; if I understood right, she broke off the engagement to marry some Russian prince or other —a better match, Dick Bradshaw told me. I assure you," continued Mr Farquhar, smiling, "I am a very passive recipient of all such intelligence, and might very probably have forgotten all about it, if the *Times*, of this morning, had not been so full of the disgrace of the young lady's father."

"Richard Bradshaw has quite left London, has he ?" asked Mr Benson, who felt far more interest in his old patron's family than in all the Campbells that ever were or ever would be.

"Yes. He has come to settle down here. I hope he may do well, and not disappoint his father, who has formed very high expectations from him ; I am not sure if they are not too high for any young man to realize." Mr Farquhar could have said more, but Dick Bradshaw was Jemima's brother, and an object of anxiety to her.

"I am sure, I trust such a mortification—such a grief as any disappointment in Richard, may not befall his father," replied Mr Benson.

"Jemima—Miss Bradshaw," said Mr Farquhar, hesitating, "was most anxious to hear of you all. I hope I may tell her you are all well" (with an emphasis on *all*) ; "that——"

"Thank you. Thank her for us. We are all well ;

all except Leonard, who is not strong, as I said before.
But we must be patient. Time, and such devoted,
tender love as he has from his mother, must do much."

Mr Farquhar was silent.

"Send him to my house for the papers. It will be
a little necessity for him to have some regular exercise,
and to face the world. He must do it, sooner or later."

The two gentlemen shook hands with each other on
parting; but no further allusion was made to either
Ruth or Leonard.

So Leonard went for the papers. Stealing along by
back streets—running with his head bent down—his
little heart panting with dread of being pointed out as
his mother's child—so he used to come back, and run
trembling to Sally, who would hush him up to her
breast with many a rough-spoken word of pity and
sympathy.

Mr Farquhar tried to catch him to speak to him, and
tame him as it were; and, by and by, he contrived to
interest him sufficiently to induce the boy to stay a
little while in the house, or stables, or garden. But
the race through the streets was always to be dreaded
as the end of ever so pleasant a visit.

Mr Farquhar kept up the intercourse with the Bensons which he had thus begun. He persevered in
paying calls—quiet visits, where not much was said,
political or local news talked about, and the same
inquiries always made and answered as to the welfare
of the two families, who were estranged from each
other. Mr Farquhar's reports were so little varied
that Jemima grew anxious to know more particulars.

"Oh, Mr Farquhar!" said she; "do you think
they tell you the truth? I wonder what Ruth can
be doing to support herself and Leonard? Nothing
that you can hear of, you say; and, of course, one
must not ask the downright question. And yet I
am sure they must be pinched in some way. Do you
think Leonard is stronger?"

"I am not sure. He is growing fast; and such
a blow as he has had will be certain to make him

more thoughtful and full of care than most boys of
his age; both these circumstances may make him
thin and pale, which he certainly is."

"Oh! how I wish I might go and see them all!
I could tell in a twinkling the real state of things."
She spoke with a tinge of her old impatience.

"I will go again, and pay particular attention to
anything you wish me to observe. You see, of
course, I feel a delicacy about asking any direct
questions, or even alluding in any way to these late
occurrences."

"And you never see Ruth by any chance?"

"Never!"

They did not look at each other while this last
question was asked and answered.

"I will take the paper to-morrow myself; it will
be an excuse for calling again, and I will try to be
very penetrating; but I have not much hope of
success."

"Oh, thank you. It is giving you a great deal
of trouble; but you are very kind."

"Kind, Jemima!" he repeated, in a tone which
made her go very red and hot; "must I tell you how
you can reward me?—Will you call me Walter?—
say, thank you, Walter—just for once."

Jemima felt herself yielding to the voice and tone
in which this was spoken; but her very consciousness of the depth of her love made her afraid of
giving way, an' anxious to be wooed, that she might
be reinstated in her self-esteem.

"No!" said she, "I don't think I can call you
so. You are too old. It would not be respectful."
She meant it half in joke, and had no idea he would
take the allusion to his age so seriously as he did.
He rose up, and coldly, as a matter of form, in a
changed voice, wished her "Good-bye." Her heart
sank; yet the old pride was there. But, as he was
at the very door, some sudden impulse made her
speak:

"I have not vexed you, have I, Walter?"

He turned round, glowing with a thrill of delight. She was as red as any rose; her looks dropped down to the ground.

They were not raised when, half an hour afterwards, she said, "You won't forbid my going to see Ruth, will you? because if you do, I give you notice I shall disobey you." The arm around her waist clasped her yet more fondly at the idea suggested by this speech, of the control which he should have a right to exercise over her actions at some future day.

"Tell me," said he, "how much of your goodness to me, this last happy hour, has been owing to the desire of having more freedom as a wife than as a daughter?"

She was almost glad that he should think she needed any additional motive to her love for him before she could have accepted him. She was afraid that she had betrayed the deep, passionate regard with which she had long looked upon him. She was lost in delight at her own happiness. She was silent for a time. At length she said:

"I don't think you know how faithful I have been to you ever since the days when you first brought me pistachio-candy from London—when I was quite a little girl."

"Not more faithful than I have been to you," for in truth, the recollection of his love for Ruth had utterly faded away, and he thought himself a model of constancy; "and you have tried me pretty well. What a vixen you have been!"

Jemima sighed; smitten with the consciousness of how little she had deserved her present happiness; humble with the recollection of the evil thoughts that had raged in her heart during the time (which she remembered well, though he might have forgotten it) when Ruth had had the affection which her jealous rival coveted.

"I may speak to your father, may not I, Jemima?"

No! for some reason or fancy which she could not define, and could not be persuaded out of, she wished

to keep their mutal understanding a secret. She had
a natural desire to avoid the congratulations she expected from her family. She dreaded her father's
consideration of the whole affair as a satisfactory dis-
posal of his daughter to a worthy man, who, being
his partner, would not require any abstraction of
capital from the concern; and Richard's more noisy
delight at his sister's having "hooked" so good a
match. It was only her simple-hearted mother that
she longed to tell. She knew that her mother's congratulations would not jar upon her, though they
might not sound the full organ-peal of her love. But
all that her mother knew passed onwards to her
father; so for the present, at any rate, she determined
to realize her secret position alone. Somehow, the
sympathy of all others that she most longed for was
Ruth's; but the first communication of such an event
was due to her parents. She imposed very strict re-
gulations on Mr Farquhar's behaviour; and quarrelled
and differed from him more than ever, but with a
secret joyful understanding with him in her heart,
even while they disagreed with each other—for simi-
larity of opinion is not always—I think not often—
needed for fulness and perfection of love.

After Ruth's "detection," as Mr Bradshaw used
to call it, he said he could never trust another governess again; so Mary and Elizabeth had been sent to
school the following Christmas, and their place in
the family was but poorly supplied by the return of
Mr Richard Bradshaw, who had left London, and
been received as a partner.

CHAPTER XXIX

THE conversation narrated in the last chapter as
taking place between Mr Farquhar and Jemima,
occurred about a year after Ruth's dismissal from her
situation. That year, full of small events, and change
of place to the Bradshaws, had been monotonous and

long in its course to the other household.   There had
been no want of peace and tranquillity ; there had,
perhaps, been more of them than in the preceding
years, when, though unacknowledged by any, all must
have occasionally felt the oppression of the falsehood—
and a slight glancing dread must have flashed across
their most prosperous state, lest, somehow or another,
the mystery should be disclosed.   But now, as the
shepherd-boy in John Bunyan sweetly sang,* " He that
is low need fear no fall."

Still their peace was as the stillness of a grey
autumnal day, where no sun is to be seen above, and
when a quiet film seems drawn before both sky and
earth, as if to rest the wearied eyes after the summer's
glare.   Few events broke the monotony of their lives,
and those events were of a depressing kind.   They
consisted in Ruth's futile endeavours to obtain some
employment, however humble ; in Leonard's fluctua-
tions of spirits and health ; in Sally's increasing
deafness ; in the final and unmendable wearing-out
of the parlour carpet, which there was no spare money
to replace, and so they cheerfully supplied its want by
a large hearth-rug that Ruth made out of ends of list;*
and, what was more a subject of unceasing regret to
Mr Benson than all, the defection of some of the
members of his congregation, who followed Mr Bradshaw's lead.   Their places, to be sure, were more than
filled up by the poor, who thronged to his chapel ; but
still it was a disappointment to find that people about
whom he had been earnestly thinking—to whom he had
laboured to do good—should dissolve the connexion
without a word of farewell or explanation.   Mr Benson
did not wonder that they should go ; nay, he even felt
it right that they should seek that spiritual help from
another, which he, by his error, had forfeited his power
to offer ; he only wished they had spoken of their
intention to him in an open and manly way.   But not
the less did he labour on among those to whom God
permitted him to be of use.   He felt age stealing upon
him apace, although he said nothing about it, and no

one seemed to be aware of it ; and he worked the more
diligently while "it was yet day." It was not the
number of his years that made him feel old, for he was
only sixty, and many men are hale and strong at that
time of life ; in all probability, it was that early injury
to his spine which affected the constitution of his mind
as well as his body, and predisposed him, in the opinion
of some at least, to a feminine morbidness of conscience.
He had shaken off somewhat of this since the affair with
Mr Bradshaw ; he was simpler and more dignified than
he had been for several years before, during which time
he had been anxious and uncertain in his manner, and
more given to thought than to action.

The one happy bright spot in this grey year, was
owing to Sally. As she said of herself, she believed
she grew more "nattered"*as she grew older ; but that
she was conscious of her "natteredness" was a new
thing, and a great gain to the comfort of the house,
for it made her very grateful for forbearance, and more
aware of kindness than she had ever been before. She
had become very deaf ; yet she was uneasy and jealous
if she were not informed of all the family thoughts,
plans, and proceedings, which often had (however
private in their details) to be shouted to her at the full
pitch of the voice. But she always heard Leonard
perfectly. His clear and bell-like voice, which was
similar to his mother's, till sorrow had taken the ring
out of it, was sure to be heard by the old servant,
though everyone else had failed. Sometimes, however,
she "got her hearing sudden," as she phrased it, and
was alive to every word and noise, more particularly
when they did not want her to hear, and at such times
she resented their continuance of the habit of speaking
loud as a mortal offence. One day, her indignation at
being thought deaf called out one of the rare smiles on
Leonard's face ; she saw it, and said, " Bless thee, lad !
if it but amuses thee, they may shout through a ram's
horn to me, and I'll never let on I'm not deaf. It's as
good a use as I can be of," she continued to herself,
"if I can make that poor lad smile a bit."

If she expected to be everybody's confidante, she
made Leonard hers. "There!" said she, when she
came home from her marketing one Saturday night,
"look here, lad! Here's forty-two pound, seven
shillings, and twopence! It's a mint of money, isn't
it? I took it all in sovereigns for fear of fire."

"What is it all for, Sally?" said he.

"Aye, lad! that's asking. It's Mr Benson's money,"
said she, mysteriously, "that I've been keeping for
him. Is he in the study, think ye?"

"Yes! I think so. Where have you been keeping
it?"

"Never you mind!" She went towards the study,
but thinking she might have been hard on her darling
in refusing to gratify his curiosity, she turned back, and
said:

"I say—if thou wilt, thou mayst do me a job of work
some day. I'm wanting a frame made for a piece of
writing."

And then she returned to go into the study, carrying
her sovereigns in her apron.

"Here, Master Thurstan," said she, pouring them
out on the table before her astonished master. "Take
it, it's all yours."

"All mine! What can you mean?" asked he,
bewildered.

She did not hear him, and went on:

"Lock it up safe, out o' the way. Dunnot go and
leave it about to tempt folks. I'll not answer for
myself if money's left about. I may be cribbing a
sovereign."

"But where does it come from?" said he.

"Come from!" she replied. "Where does all
money come from, but the Bank, to be sure? I
thought anyone could tell that."

"I have no money in the Bank!" said he, more and
more perplexed.

"No! I knowed that; but I had. Dunnot ye remember how you would raise my wage, last Martinmas
eighteen year? You and Faith were very headstrong,

but I was too deep for you. See thee! I went and put it i' th' Bank. I was never going to touch it; and if I had died it would have been all right, for I'd a will made, all regular and tight—made by a lawyer (leastways he would have been a lawyer, if he hadn't got transported first). And now, thinks I, I think I'll just go and get it out and give it 'em. Banks is not always safe."

"I'll take care of it for you with the greatest pleasure. Still, you know, banks allow interest."

"D'ye suppose I don't know all about interest, and compound interest too, by this time? I tell ye I want ye to spend it. It's your own. It's not mine. It always was yours. Now you're not going to fret me by saying you think it mine."

Mr Benson held out his hand to her, for he could not speak. She bent forward to him as he sat there, and kissed him.

"Eh, bless ye, lad! It's the first kiss I've had of ye sin' ye were a little lad, and it's a great refreshment. Now don't you and Faith go and bother me with talking about it. It's just yours, and make no more ado."

She went back into the kitchen, and brought out her will, and gave Leonard directions how to make a frame for it; for the boy was a very tolerable joiner, and had a box of tools which Mr Bradshaw had given him some years ago.

"It's a pity to lose such fine writing," said she; "though I can't say as I can read it. Perhaps you'd just read it for me, Leonard." She sat open-mouthed with admiration at all the long words.

The frame was made, and the will hung up opposite to her bed, unknown to anyone but Leonard; and, by dint of his repeated reading it over to her, she learnt all the words, except "testatrix," which she would always call "testy tricks." Mr Benson had been too much gratified and touched, by her unconditional gift of all she had in the world, to reject it; but he only held it in his hands as a deposit until he could find a

safe investment befitting so small a sum. The little
re-arrangements of the household expenditure had not
touched him as they had done the women. He was
aware that meat dinners were not now every-day occurrences; but he preferred puddings and vegetables, and
was glad of the exchange. He observed, too, that they
all sat together in the kitchen in the evenings; but
the kitchen, with the well-scoured dresser, the shining
saucepans, the well-blacked grate and whitened hearth,
and the warmth which seemed to rise up from the very
flags, and ruddily cheer the most distant corners,
appeared a very cozy and charming sitting-room; and,
besides, it appeared but right that Sally, in her old
age, should have the companionship of those with
whom she had lived in love and faithfulness for many
years. He only wished he could more frequently leave
the solitary comfort of his study, and join the kitchen
party; where Sally sat as mistress in the chimney-
corner, knitting by fire-light, and Miss Benson and
Ruth, with the candle between them, stitched away at
their work; while Leonard strewed the ample dresser
with his slate and books. He did not mope and pine
over his lessons; they were the one thing that took
him out of himself. As yet his mother could teach
him, though in some respects it was becoming a strain
upon her acquirements and powers. Mr Benson saw
this, but reserved his offers of help as long as he could,
hoping that before his assistance became absolutely
necessary, some mode of employment beyond that
of occasional plain-work might be laid open to Ruth.

In spite of the communication they occasionally had
with Mr Farquhar, when he gave them the intelligence
of his engagement to Jemima, it seemed like a glimpse
into a world from which they were shut out. They
wondered—Miss Benson and Ruth did at least—much
about the details. Ruth sat over her sewing, fancying
how all had taken place; and as soon as she had
arranged the events which were going on among people
and places once so familiar to her, she found some dis-
crepancy, and set-to afresh to picture the declaration

of love, and the yielding, blushing acceptance; for Mr
Farquhar had told little beyond the mere fact that
there was an engagement between himself and Jemima
which had existed for some time, but which had been
kept secret until now, when it was acknowledged, sanctioned, and to be fulfilled as soon as he returned from
an arrangement of family affairs in Scotland. This
intelligence had been enough for Mr Benson, who was
the only person Mr Farquhar saw; as Ruth always
shrank from the post of opening the door, and Mr
Benson was apt at recognizing individual knocks, and
always prompt to welcome Mr Farquhar.

Miss Benson occasionally thought—and what she
thought she was in the habit of saying—that Jemima
might have come herself to announce such an event to
old friends; but Mr Benson decidedly vindicated her
from any charge of neglect, by expressing his strong
conviction that to her they owed Mr Farquhar's calls—
his all but outspoken offers of service—his quiet, steady
interest in Leonard; and, moreover (repeating the
conversation he had had with her in the street, the
first time they met after the disclosure), Mr Benson
told his sister how glad he was to find that, with all
the warmth of her impetuous disposition hurrying her
on to rebellion against her father, she was now attain-
ing to that just self-control which can distinguish
between mere wishes and true reasons—that she could
abstain from coming to see Ruth while she could do
but little good, reserving herself for some great occasion or strong emergency.

Ruth said nothing, but she yearned all the more in
silence to see Jemima. In her recollection of that
fearful interview with Mr Bradshaw, which haunted
her yet, sleeping or waking, she was painfully conscious that she had not thanked Jemima for her
generous, loving advocacy; it had passed unregarded
at the time in intensity of agony—but now she recollected that by no word, or tone, or touch, had she
given any sign of gratitude. Mr Benson had never
told her of his meeting with Jemima; so it seemed as

if there were no hope of any future opportunity : for it
is strange how two households, rent apart by some
dissension, can go through life, their parallel exist-
ences running side by side, yet never touching each
other, near neighbours as they are, habitual and
familiar guests as they may have been.

Ruth's only point of hope was Leonard. She was
weary of looking for work and employment, which
everywhere seemed held above her reach. She was
not impatient of this, but she was very, very sorry.
She felt within her such capability, and all ignored
her, and passed her by on the other side. But she
saw some progress in Leonard.   Not that he could
continue to have the happy development, and genial
ripening, which other boys have ; leaping from
childhood to boyhood, and thence to youth, with
glad bounds, and unconsciously enjoying every
age. At present there was no harmony in Leonard's
character ; he was as full of thought and self-
consciousness as many men, planning his actions long
beforehand, so as to avoid what he dreaded, and
what she could not yet give him strength to face,
coward as she was herself, and shrinking from hard
remarks. Yet Leonard was regaining some of his
lost tenderness towards his mother ; when they were
alone he would throw himself on her neck and
smother her with kisses, without any apparent cause
for such a passionate impulse. If anyone was by, his
manner was cold and reserved. The hopeful parts of
his character were the determination evident in him to
be a "law unto himself," and the serious thought
which he gave to the formation of this law. There
was an inclination in him to reason, especially and
principally with Mr Benson, on the great questions
of ethics which the majority of the world have settled
long ago. But I do not think he ever so argued with
his mother. Her lovely patience, and her humility,
was earning its reward ; and from her quiet piety,
bearing sweetly the denial of her wishes—the refusal
of her begging—the disgrace in which she lay, while

others, less worthy, were employed—this, which perplexed him, and almost angered him at first, called
out his reverence at last, and what she said he took
for his law with proud humility; and thus softly, she
was leading him up to God.   His health was not
strong; it was not likely to be.   He moaned and
talked in his sleep, and his appetite was still variable,
part of which might be owing to his preference of the
hardest lessons to any outdoor exercise.   But this last
unnatural symptom was vanishing before the assiduous
kindness of Mr Farquhar, and the quiet but firm desire
of his mother.   Next to Ruth, Sally had perhaps the
most influence over him; but he dearly loved both Mr
and Miss Benson; although he was reserved on this, as
on every point not purely intellectual.   His was a hard
childhood, and his mother felt that it was so.   Children
bear any moderate degree of poverty and privation
cheerfully; but, in addition to a good deal of this,
Leonard had to bear a sense of disgrace attaching
to him and to the creature he loved best; this it
was that took out of him the buoyancy and natural
gladness of youth, in a way which no scantiness of
food or clothing, or want of any outward comfort,
could ever have done.

Two years had passed away—two long, eventless
years.   Something was now going to happen, which
touched their hearts very nearly, though out of their
sight and hearing.   Jemima was going to be married
this August, and by and by the very day was fixed.   It
was to be on the 14th.   On the evening of the 13th,
Ruth was sitting alone in the parlour, idly gazing out
on the darkening shadows in the little garden; her
eyes kept filling with quiet tears, that rose, not for her
own isolation from all that was going on of bustle
and preparation for the morrow's event, but because
she had seen how Miss Benson had felt that she and
her brother were left out from the gathering of old
friends in the Bradshaw family.   As Ruth sat, suddenly she was aware of a figure by her; she started
up, and in the gloom of the apartment she recognized

Jemima.   In an instant they were in each other's
arms—a long, fast embrace.

"Can you forgive me?" whispered Jemima in
Ruth's ear.

"Forgive you!   What do you mean?   What have
I to forgive?   The question is, can I ever thank you
as I long to do, if I could find words?"

"Oh, Ruth, how I hated you once!"

"It was all the more noble in you to stand by me
as you did.   You must have hated me when you knew
how I was deceiving you all!"

"No, that was not it that made me hate you.   It
was before that.   Oh, Ruth, I did hate you!"

They were silent for some time, still holding each
other's hands.   Ruth spoke first.

"And you are going to be married to-morrow!"

"Yes," said Jemima.   "To-morrow, at nine o'clock.
But I don't think I could have been married without
coming to wish Mr Benson and Miss Faith good-bye."

"I will go for them," said Ruth.

"No, not just yet.   I want to ask you one or two
questions first.   Nothing very particular; only it
seems as if there had been such a strange, long
separation between us.   Ruth," said she, dropping
her voice, "is Leonard stronger than he was?   I
was so sorry to hear about him from Walter.   But
he is better?" asked she anxiously.

"Yes, he is better.   Not what a boy of his age
should be," replied his mother, in a tone of quiet
but deep mournfulness.   "Oh, Jemima!" continued
she, "my sharpest punishment comes through him.
To think what he might have been, and what he
is!"

"But Walter says he is both stronger in health,
and not so—nervous and shy."   Jemima added the
last words in a hesitating and doubtful manner, as if
she did not know how to express her full meaning
without hurting Ruth.

"He does not show that he feels his disgrace so
much.   I cannot talk about it, Jemima, my heart

aches so about him. But he is better," she continued,
feeling that Jemima's kind anxiety required an answer
at any cost of pain to herself. "He is only studying
too closely now; he takes to his lessons evidently as a
relief from thought. He is very clever, and I hope
and trust, yet I tremble to say it, I believe he is very
good."

"You must let him come and see us very often
when we come back. We shall be two months away.
We are going to Germany, partly on Walter's business. Ruth, I have been talking to papa to-night,
very seriously and quietly, and it has made me love
him so much more, and understand him so much
better."

"Does he know of your coming here? I hope he
does," said Ruth.

"Yes. Not that he liked my doing it at all. But,
somehow, I can always do things against a person's
wishes more easily when I am on good terms with
them—that's not exactly what I meant; but now
to-night, after papa had been showing me that he
really loved me more than I ever thought he had
done (for I always fancied he was so absorbed
in Dick, he did not care much for us girls), I felt
brave enough to say that I intended to come here and
bid you all good-bye. He was silent for a minute, and
then said I might do it, but I must remember he did
not approve of it, and was not to be compromised by
my coming; still I can tell that, at the bottom of his
heart, there is some of the old kindly feeling to Mr and
Miss Benson, and I don't despair of its all being
made up, though, perhaps, I ought to say that
mamma does."

"Mr and Miss Benson won't hear of my going
away," said Ruth, sadly.

"They are quite right."

"But I am earning nothing. I cannot get any employment. I am only a burden and an expense."

"Are you not also a pleasure? And Leonard, is he
not a dear object of love? It is easy for me to talk, I

know, who am so impatient. Oh, I never deserved to be happy as I am! You don't know how good Walter is. I used to think him so cold and cautious. But now, Ruth, will you tell Mr and Miss Benson that I am here? There is signing of papers, and I don't know what to be done at home. And when I come back, I hope to see you often, if you'll let me."

Mr and Miss Benson gave her a warm greeting. Sally was called in, and would bring a candle with her, to have a close inspection of her, in order to see if she was changed—she had not seen her for so long a time, she said; and Jemima stood laughing and blushing in the middle of the room, while Sally studied her all over, and would not be convinced that the old gown which she was wearing for the last time was not one of the new wedding ones. The consequence of which misunderstanding was, that Sally, in her short petticoats and bedgown, turned up her nose at the old-fashioned way in which Miss Bradshaw's gown was made. But Jemima knew the old woman, and rather enjoyed the contempt for her dress. At last she kissed them all, and ran away to her impatient Mr Farquhar, who was awaiting her.

Not many weeks after this, the poor old woman whom I have named as having become a friend of Ruth's, during Leonard's illness three years ago, fell down and broke her hip-bone. It was a serious—probably a fatal injury, for one so old; and as soon as Ruth heard of it she devoted all her leisure time to old Ann Fleming. Leonard had now outstript his mother's powers of teaching, and Mr Benson gave him his lessons; so Ruth was a great deal at the cottage both night and day.

There Jemima found her one November evening, the second after their return from their prolonged stay on the Continent. She and Mr Farquhar had been to the Bensons, and had sat there some time; and now Jemima had come on just to see Ruth for five minutes, before the evening was too dark for her to return alone. She found Ruth sitting on a stool before the fire, which was composed of a few sticks on the hearth. The blaze they gave was, however, enough to enable her to read ; and she was deep in study of the Bible, in which she had read aloud to the poor old woman, until the latter had fallen asleep. Jemima beckoned her out, and they stood on the green just before the open door, so that Ruth could see if Ann awoke.

"I have not many minutes to stay, only I felt as if I must see you. And we want Leonard to come to us to see all our German purchases, and hear all our German adventures. May he come to-morrow?"

"Yes; thank you. Oh! Jemima, I have heard something—I have got a plan that makes me so happy ! I have not told anyone yet. But Mr Wynne (the parish doctor, you know) has asked me if I would go out as a sick nurse—he thinks he could find me employment."

"You, a sick nurse!" said Jemima, involuntarily glancing over the beautiful lithe figure, and the lovely refinement of Ruth's face, as the light of the rising moon fell upon it. "My dear Ruth, I don't think you are fitted for it!"

"Don't you?" said Ruth, a little disappointed. "I think I am ; at least, that I should be very soon. I like being about sick and helpless people ; I always feel so sorry for them ; and then I think I have the gift of a very delicate touch, which is such a comfort in many cases. And I should try to be very watchful and patient. Mr Wynne proposed it himself."

"It was not in that way I meant you were not fitted for it. I meant that you were fitted for something better. Why, Ruth, you are better educated than I am!"

"But if nobody will allow me to teach?—for that is what I suppose you mean. Besides, I feel as if all my education would be needed to make me a good sick nurse."

"Your knowledge of Latin, for instance," said Jemima, hitting, in her vexation at the plan, on the first acquirement of Ruth she could think of.

"Well!" said Ruth, "that won't come amiss; I can read the prescriptions."

"Which the doctors would rather you did not do."

"Still, you can't say that any knowledge of any kind will be in my way, or will unfit me for my work."

"Perhaps not. But all your taste and refinement will be in your way, and will unfit you."

"You have not thought about this so much as I have, or you would not say so. Any fastidiousness I shall have to get rid of, and I shall be better without; but any true refinement I am sure I shall find of use; for don't you think that every power we have may be made to help us in any right work, whatever that is? Would you not rather be nursed by a person who spoke gently and moved quietly about than by a loud bustling woman?"

"Yes! to be sure; but a person unfit for anything else may move quietly, and speak gently, and give medicine when the doctor orders it, and keep awake at night; and those are the best qualities I ever heard of in a sick nurse."

Ruth was quite silent for some time. At last she said: "At any rate it is work, and as such I am thankful for it. You cannot discourage me — and perhaps you know too little of what my life has been —how set apart in idleness I have been—to sympathize with me fully."

"And I wanted you to come to see us—me in my new home. Walter and I had planned that we would persuade you to come to us very often" (she had planned, and Mr Farquhar had consented); "and now you will have to be fastened up in a sick room."

"I could not have come," said Ruth quickly. "Dear Jemima! it is like you to have thought of it— but I could not come to your house. It is not a thing to reason about. It is just feeling. But I do feel as if I could not go. Dear Jemima! if you are ill or sorrowful, and want me, I will come——"

"So you would and must to anyone, if you take up that calling."

"But I should come to you, love, in quite a different way; I should go to you with my heart full of love—so full that I am afraid I should be too anxious."

"I almost wish I were ill, that I might make you come at once."

"And I am almost ashamed to think how I should like you to be in some position in which I could show you how well I remember that day—that terrible day in the schoolroom. God bless you for it, Jemima!"

CHAPTER XXX

MR WYNNE, the parish surgeon, was right. He could and did obtain employment for Ruth as a sick nurse. Her home was with the Bensons; every spare moment was given to Leonard and to them; but she was at the call of all the invalids in the town. At first her work lay exclusively among the paupers. At first, too, there was a recoil from many circumstances, which impressed upon her the most fully the physical sufferings of those whom she tended. But she tried to lose the sense of these—or rather to lessen them, and make them take their appointed places—in thinking of the individuals themselves, as separate from their decaying frames; and all along she had enough self-command to control herself from expressing any sign of repugnance. She allowed herself no nervous haste of movement or touch that should hurt the feelings of the poorest, most friendless creature, who ever lay a victim to disease. There was no rough getting over of all the disagreeable and painful work of her employment. When it was a lessening of pain to have the touch careful and delicate, and the ministration performed with gradual skill, Ruth thought of her charge and not of herself. As she had foretold, she found a use for all her powers. The poor patients themselves were unconsciously gratified and soothed by her harmony and refinement of manner, voice, and gesture. If this harmony and refinement had been merely superficial, it would not have had this balmy effect. That arose from its being the true expression of a kind, modest, and humble spirit. By degrees her reputation as a nurse spread upwards, and many sought her good offices who could well afford to pay for them. Whatever remuneration was offered to her, she took it simply and without comment : for she felt that it was not hers to refuse ; that it was, in fact, owing to the Bensons for her and her child's subsistence. She went wherever her services were first called for. If the poor bricklayer who broke both his legs in a fall from the scaffolding sent for her when she was disengaged, she went and remained with him until he could spare her, let who would be the next claimant. From the happy and prosperous in all but health, she would occasionally beg off, when some one less happy and more friendless wished for her ; and sometimes she would ask for a little money from Mr Benson to give to such in their time of need. But it was astonishing how much she was able to do without money.

Her ways were very quiet ; she never spoke much. Anyone who has been oppressed with the weight of a vital secret for years, and much more anyone the character of whose life has been stamped by one event, and that producing sorrow and shame, is naturally reserved. And yet Ruth's silence was not like reserve ; it was too gentle and tender for that. It had more the effect of a hush of all loud or disturbing emotions, and out of the deep calm the words that came forth had a beautiful power. She did not talk much about religion ; but those who noticed her knew that it was the unseen banner which she was following. The low-breathed sentences which she spoke into the ear of the sufferer and the dying carried them upwards to God.

She gradually became known and respected among the roughest boys of the rough populace of the town. They would make way for her when she passed along

the streets with more deference than they used to
most ; for all knew something of the tender care with
which she had attended this or that sick person, and,
besides, she was so often in connexion with Death that
something of the superstitious awe with which the dead
were regarded by those rough boys in the midst of
their strong life, surrounded her.

She herself did not feel changed. She felt just as
faulty—as far from being what she wanted to be, as
ever. She best knew how many of her good actions
were incomplete, and marred with evil. She did not
feel much change from the earliest Ruth she could
remember. Everything seemed to change but herself.
Mr and Miss Benson grew old, and Sally grew deaf,
and Leonard was shooting up, and Jemima was a
mother. She and the distant hills that she saw from
her chamber window, seemed the only things which
were the same as when she first came to Eccleston.
As she sat looking out, and taking her fill of solitude,
which sometimes was her most thorough rest—as she
sat at the attic window looking abroad—she saw their
next-door neighbour carried out to sun himself in his
garden. When she first came to Eccleston, this
neighbour and his daughter were often seen taking
long and regular walks ; by and by, his walks became
shorter, and the attentive daughter would convoy him
home, and set out afresh to finish her own. Of late
years he had only gone out in the garden behind his
house ; but at first he had walked pretty briskly there
by his daughter's help—now he was carried, and placed
in a large, cushioned, easy chair, his head remaining
where it was placed against the pillow, and hardly
moving when his kind daughter, who was now middle-
aged, brought him the first roses of the summer. This
told Ruth of the lapse of life and time.

Mr and Mrs Farquhar were constant in their attentions ; but there was no sign of Mr Bradshaw ever for-
giving the imposition which had been practised upon
him, and Mr Benson ceased to hope for any renewal of
their intercourse. Still, he thought that he must know

of all the kind attentions which Jemima paid to them, and of the fond regard which both she and her husband bestowed on Leonard. This latter feeling even went so far that Mr Farquhar called one day, and with much diffidence begged Mr Benson to urge Ruth to let him be sent to school at his (Mr Farquhar's) expense.

Mr Benson was taken by surprise, and hesitated. "I do not know. It would be a great advantage in some respects; and yet I doubt whether it would in others. His mother's influence over him is thoroughly good, and I should fear that any thoughtless allusions to his peculiar position might touch the raw spot in his mind."

"But he is so unusually clever, it seems a shame not to give him all the advantages he can have. Besides, does he see much of his mother now?"

"Hardly a day passes without her coming home to be an hour or so with him, even at her busiest times; she says it is her best refreshment. And often, you know, she is disengaged for a week or two, except the occasional services which she is always rendering to those who need her. Your offer is very tempting, but there is so decidedly another view of the question to be considered, that I believe we must refer it to her."

"With all my heart. Don't hurry her to a decision. Let her weigh it well. I think she will find the advantages preponderate."

"I wonder if I might trouble you with a little business, Mr Farquhar, as you are here?"

"Certainly; I am only too glad to be of any use to you."

"Why, I see from the report of the Star Life Assurance Company in the *Times*, which you are so good as to send me, that they have declared a bonus on the shares; now it seems strange that I have received no notification of it, and I thought that perhaps it might be lying at your office, as Mr Bradshaw was the purchaser of the shares, and I have always received the dividends through your firm."

Mr Farquhar took the newspaper, and ran his eye over the report.

"I've no doubt that's the way of it," said he. "Some of our clerks have been careless about it; or it may be Richard himself. He is not always the most punctual and exact of mortals; but I'll see about it. Perhaps after all it mayn't come for a day or two; they have always such numbers of these circulars to send out."

"Oh! I'm in no hurry about it. I only want to receive it some time before I incur any expenses, which the promise of this bonus may tempt me to indulge in."

Mr Farquhar took his leave. That evening there was a long conference, for, as it happened, Ruth was at home. She was strenuously against the school plan. She could see no advantages that would counterbalance the evil which she dreaded from any school for Leonard; namely, that the good opinion and regard of the world would assume too high an importance in his eyes. The very idea seemed to produce in her so much shrinking affright, that by mutual consent the subject was dropped; to be taken up again, or not, according to circumstances.

Mr Farquhar wrote the next morning, on Mr Benson's behalf, to the Insurance Company, to inquire about the bonus. Although he wrote in the usual formal way, he did not think it necessary to tell Mr Bradshaw what he had done; for Mr Benson's name was rarely mentioned between the partners; each had been made fully aware of the views which the other entertained on the subject that had caused the estrangement; and Mr Farquhar felt that no external argument could affect Mr Bradshaw's resolved disapproval and avoidance of his former minister.

As it happened, the answer from the Insurance Company (directed to the firm) was given to Mr Bradshaw along with the other business letters. It was to the effect that Mr Benson's shares had been sold and transferred above a twelvemonth ago, which sufficiently accounted for the circumstance that no notification of the bonus had been sent to him.

Mr Bradshaw tossed the letter on one side, not displeased to have a good reason for feeling a little contempt at the unbusiness-like forgetfulness of Mr Benson, at whose instance some one had evidently been writing to the Insurance Company. On Mr Farquhar's entrance he expressed this feeling to him.

"Really," he said, "these Dissenting ministers have no more notion of exactitude in their affairs than a child! The idea of forgetting that he has sold his shares, and applying for the bonus, when it seems he had transferred them only a year ago!"

Mr Farquhar was reading the letter while Mr Bradshaw spoke.

"I don't quite understand it," said he. "Mr Benson was quite clear about it. He could not have received his half-yearly dividends unless he had been possessed of these shares; and I don't suppose Dissenting ministers, with all their ignorance of business, are unlike other men in knowing whether or not they receive the money that they believe to be owing to them."

"I should not wonder if they were—if Benson was, at any rate. Why, I never knew his watch to be right in all my life—it was always too fast or too slow; it must have been a daily discomfort to him. It ought to have been. Depend upon it, his money matters are just in the same irregular state; no accounts kept, I'll be bound."

"I don't see that that follows," said Mr Farquhar, half amused. "That watch of his is a very curious one—belonged to his father and grandfather, I don't know how far back."

"And the sentimental feelings which he is guided by prompt him to keep it, to the inconvenience of himself and every one else."

Mr Farquhar gave up the subject of the watch as hopeless.

"But about this letter. I wrote, at Mr Benson's desire, to the Insurance Office, and I am not satisfied with this answer. All the transaction has passed

through our hands. I do not think it is likely Mr
Benson would write and sell the shares without, at any
rate, informing us at the time, even though he forgot
all about it afterwards."

"Probably he told Richard, or Mr Watson."

"We can ask Mr Watson at once. I am afraid we
must wait till Richard comes home, for I don't know
where a letter would catch him."

Mr Bradshaw pulled the bell that rang into the head
clerk's room, saying as he did so,

"You may depend upon it, Farquhar, the blunder
lies with Benson himself. He is just the man to
muddle away his money in indiscriminate charity, and
then to wonder what has become of it."

Mr Farquhar was discreet enough to hold his
tongue.

"Mr Watson," said Mr Bradshaw, as the old clerk
made his appearance, "here is some mistake about
those Insurance shares we purchased for Benson, ten
or a dozen years ago. He spoke to Mr Farquhar
about some bonus they are paying to the shareholders,
it seems; and, in reply to Mr Farquhar's letter, the
Insurance Company say the shares were sold twelve
months since. Have you any knowledge of the
transaction? Has the transfer passed through your
hands? By the way" (turning to Mr Farquhar),
"who kept the certificates? Did Benson or we?"

"I really don't know," said Mr Farquhar. "Perhaps Mr Watson can tell us."

Mr Watson meanwhile was studying the letter.
When he had ended it, he took off his spectacles,
wiped them, and replacing them, he read it again.

"It seems very strange, sir," he said at length,
with his trembling, aged voice, "for I paid Mr Benson
the account of the dividends myself last June, and got
a receipt in form, and that is since the date of the
alleged transfer."

"Pretty nearly twelve months after it took place,"
said Mr Farquhar.

"How did you receive the dividends? An order on

the Bank, along with old Mrs Cranmer's?" asked Mr
Bradshaw, sharply.

"I don't know how they came. Mr Richard gave
me the money, and desired me to get the receipt."

"It's unlucky Richard is from home," said Mr
Bradshaw. "He could have cleared up this mystery
for us."

Mr Farquhar was silent.

"Do you know where the certificates were kept, Mr
Watson?" said he.

"I'll not be sure, but I think they were with Mrs
Cranmer's papers and deeds in box A, 24."

"I wish old Cranmer would have made any other
man his executor. She, too, is always coming with
some unreasonable request or other."

"Mr Benson's inquiry about his bonus is perfectly
reasonable, at any rate."

Mr Watson, who was dwelling in the slow fashion
of age on what had been said before, now spoke:

"I'll not be sure, but I am almost certain, Mr
Benson said, when I paid him last June, that he
thought he ought to give the receipt on a stamp, and
had spoken about it to Mr Richard the time before,
but that Mr Richard said it was of no consequence.
Yes," continued he, gathering up his memory as he
went on, "he did—I remember now—and I thought
to myself that Mr Richard was but a young man. Mr
Richard will know all about it."

"Yes," said Mr Farquhar, gravely.

"I shan't wait till Richard's return," said Mr Bradshaw. "We can soon see if the certificates are in the
box Watson points out; if they are there, the Insurance people are no more fit to manage their concern
than that cat, and I shall tell them so. If they are
not there (as I suspect will prove to be the case), it is
just forgetfulness on Benson's part, as I have said from
the first."

"You forget the payment of the dividends," said
Mr Farquhar, in a low voice.

"Well, sir! what then?" said Mr Bradshaw,

abruptly. While he spoke—while his eye met Mr
Farquhar's—the hinted meaning of the latter flashed
through his mind; but he was only made angry to
find that such a suspicion could pass through anyone's imagination.

"I suppose I may go, sir," said Watson, respectfully, an uneasy consciousness of what was in Mr
Farquhar's thoughts troubling the faithful old clerk.

"Yes. Go. What do you mean about the dividends?" asked Mr Bradshaw, impetuously of Mr
Farquhar.

"Simply, that I think there can have been no forgetfulness—no mistake on Mr Benson's part," said Mr
Farquhar, unwilling to put his dim suspicion into
words.

"Then of course it is some blunder of that confounded Insurance Company. I will write to them
to-day, and make them a little brisker and more
correct in their statements."

"Don't you think it would be better to wait till
Richard's return? He may be able to explain it."

"No, sir!" said Mr Bradshaw, sharply. "I do not
think it would be better. It has not been my way of
doing business to spare anyone, or any company, the
consequences of their own carelessness; nor to obtain
information second-hand when I could have it direct
from the source. I shall write to the Insurance Office
by the next post."

Mr Farquhar saw that any further remonstrance on
his part would only aggravate his partner's obstinacy;
and, besides, it was but a suspicion, an uncomfortable
suspicion. It was possible that some of the clerks at
the Insurance Office might have made a mistake.
Watson was not sure, after all, that the certificates
had been deposited in box A, 24; and when he and
Mr Farquhar could not find them there, the old man
drew more and yet more back from his first assertion
of belief that they had been placed there.

Mr Bradshaw wrote an angry and indignant reproach of carelessness to the Insurance Company.

By the next mail one of their clerks came down to
Eccleston ; and having leisurely refreshed himself at
the inn, and ordered his dinner with care, he walked
up to the great warehouse of Bradshaw and Co., and
sent in his card, with a pencil notification, " On the
part of the Star Insurance Company," to Mr Bradshaw
himself.

Mr Bradshaw held the card in his hand for a minute
or two without raising his eyes. Then he spoke out
loud and firm :

" Desire the gentleman to walk up. Stay ! I will
ring my bell in a minute or two, and then show him
upstairs."

When the errand boy had closed the door, Mr Bradshaw went to a cupboard where he usually kept a glass,
and a bottle of wine (of which he very seldom partook,
for he was an abstemious man). He intended now to
take a glass, but the bottle was empty ; and though
there was plenty more to be had for ringing, or even
simply going into another room, he would not allow
himself to do this. He stood and lectured himself in
thought.

" After all, I am a fool for once in my life. If the
certificates are in no box which I have yet examined,
that does not imply they may not be in some one
which I have not had time to search. Farquhar would
stay so late last night ! And even if they are in none
of the boxes here, that does not prove——" He gave
the bell a jerking ring, and it was yet sounding when
Mr Smith, the insurance clerk, entered.

The manager of the Insurance Company had been
considerably nettled at the tone of Mr Bradshaw's
letter ; and had instructed the clerk to assume some
dignity at first in vindicating (as it was well in his
power to do) the character of the proceedings of the
company, but at the same time he was not to go too
far, for the firm of Bradshaw and Co. was daily looming larger in the commercial world, and if any reasonable explanation could be given it was to be received,
and bygones be bygones.

"Sit down, sir!" said Mr Bradshaw.

"You are aware, sir, I presume, that I come on the part of Mr Dennison, the manager of the Star Insurance Company, to reply in person to a letter of yours, of the 29th, addressed to him?"

Mr Bradshaw bowed. "A very careless piece of business," he said, stiffly.

"Mr Dennison does not think you will consider it as such when you have seen the deed of transfer, which I am commissioned to show you."

Mr Bradshaw took the deed with a steady hand. He wiped his spectacles quietly, without delay, and without hurry, and adjusted them on his nose. It is possible that he was rather long in looking over the document—at least, the clerk had just begun to wonder if he was reading through the whole of it, instead of merely looking at the signature, when Mr Bradshaw said: "It is possible that it may be——of course, you will allow me to take this paper to Mr Benson, to—to inquire if this be his signature?"

"There can be no doubt of it, I think, sir," said the clerk, calmly smiling, for he knew Mr Benson's signature well.

"I don't know, sir—I don't know." (He was speaking as if the pronunciation of every word required a separate effort of will, like a man who has received a slight paralytic stroke.)

"You have heard, sir, of such a thing as forgery—forgery, sir?" said he, repeating the last word very distinctly; for he feared that the first time he had said it, it was rather slurred over.

"Oh, sir! there is no room for imagining such a thing, I assure you. In our affairs we become aware of curious forgetfulness on the part of those who are not of business habits."

"Still I should like to show it Mr Benson, to prove to him his forgetfulness, you know. I believe on my soul it is some of his careless forgetfulness—I do, sir," said he. Now he spoke very quickly. "It must have been. Allow me to convince myself.

You shall have it back to-night, or the first thing in the morning."

The clerk did not quite like to relinquish the deed, nor yet did he like to refuse Mr Bradshaw. If that very uncomfortable idea of forgery should have any foundation in truth—and he had given up the writing! There were a thousand chances to one against its being anything but a stupid blunder; the risk was more imminent of offending one of the directors.

As he hesitated, Mr Bradshaw spoke, very calmly, and almost with a smile on his face. He had regained his self-command. "You are afraid, I see. I assure you, you may trust me. If there has been any fraud— if I have the slightest suspicion of the truth of the surmise I threw out just now"—he could not quite speak the bare naked word that was chilling his heart —"I will not fail to aid the ends of justice, even though the culprit should be my own son."

He ended, as he began, with a smile—such a smile! —the stiff lips refused to relax and cover the teeth. But all the time he kept saying to himself:

"I don't believe it—I don't believe it. I'm convinced it's a blunder of that old fool Benson."

But when he had dismissed the clerk, and secured the piece of paper, he went and locked the door, and laid his head on his desk, and moaned aloud.

He had lingered in the office for the two previous nights; at first, occupying himself in searching for the certificates of the Insurance shares; but, when all the boxes and other repositories for papers had been ransacked, the thought took hold of him that they might be in Richard's private desk; and, with the determination which overlooks the means to get at the end, he had first tried all his own keys on the complicated lock, and then broken it open with two decided blows of a poker, the instrument nearest at hand. He did not find the certificates. Richard had always considered himself careful in destroying any dangerous or tell-tale papers; but the stern father found enough, in what remained, to convince him that his pattern son—

more even than his pattern son, his beloved pride—
was far other than what he seemed.

Mr Bradshaw did not skip or miss a word. He did
not shrink while he read. He folded up letter by
letter; he snuffed the candle just when its light began
to wane, and no sooner; but he did not miss or omit
one paper—he read every word. Then, leaving the
letters in a heap upon the table, and the broken desk
to tell its own tale, he locked the door of the room
which was appropriated to his son as junior partner,
and carried the key away with him.

There was a faint hope, even after this discovery of
many circumstances of Richard's life which shocked
and dismayed his father—there was still a faint hope
that he might not be guilty of forgery—that it might
be no forgery after all—only a blunder—an omission—
a stupendous piece of forgetfulness. That hope was
the one straw that Mr Bradshaw clung to.

Late that night Mr Benson sat in his study. Everyone else in the house had gone to bed; but he was
expecting a summons to someone who was dangerously
ill. He was not startled, therefore, at the knock
which came to the front door about twelve; but he was
rather surprised at the character of the knock, so slow
and loud, with a pause between each rap. His study-
door was but a step from that which led into the street.
He opened it, and there stood—Mr Bradshaw; his
large, portly figure not to be mistaken even in the
dusky night.

He said, "That is right. It was you I wanted to
see." And he walked straight into the study. Mr
Benson followed, and shut the door. Mr Bradshaw
was standing by the table, fumbling in his pocket.
He pulled out the deed; and opening it, after a pause,
in which you might have counted five, he held it out
to Mr Benson.

"Read it!" said he. He spoke not another word until
time had been allowed for its perusal. Then he added:

"That is your signature?" The words were an
assertion, but the tone was that of question.

"No, it is not," said Mr Benson, decidedly. "It is very like my writing. I could almost say it was mine, but I know it is not."

"Recollect yourself a little. The date is August the third, of last year, fourteen months ago. You may have forgotten it." The tone of the voice had a kind of eager entreaty in it, which Mr Benson did not notice, —he was so startled at the fetch*of his own writing.

"It is most singularly like mine; but I could not have signed away these shares—all the property I have—without the slightest remembrance of it."

"Stranger things have happened. For the love of Heaven, think if you did not sign it. It's a deed of transfer for those Insurance shares, you see. You don't remember it? You did not write this name— these words?" He looked at Mr Benson with craving wistfulness for one particular answer. Mr Benson was struck at last by the whole proceeding, and glanced anxiously at Mr Bradshaw, whose manner, gait, and voice were so different from usual that he might well excite attention. But as soon as the latter was aware of this momentary inspection, he changed his tone all at once.

"Don't imagine, sir, I wish to force any invention upon you as a remembrance. If you did not write this name, I know who did. Once more I ask you,—does no glimmering recollection of—having needed money, we'll say—I never wanted you to refuse my subscription to the chapel, God knows !—of having sold these accursed shares?—Oh ! I see by your face you did not write it ; you need not speak to me—I know."

He sank down into a chair near him. His whole figure drooped. In a moment he was up, and standing straight as an arrow, confronting Mr Benson, who could find no clue to this stern man's agitation.

"You say you did not write these words?" pointing to the signature, with an untrembling finger. ' I believe you ; Richard Bradshaw did write them."

"My dear sir—my dear old friend !" exclaimed Mr Benson, "you are rushing to a conclusion for which, I

am convinced, there is no foundation ; there is no
reason to suppose that because——"

"There is reason, sir. Do not distress yourself—I
am perfectly calm." His stony eyes and immovable
face did indeed look rigid. "What we have now to
do is to punish the offence. I have not one standard
for myself and those I love—(and Mr Benson, I did
love him)—and another for the rest of the world. If
a stranger had forged my name, I should have known
it was my duty to prosecute him. You must prosecute
Richard."

"I will not," said Mr Benson.

"You think, perhaps, that I shall feel it acutely.
You are mistaken. He is no longer as my son to me.
I have always resolved to disown any child of mine who
was guilty of sin. I disown Richard. He is as a stranger
to me. I shall feel no more at his exposure—his
punishment——" He could not go on, for his voice
was choking. "Of course, you understand that I
must feel shame at our connexion ; it is that that is
troubling me ; that is but consistent with a man who
has always prided himself on the integrity of his name;
but as for that boy, who has been brought up all his
life as I have brought up my children, it must be some
innate wickedness ! Sir, I can cut him off, though he
has been as my right hand—beloved. Let me be no
hindrance to the course of justice, I beg. He has
forged your name—he has defrauded you of money—of
your all, I think you said."

"Someone has forged my name. I am not convinced that it was your son. Until I know all the
circumstances, I decline to prosecute."

"What circumstances?" asked Mr Bradshaw, in an
authoritative manner, which would have shown irritation but for his self-command.

"The force of the temptation—the previous habits
of the person——"

"Of Richard. He is the person," Mr Bradshaw
put in.

Mr Benson went on, without taking any notice. "I

should think it right to prosecute, if I found out that
this offence against me was only one of a series committed, with premeditation, against society. I should
then feel, as a protector of others more helpless than
myself——"

"It was your all," said Mr Bradshaw.

"It was all my money; it was not my all," replied
Mr Benson; and then he went on as if the interruption had never been: "Against an habitual offender.
I shall not prosecute Richard. Not because he is your
son—do not imagine that! I should decline taking
such a step against any young man without first ascertaining the particulars about him, which I know already
about Richard, and which determine me against doing
what would blast his character for life—would destroy
every good quality he has."

"What good quality remains to him?" asked Mr
Bradshaw. "He has deceived me—he has offended
God."

"Have we not all offended Him?" Mr Benson said,
in a low tone.

"Not consciously. I never do wrong consciously.
But Richard—Richard." The remembrance of the
undeceiving letters—the forgery—filled up his heart
so completely that he could not speak for a minute or
two. Yet when he saw Mr Benson on the point of
saying something, he broke in:

"It is no use talking, sir. You and I cannot agree
on these subjects. Once more, I desire you to prosecute that boy, who is no longer a child of mine."

"Mr Bradshaw, I shall not prosecute him. I have
said it once for all. To-morrow you will be glad that
I do not listen to you. I should only do harm by saying more at present."

There is always something aggravating in being told,
that the mood in which we are now viewing things
strongly will not be our mood at some other time. It
implies that our present feelings are blinding us, and
that some more clear-sighted spectator is able to distinguish our future better than we do ourselves. The

most shallow person dislikes to be told that anyone
can gauge his depth.   Mr Bradshaw was not soothed
by this last remark of Mr Benson's.   He stooped down
to take up his hat and be gone.   Mr Benson saw his
dizzy way of groping, and gave him what he sought
for ; but he received no word of thanks.   Mr Bradshaw
went silently towards the door, but, just as he got
there, he turned round, and said :

"If there were more people like me, and fewer like
you, there would be less evil in the world, sir.   It's
your sentimentalists that nurse up sin."

Although Mr Benson had been very calm during this
interview, he had been much shocked by what had been
let out respecting Richard's forgery ; not by the fact
itself so much as by what it was a sign of.   Still he had
known the young man from childhood, and had seen,
and often regretted, that his want of moral courage had
rendered him peculiarly liable to all the bad effects
arising from his father's severe and arbitrary mode of
treatment.   Dick would never have had "pluck"
enough to be a hardened villain, under any circumstances ; but, unless some good influence, some
strength, was brought upon him, he might easily sink
into the sneaking scoundrel.   Mr Benson determined
to go to Mr Farquhar's the first thing in the morning,
and consult him as a calm, clear-headed family friend—
partner in the business, as well as son and brother-in-
law to the people concerned.

CHAPTER XXXI

WHILE Mr Benson lay awake for fear of oversleeping
himself, and so being late at Mr Farquhar's (it was
somewhere about six o'clock—dark as an October
morning is at that time), Sally came to his door and
knocked.   She was always an early riser : and if she
had not been gone to bed long before Mr Bradshaw's
visit last night, Mr Benson might safely have trusted
to her calling him.

"Here's a woman down below as must see you directly. She'll be upstairs after me if you're not down quick."

"Is it anyone from Clarke's?"

"No, no! not it, master," said she, through the keyhole; "I reckon it's Mrs Bradshaw, for all she's muffled up."

He needed no other word. When he went down, Mrs Bradshaw sat in his easy chair, swaying her body to and fro, and crying without restraint. Mr Benson came up to her, before she was aware that he was there.

"Oh! sir," said she, getting up and taking hold of both his hands, "you won't be so cruel, will you? I have got some money somewhere—some money my father settled on me, sir; I don't know how much, but I think it's more than two thousand pounds, and you shall have it all. If I can't give it you now, I'll make a will, sir. Only be merciful to poor Dick—don't go and prosecute him, sir."

"My dear Mrs Bradshaw, don't agitate yourself in this way. I never meant to prosecute him."

"But Mr Bradshaw says that you must."

"I shall not, indeed. I have told Mr Bradshaw so."

"Has he been here? Oh! is not he cruel? I don't care. I've been a good wife till now. I know I have. I have done all he bid me, ever since we were married. But now I will speak my mind, and say to everybody how cruel he is—how hard to his own flesh and blood! If he puts poor Dick in prison, I will go too. If I'm to choose between my husband and son, I choose my son; for he will have no friends, unless I am with him."

"Mr Bradshaw will think better of it. You will see, that, when his first anger and disappointment are over, he will not be hard or cruel."

"You don't know Mr Bradshaw," said she, mournfully, "if you think he'll change. I might beg and beg—I have done many a time, when we had little

children, and I wanted to save them a whipping—but
no begging ever did any good. At last I left it off.
He'll not change."

"Perhaps not for human entreaty. Mrs Bradshaw,
is there nothing more powerful?"

The tone of his voice suggested what he did not say.

"If you mean that God may soften his heart,"
replied she, humbly, "I'm not going to deny God's
power—I have need to think of Him," she continued,
bursting into fresh tears, "for I am a very miserable
woman. Only think! he cast it up against me last
night, and said, if I had not spoilt Dick this never
would have happened."

"He hardly knew what he was saying, last night.
I will go to Mr Farquhar's directly, and see him; and
you had better go home, my dear Mrs Bradshaw; you
may rely upon our doing all that we can."

With some difficulty he persuaded her not to accompany him to Mr Farquhar's; but he had, indeed, to
take her to her own door before he could convince
her that, at present, she could do nothing but wait the
result of the consultation of others.

It was before breakfast, and Mr Farquhar was alone;
so Mr Benson had a quiet opportunity of telling the
whole story to the husband before the wife came down.
Mr Farquhar was not much surprised, though greatly
distressed. The general opinion he had always entertained of Richard's character had predisposed him to
fear, even before the inquiry respecting the Insurance
shares. But it was still a shock when it came, however
much it might have been anticipated.

"What can we do?" said Mr Benson, as Mr
Farquhar sat gloomily silent.

"That is just what I was asking myself. I think I
must see Mr Bradshaw, and try and bring him a little
out of this unmerciful frame of mind. That must be
the first thing. Will you object to accompany me
at once? It seems of particular consequence that
we should subdue his obduracy before the affair gets
wind."

"I will go with you willingly. But I believe I rather serve to irritate Mr Bradshaw; he is reminded of things he has said to me formerly, and which he thinks he is bound to act up to. However, I can walk with you to the door, and wait for you (if you'll allow me) in the street. I want to know how he is to-day, both bodily and mentally; for indeed, Mr Farquhar, I should not have been surprised last night if he had dropped down dead, so terrible was his strain upon himself."

Mr Benson was left at the door as he had desired, while Mr Farquhar went in.

"Oh, Mr Farquhar, what is the matter?" exclaimed the girls running to him. "Mamma sits crying in the old nursery. We believe she has been there all night. She will not tell us what it is, nor let us be with her; and papa is locked up in his room, and won't even answer us when we speak, though we know he is up and awake, for we heard him tramping about all night."

"Let me go up to him!" said Mr Farquhar.

"He won't let you in. It will be of no use." But in spite of what they said, he went up; and to their surprise, after hearing who it was, their father opened the door, and admitted their brother-in-law. He remained with Mr Bradshaw about half an hour, and then came into the dining-room, where the two girls stood huddled over the fire, regardless of the untasted breakfast behind them; and, writing a few lines he desired them to take his note up to their mother, saying it would comfort her a little, and that he should send Jemima, in two or three hours with the baby—perhaps to remain some days with them. He had no time to tell them more; Jemima would.

He left them, and rejoined Mr Benson. "Come home and breakfast with me. I am off to London in an hour or two, and must speak with you first."

On reaching his house, he ran upstairs to ask Jemima to breakfast alone in her dressing-room, and returned in five minutes or less.

"Now I can tell you about it," said he. "I see my way clearly to a certain point. We must prevent Dick and his father meeting just now, or all hope of Dick's reformation is gone for ever. His father is as hard as the nether mill-stone. He has forbidden me his house."

"Forbidden you!"

"Yes; because I would not give up Dick as utterly lost and bad; and because I said I should return to London with the clerk, and fairly tell Dennison (he's a Scotchman, and a man of sense and feeling) the real state of the case. By the way, we must not say a word to the clerk; otherwise he will expect an answer, and make out all sorts of inferences for himself, from the unsatisfactory reply he must have. Dennison will be upon honour—will see every side of the case—will know you refuse to prosecute; the company of which he is manager are no losers. Well! when I said what I thought wise, of all this—when I spoke as if my course were a settled and decided thing, the grim old man asked me if he was to be an automaton in his own house. He assured me he had no feeling for Dick—all the time he was shaking like an aspen; in short, repeated much the same things he must have said to you last night. However, I defied him; and the consequence is, I'm forbidden the house, and, what is more, he says he will not come to the office while I remain a partner."

"What shall you do?"

"Send Jemima and the baby. There's nothing like a young child for bringing people round to a healthy state of feeling; and you don't know what Jemima is, Mr Benson! No! though you've known her from her birth. If she can't comfort her mother, and if the baby can't steal into her grandfather's heart, why—I don't know what you may do to me. I shall tell Jemima all, and trust to her wit and wisdom to work at this end, while I do my best at the other."

"Richard is abroad, is not he?"

"He will be in England to-morrow. I must catch

him somewhere; but that I can easily do. The difficult point will be, what to do with him—what to say
to him, when I find him. He must give up his partnership, that's clear. I did not tell his father so, but I
am resolved upon it. There shall be no tampering
with the honour of the firm to which I belong."

"But what will become of him?" asked Mr Benson,
anxiously.

"I do not yet know. But, for Jemima's sake—for
his dear old father's sake—I will not leave him adrift.
I will find him some occupation as clear from temptation
as I can. I will do all in my power. And he will do
much better, if he has any good in him, as a freer
agent, not cowed by his father into a want of indi-
viduality and self-respect. I believe I must dismiss
you, Mr Benson," said he, looking at his watch; "I
have to explain all to my wife, and to go to that clerk.
You shall hear from me in a day or two."

Mr Benson half envied the younger man's elasticity
of mind, and power of acting promptly. He himself
felt as if he wanted to sit down in his quiet study, and
think over the revelations and events of the last
twenty-four hours. It made him dizzy even to follow
Mr Farquhar's plans, as he had briefly detailed them;
and some solitude and consideration would be required
before Mr Benson could decide upon their justice and
wisdom. He had been much shocked by the discovery
of the overt act of guilt which Richard had perpe-
trated, low as his opinion of that young man had been
for some time; and the consequence was, that he felt
depressed, and unable to rally for the next few days.
He had not even the comfort of his sister's sympathy,
as he felt bound in honour not to tell her anything;
and she was luckily so much absorbed in some household contest with Sally that she did not notice her
brother's quiet languor.

Mr Benson felt that he had no right at this time to
intrude into the house which he had been once tacitly
forbidden. If he went now to Mr Bradshaw's without
being asked, or sent for, he thought it would seem

like presuming on his knowledge of the hidden disgrace of one of the family. Yet he longed to go: he knew that Mr Farquhar must be writing almost daily to Jemima, and he wanted to hear what he was doing. The fourth day after her husband's departure she came, within half an hour of the post-delivery, and asked to speak to Mr Benson alone.

She was in a state of great agitation, and had evidently been crying very much.

"Oh, Mr Benson!" said she, "will you come with me, and tell papa this sad news about Dick. Walter has written me a letter at last to say he has found him —he could not at first; but now it seems that, the day before yesterday, he heard of an accident which had happened to the Dover coach; it was overturned —two passengers killed, and several badly hurt. Walter says we ought to be thankful, as he is, that Dick was not killed. He says it was such a relief to him on going to the place—the little inn nearest to where the coach was overturned—to find that Dick was only severely injured; not one of those who was killed. But it is a terrible shock to us all. We had had no more dreadful fear to lessen the shock; mamma is quite unfit for anything, and we none of us dare to tell papa." Jemima had hard work to keep down her sobs thus far, and now they overmastered her.

"How is your father? I have wanted to hear every day," asked Mr Benson, tenderly.

"It was careless of me not to come and tell you; but, indeed, I have had so much to do. Mamma would not go near him. He has said something which she seems as if she could not forgive. Because he came to meals, she would not. She has almost lived in the nursery; taking out all Dick's old playthings, and what clothes of his were left, and turning them over, and crying over them."

"Then Mr Bradshaw has joined you again; I was afraid, from what Mr Farquhar said, he was going to isolate himself from you all?"

" I wish he had," said Jemima, crying afresh. " It would have been more natural than the way he has gone on ; the only difference from his usual habits is, that he has never gone near the office, or else he has come to meals just as usual, and talked just as usual ; and even done what I never knew him do before, tried to make jokes—all in order to show us how little he cares."

" Does he not go out at all ?"

" Only in the garden. I am sure he does care after all ; he must care ; he cannot shake off a child in this way, though he thinks he can ; and that makes me so afraid of telling him of this accident. Will you come, Mr Benson ?"

He needed no other word. He went with her, as she rapidly threaded her way through the by-streets. When they reached the house, she went in without knocking, and putting her husband's letter into Mr Benson's hand, she opened the door of her father's room, and saying—" Papa, here is Mr Benson," left them alone.

Mr Benson felt nervously incapable of knowing what to do, or to say. He had surprised Mr Bradshaw sitting idly over the fire—gazing dreamily into the embers. But he had started up, and drawn his chair to the table, on seeing his visitor ; and, after the first necessary words of politeness were over, he seemed to expect him to open the conversation.

" Mrs Farquhar has asked me," said Mr Benson, plunging into the subject with a trembling heart, " to tell you about a letter she has received from her husband " ; he stopped for an instant, for he felt that he did not get nearer the real difficulty, and yet could not tell the best way of approaching it.

" She need not have given you that trouble. I am aware of the reason of Mr Farquhar's absence. I entirely disapprove of his conduct. He is regardless of my wishes ; and disobedient to the commands which, as my son-in-law, I thought he would have felt bound to respect. If there is any more agreeable subject that you can introduce, I shall be glad to hear you, sir."

"Neither you, nor I, must think of what we like to hear or to say. You must hear what concerns your son."

"I have disowned the young man who was my son," replied he, coldly.

"The Dover coach has been overturned," said Mr Benson, stimulated into abruptness by the icy sternness of the father. But, in a flash, he saw what lay below that terrible assumption of indifference. Mr Bradshaw glanced up in his face one look of agony—and then went grey-pale; so livid that Mr Benson got up to ring the bell in affright, but Mr Bradshaw motioned to him to sit still.

"Oh! I have been too sudden, sir—he is alive, he is alive!" he exclaimed, as he saw the ashy face working in a vain attempt to speak; but the poor lips (so wooden, not a minute ago) went working on and on, as if Mr Benson's words did not sink down into the mind, or reach the understanding. Mr Benson went hastily for Mrs Farquhar.

"Oh, Jemima!" said he, "I have done it so badly —I have been so cruel—he is very ill, I fear—bring water, brandy——" and he returned with all speed into the room. Mr Bradshaw—the great, strong, iron man—lay back in his chair in a swoon, a fit.

"Fetch my mother, Mary. Send for the doctor, Elizabeth," said Jemima, rushing to her father. She and Mr Benson did all in their power to restore him. Mrs Bradshaw forgot all her vows of estrangement from the dead-like husband, who might never speak to her, or hear her again, and bitterly accused herself for every angry word she had spoken against him during these last few miserable days.

Before the doctor came, Mr Bradshaw had opened his eyes and partially rallied, although he either did not, or could not speak. He looked struck down into old age. His eyes were sensible in their expression, but had the dim glaze of many years of life upon them.

His lower jaw fell from his upper one, giving a look of melancholy depression to the face, although the lips hid the unclosed teeth. But he answered correctly (in monosyllables, it is true) all the questions which the doctor chose to ask. And the medical man was not so much impressed with the serious character of the seizure as the family, who knew all the hidden mystery behind, and had seen their father lie for the first time with the precursor aspect of death upon his face. Rest, watching, and a little medicine were what the doctor prescribed; it was so slight a prescription, for what had appeared to Mr Benson so serious an attack, that he wished to follow the medical man out of the room to make further inquiries, and learn the real opinion which he thought must lurk behind. But as he was following the doctor, he—they all— were aware of the effort Mr Bradshaw was making to rise, in order to arrest Mr Benson's departure. He did stand up, supporting himself with one hand on the table, for his legs shook under him. Mr Benson came back instantly to the spot where he was. For a moment, it seemed as if he had not the right command of his voice: but at last he said, with a tone of humble, wistful entreaty, which was very touching:

"He is alive, sir, is he not?"

"Yes, sir—indeed he is; he is only hurt. He is sure to do well. Mr Farquhar is with him," said Mr Benson, almost unable to speak for tears.

Mr Bradshaw did not remove his eyes from Mr Benson's face for more than a minute after his question had been answered. He seemed as though he would read his very soul, and there see if he spoke the truth. Satisfied at last, he sank slowly into his chair; and they were silent for a little space, waiting to perceive if he would wish for any further information just then. At length he put his hands slowly together in the clasped attitude of prayer, and said—"Thank God!"

CHAPTER XXXII

IF Jemima allowed herself now and then to imagine
that one good would result from the discovery of
Richard's delinquency, in the return of her father
and Mr Benson to something of their old understanding and their old intercourse—if this hope fluttered
through her mind, it was doomed to disappointment
Mr Benson would have been most happy to go, if
Mr Bradshaw had sent for him; he was on the watch
for what might be even the shadow of such an invitation—but none came. Mr Bradshaw, on his part,
would have been thoroughly glad if the wilful seclusion
of his present life could have been broken by the
occasional visits of the old friend whom he had once
forbidden the house; but this prohibition having passed
his lips, he stubbornly refused to do anything which
might be constructed into unsaying it. Jemima was
for some time in despair of his ever returning to the
office, or resuming his old habits of business. He
had evidently threatened as much to her husband.
All that Jemima could do was to turn a deaf ear to
every allusion to this menace, which he threw out
from time to time, evidently with a view to see if it
had struck deep enough into her husband's mind for
him to have repeated it to his wife. If Mr Farquhar
had named it—if it was known only to two or three
to have been, but for one half hour even, his resolution—Mr Bradshaw could have adhered to it, without any other reason than the maintenance of what
he called consistency, but which was in fact dogged-
ness. Jemima was often thankful that her mother
was absent, and gone to nurse her son. If she had
been at home, she would have entreated and implored
her husband to fall back into his usual habits, and
would have shown such a dread of his being as good
as his word, that he would have been compelled to
adhere to it by the very consequence affixed to it.
Mr Farquhar had hard work, as it was, in passing

rapidly enough between the two places—attending
to his business at Eccleston; and deciding, comforting, and earnestly talking, in Richard's sick-room.
During an absence of his, it was necessary to apply
to one of the partners on some matter of importance;
and accordingly, to Jemima's secret joy, Mr Watson
came up and asked, if her father was well enough
to see him on business? Jemima carried in this inquiry literally; and the hesitating answer which her
father gave was in the affirmative. It was not long before she saw him leave the house, accompanied by the
faithful old clerk; and when he met her at dinner,
he made no allusion to his morning visitor, or to his
subsequent going out. But from that time forwards
he went regularly to the office. He received all the
information about Dick's accident, and his progress
towards recovery, in perfect silence, and in as indifferent a manner as he could assume; but yet he
lingered about the family sitting-room every morning
until the post had come in which brought all letters
from the south.

When Mr Farquhar at last returned to bring the
news of Dick's perfect convalescence, he resolved to
tell Mr Bradshaw all that he had done and arranged
for his son's future career; but, as Mr Farquhar told
Mr Benson afterwards, he could not really say if Mr
Bradshaw had attended to one word that he said.

"Rely upon it," said Mr Benson, "he has not
only attended to it, but treasured up every expression you have used."

"Well, I tried to get some opinion, or sign of
emotion, out of him. I had not much hope of the
latter, I must own; but I thought he would have
said whether I had done wisely or not in procuring
that Glasgow situation for Dick—that he would,
perhaps, have been indignant at my ousting him
from the partnership so entirely on my own responsibility."

"How did Richard take it?"

"Oh, nothing could exceed his penitence. If one

had never heard of the proverb, ' When the devil was sick, the devil a monk would be,'*I should have had greater faith in him ; or if he had had more strength of character to begin with, or more reality and less outward appearance of good principle instilled into him. However, this Glasgow situation is the very thing ; clear, defined duties, no great trust reposed in him, a kind and watchful head, and introductions to a better class of associates than I fancy he has ever been thrown amongst before. For, you know, Mr Bradshaw dreaded all intimacies for his son, and wanted him to eschew all society beyond his own family—would never allow him to ask a friend home. Really, when I think of the unnatural life Mr Bradshaw expected him to lead, I get into charity with him, and have hopes. By the way, have you ever succeeded in persuading his mother to send Leonard to school? He may run the same risk from isolation as Dick : not be able to choose his companions wisely when he grows up, but be too much overcome by the excitement of society to be very discreet as to who are his associates. Have you spoken to her about my plan?"

" Yes! but to no purpose. I cannot say that she would even admit an argument on the subject. She seemed to have an invincible repugnance to the idea of exposing him to the remarks of other boys on his peculiar position."

" They need never know of it. Besides, sooner or later, he must step out of his narrow circle, and encounter remark and scorn."

" True," said Mr Benson, mournfully. " And you may depend upon it, if it really is the best for Leonard, she will come round to it by and by. It is almost extraordinary to see the way in which her earnest and most unselfish devotion to this boy's real welfare leads her to right and wise conclusions."

" I wish I could tame her so as to let me meet her as a friend. Since the baby was born, she comes to see Jemima. My wife tells me, that she sits and holds

it soft in her arms, and talks to it as if her whole soul
went out to the little infant. But if she hears a strange
footstep on the stair, what Jemima calls the 'wild-
animal look' comes back into her eyes, and she steals
away like some frightened creature. With all that she
has done to redeem her character, she should not be so
timid of observation."

"You may well say 'with all that she has done!'
We of our own household hear little or nothing of what
she does. If she wants help, she simply tells us how
and why; but if not—perhaps because it is some relief
to her to forget for a time the scenes of suffering in
which she has been acting the part of comforter, and
perhaps because there always was a shy, sweet reticence
about her—we never should know what she is and what
she does, except from the poor people themselves, who
would bless her in words if the very thought of her did
not choke them with tears. Yet, I do assure you, she
passes out of all this gloom, and makes sunlight in our
house. We are never so cheerful as when she is at
home. She always had the art of diffusing peace, but
now it is positive cheerfulness. And about Leonard;
I doubt if the wisest and most thoughtful schoolmaster
could teach half as much directly, as his mother does
unconsciously and indirectly every hour that he is with
her. Her noble, humble, pious endurance of the consequences of what was wrong in her early life, seems
expressly fitted to act upon him, whose position is
(unjustly, for he has done no harm) so similar to
hers."

"Well! I suppose we must leave it alone for the
present. You will think me a hard practical man when
I own to you, that all I expect from Leonard's remaining a home-bird is that, with such a mother, it will do
him no harm. At any rate, remember my offer is the
same for a year—two years hence, as now. What
does she look forward to making him into, finally?"

"I don't know. The wonder comes into my mind
sometimes; but never into hers, I think. It is part of
her character—part perhaps of that which made her

what she was—that she never looks forward, and
seldom back. The present is enough for her."

And so the conversation ended. When Mr Benson
repeated the substance of it to his sister, she mused
awhile, breaking out into an occasional whistle
(although she had cured herself of this habit in a great
measure), and at last she said :

"Now, do you know, I never liked poor Dick ; and
yet I'm angry with Mr Farquhar for getting him out
of the partnership in such a summary way. I can't get
over it, even though he has offered to send Leonard to
school. And here he's reigning lord-paramount at the
office ! As if you, Thurstan, weren't as well able to
teach him as any schoolmaster in England ! But I
should not mind that affront, if I were not sorry to
think of Dick (though I never could abide him) labouring away in Glasgow for a petty salary of nobody knows
how little, while Mr Farquhar is taking halves, instead
of thirds, of the profits here !"

But her brother could not tell her—and even Jemima
did not know, till long afterwards—that the portion of
income which would have been Dick's as a junior
partner, if he had remained in the business, was carefully laid aside for him by Mr Farquhar ; to be
delivered up, with all its accumulated interest, when
the prodigal should have proved his penitence by his
conduct.

When Ruth had no call upon her time, it was indeed
a holiday at Chapel-house. She threw off as much as
she could of the care and the sadness in which she had
been sharing ; and returned fresh and helpful, ready
to go about in her soft quiet way, and fill up every
measure of service, and heap it with the fragrance of
her own sweet nature. The delicate mending, that
the elder women could no longer see to do, was put by
for Ruth's swift and nimble fingers. The occasional
copying, or patient writing to dictation, that gave rest
to Mr Benson's weary spine, was done by her with
sunny alacrity. But, most of all, Leonard's heart
rejoiced when his mother came home. Then came the

quiet confidences, the tender exchange of love, the happy walks from which he returned stronger and stronger—going from strength to strength as his mother led the way. It was well, as they saw now, that the great shock of the disclosure had taken place when it did. She, for her part, wondered at her own cowardliness in having even striven to keep back the truth from her child—the truth that was so certain to be made clear, sooner or later, and which it was only owing to God's mercy that she was alive to encounter with him, and, by so encountering, shield and give him good courage. Moreover, in her secret heart, she was thankful that all occurred while he was yet too young to have much curiosity as to his father. If an unsatisfied feeling of this kind occasionally stole into his mind, at any rate she never heard any expression of it; for the past was a sealed book between them. And so, in the bright strength of good endeavour, the days went on, and grew again to months and years.

Perhaps one little circumstance which occurred during this time had scarcely external importance enough to be called an event; but in Mr Benson's mind it took rank as such. One day, about a year after Richard Bradshaw had ceased to be a partner in his father's house, Mr Benson encountered Mr Farquhar in the street, and heard from him of the creditable and respectable manner in which Richard was conducting himself in Glasgow, where Mr Farquhar had lately been on business.

"I am determined to tell his father of this," said he; "I think his family are far too obedient to his tacit prohibition of all mention of Richard's name."

"Tacit prohibition?" inquired Mr Benson.

"Oh! I dare say I use the words in a wrong sense for the correctness of a scholar; but what I mean is, that he made a point of immediately leaving the room if Richard's name was mentioned; and did it in so marked a manner, that by degrees they understood that it was their father's desire that he should never be alluded to; which was all very well as long as there

was nothing pleasant to be said about him; but to-night
I am going there, and shall take good care he does not
escape me before I have told him all I have heard and
observed about Richard. He will never be a hero of
virtue, for his education has drained him of all moral
courage; but with care, and the absence of all strong
temptation for a time, he will do very well; nothing
to gratify paternal pride, but certainly nothing to be
ashamed of."

It was on the Sunday after this that the little circumstance to which I have alluded took place.

During the afternoon service, Mr Benson became
aware that the large Bradshaw pew was no longer unoccupied. In a dark corner Mr Bradshaw's white head
was to be seen, bowed down low in prayer. When
last he had worshipped there, the hair on that head
was iron-grey, and even in prayer he had stood erect,
with an air of conscious righteousness sufficient for all
his wants, and even some to spare with which to judge
others. Now, that white and hoary head was never
uplifted; part of his unobtrusiveness might, it is true,
be attributed to the uncomfortable feeling which was
sure to attend any open withdrawal of the declaration
he had once made, never to enter the chapel in which
Mr Benson was minister again; and, as such a feeling
was natural to all men, and especially to such a one as
Mr Bradshaw, Mr Benson instinctively respected it,
and passed out of the chapel with his household, without ever directing his regards to the obscure place
where Mr Bradshaw still remained immovable.

From this day Mr Benson felt sure that the old
friendly feeling existed once more between them,
although some time might elapse before any circumstance gave the signal for a renewal of their intercourse.

CHAPTER XXXIII

OLD people tell of certain years when typhus fever
swept over the country like a pestilence; years that

bring back the remembrance of deep sorrow—refusing
to be comforted—to many a household; and which
those whose beloved passed through the fiery time un-
scathed, shrink from recalling: for great and tremulous
was the anxiety—miserable the constant watching for
evil symptoms; and beyond the threshold of home a
dense cloud of depression hung over society at large.
It seemed as if the alarm was proportionate to the
previous light-heartedness of fancied security—and
indeed it was so; for, since the days of King Belshazzar,* the solemn decrees of Doom have ever seemed
most terrible when they awe into silence the merry
revellers of life. So it was this year to which I come
in the progress of my story.

The summer had been unusually gorgeous. Some
had complained of the steaming heat, but others had
pointed to the lush vegetation, which was profuse and
luxuriant. The early autumn was wet and cold, but
people did not regard it, in contemplation of some
proud rejoicing of the nation, which filled every newspaper and gave food to every tongue. In Eccleston
these rejoicings were greater than in most places; for,
by the national triumph of arms, it was supposed that
a new market for the staple manufacture of the place
would be opened; and so the trade, which had for a
year or two been languishing, would now revive with
redoubled vigour. Besides these legitimate causes of
good spirits, there was the rank excitement of a coming
election, in consequence of Mr Donne having accepted
a Government office, procured for him by one of his
influential relations. This time, the Cranworths roused
themselves from their magnificent torpor of security in
good season, and were going through a series of pompous
and ponderous hospitalities, in order to bring back the
Eccleston voters to their allegiance.

While the town was full of these subjects by turn—
now thinking and speaking of the great revival of trade
—now of the chances of the election, as yet some weeks
distant—now of the balls at Cranworth Court, in which
Mr Cranworth Cranworth had danced with all the belles

of the shopocracy of Eccleston—there came creeping,
creeping, in hidden, slimy courses, the terrible fever—
that fever which is never utterly banished from the sad
haunts of vice and misery, but lives in such darkness,
like a wild beast in the recesses of his den.   It had
begun in the low Irish lodging-houses ;* but there it
was so common it excited little attention.   The poor
creatures died almost without the attendance of the
unwarned medical men, who received their first notice
of the spreading plague from the Roman Catholic
priests.

Before the medical men of Eccleston had had time
to meet together and consult, and compare the knowledge of the fever which they had severally gained, it
had, like the blaze of a fire which had long smouldered,
burst forth in many places at once—not merely among
the loose-living and vicious, but among the decently
poor—nay, even among the well-to-do and respectable.
And, to add to the horror, like all similar pestilences,
its course was most rapid at first, and was fatal in the
great majority of cases—hopeless from the beginning.
There was a cry, and then a deep silence, and then
rose the long wail of the survivors.

A portion of the Infirmary of the town was added to
that already set apart for a fever ward ; the smitten
were carried thither at once, whenever it was possible,
in order to prevent the spread of infection ; and on
that lazar-house was concentrated all the medical skill
and force of the place.

But when one of the physicians had died, in consequence of his attendance—when the customary staff of
matrons and nurses had been swept off in two days—
and the nurses belonging to the Infirmary had shrunk
from being drafted into the pestilential fever-ward—
when high wages had failed to tempt any to what, in
their panic, they considered as certain death—when
the doctors stood aghast at the swift mortality among
the untended sufferers, who were dependent only on
the care of the most ignorant hirelings, too brutal to
recognize the solemnity of Death (all this had happened

within a week from the first acknowledgment of the presence of the plague)—Ruth came one day, with a quieter step than usual, into Mr Benson's study, and told him she wanted to speak to him for a few minutes.

"To be sure, my dear! Sit down!" said he; for she was standing and leaning her head against the chimney-piece, idly gazing into the fire. She went on standing there, as if she had not heard his words; and it was a few moments before she began to speak. Then she said:

"I want to tell you, that I have been this morning and offered myself as matron to the fever-ward while it is so full. They have accepted me; and I am going this evening."

"Oh, Ruth! I feared this; I saw your look this morning as we spoke of this terrible illness."

"Why do you say 'fear,' Mr Benson? You yourself have been with John Harrison, and old Betty, and many others, I dare say, of whom we have not heard."

"But this is so different! in such poisoned air! among such malignant cases! Have you thought and weighed it enough, Ruth?"

She was quite still for a moment, but her eyes grew full of tears. At last she said, very softly, with a kind of still solemnity:

"Yes! I have thought, and I have weighed. But through the very midst of all my fears and thoughts I have felt that I must go."

The remembrance of Leonard was present in both their minds; but for a few moments longer they neither of them spoke. Then Ruth said:

"I believe I have no fear. That is a great pre-servative, they say. At any rate, if I have a little natural shrinking, it is quite gone when I remember that I am in God's hands! Oh, Mr Benson," con-tinued she, breaking out into the irrepressible tears —"Leonard, Leonard!"

And now it was his turn to speak out the brave words of faith.

"Poor, poor mother!" said he. "Be of good heart. He, too, is in God's hands. Think what a flash of time only will separate you from him, if you should die in this work!"

"But he—but he—it will be long to him, Mr Benson! He will be alone!"

"No, Ruth, he will not. God and all good men will watch over him. But if you cannot still this agony of fear as to what will become of him, you ought not to go. Such tremulous passion will predispose you to take the fever."

"I will not be afraid," she replied, lifting up her face, over which a bright light shone, as of God's radiance. "I am not afraid for myself. I will not be so for my darling."

After a little pause, they began to arrange the manner of her going; and to speak of the length of time that she might be absent on her temporary duties. In talking of her return, they assumed it to be certain, although the exact time when was to them unknown, and would be dependent entirely on the duration of the fever; but not the less in their secret hearts, did they feel where alone the issue lay. Ruth was to communicate with Leonard and Miss Faith through Mr Benson alone, who insisted on his determination to go every evening to the Hospital to learn the proceedings of the day, and the state of Ruth's health.

"It is not alone on your account, my dear! There may be many sick people of whom, if I can give no other comfort, I can take intelligence to their friends."

All was settled with grave composure; yet still Ruth lingered, as if nerving herself up for some effort. At length she said, with a faint smile upon her pale face:

"I believe I am a great coward. I stand here talking because I dread to tell Leonard."

"You must not think of it," exclaimed he. "Leave it to me. It is sure to unnerve you."

"I must think of it.   I shall have self-control
enough in a minute to do it calmly—to speak hopefully.   For only think," continued she, smiling
through the tears that would gather in her eyes,
"what a comfort the remembrance of the last few
words may be to the poor fellow, if——" The words
were choked, but she smiled bravely on.   "No!"
said she, "that must be done; but perhaps you will
spare me one thing—will you tell Aunt Faith? I
suppose I am very weak, but, knowing that I must
go, and not knowing what may be the end, I feel as
if I could not bear to resist her entreaties just at last.
Will you tell her, sir, while I go to Leonard?"

Silently he consented, and the two rose up and came
forth, calm and serene.   And calmly and gently did
Ruth tell her boy of her purpose; not daring even to
use any unaccustomed tenderness of voice or gesture,
lest, by so doing, she should alarm him unnecessarily
as to the result.   She spoke hopefully, and bade him
be of good courage; and he caught her bravery,
though his, poor boy! had root rather in his
ignorance of the actual imminent danger than in her
deep faith.

When he had gone down, Ruth began to arrange her
dress.   When she came downstairs she went into the
old familiar garden and gathered a nosegay of the last
lingering autumn flowers—a few roses and the like.

Mr Benson had tutored his sister well; and although
Miss Faith's face was swollen with crying, she spoke
with almost exaggerated cheerfulness to Ruth.   Indeed, as they all stood at the front door, making-
believe to have careless nothings to say, just as at
an ordinary leave-taking, you would not have guessed
the strained chords of feeling there were in each heart.
They lingered on, the last rays of the setting sun
falling on the group.   Ruth once or twice had roused
herself to the pitch of saying "Good-bye," but when
her eye fell on Leonard she was forced to hide the
quivering of her lips, and conceal her trembling mouth
amid the bunch of roses.

" They won't let you have your flowers, I'm afraid,"
said Miss Benson. " Doctors so often object to the
smell."

" No ; perhaps not," said Ruth, hurriedly. " I did
did not think of it. I will only keep this one rose.
Here, Leonard, darling ! " She gave the rest to him.
It was her farewell ; for having now no veil to hide
her emotion, she summoned all her bravery for one
parting smile, and, smiling, turned away. But she
gave one look back from the street, just from the last
point at which the door could be seen, and catching a
glimpse of Leonard standing foremost on the step, she
ran back, and he met her half-way, and mother and
child spoke never a word in that close embrace.

" Now, Leonard," said Miss Faith, " be a brave
boy. I feel sure she will come back to us before
very long."

But she was very near crying herself ; and she
would have given way, I believe, if she had not found
the wholesome outlet of scolding Sally, for expressing
just the same opinion respecting Ruth's proceedings as
she herself had done not two hours before. Taking
what her brother had said to her as a text, she
delivered such a lecture to Sally on want of
faith that she was astonished at herself, and so much
affected by what she had said that she had to shut the
door of communication between the kitchen and the
parlour pretty hastily, in order to prevent Sally's
threatened reply from weakening her belief in the
righteousness of what Ruth had done. Her words
had gone beyond her conviction.

Evening after evening, Mr Benson went forth to
gain news of Ruth ; and night after night he returned
with good tidings. The fever, it is true, raged ; but
no plague came nigh her. He said her face was ever
calm and bright, except when clouded by sorrow as
she gave the accounts of the deaths which occurred in
spite of every care. He said he had never seen her
face so fair and gentle as it was now, when she was
living in the midst of disease and woe.

One evening Leonard (for they had grown bolder as
to the infection) accompanied him to the street on which
the hospital abutted.   Mr Benson left him there, and
told him to return home ; but the boy lingered,
attracted by the crowd that had gathered, and were
gazing up intently towards the lighted windows of the
hospital.   There was nothing beyond to be seen ; but
the greater part of these poor people had friends or
relations in that palace of Death.

Leonard stood and listened.   At first their talk consisted of vague and exaggerated accounts (if such could
be exaggerated) of the horrors of the fever.   Then they
spoke of Ruth—of his mother ; and Leonard held his
breath to hear.

"They say she has been a great sinner, and that this
is her penance," quoth one.   And as Leonard gasped,
before rushing forward to give the speaker straight the
lie, an old man spoke :

"Such a one as her has never been a great sinner ;
nor does she do her work as a penance, but for the love
of God, and of the blessed Jesus.   She will be in the
light of God's countenance when you and I will be
standing afar off.   I tell you, man, when my poor
wench died, as no one would come near, her head lay
at that hour on this woman's sweet breast.   I could
fell you," the old man went on, lifting his shaking
arm, "for calling that woman a great sinner.   The
blessing of them who were ready to perish is upon
her."

Immediately there arose a clamour of tongues, each
with some tale of his mother's gentle doings, till
Leonard grew dizzy with the beatings of his glad,
proud heart.   Few were aware how much Ruth had
done ; she never spoke of it, shrinking with sweet
shyness from over-much allusion to her own work at
all times.   Her left hand truly knew not what her
right hand did ; and Leonard was overwhelmed now to
hear of the love and the reverence with which the poor
and outcast had surrounded her.   It was irrepressible.
He stepped forward with a proud bearing, and touching

the old man's arm, who had first spoken, Leonard tried
to speak ; but for an instant he could not, his heart
was too full : tears came before words, but at length
he managed to say :

"Sir, I am her son !"

"Thou ! thou her bairn ! God bless you, lad," said
an old woman, pushing through the crowd. "It was
but last night she kept my child quiet with singing
psalms the night through. Low and sweet, low and
sweet, they tell me—till many poor things were
hushed, though they were out of their minds, and had
not heard psalms this many a year. God in heaven
bless you, lad !"

Many other wild, woe-begone creatures pressed forward with blessings on Ruth's son, while he could only
repeat :

"She is my mother."

From that day forward Leonard walked erect in the
streets of Eccleston, where "many arose and called
her blessed."*

After some weeks the virulence of the fever abated ;
and the general panic subsided— indeed, a kind of fool-
hardiness succeeded. To be sure, in some instances
the panic still held possession of individuals to an
exaggerated extent. But the number of patients in
the hospital was rapidly diminishing, and, for money,
those were to be found who could supply Ruth's place.
But to her it was owing that the overwrought fear of
the town was subdued ; it was she who had gone volun-
tarily, and, with no thought of greed or gain, right
into the very jaws of the fierce disease. She bade the
inmates of the hospital farewell, and after carefully
submitting herself to the purification recommended by
Mr Davis, the principal surgeon of the place, who had
always attended Leonard, she returned to Mr Benson's
just at gloaming time.

They each vied with the other in the tenderest cares.
They hastened tea ; they wheeled the sofa to the fire ;
they made her lie down ; and to all she submitted with
the docility of a child ; and when the candles came,

even Mr Benson's anxious eye could see no change in
her looks, but that she seemed a little paler. The eyes
were as full of spiritual light, the gently parted lips as
rosy, and the smile, if more rare, yet as sweet as ever.

CHAPTER XXXIV

THE next morning, Miss Benson would insist upon
making Ruth lie down on the sofa. Ruth longed to
do many things; to be much more active; but she
submitted, when she found that it would gratify Miss
Faith if she remained as quiet as if she were really an
invalid.

Leonard sat by her holding her hand. Every now
and then he looked up from his book, as if to make
sure that she indeed was restored to him. He had
brought her down the flowers which she had given him
the day of her departure, and which he had kept in
water as long as they had any greenness or fragrance,
and then had carefully dried and put by. She too,
smiling, had produced the one rose which she had
carried away to the hospital. Never had the bond
between her and her boy been drawn so firm and
strong.

Many visitors came this day to the quiet Chapel-
house. First of all Mrs Farquhar appeared. She
looked very different from the Jemima Bradshaw of
three years ago. Happiness had called out beauty;
the colouring of her face was lovely, and vivid as that
of an autumn day; her berry-red lips scarce closed
over the short white teeth for her smiles; and her
large dark eyes glowed and sparkled with daily happiness. They were softened by a mist of tears as she
looked upon Ruth.

" Lie still ! Don't move ! You must be content
to-day to be waited upon, and nursed ! I have just
seen Miss Benson in the lobby, and had charge upon
charge not to fatigue you. Oh, Ruth ! how we all

love you, now we have you back again ! Do you know,
I taught Rosa to say her prayers as soon as ever you
were gone to that horrid place, just on purpose that
her little innocent lips might pray for you—I wish you
could hear her say it—' Please, dear God, keep Ruth
safe.' Oh, Leonard ! are not you proud of your
mother ? "

Leonard said " Yes," rather shortly, as if he were
annoyed that anyone else should know, or even have
a right to imagine, how proud he was. Jemima went
on :

" Now, Ruth ! I have got a plan for you. Walter
and I have partly made it ; and partly it's papa's doing.
Yes, dear ! papa has been quite anxious to show his
respect for you. We all want you to go to the dear
Eagle's Crag for this next month, and get strong, and
have some change in that fine air at Abermouth. I am
going to take little Rosa there. Papa has lent it to us.
And the weather is often very beautiful in November."

"Thank you very much. It is very tempting ; for
I have been almost longing for some such change. I
cannot tell all at once whether I can go ; but I will see
about it, if you will let me leave it open a little."

"Oh ! as long as you like, so that you will but go at
last. And, Master Leonard ! you are to come too.
Now, I know I have you on my side."

Ruth thought of the place. Her only reluctance
arose from the remembrance of that one interview on
the sands. That walk she could never go again ; but
how much remained ! How much that would be a
charming balm and refreshment to her !

"What happy evenings we shall have together !
Do you know, I think Mary and Elizabeth may perhaps come."

A bright gleam of sunshine came into the room.
"Look ! how bright and propitious for our plans.
Dear Ruth, it seems like an omen for the future ! "

Almost while she spoke, Miss Benson entered,
bringing with her Mr Grey, the rector of Eccleston.
He was an elderly man, short and stoutly-built, with

something very formal in his manner; but anyone might feel sure of his steady benevolence who noticed the expression of his face, and especially of the kindly black eyes that gleamed beneath his grey and shaggy eyebrows. Ruth had seen him at the hospital once or twice, and Mrs Farquhar had met him pretty frequently in general society.

"Go and tell your uncle," said Miss Benson to Leonard.

"Stop, my boy! I have just met Mr Benson in the street, and my errand now is to your mother. I should like you to remain and hear what it is; and I am sure that my business will give these ladies"—bowing to Miss Benson and Jemima—"so much pleasure, that I need not apologize for entering upon it in their presence."

He pulled out his double eyeglass, saying, with a grave smile:

"You ran away from us yesterday so quietly and cunningly, Mrs Denbigh, that you were, perhaps, not aware that the Board was sitting at that very time, and trying to form a vote sufficiently expressive of our gratitude to you. As Chairman, they requested me to present you with this letter, which I shall have the pleasure of reading."

With all due emphasis he read aloud a formal letter from the Secretary to the Infirmary, conveying a vote of thanks to Ruth.

The good rector did not spare her one word, from date to signature; and then, folding the letter up, he gave it to Leonard, saying:

"There, sir! when you are an old man, you may read that testimony to your mother's noble conduct with pride and pleasure. For, indeed," continued he, turning to Jemima, "no words can express the relief it was to us. I speak of the gentlemen composing the Board of the Infirmary. When Mrs Denbigh came forward, the panic was at its height, and the alarm of course aggravated the disorder. The poor creatures died rapidly; there was hardly time to remove the

dead bodies before others were brought in to occupy
the beds, so little help was to be procured on account
of the universal terror ; and the morning when Mrs
Denbigh offered us her services, we seemed at the very
worst.   I shall never forget the sensation of relief in
my mind when she told us what she proposed to do ;
but we thought it right to warn her to the full
extent——

"Nay, madam," said he, catching a glimpse of
Ruth's changing colour, "I will spare you any more
praises.   I will only say, if I can be a friend to you, or
a friend to your child, you may command my poor
powers to the utmost."

He got up, and bowing formally, he took his leave.
Jemima came and kissed Ruth.   Leonard went upstairs to put the precious letter away.   Miss Benson sat
crying heartily in a corner of the room.   Ruth went
to her and threw her arms round her neck, and said :

"I could not tell him just then.   I durst not speak
for fear of breaking down ; but if I have done right, it
was all owing to you and Mr Benson.   Oh ! I wish I
had said how the thought first came into my head from
seeing the things Mr Benson has done so quietly ever
since the fever first came amongst us.   I could not
speak ; and it seemed as if I was taking those praises to
myself, when all the time I was feeling how little I
deserved them—how it was all owing to you."

"Under God, Ruth," said Miss Benson, speaking
through her tears.

"Oh ! I think there is nothing humbles one so much
as undue praise.   While he was reading that letter, I
could not help feeling how many things I had done
wrong !   Could he know of—of what I have been?"
asked she, dropping her voice very low.

"Yes !" said Jemima, "he knew—everybody in
Eccleston did know—but the remembrance of those
days is swept away.   Miss Benson," she continued, for
she was anxious to turn the subject, "you must be on
my side, and persuade Ruth to come to Abermouth for
a few weeks.   I want her and Leonard both to come."

"I'm afraid my brother will think that Leonard is missing his lessons sadly. Just of late we could not wonder that the poor child's heart was so full; but he must make haste, and get on all the more for his idleness." Miss Benson piqued herself on being a disciplinarian.

"Oh, as for lessons, Walter is so very anxious that you should give way to his superior wisdom, Ruth, and let Leonard go to school. He will send him to any school you fix upon, according to the mode of life you plan for him."

"I have no plan," said Ruth. "I have no means of planning. All I can do is to try and make him ready for anything."

"Well," said Jemima, "we must talk it over at Abermouth; for I am sure you won't refuse to come, dearest, dear Ruth! Think of the quiet, sunny days, and the still evenings, that we shall have together, with little Rosa to tumble about among the fallen leaves; and there's Leonard to have his first sight of the sea."

"I do think of it," said Ruth, smiling at the happy picture Jemima drew. And both smiling at the hopeful prospect before them, they parted—never to meet again in life.

No sooner had Mrs Farquhar gone than Sally burst in.

"Oh! dear, dear!" said she, looking around her. "If I had but known that the rector was coming to call, I'd ha' put on the best covers, and the Sunday tablecloth! You're well enough," continued she, surveying Ruth from head to foot; "you're always trim and dainty in your gowns, though I reckon they cost but tuppence a yard, and you've a face to set 'em off; but as for you" (as she turned to Miss Benson), "I think you might ha' had something better on than that old stuff, if it had only been to do credit to a parishioner like me, whom he has known ever sin' my father was his clerk."

"You forget, Sally, I have been making jelly all the

morning. How could I tell it was Mr Grey when there
was a knock at the door?" Miss Benson replied.

"You might ha' letten me do the jelly; I'se warrant
I could ha' pleased Ruth as well as you. If I had but
known he was coming, I'd ha' slipped round the corner
and bought ye a neck-ribbon, or summut to lighten ye
up. I'se loath he should think I'm living with Dissenters, that don't know how to keep themselves trig*
and smart."

"Never mind, Sally; he never thought of me.
What he came for, was to see Ruth; and, as you say,
she's always neat and dainty."

"Well! I reckon it cannot be helped now; but if I
buy ye a ribbon, will you promise to wear it when
church-folks come? for I cannot abide the way they
have of scoffing at the Dissenters about their dress."

"Very well! we'll make that bargain," said Miss
Benson; "and now, Ruth, I'll go and fetch you a cup
of warm jelly."

"Oh! indeed, Aunt Faith," said Ruth, "I am very
sorry to balk you; but, if you're going to treat me as
an invalid, I am afraid I shall rebel."

But when she found that Aunt Faith's heart was set
upon it, she submitted very graciously; only dimpling
up a little, as she found that she must consent to lie on
the sofa, and be fed, when, in truth, she felt full of
health, with a luxurious sensation of languor stealing
over her now and then, just enough to make it very
pleasant to think of the salt breezes, and the sea beauty
which awaited her at Abermouth.

Mr Davis called in the afternoon, and his visit was
also to Ruth. Mr and Miss Benson were sitting with
her in the parlour, and watching her with contented
love, as she employed herself in household sewing, and
hopefully spoke about the Abermouth plan.

"Well! so you had our worthy rector here to-day;
I am come on something of the same kind of errand;
only I shall spare you the reading of my letter, which,
I'll answer for it, he did not. Please to take notice,"
said he, putting down a sealed letter, "that I have

delivered you a vote of thanks from my medical brothers; and open and read it at your leisure; only rest now, for I want to have a little talk with you on my own behoof. I want to ask you a favour, Mrs Denbigh."

"A favour!" exclaimed Ruth; "what can I do for you? I think I may say I will do it, without hearing what it is."

"Then you're a very imprudent woman," replied he; "however, I'll take you at your word. I want you to give me your boy."

"Leonard!"

"Aye! there it is, you see, Mr Benson. One minute she is as ready as can be, and the next, she looks at me as if I was an ogre!"

"Perhaps we don't understand what you mean," said Mr Benson.

"The thing is this. You know I've no children; and I can't say I've ever fretted over it much; but my wife has; and whether it is that she has infected me, or that I grieve over my good practice going to a stranger, when I ought to have had a son to take it after me, I don't know; but, of late, I've got to look with covetous eyes on all healthy boys, and at last I've settled down my wishes on this Leonard of yours, Mrs Denbigh."

Ruth could not speak; for, even yet, she did not understand what he meant. He went on:

"Now, how old is the lad?" He asked Ruth, but Miss Benson replied:

"He'll be twelve next February."

"Umph! only twelve! He's tall and old looking for his age. You look young enough, it is true." He said this last sentence as if to himself, but seeing Ruth crimson up, he abruptly changed his tone.

"Twelve, is he! Well, I take him from now. I don't mean that I really take him away from you," said he, softening all at once, and becoming grave and considerate. "His being your son—the son of one whom I have seen—as I have seen you, Mrs Den-

bigh (out and out the best nurse I ever met with, Miss
Benson ; and good nurses are things we doctors know
how to value)—his being your son is his great recom-
mendation to me ; not but what the lad himself is a
noble boy. I shall be glad to leave him with you as
long and as much as we can ; he could not be tied to
your apron-string all his life, you know. Only I provide for his education, subject to your consent and
good pleasure, and he is bound apprentice to me. I,
his guardian, bind him to myself, the first surgeon in
Eccleston, be the other who he may ; and in process
of time he becomes partner, and some day or other
succeeds me. Now, Mrs Denbigh, what have you got
to say against this plan ? My wife is just as full of it
as me. Come ! begin with your objections. You're
not a woman if you have not a whole bag-full
of them ready to turn out against any reasonable
proposal."

"I don't know," faltered Ruth. "It is so
sudden——"

"It is very, very kind of you, Mr Davis," said Miss
Benson, a little scandalized at Ruth's non-expression
of gratitude.

"Pooh ! pooh ! I'll answer for it, in the long run,
I am taking good care of my own interests. Come,
Mrs Denbigh, is it a bargain ?"

Now Mr Benson spoke.

"Mr Davis, it is rather sudden, as she says. As
far as I can see, it is the best as well as the kindest
proposal that could have been made ; but I think we
must give her a little time to think about it."

"Well, twenty-four hours ! Will that do ?"

Ruth lifted up her head. "Mr Davis, I am not un-
grateful because I can't thank you" (she was crying
while she spoke) ; "let me have a fortnight to consider about it. In a fortnight I will make up my
mind. Oh, how good you all are !"

"Very well. Then this day fortnight—Thursday
the 28th—you will let me know your decision. Mind !
if it's against me, I shan't consider it a decision, for

I'm determined to carry my point. I'm not going to make Mrs Denbigh blush, Mr Benson, by telling you, in her presence, of all I have observed about her this last three weeks, that has made me sure of the good qualities I shall find in this boy of hers. I was watching her when she little thought it. Do you remember that night when Hector O'Brien was so furiously delirious, Mrs Denbigh?"

Ruth went very white at the remembrance.

"Why now, look there! how pale she is at the very thought of it. And yet, I assure you, she was the one to go up and take the piece of glass from him which he had broken out of the window for the sole purpose of cutting his throat, or the throat of anyone else, for that matter. I wish we had some others as brave as she is."

"I thought the great panic was passed away!" said Mr Benson.

"Aye! the general feeling of alarm is much weaker; but, here and there, there are as great fools as ever. Why, when I leave here, I am going to see our precious member, Mr Donne——"

"Mr Donne?" said Ruth.

"Mr Donne, who lies ill at the Queen's—came last week, with the intention of canvassing, but was too much alarmed by what he heard of the fever to set to work; and, in spite of all his precautions, he has taken it; and you should see the terror they are in at the hotel; landlord, landlady, waiters, servants—all; there's not a creature will go near him, if they can help it; and there's only his groom—a lad he saved from drowning, I'm told—to do anything for him. I must get him a proper nurse, somehow or somewhere, for all my being a Cranworth man. Ah, Mr Benson! you don't know the temptations we medical men have. Think, if I allowed your member to die now, as he might very well, if he had no nurse—how famously Mr Cranworth would walk over the course!—Where's Mrs Denbigh gone to? I hope I've not frightened her away by reminding her of Hector O'Brien, and

that awful night, when I do assure you she behaved
like a heroine!"

As Mr Benson was showing Mr Davis out, Ruth
opened the study door, and said, in a very calm, low
voice:

"Mr Benson! will you allow me to speak to Mr
Davis alone?"

Mr Benson immediately consented, thinking that,
in all probability, she wished to ask some further
questions about Leonard; but as Mr Davis came into
the room, and shut the door, he was struck by her
pale, stern face of determination, and awaited her
speaking first.

"Mr Davis! I must go and nurse Mr Bellingham,"
said she at last, clenching her hands tight together,
but no other part of her body moving from its intense
stillness.

"Mr Bellingham?" asked he, astonished at the name.

"Mr Donne, I mean," said she, hurriedly. "His
name was Bellingham."

"Oh! I remember hearing he had changed his
name for some property. But you must not think of
any more such work just now. You are not fit for it.
You are looking as white as ashes."

"I must go," she repeated.

"Nonsense! Here's a man who can pay for the
care of the first hospital nurses in London—and I
doubt if his life is worth the risk of one of theirs even,
much more of yours."

"We have no right to weigh human lives against
each other."

"No! I know we have not. But it's a way we
doctors are apt to get into; and, at any rate, it's
ridiculous of you to think of such a thing. Just listen
to reason."

"I can't! I can't!" cried she, with sharp pain in
her voice. "You must let me go, dear Mr Davis!"
said she, now speaking with soft entreaty.

"No!" said he, shaking his head authoritatively.
"I'll do no such thing."

"Listen ." said she, dropping her voice, and going all over the deepest scarlet; "he is Leonard's father! Now! you will let me go!"

Mr Davis was indeed staggered by what she said, and for a moment he did not speak. So she went on:

"You will not tell! You must not tell! No one knows, not even Mr Benson, who it was. And now— it might do him so much harm to have it known. You will not tell!"

"No! I will not tell," replied he. "But, Mrs Denbigh, you must answer me this one question, which I ask you in all true respect, but which I must ask, in order to guide both myself and you aright—Of course I knew Leonard was illegitimate—in fact, I will give you secret for secret: it was being so myself that first made me sympathize with him, and desire to adopt him. I knew that much of your history; but tell me, do you now care for this man? Answer me truly—do you love him?"

For a moment or two she did not speak; her head was bent down; then she raised it up, and looked with clear and honest eyes into his face.

"I have been thinking—but I do not know—I cannot tell—I don't think I should love him, if he were well and happy—but you said he was ill—and alone—how can I help caring for him?—how can I help caring for him?" repeated she, covering her face with her hands, and the quick hot tears stealing through her fingers. "He is Leonard's father," continued she, looking up at Mr Davis suddenly. "He need not know—he shall not—that I have ever been near him. If he is like the others, he must be delirious—I will leave him before he comes to himself—but now let me go—I must go."

"I wish my tongue had been bitten out before I had named him to you. He would do well enough without you; and, I dare say, if he recognizes you, he will only be annoyed."

"It is very likely!" said Ruth, heavily.

"Annoyed,—why! he may curse you for your un-

asked-for care of him. I have heard my poor mother
—and she was as pretty and delicate a creature as you
are—cursed for showing tenderness when it was not
wanted. Now, be persuaded by an old man like me,
who has seen enough of life to make his heart ache—
leave this fine gentleman to his fate. I'll promise you
to get him as good a nurse as can be had for money."

"No!" said Ruth, with dull persistency—as if she
had not attended to his dissuasions ; "I must go. I
will leave him before he recognizes me."

"Why, then," said the old surgeon, "if you're so
bent upon it, I suppose I must let you. It is but what
my mother would have done—poor, heart-broken
thing! However, come along, and let us make the
best of it. It saves me a deal of trouble, I know ; for,
if I have you for a right hand, I need not worry myself
continually with wondering how he is taken care of.
Go! get your bonnet, you tender-hearted fool of a
woman! Let us get you out of the house without any
more scenes or explanations ; I'll make all straight
with the Bensons."

"You will not tell my secret, Mr Davis," she said,
abruptly.

"No! not I! Does the woman think I had never
to keep a secret of the kind before? I only hope he'll
lose his election, and never come near the place again.
After all," continued he, sighing, "I suppose it is but
human nature!" He began recalling the circumstances of his own early life, and dreamily picturing
scenes in the grey dying embers of the fire ; and he
was almost startled when she stood before him, ready
equipped, grave, pale, and quiet.

"Come along!" said he. "If you're to do any good
at all, it must be in these next three days. After that,
I'll ensure his life for this bout ; and mind! I shall
send you home then ; for he might know you, and I'll
have no excitement to throw him back again, and no
sobbing and crying from you. But now every moment
your care is precious to him. I shall tell my own
story to the Bensons, as soon as I have installed you."

Mr Donne lay in the best room of the Queen's Hotel —no one with him but his faithful, ignorant servant, who was as much afraid of the fever as anyone else could be, but who, nevertheless, would not leave his master—his master who had saved his life as a child, and afterwards put him in the stables at Bellingham Hall, where he learnt all that he knew. He stood in a farther corner of the room, watching his delirious master with affrighted eyes, not daring to come near him, nor yet willing to leave him.

"Oh! if that doctor would but come! He'll kill himself or me—and them stupid servants won't stir a step over the threshold; how shall I get over the night? Blessings on him—here's the old doctor back again! I hear him creaking and scolding up the stairs!"

The door opened, and Mr Davis entered, followed by Ruth.

"Here's the nurse, my good man—such a nurse as there is not in the three counties. Now, all you'll have to do is to mind what she says."

"Oh, sir! he's mortal bad! won't you stay with us through the night, sir?"

"Look there!" whispered Mr Davis to the man, "see how she knows how to manage him! why, I could not do it better myself!"

She had gone up to the wild, raging figure, and with soft authority had made him lie down: and then, placing a basin of cold water by the bedside, she had dipped in it her pretty hands, and was laying their cool dampness on his hot brow, speaking in a low soothing voice all the time, in a way that acted like a charm in hushing his mad talk.

"But I will stay!" said the doctor, after he had examined his patient; "as much on her account as his! and partly to quieten the fears of this poor, faithful fellow."

CHAPTER XXXV

THE third night after this was to be the crisis—the
turning point between Life and Death. Mr Davis
came again to pass it by the bedside of the sufferer.
Ruth was there, constant and still, intent upon watching the symptoms, and acting according to them, in
obedience to Mr Davis's directions. She had never left
the room. Every sense had been strained in watching
—every power of thought or judgement had been kept
on the full stretch. Now that Mr Davis came and took
her place, and that the room was quiet for the night,
she became oppressed with heaviness, which yet did
not tend to sleep. She could not remember the present
time, or where she was. All times of her earliest
youth—the days of her childhood—were in her memory
with a minuteness and fulness of detail which was
miserable; for all along she felt that she had no real
grasp on the scenes that were passing through her
mind—that, somehow, they were long gone by, and
gone by for ever—and yet she could not remember
who she was now, nor where she was, and whether she
had now any interests in life to take the place of those
which she was conscious had passed away, although
their remembrance filled her mind with painful acute-
ness. Her head lay on her arms, and they rested on
the table. Every now and then she opened her eyes,
and saw the large room, handsomely furnished with
articles that were each one incongruous with the other,
as if bought at sales. She saw the flickering night-
light—she heard the ticking of the watch, and the two
breathings, each going on at a separate rate—one
hurried, abruptly stopping, and then panting violently,
as if to make up for lost time; and the other slow,
steady and regular, as if the breather was asleep; but
this supposition was contradicted by an occasional
repressed sound of yawning. The sky through the un-
curtained window looked dark and black—would this
night never have an end? Had the sun gone down for

ever, and would the world at last awaken to a general
sense of everlasting night?

Then she felt as if she ought to get up, and go and
see how the troubled sleeper in yonder bed was
struggling through his illness; but she could not remember who the sleeper was, and she shrunk from
seeing some phantom-face on the pillow, such as now
began to haunt the dark corners of the room, and look
at her, jibbering and mowing as they looked. So she
covered her face again, and sank into a whirling
stupor of sense and feeling. By and by she heard her
fellow-watcher stirring, and a dull wonder stole over
her as to what he was doing; but the heavy languor
pressed her down, and kept her still. At last she
heard the words, "Come here," and listlessly obeyed
the command. She had to steady herself in the rocking chamber before she could walk to the bed by
which Mr Davis stood; but the effort to do so roused
her, and, although conscious of an oppressive headache, she viewed with sudden and clear vision all the
circumstances of her present position. Mr Davis was
near the head of the bed, holding the night-lamp
high, and shading it with his hand, that it might not
disturb the sick person, who lay with his face towards
them, in feeble exhaustion, but with every sign that
the violence of the fever had left him. It so happened
that the rays of the lamp fell bright and full upon
Ruth's countenance, as she stood with her crimson
lips parted with the hurrying breath, and the fever-
flush brilliant on her cheeks. Her eyes were wide
open, and their pupils distended. She looked on the
invalid in silence, and hardly understood why Mr
Davis had summoned her there.

"Don't you see the change? He is better!—the
crisis is past!"

But she did not speak; her looks were riveted on
his softly-unclosing eyes, which met hers as they
opened languidly. She could not stir or speak. She
was held fast by that gaze of his, in which a faint
recognition dawned, and grew to strength.

He murmured some words. They strained their
sense to hear. He repeated them even lower than
before; but this time they caught what he was
saying.

"Where are the water-lilies? Where are the lilies
in her hair?"

Mr Davis drew Ruth away.

"He is still rambling," said he, "but the fever has
left him."

The grey dawn was now filling the room with its
cold light; was it that made Ruth's cheek so deadly
pale? Could that call out the wild entreaty of her
look, as if imploring help against some cruel foe that
held her fast, and was wrestling with her Spirit of
Life? She held Mr Davis's arm. If she had let it go,
she would have fallen.

"Take me home," she said, and fainted dead away.

Mr Davis carried her out of the chamber, and sent
the groom to keep watch by his master. He ordered
a fly to convey her to Mr Benson's, and lifted her in
when it came, for she was still half unconscious. It
was he who carried her upstairs to her room; where
Miss Benson and Sally undressed and laid her in her
bed.

He awaited their proceedings in Mr Benson's study.
When Mr Benson came in, Mr Davis said:

"Don't blame me. Don't add to my self-reproach.
I have killled her. I was a cruel fool to let her go.
Don't speak to me."

"It may not be so bad," said Mr Benson, himself
needing comfort in that shock. "She may recover.
She surely will recover. I believe she will."

"No, no! she won't. But by —— she shall, if I
can save her." Mr Davis looked defiantly at Mr Benson, as if he were Fate. "I tell you she shall recover,
or else I am a murderer. What business had I to take
her to nurse him——"

He was cut short by Sally's entrance, and announce-
ment that Ruth was now prepared to see him.

From that time forward Mr Davis devoted all his

leisure, his skill, his energy to save her. He called
on the rival surgeon to beg him to undertake the
management of Mr Donne's recovery, saying, with his
usual self-mockery, "I could not answer it to Mr
Cranworth if I had brought his opponent round, you
know, when I had had such a fine opportunity in my
power. Now, with your patients, and general Radical
interest, it will be rather a feather in your cap ; for
he may want a good deal of care yet, though he is
getting on famously—so rapidly, in fact, that it's a
strong temptation to me to throw him back—a relapse,
you know."

The other surgeon bowed gravely, apparently taking
Mr Davis in earnest, but certainly very glad of the
job thus opportunely thrown in his way. In spite of
Mr Davis's real and deep anxiety about Ruth, he
could not help chuckling over his rival's literal inter-
pretation of all he had said.

"To be sure, what fools men are ! I don't know
why one should watch and strive to keep them in the
world. I have given this fellow something to talk
about confidentially to all his patients ; I wonder how
much stronger a dose the man would have swallowed !
I must begin to take care of my practice for that lad
yonder. Well-a-day ! well-a-day ! What was this sick
fine gentleman sent here for, that she should run a
chance of her life for him? or why was he sent into
the world at all, for that matter ?"

Indeed, however much Mr Davis might labour with
all his professional skill—however much they might
all watch—and pray—and weep—it was but too evident that Ruth "home must go, and take her wages."*
Poor, poor Ruth !

It might be that, utterly exhausted by watching and
nursing, first in the hospital, and then by the bedside
of her former lover, the power of her constitution was
worn out ; or, it might be, her gentle, pliant sweetness, but she displayed no outrage or discord even in
her delirium. There she lay in the attic room in
which her baby had been born, her watch over him

kept, her confession to him made; and now she was stretched on the bed in utter helplessness, softly gazing at vacancy with her open, unconscious eyes, from which all the depth of their meaning had fled, and all they told was of a sweet, childlike insanity within. The watchers could not touch her with their sympathy, or come near her in her dim world;—so, mutely, but looking at each other from time to time with tearful eyes, they took a poor comfort from the one evident fact that, though lost and gone astray, she was happy and at peace. They had never heard her sing; indeed the simple art which her mother had taught her, had died, with her early joyousness, at that dear mother's death. But now she sang continually, very soft and low. She went from one childish ditty to another without let or pause, keeping a strange sort of time with her pretty fingers, as they closed and unclosed themselves upon the counterpane. She never looked at anyone with the slightest glimpse of memory or intelligence in her face; no, not even at Leonard.

Her strength faded day by day; but she knew it not. Her sweet lips were parted to sing, even after the breath and the power to do so had left her, and her fingers fell idly on the bed. Two days she lingered thus—all but gone from them, and yet still there.

They stood around her bedside, not speaking, or sighing, or moaning; they were too much awed by the exquisite peacefulness of her look for that. Suddenly she opened wide her eyes, and gazed intently forwards, as if she saw some happy vision, which called out a lovely, rapturous, breathless smile. They held their very breaths.

"I see the Light coming," said she. "The Light is coming," she said. And, raising herself slowly, she stretched out her arms, and then fell back, very still for evermore.

They did not speak. Mr Davis was the first to utter a word.

" It is over ! " said he.   " She is dead ! "

Outrang through the room the cry of Leonard :

" Mother ! mother ! mother !   You have not left me alone !   You will not leave me alone !   You are not dead !   Mother !   Mother ! "

They had pent in his agony of apprehension till then, that no wail of her child might disturb her ineffable calm.   But now there was a cry heard through the house, of one refusing to be comforted : " Mother ! Mother ! "

But Ruth lay dead.

CHAPTER XXXVI

A STUPOR of grief succeeded to Leonard's passionate cries.   He became so much depressed, physically as well as mentally, before the end of the day, that Mr Davis was seriously alarmed for the consequences. He hailed with gladness a proposal made by the Farquhars, that the boy should be removed to their house, and placed under the fond care of his mother's friend, who sent her own child to Abermouth the better to devote herself to Leonard.

When they told him of this arrangement, he at first refused to go and leave *her*; but when Mr Benson said: " *She* would have wished it, Leonard !   Do it for her sake ! " he went away very quietly ; not speaking a word, after Mr Benson had made the voluntary promise that he should see her once again.   He neither spoke nor cried for many hours ; and all Jemima's delicate wiles were called forth, before his heavy heart could find the relief of tears.   And then he was so weak, and his pulse so low, that all who loved him feared for his life.

Anxiety about him made a sad distraction from the sorrow for the dead.   The three old people who now formed the household in the Chapel-house, went about slowly and dreamily, each with a dull wonder at their

hearts why they, the infirm and worn-out, were left,
while she was taken in her lovely prime.

The third day after Ruth's death, a gentleman came
to the door and asked to speak to Mr Benson. He was
very much wrapped up in furs and cloaks, and the
upper exposed part of his face was sunk and hollow,
like that of one but partially recovered from illness.
Mr and Miss Benson were at Mr Farquhar's, gone to
see Leonard, and poor old Sally had been having a
hearty cry over the kitchen fire before answering the
door-knock. Her heart was tenderly inclined just then
towards anyone who had the aspect of suffering ; so,
although her master was out, and she was usually chary
of admitting strangers, she proposed·to Mr Donne (for
it was he) that he should come in and await Mr Benson's return in the study. He was glad enough to
avail himself of her offer ; for he was feeble and
nervous, and come on a piece of business which he exceedingly disliked, and about which he felt very
awkward. The fire was nearly, if not quite, out ; nor
did Sally's vigorous blows do much good, although she
left the room with an assurance that it would soon burn
up. He leant against the chimney-piece, thinking over
events, and with a sensation of discomfort, both external and internal, growing and gathering upon him.
He almost wondered whether the proposal he meant to
make with regard to Leonard could not be better
arranged by letter than by an interview. He became
very shivery, and impatient of the state of indecision
to which his bodily weakness had reduced him.

Sally opened the door, and came in. "Would you
like to walk upstairs, sir?" asked she, in a trembling
voice, for she had learnt who the visitor was from the
driver of the fly, who had run up to the house to
inquire what was detaining the gentleman that he had
brought from the Queen's Hotel ; and, knowing that
Ruth had caught the fatal fever from her attendance
on Mr Donne, Sally imagined that it was but a piece of
sad civility to invite him upstairs to see the poor dead
body, which she had laid out and decked for the grave,

with such fond care that she had grown strangely proud
of its marble beauty.

Mr Donne was glad enough of any proposal of a
change from the cold and comfortless room where he
had thought uneasy, remorseful thoughts. He fancied
that a change of place would banish the train of reflection that was troubling him; but the change he anticipated was to a well-warmed, cheerful sitting-room,
with signs of life, and a bright fire therein; and he was
on the last flight of stairs,—at the door of the room
where Ruth lay—before he understood whither Sally
was conducting him. He shrank back for an instant,
and then a strange sting of curiosity impelled him on.
He stood in the humble low-roofed attic, the window
open, and the tops of the distant snow-covered hills
filling up the whiteness of the general aspect. He
muffled himself up in his cloak, and shuddered, while
Sally reverently drew down the sheet, and showed the
beautiful, calm, still face, on which the last rapturous
smile still lingered, giving an ineffable look of bright
serenity. Her arms were crossed over her breast; the
wimple-like cap marked the perfect oval of her face,
while two braids of the waving auburn hair peeped
out of the narrow border, and lay on the delicate
cheeks.

He was awed into admiration by the wonderful
beauty of that dead woman.

"How beautiful she is!" said he, beneath his
breath. "Do all dead people look so peaceful—so
happy?"

"Not all," replied Sally, crying. "Few has been
as good and as gentle as she was in their lives." She
quite shook with her sobbing.

Mr Donne was disturbed by her distress.

"Come, my good woman! we must all die——" he
did not know wnat to say, and was becoming infected
by her sorrow. "I am sure you loved her very much,
and were very kind to her in her lifetime; you must
take this from me to buy yourself some remembrance
of her." He had pulled out a sovereign, and really

2 f*

had a kindly desire to console her, and reward her, in offering it to her.

But she took her apron from her eyes, as soon as she became aware of what he was doing, and, still holding it midway in her hands, she looked at him indignantly, before she burst out:

"And who are you, that think to pay for my kindness to her by money? And I was not kind to you, my darling," said she, passionately addressing the motionless, serene body—"I was not kind to you. I frabbed you, and plagued you from the first, my lamb! I came and cut off your pretty locks in this very room —I did—and you said never an angry word to me ;— no! not then, nor many a time at after, when I was very sharp and cross to you.—No! I never was kind to you, and I dunnot think the world was kind to you, my darling,—but you are gone where the angels are very tender to such as you—you are, my poor wench!" She bent down and kissed the lips, from whose marble, unyielding touch Mr Donne recoiled, even in thought.

Just then, Mr Benson entered the room. He had returned home before his sister, and come upstairs in search of Sally, to whom he wanted to speak on some subject relating to the funeral. He bowed in recognition of Mr Donne, whom he knew as the member for the town, and whose presence impressed him painfully, as his illness had been the proximate cause of Ruth's death   But he tried to check this feeling, as it was no fault of Mr Donne's. Sally stole out of the room, to cry at leisure in her kitchen.

"I must apologize for being here," said Mr Donne. "I was hardly conscious where your servant was leading me to, when she expressed her wish that I should walk upstairs."

"It is a very common idea in this town, that it is a gratification to be asked to take a last look at the dead," replied Mr Benson.

"And in this case, I am glad to have seen her once more," said Mr Donne. "Poor Ruth!"

Mr Benson glanced up at him at the last word. How did he know her name? To him she had only been Mrs Denbigh. But Mr Donne had no idea that he was talking to one unaware of the connexion that had formerly existed between them; and, though he would have preferred carrying on the conversation in a warmer room, yet, as Mr Benson was still gazing at her with sad, lingering love, he went on:

"I did not recognize her when she came to nurse me; I believe I was delirious. My servant, who had known her long ago, in Fordham, told me who she was. I cannot tell how I regret that she should have died in consequence of her love of me."

Mr Benson looked up at him again, a stern light filling his eyes as he did so. He waited impatiently to hear more, either to quench or confirm his suspicions. If she had not been lying there, very still and calm, he would have forced the words out of Mr Donne, by some abrupt question. As it was, he listened silently, his heart quick-beating.

"I know that money is but a poor compensation,— is no remedy for this event, or for my youthful folly."

Mr Benson set his teeth hard together, to keep in words little short of a curse.

"Indeed, I offered her money to almost any amount before;—do me justice, sir," catching the gleam of indignation on Mr Benson's face: "I offered to marry her, and provide for the boy as if he had been legitimate. It's of no use recurring to that time," said he, his voice faltering; "what is done cannot be undone. But I came now to say, that I should be glad to leave the boy still under your charge, and that every expense you think it right to incur in his education I will defray;—and place a sum of money in trust for him —say, two thousand pounds—or more. fix what you will. Of course, if you decline retaining him, I must find some one else; but the provision for him shall be the same, for my poor Ruth's sake."

Mr Benson did not speak. He could not, till he

had gathered some peace from looking at the ineffable repose of the Dead.

Then, before he answered, he covered up her face; and in his voice there was the stillness of ice.

"Leonard is not unprovided for. Those that honoured his mother will take care of him. He shall never touch a penny of your money. Every offer of service you have made, I reject in his name, —and in her presence," said he, bending towards the Dead. "Men may call such actions as yours, youthful follies! There is another name for them with God. Sir! I will follow you downstairs."

All the way down, Mr Benson heard Mr Donne's voice urging and entreating, but the words he could not recognize for the thoughts that filled his brain— the rapid putting together of events that was going on there. And when Mr Donne turned at the door, to speak again, and repeat his offers of service to Leonard, Mr Benson made answer, without well knowing whether the answer fitted the question or not:

"I thank God, you have no right, legal or other-wise, over the child. And for her sake, I will spare him the shame of ever hearing your name as his father."

He shut the door in Mr Donne's face.

"An ill-bred, puritanical old fellow! He may have the boy, I am sure, for aught I care. I have done my duty, and will get out of this abomin-able place as soon as I can. I wish my last remem-brance of my beautiful Ruth was not mixed up with all these people."

Mr Benson was bitterly oppressed with this inter-view; it disturbed the peace with which he was beginning to contemplate events. His anger ruffled him, although such anger had been just, and such indignation well deserved; and both had been uncon-sciously present in his heart for years against the unknown seducer, whom he met face to face by the death-bed of Ruth.

It gave him a shock which he did not recover from for many days. He was nervously afraid lest Mr Donne should appear at the funeral; and not all the reasons he alleged to himself against this apprehension, put it utterly away from him. Before then, however, he heard casually (for he would allow himself no inquiries) that he had left the town. No! Ruth's funeral passed over in calm and simple solemnity. Her child, her own household, her friend, and Mr Farquhar, quietly walked after the bier, which was borne by some of the poor to whom she had been very kind in her lifetime. And many others stood aloof in the little burying-ground, sadly watching that last ceremony.

They slowly dispersed; Mr Benson leading Leonard by the hand, and secretly wondering at his self-restraint. Almost as soon as they had let themselves into the Chapel-house, a messenger brought a note from Mrs Bradshaw, with a pot of quince marmalade, which, she said to Miss Benson, she thought that Leonard might fancy, and if he did, they were to be sure and let her know, as she had plenty more; or, was there anything else that he would like? She would gladly make him whatever he fancied.

Poor Leonard! he lay stretched on the sofa, white and tearless, beyond the power of any such comfort, however kindly offered; but this was only one of the many homely, simple attentions, which all came round him to offer, from Mr Grey, the rector, down to the nameless poor who called at the back door to inquire how it fared with *her* child.

Mr Benson was anxious, according to Dissenting custom, to preach an appropriate funeral sermon. It was the last office he could render to her; it should be done well and carefully. Moreover, it was possible that the circumstances of her life, which were known to all, might be made effective in this manner to work conviction of many truths. Accordingly, he made great preparation of thought and paper; he laboured hard, destroying sheet after sheet—his eyes filling with

tears between-whiles, as he remembered some fresh
proof of the humility and sweetness of her life. Oh,
that he could do her justice ! but words seemed hard
and inflexible, and refused to fit themselves to his
ideas. He sat late on Saturday, writing ; he watched
through the night till Sunday morning was far advanced. He had never taken such pains with any
sermon, and he was only half satisfied with it after
all.

Mrs Farquhar had comforted the bitterness of Sally's
grief by giving her very handsome mourning. At any
rate, she felt oddly proud and exulting when she
thought of her new black gown ; but when she remembered why she wore it, she scolded herself pretty
sharply for her satisfaction, and took to crying afresh
with redoubled vigour. She spent the Sunday morning in alternately smoothing down her skirts, and
adjusting her broad hemmed collar, or bemoaning the
occasion with tearful earnestness. But the sorrow
overcame the little quaint vanity of her heart, as she
saw troop after troop of humbly-dressed mourners pass
by into the old chapel. They were very poor—but
each had mounted some rusty piece of crape, or some
faded black ribbon. The old came halting and slow—
the mothers carried their quiet, awe-struck babes.

And not only these were there—but others—equally
unaccustomed to nonconformist worship : Mr Davis,
for instance, to whom Sally acted as chaperone ; for
he sat in the minister's pew, as a stranger ; and, as
she afterwards said, she had a fellow-feeling with him,
being a Church-woman herself, and Dissenters had
such awkward ways ; however, she had been there
before, so she could set him to rights about their
fashions.

From the pulpit, Mr Benson saw one and all—the
well-filled Bradshaw pew—all in deep mourning, Mr
Bradshaw conspicuously so (he would have attended
the funeral gladly if they would have asked him)—
the Farquhars—the many strangers—the still more
numerous poor—one or two wild-looking outcasts, who

stood afar off, but wept silently and continually. Mr Benson's heart grew very full.

His voice trembled as he read and prayed. But he steadied it as he opened his sermon—his great, last effort in her honour—the labour that he had prayed God to bless to the hearts of many. For an instant the old man looked on all the upturned faces, listening, with wet eyes, to hear what he could say to interpret that which was in their hearts, dumb and unshaped, of God's doings as shown in her life. He looked, and, as he gazed, a mist came before him, and he could not see his sermon, nor his hearers, but only Ruth, as she had been—stricken low, and crouching from sight, in the upland field by Llan-dhu — like a woeful, hunted creature. And now her life was over! her struggle ended! Sermon and all was forgotten. He sat down, and hid his face in his hands for a minute or so. Then he arose, pale and serene. He put the sermon away, and opened the Bible, and read the seventh chapter of Revelations,* beginning at the ninth verse.

Before it was finished, most of his hearers were in tears. It came home to them as more appropriate than any sermon could have been. Even Sally, though full of anxiety as to what her fellow-Churchman would think of such proceedings, let the sobs come freely as she heard the words :

" And he said to me, These are they which came out of great tribulation, and have washed their robes, and made them white in the blood of the Lamb.

" Therefore are they before the throne of God, and serve him day and night in his temple ; and he that sitteth on the throne shall dwell among them.

" They shall hunger no more, neither thirst any more ; neither shall the sun light on them, nor any heat.

" For the Lamb which is in the midst of the throne shall feed them, and shall lead them unto living fountains of waters, and God shall wipe away all tears from their eyes."

"He preaches sermons sometimes," said Sally, nudging Mr Davis, as they rose from their knees at last. "I make no doubt there was as grand a sermon in yon paper-book as ever we hear in church. I've heard him pray uncommon fine—quite beyond any but learned folk."

Mr Bradshaw had been anxious to do something to testify his respect for the woman, who, if all had entertained his opinions, would have been driven into hopeless sin. Accordingly, he ordered the first stone-mason of the town to meet him in the chapel-yard on Monday morning, to take measurement and receive directions for a tombstone. They threaded their way among the grassy heaps to where Ruth was buried, in the south corner, beneath the great Wych-elm. When they got there, Leonard raised himself up from the new-stirred turf. His face was swollen with weeping; but when he saw Mr Bradshaw he calmed himself, and checked his sobs, and, as an explanation of being where he was when thus surprised, he could find nothing to say but the simple words:

"My mother is dead, sir."

His eyes sought those of Mr Bradshaw with a wild look of agony, as if to find comfort for that great loss in human sympathy; and at the first word—the first touch of Mr Bradshaw's hand on his shoulder—he burst out afresh.

"Come, come! my boy!—Mr Francis, I will see you about this to-morrow—I will call at your house.—Let me take you home, my poor fellow. Come, my lad, come!"

The first time, for years, that he had entered Mr Benson's house, he came leading and comforting her son—and, for a moment, he could not speak to his old friend, for the sympathy which choked up his voice, and filled his eyes with tears.

THE END.

EXPLANATORY NOTES

IT was Mrs Gaskell's writing practice to refer, with varying degrees of accuracy, to a wide range of popular, literary and biblical sources. Sometimes she indicates that she has done so: more often she simply absorbs these references into her text. For the purposes of this edition I have adopted the general principle of attempting to identify only those references to which she draws attention by her use of quotation marks. In this I have been greatly helped by the work of Dr Michael Wheeler of the University of Lancaster, whose Ph.D. thesis, *Elizabeth Gaskell's use of literary sources in 'Mary Barton' and 'Ruth'* (University of London, 1975), is a mine of information on this aspect of Mrs Gaskell's work. Where a note would not have been possible without Dr Wheeler's specialist knowledge I have appended his initials (MW). I should also acknowledge the help I have received from Mr Glynn Morris, the Revd William Strachan and Mrs Marjorie Cox in particular amongst the many friends and colleagues who have responded to my queries.

iii *Title-page*: Mrs Gaskell takes as her motto Phineas Fletcher's 'Hymne', from *Poetical Miscellanies* (1633).

1 *an assize-town in one of the eastern counties*: throughout *Ruth* Mrs Gaskell fictionalizes her locations, but often only thinly. In this case I suspect the reference is to Chelmsford, the nearest town to the Essex home of the Shaen family, with whom she stayed on several occasions, although the details of the description are in all probability imaginary.

2 *before Mr Pitt's days of taxation*: Pitt's Commutation Act of 1784 substantially reshaped the tax system. Notably it reduced tea-duty and in compensation increased the direct tax on windows in houses to an extent that seriously affected wealthy householders. As a consequence large houses built after this time tended to have fewer windows.

3 *now many years ago*: this is perhaps misleading. At this point Mrs Gaskell is imprecise about the dating of the action, but the election described in Chapter 21 would seem to have taken place under the provisions of the 1832 Reform Bill (see note to p. 249), while there are references later in the novel to rail travel (e.g., in Chapter 23) which confirm that the action cannot have been earlier than the late 1830s.

7 *Monnoyer*: Jean-Baptiste Monnoyer (1635–99), a French painter

famous for his paintings of fruit and flowers. As well as the Palace of Versailles he decorated a number of historic houses in England: there are several of his designs, for example, at Hampton Court.

8 *"Oh! how shall I get through five years of these terrible nights! . . ."*: the situation of milliners' apprentices attracted considerable comment in mid-Victorian England: they were a byword for both the hardships of their work and their exposure to temptation. Mrs Gaskell had approached the subject in her first novel, *Mary Barton*, where the heroine's aunt, herself a woman of the streets, says of her becoming a dressmaker's apprentice: 'I began to be frightened for her; for it's a bad life for a girl to be out late at night in the streets, and, after many an hour of weary work, they're ready to follow after any novelty that makes a little change.' (*Mary Barton*, Chapter 14) The remark is prophetic of Ruth Hilton's fate. On this issue see Wanda Neff, *Victorian Working Women* (London, 1929).

18 *grey satin pelisse*: a pelisse was a woman's over-garment, reaching to the ankles and with armholes rather than sleeves.

21 *craddy*: a difficult or dangerous feat (dial.). *The English Dialect Dictionary* records this as a usage found in Yorkshire, Lancashire, Cheshire and Lincolnshire, but not in Essex: Mrs Gaskell has perhaps erred in translating a predominantly northern term to her 'eastern' county.

28 *Alnaschar visions*: a popular nineteenth-century reference. Alnaschar was a figure of legend who invested all his money in glassware, in the belief that by trading upon it he would become rich enough to marry a vizier's daughter. While dreaming about his future he overturned his basket of goods, thus destroying his own prospects.

31 *to recruit*: i.e., to recuperate. This usage has now effectively disappeared.

33 *agaceries*: flirtatious behaviour.

37 *the gold mines of Potosi*: Potosi was a region in Bolivia famous since the discovery of the Americas for its mines, notably of silver but also of gold.

40 *the Leasowes*: strictly applied, the term denotes pasture or grazing-land.

"February fill-dyke": the phrase is proverbial. A possible source is Thomas Tusser (1524–80), *February's Husbandry*:

> Feb, fill the dyke
> With what thou dost like.

41 *Mrs Brownrigg*: Elizabeth Brownrigg, a midwife and workhouse overseer, who was hanged in 1767 for the murder of an apprentice

whom she had maltreated. Various accounts of her career circulated in the eighteenth and nineteeth centuries.

46 *"Why art thou so vexed . . .?"; "O put thy trust in God . . .":* Psalms 43:5. Mrs Gaskell's rendering of the text differs slightly from that of the Prayer Book, from which, as she says, the old man is reading, but is closer to it than it is to that of the Authorized Version.

47 *"blood of all the Howards":* i.e., noble birth. Pope, *Essay on Man,* IV. lines 215–16:

> What can ennoble sots, or slaves, or cowards?
> Alas! not all the blood of all the Howards.

48 *shovel-board:* a table on which the game of shovel-board, or shove-halfpenny, was played. Here the term simply means a plain smooth table.

50 *manty-maker's:* From 'mantua-maker', an archaic term for a dressmaker, deriving from the term 'mantua', the name given to a type of silk from which dresses were sometimes made, and hence to the dresses themselves.

51 *the devil goeth about as a roaring lion:* 1 Peter 5:8.

"God judgeth not as man judgeth": cf. 1 Samuel 16:7, 'the Lord seeth not as man seeth'.

the hundred: the sub-division of a county, or shire.

52 *"such tents the patriarchs loved":* Coleridge, 'Inscription for a fountain on a heath' (1802).

King Charles in the oak: the reference is to the traditional story of Charles II's escape after the battle of Worcester (1651), during the course of which he is said to have hidden in an oak tree. The story is the origin of the popular inn-name, the 'Royal Oak'.

62 *Pen trê Voelas:* Mrs Gaskell had particularly poignant memories of North Wales. She had spent her honeymoon there, and in 1844 her infant son William died there during a family holiday. Her description of North Wales in the chapters that follow is only thinly fictionalized, and she would seem to have used a mixture of real and fictionalized place-names. Pentrefoelas (Mrs Gaskell's usage here is an archaism) is a village on the A5 between Betwys-y-coed and Corwen.

64 *"But can she take us in, sir? . . .":* in a letter dated 3 May 1853 Dickens wrote to Mrs Gaskell of *Ruth*: 'I will now mention one word that I wish you would take out whenever you reprint that book. She would never—I am ready to make affidavit before any authority in the land—have called her seducer "Sir" when they were living at that hotel in Wales. A girl pretending to be what she really was would have done it, but she—never!' Mrs Gaskell took

Dickens's advice, and deleted the 'one word' in this instance and elsewhere in subsequent editions of *Ruth*, but it may be questioned, I think, whether she was right to do so. Ruth's formal address to Bellingham, as originally described, defines the relationship rather more precisely than Dickens's comment allows for, and in particular it emphasizes the naïvety of Ruth's deference—a quality very different from what Dickens would seem to infer.

69 *"There are in this loud stunning tide . . . a holy strain repeat"*: I have been unable to trace the source of these lines: I suspect them to have been taken from one of the many common-place books or annuals that were popular in the period.

Maneg Ellyllyn: strictly speaking, 'Maneg Ellyllon', the name by which the foxglove is popularly known in Wales, means 'goblin's glove'. Mrs Gaskell's enthusiasm for this kind of detail has perhaps been undermined by her limited knowledge of Welsh.

70 *Riquet-with-the-tuft*: a dwarf in the fairy-tales of Perrault. He is extremely ugly, but has the power of endowing the person he loves with wit and intelligence. He falls in love with a beautiful but unintelligent woman who marries him in spite of his ugliness: she becomes intelligent, he handsome.

tout ensemble: overall appearance.

"bridal of the earth and sky": the phrase is from George Herbert's poem 'Virtue'.

77 *Llanglâs*: this name does not appear on contemporary maps of the area. Literally translated, it means 'Blue church'. It is, I suspect, a coinage of Mrs Gaskell's.

81 *Gelert*: the name of a dog owned by the Welsh chieftain Llewellyn. In the ballad 'The Grave of the Greyhound' by William Robert Spencer (1770–1834) the story is told of how the dog was killed by his master who wrongly believed it to have savaged his child. In fact the dog had killed a wolf which had threatened the child. Its master realizes his error when the death-howl of the dog awakens the child.

92 *some penitentiary*: see note to page 108.

Yspytty road: the road south from Pentrefoelas through the village of Ysbyty Ifan to Blaenau Ffestiniog.

94 *ling*: a kind of heather.

100 *"What have I to do with Thee?"*: this phrase appears variously in the Bible. Given the context here, the most appropriate references are Mark 5:7 and Luke 8:28, which record the story of the man possessed by devils and the Gadarene swine.

103 *"It blesses him that gives, and him that takes."*: Shakespeare, *Merchant of Venice*, IV. i. 187.

108 *the Fordham Penitentiary*: Mrs Gaskell was familar with the Asylum for Female Penitents, or 'Penitentiary' as it was generally known, which existed for the shelter of unmarried mothers in Manchester in the early nineteenth century. It was sustained by charitable contributions.

109 *Facciolati*: Jacopo Facciolate (1682–1769) was a distinguished lexicographer and philologist. The reference here is perhaps to a copy of his *magnum opus*, *Lexicon Septum Linguarum*, or to his *Totius Latinitatis Lexicon*, which ran to four editions between 1771 and 1835.

110 *Llan-dhu*: probably another Gaskell coinage, this time meaning 'Black church'.

111 *"Dim Saesoneg"*: this translates literally as 'No English', but the sense demanded is clearly that the speaker should use English— 'Aren't you going to speak to me in English?' perhaps. The 'o' in 'Saesoneg' is redundant. Again, I suspect the phrase to represent what can only have been an imperfect knowledge of Welsh on Mrs Gaskell's part.

119 *the tenderness which led the Magdalen aright*: the western Christian tradition has popularly associated the figure of Mary Magdalen, the disciple of Jesus who wept with Mary at the foot of the cross, and who was the first to see him after he had risen, with the fallen woman whom Jesus allowed to wash his feet with her tears (Luke 7: 36–50). Hence the use of the word 'Magdalen' to signify a fallen woman. There is, however, no scriptural authority for the confusion of the two.

121 *the registry of his birth and baptism*: at a time when all children were baptized the circumstances of a child's parentage could not be concealed in the baptismal register, which recorded the specific details of the names and status of its known parents.

132 *manty-makers*: dressmakers. See note to p. 50.

133 *A low grey cloud was the first sign of Eccleston*: in general terms the originals of Mrs Gaskell's fictional locations are invariably easy to identify, but it has not, I think, been previously suggested that in her account of 'Eccleston' she may have had Macclesfield, a town in Cheshire less than ten miles from Knutsford, in mind. Coming to Macclesfield from North Wales one would indeed travel 'across the plain' and approaching 'moors and rising ground' (p. 132). The description here of what is later called 'a small town' (p. 229) as being set in surrounding hills is appropriate to Macclesfield, as is the fact that amongst Benson's congregation are farmers and their labourers, shopkeepers, and the Bradshaws, members of the business interest (pp. 152–3). Nineteenth-century Macclesfield— unlike Knutsford, which had no manufacturing community—would

have provided just such a mix. Eccleston, we are told, had six hundred electors (p. 250): after the Reform Bill of 1832 Macclesfield had just over one thousand. Macclesfield, however, was not represented on its own account in Parliament before the Bill, as Eccleston would seem to have been (see note to p. 249). Furthermore, there was no Public Infirmary, as required by the conclusion of the novel, in Macclesfield until 1860. Yet again, Eccleston is described as being 'within twenty miles' distance of the sea, a point of detail impossible to reconcile with the fictional geography of the novel, let alone any possible real-life precedent (see note to p. 249). But such correspondences are of their nature a matter of general conception rather than of detail, which can always be imposed as the novel requires it. J. G. Sharps, for example, has suggested that the cholera epidemic at the end of the novel is drawn from Mrs Gaskell's experience in Newcastle in 1831 (*Mrs Gaskell's Observation and Invention*, Fontwell, Sussex, 1970, p. 157). Sharps, like other commentators, automatically associates Benson's chapel with that at Knutsford, whose features it reproduces, but the chapel can equally well be identified with an identical chapel at Macclesfield (see note to p. 151). Undoubtedly 'Eccleston' embodies much of the emotional feeling associated with Knutsford by Mrs Gaskell: what I believe has happened is that she has given us the circumstances of Macclesfield as a town more suited to her fictional requirements. Finally, the approximation of the name is a factor in Macclesfield's favour: Eccleston may well stand to Macclesfield as does Cranford or Hollingford (in *Wives and Daughters*) to Knutsford.

134 *as effectually as . . . the coming of Abdallah*: historically, Abdallah was the father of Mahomet. I have been unable to identify the source of Mrs Gaskell's quotation though, and it is not clear whether it is to him that she refers.

136 *linsey-woolsey*: coarse woollen material of an inferior standard.

  a "mutch": an old woman's cap (dial.).

140 *"them that had gone astray"*: the reference is to the parable of the lost sheep, Matthew 18:12–14.

142 *Who ask not if Thine eye/Be on them . . .*: Wordsworth, 'Ode to Duty', *Poems* (1807). The lines cited begin the second stanza of the poem.

  "God be merciful to me a sinner!": Luke 18:13.

144 *Queen Eleanor herself . . . fair Rosamond*: 'Fair Rosamond', daughter of Lord Clifford and mistress of Henry II, was traditionally held to have been poisoned by Queen Eleanor at Woodstock. The story is told in the ballad 'Fair Rosamond' in Percy's *Reliques of Ancient English Poetry*.

147 *farred*: literally, 'sent afar off' (dial.), although here it seems to be used as a more general expletive.

148 *th'overseer*: a parish official, appointed to perform administrative duties largely in connection with the relief of the poor. The office was abolished under the terms of the Poor Law Amendment Act of 1834.

151 *The chapel . . . close by*: the chapel described here has generally been taken to be based upon the Unitarian chapel at Knutsford, built in 1689, where Mrs Gaskell worshipped in her early years, and where she was buried. Certainly the description corresponds in fairly precise detail to the Knutsford chapel, notably regarding the outside staircases, the leaded windows, and the interior, with its whitewashed walls, its plain timbers, and its galleries. There are, however, virtually identical chapels at the nearby towns of Wilmslow and Macclesfield, and the setting of the latter in fact corresponds in some ways more closely with the situation described here than does that of the Knutsford chapel. The building at Macclesfield is indeed approached by a cul-de-sac, whereas the Knutsford chapel stands on open ground on the main road leading out of the town. The Macclesfield chapel may more legitimately be described as being 'on the outskirts' of the town, if not now 'almost in fields', and there are still 'buildings immediately surrounding' of a similar period. Furthermore there is no record of an adjoining minister's house of the kind described in *Ruth* where Knutsford is concerned: such a house did apparently stand at Macclesfield. The one point of difference between the chapel in the novel and that at Macclesfield is that there is no graveyard there: there is one at Knutsford. Finally, it should be mentioned that Mrs Gaskell records having worshipped at Macclesfield: in a letter to her daughter Marianne, dated ?February 1852, she describes how 'the little chapel' there 'was so very hot that it has made me sleepy ever since' (*The Letters of Mrs Gaskell*, ed. J. A. V. Chapple and Arthur Pollard, Manchester, 1966, p. 178).

Matthew and Philip Henry: nonconformist divines, father and son, of the seventeenth century. Philip Henry in particular came into conflict with authority over his right to preach; Matthew Henry was well known for his preaching in the Knutsford and Macclesfield areas, and in fact preached at the chapels there.

153 *the dear old Scottish paraphrase*: the Scottish Psalter, a metrical version of the Psalms much used in dissenting congregations.

in Poussin's beautiful picture: there is apparently no record of a painting by Poussin of the Good Shepherd. Mrs Gaskell would seem to be in error.

154 *"Father! I have sinned against Heaven and before Thee . . .":* Luke 15:18–19.

157 *"Do unto others as ye would that they should do unto you?":* cf. Luke 6:31, 'And as ye would that men should do to you, do ye also to them likewise.'

160 *"hiding her guilty front with innocent snow":* Milton, 'On the Morning of Christ's Nativity'.

163 *"tormented in this flame":* Luke 16:24.

169 *the old song of Barbary Allen:* there are two Scottish ballads of Barbara Allen: both tell of how her lover Sir John Graeme died of his unrequited love for her. The line quoted here, 'wi' deadly sorrow sighing', appears in the version recorded in Percy's *Reliques of Ancient English Poetry*.

174 *thole:* endure.

176 *"to do my duty in that station of life unto which it shall please God to call me":* this concludes the answer in the Catechism to the question, 'What is thy duty towards thy neighbour?'

178 *In that body of Dissenters to which Mr Benson belonged:* Thurstan Benson, it is generally accepted, is based upon the Revd William Turner, Unitarian minister of Newcastle-upon-Tyne, with whom Mrs Gaskell stayed when a young woman on two occasions between 1829 and 1831. Benson is nowhere defined in *Ruth* as a Unitarian and Mrs Gaskell was perhaps deliberately vague about his explicit denomination, but the practice of deferring infant baptism described here is characteristic of Unitarian practice at the time.

184 *coucher:* an evening reception. Mrs Gaskell's use of the term here is gently ironic.

185 *One of Job's daughters; Jemima, Kezia, and Keren-Happuch:* Job 42:14.

188 *the Minerva press:* the Minerva Press, which published sensational and romantic fiction in the late eighteenth and early nineteenth centuries, became a byword throughout the nineteenth century for the kind of taste its productions exploited.

191 *As I was going to Derby, sir,|Upon a market-day:* the opening lines of a nonsense song, 'The Derby Ram', which appeared in a collection of songs by John Wall Callcott (1766–1821), 'a glee writer of great power and fecundity' (D.N.B.). (MW)

the old tune of "Life let us cherish": the song 'Life let us cherish' is reprinted in *The New Musical Magazine, Review and Register*, I (1809). It is a translation from the German of Johann Martin Usteri. The words 'Life let us cherish while yet the taper glows|And the fresh floweret pluck ere it close' form the refrain to a series of stanzas reflecting on the transience of human life. (MW)

192 *Old-man . . . lad's-love*: two names for the hardy deciduous shrub Southernwood (*artemesia abrotanum*), which is known for its white feathery foliage and its fragrant, slightly spicy, smell. It was much favoured for its medicinal qualities.

when missus died, we forgot to tell 'em: the tradition of telling the bees of a death in the family is recorded by John Brand in his *Observations on the Popular Antiquities of Great Britain* (New Edition, 1859, vol. II, pp. 300–1). Brand records the belief, alluded to here, that failure to inform the bees will result in their deserting the hive, and refers to the related belief that the hives themselves should be dressed with crape as a mark of mourning.

193 *mim*: affectedly modest, demure, primly silent (dial.).

194 *scomfish*: suffocate, stifle (dial.).

195 *clipped*: excluded from (dial.).

203 "*He that spareth the rod, spoileth the child*": cf. Proverbs 13:24, 'He that spareth the rod hateth his son but he that loveth him chastiseth him betimes.' Sally's reference to scripture that follows is accurate: the reign of Rehoboam, son of Solomon, is described in 2 Chronicles 10–12.

205 to "*wait patiently upon God*": cf. Psalms 37:7, 'Rest in the Lord and wait patiently for him.'

208 *a jargonelle pear tree rich in autumnal fruit*: the reference to 'rich . . . autumnal fruit' is questionable on two counts. The jargonelle is an early ripening variety of pear, and it was popular for the attractiveness of the tree rather than the quality of its fruit.

209 *Rizpah*: Rizpah was the concubine of Saul whose sons were given over to the Gibeonites by David to be hanged. The story is told in 2 Samuel 21 of how Rizpah watched over the bodies making sure that they were not approached by bird or beast.

"*Thy will, not mine, be done*": the words of Christ before the Passion, Luke 22:42. Mrs Gaskell has slightly misquoted them.

210 (*Oh, mercy! to myself I said,|If Lucy should be dead!*): Wordsworth, 'Strange fits of passion I have known', *Lyrical Ballads* (1800).

230 *a delicate pair of Limerick ones . . . walnut-shell*: Limerick gloves were traditionally made of the skins of unborn calves, and were thus very fine. Sally's suggestion that they were made of chicken skin is therefore inaccurate, although this material was used for fashion accessories in the nineteenth century.

232 "*keeping a calm sough*": keeping quiet (dial.).

236 *On revient . . . premiers amours*: these lines, slightly rearanged,
    are from an opera, *Joconde*, by Charles-Guillaume Etienne
    and Nicolo Isouard (Act III, Scene 1), although it is perhaps likely
    that Mrs Gaskell would have known them from an anthology.
    (MW)

249 *Abermouth*: despite its apparently Welsh name, Gaskell com-
    mentators have traditionally associated Abermouth with Silver-
    dale, a village on the North Lancashire coast where the Gaskell
    family took their own holidays (see, for example, A. W. Ward's
    Introduction to *Ruth* in the 'Knutsford' edition). But on p. 251 it is
    described as being 'within twenty miles distance' of Eccleston. In
    that Eccleston is only 'eighteen miles' from the sight of the Welsh
    mountains (p. 132), and thus evidently in Cheshire, Mrs Gaskell
    would seem drastically to have telescoped her geography. (See
    note to p. 133.)

    He was the mover of a project . . . election: since Mrs Gaskell goes
    on to say that there were 600 voters, the election would seem to
    take place under the provisions of the Reform Bill of 1832, a point
    confirmed when she later mentions railway facilities in connection
    with Ruth's journey to Abermouth (p. 266 and p. 289). But from
    her account of the Cranworth family, Eccleston would seem to
    have been enfranchised in pre-Reform days (see note to p. 133).

255 *if men were angels . . . we would not bribe*: that the issue of bribery
    was a central one in post-Reform Bill elections is reflected in a
    number of novels of the period. Notably, the situation here
    anticipates that described in George Eliot's *Felix Holt* (1866),
    where another dissenting minister, Rufus Lyon, finds himself
    opposed to the interests of a more morally flexible Parliamentary
    candidate, Harold Transome. Like 'Donne', Transome has only a
    superficial commitment to politics and he too acts in the Radical
    interest.

    "We are not to do evil that good may come": cf. Romans 3:8, 'And
    not rather . . . Let us do evil that good may come.' The text, of
    course, reflects on Benson's own action in protecting Ruth by a lie,
    and is thus central to the theme of the novel.

259 *the "little birds sang east, and the little birds sang west"*: Elizabeth
    Barrett Browning, 'Rhyme of the Duchess May'. The poem first
    appeared in Mrs Browning's *Poems* of 1844. The sentiments of its
    concluding lines, from which Mrs Gaskell quotes, are likely to have
    appealed to her:

    Oh, the little birds sang east, and the little birds sang west
                    Toll slowly.
    And I said in underbreath,—All our life is mixed with death,
                And who knoweth which is best?

> Oh, the little birds sang east, and the little birds sang west,
> > *Toll slowly*.
> And I smiled to think God's greatness flowed around
> > Our incompleteness,—
> > > Round our restlessness, His rest.

(Elizabeth Barrett Browning, *Poetical Works*, Smith and Elder. 1883, Vol. III, pp. 81–2)

the "*little cloud no bigger than a man's hand*": the sign given to Elijah that the drought that afflicted Israel under the rule of King Ahab would end. Cf. 1 Kings 18:44.

261 "*fluttered the Volscians in Corioli*": Shakespeare, *Coriolanus*, v. vi. 116.

274 "*stormy wind fulfilling his word*": Psalms 148:8.

"*a very present help in time of trouble*": Psalms 46:1.

276 "*Thy will be done!*": traditionally the words of Christ in the garden of Gethsemane. Cf. Luke 22:42.

279 *Mr Bradshaw always disliked going to church*: i.e., as distinct from chapel, where the order of service, if traditional, was informal and prayer extempore.

282 the "*Hills from whence cometh our help*": Psalms 121:1.

283 the *26th chapter of St Matthew's Gospel*: this gives Matthew's account of Christ's agony in the garden, which Mrs Gaskell refers to here.

286 "*for His mercy endureth for ever*": Psalms 136:1.

291 "*alley*": a glass marble.

301 *it was so once when the gentle, blessed Christ was upon earth*: a further reference to the story of how Christ allowed the fallen woman to bathe his feet with her tears (see note to p. 119).

309 *oneiromancy*: divination by dreams.

312 *A child whom all that looked on, loved*: Wordsworth, 'Six months to six years added':

> Six months to six years added he remained
> Upon this sinful earth, by sin unstained:
> O blessed Lord! whose mercy then removed
> A child whom every eye that looked on loved;
> Support us, teach us calmly to resign
> What we possessed, and now is wholly thine!

These lines were inscribed by Wordsworth on the tombstone of his son Thomas, who died in 1812, but were not published until 1837.

313 "*clave unto her*": Ruth 1:14.

470 EXPLANATORY NOTES

314 (*gioventu dell'anno*): literally, in the youth of the year. The phrase appears at the opening of the third act of *Il Pastor Fido*, by Battista Guarini (1538–1612). Guarini's play, a pastoral drama, was translated into English by Richard Fanshawe in 1647. It retained its popularity throughout Europe well into the nineteenth century.

335 the "*Delectus*": Richard Valpy's *Delectus Sententiarum et Historianum* (1800), a work which established itself as a standard Latin grammar and formed the basis of later grammars in the nineteenth century.

338 *as St Paul shook off the viper—even into the fire*: the story is told in Acts 28 of how St Paul, when on the island of Melita, shook off a viper that had fastened on his arm, and was unharmed.

350 *that gentle tender help . . . Mary Magdalen*: see note to p. 119.

358 "*Ask, and it shall be given unto you . . .*": Matthew 7:7.

367 "*accepted her penance*": cf. Leviticus 26:40–42, 'If they shall confess their iniquity . . . and they then accept of the punishment of their iniquity: Then will I remember my convenant with Jacob.'

377 *as the shepherd-boy in John Bunyan sweetly sang*: the reference is to the shepherd-boy's song in the Valley of Humiliation in *The Pilgrim's Progress*, Part II.

   ends of list: 'list' is the selvage, or border; hence, the wastage of a piece of cloth.

378 "*nattered*": irritable, fractious (dial.).

403 *the fetch of his own writing*: a 'fetch' is a traditional term for an apparition or double; hence, here, a replica.

418 "*When the devil was sick, the devil a monk would be*": proverbial; said of people who make pious resolutions in times of danger, but revert to type when the danger is past.

423 *since the days of King Belshazzar*: the story of Belshazzar's feast, at which King Belshazzar was warned of his fate by the writing on the wall, is told in Daniel 5.

424 *the low Irish lodging-houses*: Mrs Gaskell probably draws here on her Manchester experience. The Irish quarter of Manchester was notorious for its proneness to epidemics of fever, but most manufacturing towns had lodging-houses where sanitation was minimal. In Macclesfield, for example (see note to p. 133), a report on the appalling conditions of such residences was presented in 1853, the year of the publication of *Ruth*.

430 "*many arose and called her blessed*": cf. Proverbs 31:28, 'Her children arise up, and call her blessed; her husband also, and he praiseth her.'

436 *trig*: neat (dial.).

447 "*home must go, and take her wages*": from the song in *Cymbeline*, IV. ii. 'Fear no more the heat o' the sun'.

457 *the seventh chapter of Revelations . . . ninth verse*: the passage referred to describes the Evangelist's vision of the appearance of the multitude of all nations before the throne of God. Mrs Gaskell directly quotes the last four verses of the chapter.

VIRGIL: The Aeneid
Translated by C. Day Lewis
Edited by Jasper Griffin

HORACE WALPOLE : The Castle of Otranto
Edited by W. S. Lewis

IZAAK WALTON and CHARLES COTTON:
The Compleat Angler
Edited by John Buxton
Introduction by John Buchan

OSCAR WILDE: Complete Shorter Fiction
Edited by Isobel Murray

The Picture of Dorian Gray
Edited by Isobel Murray

VIRGINIA WOOLF: Orlando
Edited by Rachel Bowlby

ÉMILE ZOLA:
The Attack on the Mill and other stories
Translated by Douglas Parmée